MW00834969

MOTION OF INTERVALS

KRISTY MCGINNIS

Glassy Lake Publishing
Virginia Beach, VA, USA

1

Cover design by A.Jewel.
Edited by Nicole Neuman

Identifiers: LCCN 2023910014 | ISBN 978-1-7365367-2-8 (paperback)| ISBN 978-1-7365367-1-1 (ebook)

Mothers and daughters: when it goes right, it goes very right. This one is for my mom, the Anti-Tessa, and my dad. I love you both!

In music theory, the concept of *motion of intervals* refers to the way in which the distance between two notes in a melody or harmony changes over time.

Chapter 1

Tessa

Richard Nixon, that paranoid old prevaricator, once famously declared, "I am not a crook." Had Dick bothered to consult his friend Allister Shepherd's daughter before uttering those words, she could have saved him a whole world of trouble. There is only one acceptable way to address a scandal: you pretend it doesn't exist. Tessa was shrewder than Dick Nixon. She would project the image of a woman unburdened by the baseless speculation and gossip that currently dominated social media. She wasn't going to deny anything. On stage, she'd walk confidently and proudly. She was still Tessa, after all. She was still America's Darling.

Sara walked briskly toward her. "Let's see if you need anything refreshed, Ms. Shepherd."

The younger woman leaned in and studied her face. With a barely audible sigh, she reached over onto the makeup table and withdrew a large brush.

"A little pale today; just a little touch up and you'll be as good as new," the girl promised in a singsong voice.

Turning her head slightly to the right, Tessa glanced toward the harshly lit mirror and traced a fingertip along her brow line. Her mother's face, she'd been told. Her mother hadn't had to deal with the cruelty of time. Her skin had never grown bored and limp above her eyelids. Her eyebrows hadn't thinned themselves into imprecise shadows over time. She'd never known the emergence of cursed jowls. She'd never had to undergo the indignity of a *procedure* to correct that which had always been perfectly fine before. If she had experienced all of that, it wouldn't have been under the harsh stage lights of Shepherd Studio 1.

She glanced back at Sara's still youthful face hovering anxiously nearby. The girl didn't comment on the fact that Tessa had dared touch her own face, but her disapproval was palpable. Did she actually think that the carefully constructed mask Tessa wore was her doing? Her expert work with make-up might highlight the fine bone structure and compliment the harsh stage lights, but that was all superficial. Makeup artists could be easily replaced.

After carefully applying a setting spray, the girl stood back and studied Tessa again. This time she smiled in satisfaction.

"There you are, Ms. Shepherd! Perfect!"

"Perfect?" Tessa asked in a soft, genial tone. Someone better acquainted with her would have recognized that tone and known to be afraid. The girl smiled and nodded agreeably.

Tessa stood several inches taller in her heels and leaned toward Sara's body. With her mouth hovering just inches from the girl's right ear, she smiled and said bluntly, "Get out."

Sarah stepped back, confused, and replied, "Excuse me, Ms. Shepherd? Did I do something..."

"Get out." Tessa said, much louder this time before lowering her voice and adding softly, "And don't bother to look for another job in this city."

After the girl ran out of the room, Tessa glanced back into the mirror. The rings on her fingers glittered in the harsh dressing room lighting as she casually touched her hair. Those rings sported a few hundred thousand dollars' worth of jewels that she'd purchased with her own money, not her father's. She didn't care as much about the waning beauty of youth when she saw them. Beauty was powerful, but money trumped it in the hierarchy of status. That was why she had to kill the scandal. She had an empire to run.

Tessa stood and walked confidently toward the stage door. Before opening it, she took a deep breath and transformed her face with a carefully plotted smile.

"Three, Two, One, Go!"

As the familiar theme song began, Tessa confidently strode across the studio stage to reach her mark. She stopped and lifted both arms, perfectly timing her greeting with the signature "She's your best friend!" line. The audience erupted into a frantic, cheering mass just as they'd been instructed to do. Tessa knew that they'd have done it unprompted as well. This part was completely predictable because they adored her. Yes, Dick Nixon could have learned a few things from Tessa Shepherd.

Chapter 2

Kenna

Self-loathing is a super power. Creating an invisible layer of armor with the simple act of remembering who and what you are isn't a talent that just anyone can manifest on demand. If you hate yourself enough then public shaming can't really hurt you. The ability to stare into a mirror, before you take a liner pen to your eyes and see the ugly that hides in your pores- well, that's a gift. That's what I tell myself anyway. Break your own ankles and it doesn't matter if they smash your feet. You're not going to be wearing your pretty new Balenciaga heels anytime soon either way.

I hate myself, they can't hurt me. I hate myself, they can't hurt me.

I repeat the mantra in the same way I used to recite caustic lyrics in the back of my closet so Mother wouldn't hear. Silently. I'm not good at much. I'm good at not moving my lips when I'm singing a song though. My legs churn with the hate-hymn beat as I walk through the building entry and down the main corridor. This walk, this cadence, it's a performance. The entire point is to convince my audience that I'm unaware of their presence. I know that my cheeks betray me. Red flames crawl across them. I can't will them away with a song.

The soles of my black leather boots are nearly silent as they hit the hundred-year-old wood plank floor. I'm grateful I'd chosen a pair with whispering wedge heels. I focus on those boots. I watch as they fall on the warbled knots and blackened crevices between the well-worn floor boards. It's another thing to be grateful for. A place to hide my eyes. Windows to the soul they say, windows to my torment, I say. I feel the crowd part as I approach. I hear the way their conversations evaporate into nothingness as

I pass. I hear the whispers. I refuse to look up. Only my feet and the floor exist.

Reaching the conference style classroom, my heartbeat is a drum echoing a primal rhythm that I hope only I can hear. Through the subtle vanilla scent of my deodorant, I smell my own perspiration. Musky. Feral. It's just another scorching shame. Just another crime to add to my cumulative humiliation. Once again, the casual conversations around me abruptly halt and after a brief caesura, an allegro of conspiratorial whispers begins. I walk toward the long, oaken, collaborative table and still refuse to lift my eyes. I don't have to look; I know what I'll see in the faces of my nine classmates.

Look away, look away, my broken girl.
Blind yourself to this smirking world.

The line comes as they always do, in a whisper. I wish I could dig into my backpack for a notebook to jot it down before it disappears to that mysterious place where thousands of other unfortunate words dance untouched, but I can't. I'm sitting protected by the bulk of this table and I'm afraid to move at all. If I remain perfectly still, the attention of my classmates might be drawn elsewhere.

The silence comes to an abrupt halt as Professor Jackson, or Natasha as she prefers to be called, stomps into the room. She is the antithesis of grace. All huff and puff, her doughy arms are weighed down with a stack of manila folders. She uses the considerable girth of her polyester clad hip to power push the heavy chair at the head of the table aside. She's breathing heavily as she drops the stack of folders and I'm momentarily distracted by the sheen across her ebony forehead. It reminds me of Mother's forehead on stage when the lights are too bright. Mother's forehead before her powder is retouched.

The attention of my classmates has shifted with Natasha's arrival and I cautiously glance around. No one is looking at me and for a moment I welcome a surge of relief. That relief fades as Natasha turns in time to catch my eyes with her own. She gives the slightest of nods and I'm not sure how to read her expression. She rarely smiles and I attribute the lack of lines on her face to that trait. Owl-face. That's how I've always thought of her. She's got large, penetrating amber brown eyes that portend wisdom and patience, eyes that are too old for her smooth skin. They're focused squarely on me now.

I am not here by accident. With only 2500 students campus wide, and only a fraction of those students studying disciplines within the English department, the intimacy of Barnard's classrooms had at one time been the very thing that attracted me. My mother had championed for her own alma mater, Columbia University. Rain is wet. Grass is green. Shepherds go to Columbia. Her expectation had quickened to a frantic tempo during my final years of high school. She didn't understand my reluctance to apply. Notwithstanding her constant reminders about Columbia's superior academics and networking contacts, I'd been terrified by the institution's size and reputation.

I had spent a lifetime attempting to please my mother, usually without success. Disappointment in me was nothing new. I'd never challenged her directly though. I hadn't been mutinous; I'd just failed to thrive. I certainly hadn't ever openly rebelled against her. No one, not even her own daughter, said no to Tessa Shepherd. Yet somehow when college decision time rolled around, Columbia had seemed even bigger and more terrifying than Tessa Shepherd. I fought and won the only real battle we'd ever had.

Victory has been hollow. She'd tricked me into believing I was a victor. I realized during my first year of college that she'd finally relented because she had decided Barnard and Columbia were actually the same institution. Their proximity and close relationship gave her the rare opportunity to offer me a consolation prize. Now, I wish that I could take it back. It would have been easier to hide from my classmates' prying eyes within the larger crowds of Columbia proper.

"Miss Shepherd? Are you with us today?" Natasha's smooth voice interrupts my thoughts. She has an owl's face, but her voice is honey. It softens her effect. I find myself wanting to please her. I want her approval. I hate that want.

Feeling the heat rise to my face again, I nod reluctantly. "I... I'm sorry, I missed the question." I admit in my quiet voice, the one that I almost couldn't hear myself. This word game, it's agony. In my mind, I am coherent, I am colorful, I am intelligent. When I open my mouth though, I spit out weakness.

"As I was saying, this class is really a continuation of last semester's Gendered Writing course. One main difference is that students will be expected to focus on one primary writer for the entire semester. You will become an expert on your chosen subject and you will be able to present your knowledge of her in a very public way. Do you have anyone in mind yet?"

A roomful of eyes stares at me and I'm paralyzed. Some stare with casual amusement, while others reveal open hostility. They stare like wasps from an overhead eave. I open my mouth to reply, but the circuitry from my brain to my vocal chords has been shorted. I close my mouth and simply shake my head. Natasha's eyes narrow, but she moves onto the student next to me. This young woman is clearly eager to show off her literary chops and her words do not die before reaching her lips. I push away her smug tone and manufactured academic prowess. I'm unable to focus on her and I'm unable to focus on the topic of gendered writing. I'm surrounded by eager, engaging women who are marching with certainty toward successful career destinies. My own future is about to spectacularly implode in front of the entire world.

The rest of the class period is a game of invisibility. I hunch down, make myself smaller, and attempt to disappear completely from my classmates' view. When Natasha ends our class with her familiar, "Go forth and be bold," I grab my backpack and try to escape. I don't make it to the door before hearing Natasha's honeyed voice calling my name. Ignoring the smirks and knowing-looks of my classmates, I stand still in the middle of the small room and contemplate running away. I'm unable to actually do that –you don't spend nearly 21 years of your life being perfectly obedient to suddenly develop a spine during a moment of pressure.

I approach Natasha cautiously, practicing an apology in my head. I've spent hours rehearsing the facsimile of casual conversation. Sometimes, I am able to pull the scripts and fake an ease that I've never known. When I reach her and lift my eyes, I know this is not going to be casual. I don't see anger or contempt on her face. I see curiosity and underneath it, something softer that hints at kindness. I know her to be a tough professor, blunt in her assessment, quick with her red pen as she demands excellence from her students. As tough as she is, she's also fair. She's not a cruel woman. She's not my mother.

"Miss Shepherd, I know this is a trying time for you. How are you handling it?"

It's unlikely that she can't see how I'm handling it. I'm not. I've barely eaten or slept in the past three days. I've spent nearly every moment battling rising panic in a war I know I'll eventually lose. My bowels are twisted into cruel knots. A permanent lump has invaded my throat. I swallow hard, temporarily forcing the lump down and I reply softly, lamely, "I guess I'm okay."

She reaches a hand out toward my own and I'm stunned at the moment they connect. I haven't felt physical human contact in so long. It's as if she's pointed a gun at me and pulled the trigger. Pain slices through me and tears begin to roll down my cheeks. I instinctively jerk my hand away and rush to wipe my cheeks and hide my new shame.

"Miss Shepherd, Kenna, I can't tell you how you should handle this, but please consider your options. Perhaps I can write a letter on your behalf to the academic honor board, or to the dean if you wish to request a leave of absence."

I default to my favorite defense. I look down at my feet. Her kindness is jarring and unexpected. Somehow it's more painful than my mother's anger, my classmates' derision, the ridicule of strangers. I'm ashamed of what I've done and who I've embarrassed. Most of all, I'm ashamed of who I am. I have a mother who is adored by the entire country, a grandfather who can be found on Forbes' annual billionaire list, and I'm standing here wearing an outfit that I know must have cost more than Natasha's monthly salary. I'm a caricature, the poor little rich girl. I don't want or deserve Natasha's kindness. I want her to be oblivious to my existence. I want to disappear entirely.

"Thank you. I really don't think there's anything anyone can do at this point." I pause and force myself to breathe deeply a few times. I try to force the trembling sound from my voice and then finally manage a defiant, "I did it. I did it and I'll have to live with it."

She considers this for a moment, then nods and asks what no one else has until now, "Kenna, can I ask why you did it?"

I shake my head. She's asking too much of me. I can't explain about my mother or the ridicule I'd endured at The Crier. I can't vocalize the rising panic when the deadlines were approaching and I'd realized I would fail again. There are no words I can utter that will excuse my actions. The truth wouldn't make her more sympathetic to my situation. Instead, she would resent my ever having taken a highly sought seat at her discussion table.

"It's okay, that's your business. I just want you to know I'm here if you need an ear. You're a strong writer, Kenna, and I don't want you to give up on your education. There may be a pause, but that doesn't mean you're finished. No matter how bad things seem right now, there's going to be a new chapter eventually. Someday this too shall pass."

She wants an affirmation from me, some hint that her words matter. I owe it to her. I've been gripped by this panic for days though and even a small token of gratitude is too much. My continuing silence is clearly making her uncomfortable and I see the exact moment the sympathy in her eyes fades.

"Everyone faces trials in life. Find your people to lean on during this. That's what makes them bearable. There are resources here at Barnard to help you through times of crisis and hopefully you have some outside of school as well." She continues, her brown eyes narrowing at my paralyzed state.

This moment, interaction, interrogation- needs to end. It's not just that I want to escape; I also want to release Natasha from a duty she can't possibly actually want. Reaching deeply into my reserves I somehow manage to retrieve and then mutter a bland thank you before I turn and run.

The minutes spent shrinking beneath Natasha's unwavering gaze are minutes lost. I'm none the better for them and now I'm sure I'll be late for my next class. As I leave the building and round the corner, I finally glance at my phone screen. Class is already starting. I know from experience that walking into an already seated classroom is a cringe-worthy scenario. Showing up late in better times was awful. If a seat in the back isn't open, then everyone watches as you make your way toward the front of the room. Eyes watching, prying, judging. There is nothing worse than being stared at and *thought about* in normal times. These are no longer normal times and being late now will be a nightmare.

My pace slows- why am I still chasing my assigned schedule? It's embarrassingly simple. I'm doing it because it's expected and I've been well programmed to do what's expected. I've never cut a class in my life but today's act is a charade. I'm going to be expelled as soon as the committee met, of this I am certain. Perfect attendance isn't going to rescue me.

For the first time in my academic life, I choose to walk purposely away from the very building I should be entering. My apartment is the obvious place to escape to but the five block walk it'll require sounds impossible. I'm not sure my shaking legs can carry me the distance I need to go. Up ahead, I spied an empty bench in front of the Milstein Center. I walk wearily toward it. I haven't slept much in recent days and as I sink my body down onto the hard wooden slats I feel a wave of dizziness wash over me. Even now, even when it feels as if nothing on my body works correctly anymore, the lyrics come.

Walked twelve thousand miles between two poles
Gravel and ice wore down my soles.
Wore the soles right off my feet.
Wore the soul right outta me.

I indulge in a moment of actual rest to ride out the wave. When the tide of disorientation recedes, I turn to my phone and open my mindfulness app. The immediate aftermath of conflict is the best time to try to seize some zen. The fragrance of freshly cut grass is an aromatic balm against my anxiety and the unusually warm September air offers just a hint of solace. It's a moment that would have been enjoyable at another time in my life. The loveliness of it contrasts so severely with the ugliness of my life though, now it just makes me sadder.

When the app's timer ends the brief exercise, I stare at my screen and try to talk myself out of opening it. A portal to the larger, crueler world. I can't resist the allure though, I open a browser and type my name into Google. A few social media and older fluff pieces hit and, for a moment, I allow myself to feel relieved. If my mother has taught me anything useful, it's that it's always a bad idea to let your guard down. I realize too late that any articles out there are probably using my formal name. I replace Kenna Shepherd with Kennedy Shepherd in the search bar. Sure enough, a slew of newly published articles appear.

"Oh no, oh no, oh no..." I whisper at the headlines and close the browser without hitting any of the links. If I read the words I may not make it back to my apartment at all.

I'm not alone in my misery. I know there's one person in the world watching these headlines even more closely than me- and she isn't going to avoid opening them. I wish I was alone in my misery. Right this minute my mother would be pouring through every scandalous word. I imagine her voice, cold and brittle, capable of cutting glass, demanding that her legal team find a way to stop the media. I loathe diamonds and that's because I decided when I was a small girl that Mother's voice was made of diamonds.

Her publicists would be fielding non-stop calls right now from her stable of assistants- each of them more desperate than the last to avoid her wrath. Right this minute, a multi-media plan was being designed that would best meet Tessa's needs. That I am the center of the entire storm is entirely irrelevant. My opinion or wishes wouldn't be considered. As always, the entire world orbits Tessa Shepherd.

A pair of girls who look young enough to be first year students walk by with their arms locked together at the elbow. Skin to skin, in short sleeves, because that's how warm this September is. One of them, a pretty brunette with her hair pulled back in an artful ponytail, leans toward her companion's quadruple pierced ear and whispers something. They're suddenly both laughing and I steel myself. Is it me? They glance toward me but then look away without interest and continue walking. I exhale with relief. Even before this disaster, I had felt horribly conspicuous on campus but I have come by my paranoia honestly. I've heard the comments and whispers since first year. Maybe I'm not known by every student, but often enough there's an inevitable awkward moment of recognition.

"Oh my god, are you Tessa's daughter?"

"Kennedy, I love your mother!"

"Wow, what's Tessa like in person?"

When I'd first arrived at Barnard, I'd been incredibly naive about my own anonymity or lack thereof. Even with Tessa's impatient coaching, I hadn't been prepared for the attention I'd receive away from the protective bubble that had shielded me in childhood. I had been homeschooled by skilled teachers during my elementary years. Then in seventh grade, I'd moved from one carefully constructed bubble to another. My six years of middle and high school were spent sheltered within the wooded compound of the elite Calvin Brook Academy in rural Vermont. There at Calvin Brook I'd lived and studied alongside the offspring of other American royalty. Like me, they had been packed up and dropped off at the picturesque campus to be educated and pampered, away from the prying eyes of the media.

Being separated from Tessa and her army of nannies and housekeepers was a change I'd embraced. I hadn't gone on to become a standout student or peer at Calvin Brook, but I was safe and normal within the context of my surroundings. If I hadn't exactly made close friends, I had at least found peers who allowed me to blend in. Blending in is a gift that most people don't appreciate enough. For the first time in my life I felt almost normal. I forgot to be overly cautious. But then came graduation. I moved on to Barnard and NYC and any illusion of normalcy was shattered.

My thoughts are interrupted as the phone in my hand buzzes. I'm holding a bomb and I want to hurl it across the lawn. I know who it is before I even look at the screen. We may have missed that symbiotic mother-fetus bonding experience you read about in health class due to the circumstances of my birth, but I've always been completely attuned to my mother's needs. She's programmed me well for that. Right now, her need is to lash out and punish me. I know better than to ignore her call though and with a shaking hand I put the phone to my ear.

"Hello."

"Kennedy. Of course you're not in class. Of course this is the time you decide to make it clear to administrators that you really don't care at all about your education."

"I'm sorry." I reply and I physically wince at the words. They are the same two words I've said over and over in recent days. They're met with deaf ears every time.

"I've told you to stop saying that. Those words mean nothing, Kennedy! Your actions speak loudest. Now sit down. I have some less than disastrous news, finally. I spoke to Phil, and he thinks we have a pretty good case against the Crier. We can't fight the termination for cause, but they may have violated their contract when they went public with it. We don't want to actually go to court, we want a retraction. He also thinks they might be liable for damages against HoHo, and that might be parlayed into a little free positive publicity."

HoHo. In the end, that's what Mother really cares about. Home Honorific isn't just her publishing and broadcasting empire, it's the foundation of her entire identity. HoHo is her real child- labored over, birthed, nurtured, and matured under her skillful eye for far longer than I've existed. I am just the pale little sister.

"Mother, can't we just let this go? Maybe if we do, it'll just fade away and people will stop talking..."

Her shrill voice interrupts me, "Of course not. The entire point is making it clear you did nothing wrong, without actually saying you did nothing wrong, because you did everything wrong."

I close my eyes and hold my breath. If I hold it long enough maybe I will just die and this will all be over. This trick had never worked during my childhood though and it doesn't work today. Mother is finally quiet and I know she expects a reply, but I can't formulate anything coherent.

"Kennedy! Stay here on planet Earth. There is more good news. I spoke to Elizabeth Dutton, the President of Westminster College in Ontario. She said they can offer you a spot for the spring semester. We just have to get through the current crisis, and then we'll get you up there and hopefully by the time January rolls around the public has forgotten what you've done."

Nothing she is saying makes sense. For a brief moment I'm more confused than humiliated. "Ontario?"

"Yes, Ontario. Were you expecting Cambridge," she asks, her voice dripping with sarcasm. "There isn't a school in the states that will have you at this point, no matter how generous my gift might be. Westminster is perfect. It's very small and no one has ever heard of it. A year from now, this will all just be a horrible memory for us all."

I've got to escape the cutting edge of her diamond voice before it slices straight through my jugular vein. I murmur a lie about getting to class late and I know that she knows it's a lie. She must have a full schedule though because she actually lets the lie go. This is classic Tessa. I've always been permitted to lie if it made life more convenient for her. We hang up and I drop my face into my hands. She was doing it again. Last time I'd mustered enough of a fight to refuse Columbia, but that had been a pretty half-assed attempt at rebellion considering Barnard's relationship with Columbia. Whatever spark of defiance I might have summoned then has been completely obliterated by my humiliating experience this summer at The Crier. I'm squarely back in Tessa's control and she knows it.

Having no control is nothing new. My entire life has been not just constructed, but specifically engineered by her. Before I'd even existed, she'd planned and plotted it all with the skill of a mad scientist. My sperm donor had been carefully vetted and selected. The surrogate who carried me had undergone rigorous interviews, tests, and background checks. When four successfully fertilized eggs were ready for implantation, Tessa had taken no chances. She hadn't truly wanted one child, she certainly didn't want four. Naturally, she'd worked with an embryologist to select what was presumably the healthiest option. She chose poorly though.

My clinical conception wasn't the result of infertility on Tessa's part; it was simply an extension of who she was. Exact, leaving nothing to chance, and completely in keeping with being the most self-centered woman on the planet. Between her magazine and her books and her afternoon television show and her appearances on late night television, Tessa Shepherd didn't have time to be pregnant. That sort of unskilled labor belonged to the masses, so she'd contracted that little job out.

The construction hadn't ended with my birth. That's when the seemingly endless stream of nannies began. No one could have accused her of skimping on the best. Even her critics acknowledged her generosity with strangers after all. She could hardly present an image of being less than generous with her own child. As a result, she sought out only the most qualified candidates. Young women who spoke three, four languages. Aspiring authors. Recent Ivy League graduates who were saving for graduate programs.

Universally, I was reassured by each nanny that I was a good girl. I'd been a very docile child, eager to please my caretaker of the moment and, oh, how I tried to please them enough so that they would stay. The reality was that it didn't matter how hard I tried, they always left. No one ever left because of me. The problem was Tessa. No matter how well she paid, she quickly turned the girls off with her demands and insults, and they'd leave as soon as new employment was found.

In the years just prior to Calvin Brook, I'd graduated to household staff and private tutors rather than traditional nannies. They tended to stick around longer, because it wasn't ever intended to be a temporary career path for them. They knew that they were in their fields for the long haul, and the long haul meant staying within the good graces of Tessa Shepherd. This wasn't a storybook childhood though. A magical nanny didn't swoop in to turn household chores into a magical game. No one ever sang a ditty to me about sweeping the chimney. None of the adults who entered my life became more loyal to me than to their primary employer. Growing up, I understood my place in the household. My place was to provide others a well-paying job.

When I wasn't attending classes with my tutors or being shuttled around to ice skating lessons or gymnastics, both of which I was terrible at, I hid in my room. Within the paisley papered walls of my private quarters, I created an entire fantasy life centered around the family I never had. I wasn't Kennedy Shepherd, the pampered trophy daughter of the world-adored Tessa Shepherd and granddaughter of Allister Shepherd, heir to the Shepherd fortune. In my fantasy world, my embryo had been switched by accident.

Somewhere out there a spectacularly perfect little girl had accidentally ended up with a warm and humble family. She was really the daughter of a world renowned media personality and a mysterious tall, well-educated sperm donor. My real parents had normal jobs. He was a pilot. She was a nurse. They lived in a cozy house like the families in the movies. My real mother wasn't a woman who looked at me with frigid eyes, always searching for some hint that I might actually share her extraordinary DNA. My real mother wouldn't have found me wanting at all.

When I wasn't enacting scenes from my make-believe family world, I was curled up on my bed reading my books or penning awkward poems that I'd turn into little songs I'd softly sing as I strummed my guitar. Tessa preferred I spend my musical energy on the piano or violin, instruments she was well trained on that her own father approved of, but I loved escaping with my guitar the most. If she was in town, I'd retreat to the safety of my huge closet where I played and sang. Somehow in my juvenile mind, that closet door offered even greater protection than my bedroom door.

When middle school loomed and I was to be sent off to Calvin Brook, I said goodbye to that childhood room. I understood even then that it would never be the same. I'd be home for holidays and breaks, but those periods would be blessedly short. Then just before I was to leave, my mother dismissed our head housekeeper, Pilar, and offered to help me pack for the move. This was so out of character for her, she may as well have stripped down to her underwear and danced around the house to rock and roll. I wasn't sure what was happening, but I was weary of her offer. I knew even at that young age that Mother couldn't be trusted. As the daunting pile of suitcases and garment bags grew, she finally revealed her motive.

"Kennedy... you're a difficult child."

I stared up at her icy blue eyes, eyes that looked disturbingly similar to my own. A buzzing sound filled the background as her voice grew quieter. I'd tried so hard to stay out of her way, to bite back any requests. It wasn't enough though. She'd made it clear my entire life that I failed to measure up to her expectations. Her words were not a surprise. They stung just the same.

"I've tried to give you the tools you need. You've had a top-notch education, the best caretakers, the best instructors and tutors and guides.

You just don't seem to actually excel at anything though. You need to dig deeper and find what you can excel at Kennedy. You know that I did not build HoHo and everything that came afterward with luck. I built it all from the ground up, through hard work and perseverance."

At the tender age of 13, I didn't quite grasp how audacious her claim was. My mother had certainly worked hard, maybe it was even true that she'd worked even harder than any other woman had ever worked for anything, but she hadn't done it alone or from scratch. She'd walked right into the front doors of Columbia like she owned the place because in some ways she did. Her family had donated an actual building to the institution. Her trust fund had funded the startup costs for HoHo. Grandfather's contacts in the publishing and marketing industries had propped her and the then fledgling single publication up. My mother hadn't done any of it alone. It would take a few years before I really understood that though. Back then, I'd just accepted her version of history and allowed it to fill me with shame.

"I'm sorry. I will do so much better." I promised and meant it.

She stared at me for a moment, and then sighed and shook her head. "I hope so. You have a window of opportunity, Kennedy. It's not eternal. In just a few years you're going to be competing with people far brighter than yourself for a seat at the table. It all starts now. You need to learn and grow and be ready to seize your moment."

I'd promised to do just that, even though I didn't fully understand her advice. The one thing that was painfully clear though was that I was a disappointment. I was not the daughter that she'd paid a small fortune for. Something in my engineering had gone horribly and irreversibly wrong.

Sitting on this bench, the memory of her disappointment in me comes crashing back. This latest crisis isn't an anomaly. This isn't a terrible one-off. This is just further confirmation of what both my mother and I have always known. I'm not cut out to be Tessa Shepherd's daughter, I am a failure. This time, my failure is all too public though and that is the most unforgivable sin of all.

Chapter 3

Rachel

The muted trill of a double beep sounded from the top drawer of my desk and I glanced at the thin silver watch on my left wrist to confirm the time. There had been a time when I hadn't needed an alarm. Closing time had been an instinctive thing driven by years of unvaried practice, but ever since Delta left, this, like so many other things, has changed. Time has become a difficult thing to navigate. Minutes and hours blend together into murkiness; the distinct patterns developed over a lifetime have seemingly abandoned me. Now, I depend on alarms and calendars to keep my days organized. Still, I occasionally awake and feel momentary panic as I struggle to remember what day of the week it is. I like order- the loss of time is anything but orderly.

I turned the Open sign to Closed in the door window and carefully locked both locks. After turning off the front section of overhead lights, I opened the return drawer for a last check. Only a single book waited in the bin. After checking it back in, I studied the number on the spine and moved confidently down the dimly lit aisles.

When I reached the correct spot, I paused and glanced down at the book again. *Man's Search for Meaning*, by Viktor Frank. It was a whimsical desire that struck and I haven't been very prone to whimsy of late so I honored the impulse by flipping the book open to an arbitrary page and focusing on a random passage.

"You cannot control what happens to you in life, but you can always control what you will feel and do about what happens to you."

With a sharp intake of breath, I slammed the book shut and squeezed it into its proper place on the shelf. Yes, I understood something about the loss of control over one's own life already, didn't I? As I turned to walk away though, something made me pause. I'd been hearing Delta's voice less frequently lately- and it was bothering me more than I cared to admit, even to myself. So when she came to me, or more accurately the memory of her came to me, I stopped and listened.

"It's a riptide. You don't fight the current Rachel, that's how even strong swimmers exhaust themselves and die. Swim parallel to the coast instead. The ocean's gonna get bored of you eventually, she'll let you go if you're patient enough and don't fight her."

I turned and glanced again at the book's spine. Grudgingly, I pulled the book back off of the shelf. The shameful truth was that it had been awhile since I'd read anything. Delta would have been disappointed in my abandonment of the books that we had once loved so much, but I had not been able to bring myself to sit down and enjoy the kind of escapism that only a book offered in quite a long time. Not that I imagined Viktor Frank would offer much by way of escapism. Still, I'm a believer in signs. I craved them even. I'd give it a go.

Finally, my closing checklist was marked complete and I made my way toward the worn, old Saturn that sat illuminated beneath a perigean full moon. Although it was September, the unseasonably warm air seemed to be mocking any notion of impending autumn. Summer had issued its challenge; it wouldn't go quietly this year. This would have been a perfect evening to sit on the porch with Delta, sharing the details of our day, as we drank gin and tonics, heavy on the tonic, from small mason jars.

Those evenings hadn't been especially extraordinary but our ordinary had been more than enough. We'd swap stories and share laughter about the mundane moments of our day. Delta would stretch out, resting her tiny feet on the wicker table, bare legs shiny with insect repellant. Those short lazy moments were as relaxed as I'd ever see her- Delta was a hummingbird. A constant blur of motion. After a few minutes, she'd shift a bit and then stand to walk to the porch's rail where she'd scan the dark sky. I didn't bother standing, my stillness had always been keenly balanced with her motion.

Everything's changed. All memories hurt now. I glanced at the neon green numbers of the clock on the car's dashboard and verified them against my wristwatch. They were a minute off. I knew it already, I'd known it for weeks, but I fought the urge to correct it. Allowing the latitude of one solitary lost minute made me feel reasonable.

Gripping the steering wheel, I navigated through town, until I reached the abandoned gray clapboard house that marked the turn off for Cottage Road. In the background a reporter's voice droned in static dismemberment from the New York based news outlet that played on my a.m. radio station. It was loud enough to distract me from the noise that my car's engine had been making with alarming frequency lately. I knew I needed to replace the car, I'd had it for almost twenty years after all, but I avoided making large purchases at all costs. The radio helped me pretend that the noise was in my head. I'd only been half listening to the background hum of voices. That changed when I heard a familiar name waft through the car's speakers. Reaching down frantically, I increased the volume.

"... daughter of Tessa Shepherd reportedly admitted she invented the source. Shepherd, a student at Barnard College was about to complete the internship when the discrepancy was discovered by a Crier fact-checker. The Crier immediately corrected the story and is now...." The static increased in volume and drowned out the woman's voice and I softly muttered a single curse word.

Kennedy. It'd been many years since I'd heard that name spoken aloud and it hit with the force of a lead weight to my stomach. I hadn't uttered it myself in almost 21 years. Even Delta, a woman who had never been known for holding her tongue, hadn't violated that sacred boundary. Unable to recover the lost station, I gnashed my foot on the gas pedal harder than I normally would. I was suddenly desperate to get home so I could learn why her name was on the radio. I hadn't been able to work out exactly what had gone wrong but I was certain of one thing- Kennedy was in trouble.

*****

A very impatient Bilbo greeted me when I opened my front door. He meowed plaintively and I murmured an apology as we made our way back to the kitchen where I filled his bowl. I then quickly retreated to the guest room where we kept a small desk that housed an ancient Dell desktop computer. We'd previously used it to periodically pay bills and research trips; we could go days or even weeks without firing it up. Lately though, it had seen more frequent use as I'd started the job search process.

Tapping my foot impatiently as the ancient web browser loaded, I reminded myself that it was time to upgrade to a laptop. Like the car though, I was loath to replace a working computer even if it was operating on a less than optimal level. Finally, I was connected to the internet and was able to attempt a web search. Kennedy Shepherd.

As the results loaded, my frown deepened. Kennedy really was in trouble. According to the media, she'd spent the summer interning as a journalist at the Crier. Her program had almost reached its contracted end when the incident happened. A local reporter from the competing outlet, the NY Buzz, had been doing a series on the new harbor infrastructure project and erroneously reported the project was over budget. In his case, the error was later to be revealed as a simple typo, an erroneous extra zero, on an original memo. The data on that memo was eventually extrapolated into an entire print article. The story wasn't big news, readers expected government projects to be over budget, after all. Most readers would skim right past it and the retraction that later followed it. In almost any other circumstance, that would have been the last anyone heard about it.

Meanwhile though, the Crier had promised each intern a byline opportunity and Kennedy was assigned the relatively easy assignment. According to TMZ, Kennedy submitted a mediocre article at deadline and when a fact checker asked for her source, she'd then submitted an email that was purported to be from a mid-level city employee. The Crier ran the story and unfortunately for the newspaper and for Kennedy herself, it happened to run the very day that the Buzz retracted their story with an explanation of error. Kennedy was asked to explain herself, and it became clear that she hadn't just avoided doing her due diligence; she'd actually manufactured both the city employee and the email that he had supposedly sent.

Kennedy's journalistic integrity would be forever colored by the experience, but the story itself was relatively minor. It never would have made headlines at all if the name on the byline had been anything other than Kennedy Shepherd. When someone tipped off TMZ to the relatively minor event though, it had blown up into a full scandal. Now mainstream media everywhere was relaying the sordid tale of Tessa Shepherd's dishonest daughter.

The comments on the articles made it clear that the public wasn't going to be forgiving. I wasn't fooled by the faux outrage though. Those readers didn't actually care about the harbor project budget; this was just an opportunity to castigate both the media and the over-privileged daughter of America's Darling.

There wasn't an evening that went by that I didn't fervently wish for Delta's presence. Tonight, I needed her more than ever though. Sickened by what I'd read, I needed counsel on what to do next because I was considering doing something drastic. Something very improper. For almost 21 years, I've carefully abided by the contract I had signed; I have never attempted to contact Kennedy. At this precipitous moment though, my instinct was to reach out to the girl with an offer of comfort. I knew that she was probably facing scorn from both the public and from the very private. Tessa Shepherd would be furious with her.

My lips tightened as the woman trespassed into a space in my head, a space that normally repelled her. The world saw a handsome, smart, bitingly funny woman who could do no wrong. Her tips, advice, and opinions were heralded as gospel truth. I knew her better, though. It wasn't as if I could completely avoid her, although I'd tried. When I was younger, it had been easy enough to just ignore her magazine, HoHo, and her afternoon home decorating television show. Since then though, HoHo had spawned spin-off titles and guest television appearances. A major department store chain that I couldn't completely avoid carried a huge line of Tessa products, her smiling face emblazoned on the end caps that pushed the items.

I bit my tongue and hid my feelings whenever Tessa was mentioned by friends or patrons. I knew the real woman. I'd been at the receiving end of her abuse and fury. Twenty-one years later, I could still remember our initial meeting in vivid color. What had been described as a casual interview had in reality felt more like an inquisition. With the benefit of hindsight and age I knew now that I should have been suspicious from the onset of that meeting. I'd had to sign that ridiculous nondisclosure agreement just to attend the interview. Instead, I'd naively taken everything at face value and had been too star struck at meeting Tessa to question the request.

She'd been seated behind her monstrous oak desk, wearing a pink silk blouse adorned with a huge bow. Her ash blonde hair had been pulled back into an elegant simple clip at the back of her neck. Her makeup was expertly applied, drawing attention to the pale blue eyes that stared without compromise. She'd been flanked by an assistant and an attorney, who'd remained mostly silent through the process.

"Why Connecticut College?" Like every other question, it was asked in a probing, suspicious voice.

"Why did I pick it? I guess it just seemed like a good school and I wanted to be near the ocean and..." my voice had broken away, my nerves getting the better of me under her direct gaze.

Tessa continued to stare at me, piercing me with a prosecutorial gaze and the corners of her mouth turned up into something that resembled a smile but clearly wasn't.

"Your application says you graduated high school in Virginia Beach. No one goes to Connecticut College because it's a good school near the ocean if they live in Virginia. I'm asking again, and if we can't agree on reaching the truth here now, then I'll have Melissa escort you out. Why Connecticut College?"

I felt my face heat up and knew my cheeks would be an embarrassing patchwork of red splotches. If I told the truth, I probably wouldn't be selected. If I told a lie, this woman's relentless stare would see right through it. In the end, because I'd never been comfortable telling lies, I chose the truth.

"I followed my girlfriend here. She's in the Coast Guard and works at the academy in New London."

There it was. I'd assumed I'd be asked to leave and I'd go back to my desperate job search. My tuition deadline had been looming. I'd used up all of my savings and asking my parents for financial help wasn't an option. My federal loan only covered a portion of the tuition and fees due that semester and my job search was going dismally. I hadn't believed my luck when I'd heard back from the most improbable application of all. I wasn't exactly sure what a HoHo campus representative even did- but whatever it was, I wanted it! When I learned that the interview would be conducted by Tessa herself, I'd been shocked, yet I naively assumed it was her normal hands-on style.

When I'd answered her honestly, I had anticipated the worst. Instead, Tessa's mouth quirk twisted into a real smile. She glanced to her left, and nodded approvingly at her assistant. I had the distinct impression I'd somehow managed to pass a secret test.

"Where are your parents? Are they alive?"

Again taken aback by the personal question, I'd hesitantly answered, "Yes, they're alive. My father was also in the Coast Guard and recently retired from service. They relocated to Charleston, SC."

"Do they expect you to go to Charleston for breaks?"

That was a rather sticky issue. They certainly wanted me to come home, but that desire came with strings that I wasn't willing to agree to. Tessa tapped a pen impatiently against her desk, interrupting my thoughts.

"Not exactly. They'd like to see me, but it's complicated." I answered diplomatically.

Tessa nodded and pushed harder. "Any chance of reconciling this year?"

It was an odd question. The entire interview had been very odd though, so I'd shaken my head. Even back then, I hadn't been prone to entertaining false hopes.

The interview progressed to more conventional questions about my class load, hobbies, and goals. When I was asked about smoking, drinking, and drugs, I'd actually laughed. "I grew up in a strict Coast Guard family, now I live with a woman in the Coast Guard who also happens to be a marathon runner. We don't touch any substances that could endanger her job or her fitness level."

Just as I had finally begun to feel comfortable with the direction that the interview was heading in, Tessa had thrown me for another loop.

"Are you receiving any treatment or therapy for emotional or mental health issues?"

I didn't know everything about employment laws, but I had been pretty sure that wasn't a question an interviewer was allowed to ask. I remember Tessa looking almost bemused by my momentary silence, and I suspected that she was enjoying my discomfort. She was toying with me, batting me around softly as a cat might play with his prey.

I summoned my courage and said, "Ms. Shepherd, I really don't feel comfortable with all of these questions, I'm not sure how they can possibly relate to this position."

Tessa flashed her familiar television smile. "Dear, perhaps it's time to make my needs a little more clear. You'll have to forgive me if I gave a little bit of a false impression about this job. I'm not looking for a brand worker on campus. I'm searching for a potential surrogate for my fertilized embryo."

I'd gasped. "I don't understand. Aren't there agencies that handle that?"

Tessa explained that going to such an agency would necessarily involve a lot of staff and an easily accessible paper trail. She had no problem with the world knowing that her child had been brought into the world via a temporary surrogate vessel. She used those actual words, a temporary surrogate vessel. She didn't want a word leaked about it though until a healthy child had actually been produced. She didn't want the news to distract from her latest venture into a home goods line, and she didn't want her surrogate hounded either.

I learned that I along with over three hundred other eager applicants in the eastern CT region had already undergone basic background checks. The list had been culled down and of those invited to formally interview, I had been the first to hear the truth. Tessa stressed that this was still very much a job interview. She was seeking an employee, not a new family member or friend.

She'd have very specific and demanding expectations about everything from diet and rest, to what kind of labor would be expected.

There would be a residency requirement during the term of the pregnancy- her surrogate would be expected to remain in the state of Connecticut at all times. The contract would include all of those expectations along with a full non-disclosure agreement and a clause specifically forbidding contact with Tessa or the child after the birth. In exchange for following all conditions and delivering a healthy child, I would be very well compensated. The figure offered was enough to shock me- both then and now. I knew that I wouldn't have to work at all through my final year and half of college and could easily cover graduate school as well. There'd still be enough left over to invest, travel, and maybe buy a house someday.

I was given three days to consider the offer and was told that if I decided to continue then the next step would be a physical exam, a much more in-depth background check, including a home visit conducted by Tessa's personal investigator, and, of course, a drug test. In the end, I'd really only needed a few hours- the dollar amount I'd been offered was so staggering, I knew what I wanted to do. The only consideration I had left was Delta, and Delta had been an enthusiastic supporter of the crazy plan as soon as she heard the payout.

When the tests and investigation proved me to be a good candidate, I immediately began the required lifestyle changes. Prenatal vitamins, a strict diet, yoga and long walks became part of my daily life. I ended my enjoyment of an occasional glass of wine well before implantation was even attempted. In the end, Tessa's gut instinct proved correct and I found myself pregnant after the first round of in vitro fertilization.

The nearly forty weeks that followed are much harder to remember, not because I couldn't remember every single instant of them, but because it hurt too much to allow the memories to surface. I've done a good job of pushing the thoughts, the images, the caustic words and fears away. I've tried valiantly for over twenty years to pretend that year hadn't really happened. Delta made it easier. Delta had understood the visceral pain that any mention of that year could elicit. Delta wasn't here now to distract me and help me find peace.

I looked again at the monitor and browsed another article. It's curious that while each link has multiple pictures of Tessa, Kennedy was either not pictured at all or was represented by one of a handful of older photographs. The caption on this one indicated that it was from the daytime Emmy awards. In the photo she was twelve years old, wearing a sage green satin gown that looked about ten years too old for her thin, shapeless frame. She wasn't smiling; instead, she stood a few feet from Tessa's beaming presence, washed into the backdrop as a result.

I zoomed in to study her face. Every individual feature was a mirror of Tessa's; her eyes, her nose, her mouth, are all shaped the exact same way. Yet there was something about the way that they were placed that made her look wholly different. There was a hint of asymmetry, enough to make the overall effect less than perfect. In her youth, Tessa had been known as a great beauty. Before her empire building, when she was simply the daughter of one of the richest men in America, she'd been considered a prime catch. Kennedy is an attractive girl, but she wouldn't have enjoyed those same headlines.

The girl in the picture seemed to hover just far enough from her mother, in pale imitation, that there was an illusion of her being Tessa's barely perceptible shadow. Not for the first time, I felt the guilt wash over me. I'd brought that child into the world and then had left her with a woman I'd never believed could be a nurturing and loving mother. At the time, my financial desperation and the estrangement from my own parents muddied the waters and I'd convinced myself that if it wasn't me, it'd be some other young woman. I'd convinced myself it was ethical to agree to Tessa's plan. In retrospect though, I'd left a lamb with a wolf. It was my single greatest regret in life.

The lamb was alone now and needed someone to be on her side. The specter of Tessa and her legion of attorneys chilled me though. As much as I longed to reach out to Kennedy, I had no such right. Even if I were willing to break the contracts I'd signed, it might only make Kennedy's life more complicated and difficult. I needed to think before acting. I turned off the computer and went back downstairs to lock up the house. I'd attempt to put off any drastic decisions until after a full night's sleep.

Chapter 4

Kenna

The glossy, ink-scented pages of the annual HoHo College Years Special Edition are an homage to the art of decorating tiny student spaces. The wow factor of those tiny but extravagant spaces guarantees a flood of Instagram hearts. My third floor apartment wouldn't have made the magazine line up. Not because it isn't extravagant, but because no one would have believed it was actually a student's apartment. By Manhattan single bedroom apartment standards, it's large. By student standards, well, Mother prefers to call it an investment. I suppose financially it will eventually pay off. The real investment though, is her ego. She loves to show off photos of the *tony* apartment she's given her daughter. Mother insists on referring to it as *tony* even though absolutely no one uses that word anymore despite her efforts at giving it a comeback. She also hadn't actually given it to me - my name isn't on the deed. It's hers, just like I'm hers.

　　She'd had it expertly decorated by one of HoHo's designers, a bold young woman whose lips are permanently stained with a bright red matte lipstick. Most women intimidate me and she was no exception. I'd met her beforehand so she could consult with me about my style preferences. The velvety red Cupid's bow on her face had made me want to be brave. I'd chosen to be brave. I did something rare- I chose to share my real opinion. I'd told her I didn't have high needs. White walls, black furniture, dramatic black and white art prints would be just fine. My solitude and my music can both handle living in black and white. When I'd finally moved in a month later, I settled into the reds and oranges and ambers of the rich Moroccan palette that my mother had chosen.

Now that I'm safely back within my apartment's plush walls, I wonder how long I can hide from the world. I've never brought any fellow students back here. My mother and the daily delivery persons are the sum total of my guest list. I'm not close enough to anyone to invite them in. I don't trust anyone enough to see beyond the opulence I had never asked for to see the real me. I'm used to being alone. Back when I was at Calvin Brook I'd felt safe enough with my peers to connect with them casually. I hadn't nurtured or maintained those relationships afterward; I'm not really sure how people do that. Those relationships hadn't proven strong enough to survive the tests of time and distance. At Barnard I haven't even tried. I've just hidden in plain sight, along the periphery.

My stomach is still knotted so I curl up on my sofa and wrap a soft, burnt orange knit throw around my thin frame. Bag of bones, that's exactly what my last Nanny had called me affectionately. I never cared for that term of endearment. I feel it in my soul now though. No form or substance- just a random collection of collagen and calcium phosphate. My first day back on campus had been every bit as awful as I'd feared it would be. Mother had insisted I make an appearance. "Put on your lipstick and a nice pair of shoes, hold your head up high and act as if you did nothing wrong. Half the people you meet don't care about the truth, they only care about how you carry yourself."

Such bits of wisdom are vintage Tessa. Understand, my mother is angry most of the time. But when she isn't, she doles out nuggets of wisdom in the way that other mothers dole out hugs. I cling to those moments because they're as close as I ever get to her love. I collect the words and memorize them, but I don't actually believe them. Their power is in the giving, not the application. Mother doesn't understand that she operates on an entirely different plane than the rest of us. In Tessaworld, she can do no wrong and her word is gospel. She is America's Darling, after all. Her advice doesn't really apply to my reality.

None of this is to say that Mother doesn't have her critics. There is a certain segment of the public who love to hate her. Nothing she says or does will ever placate them. Those voices are the fringe though; they hold no real power over my mother. My mother controls the entire narrative of her life and the lives around her and she's able to ignore the voices that she's decided don't matter. I didn't inherit that trait.

I try to steel myself with a deep breath, and then I open a browser on my phone. A search results in a slew of articles, all based on or referring back to the original TMZ piece. Link after link shares my humiliation in celebratory fashion. It's as if I'm reading about a stranger. Who is this horrible young woman, Kennedy Shepherd? She's a liar and a fraud. The people who wrote the articles and blog posts are so excited to see her fall. It's obvious that some of them were really excited to see a chink in Tessa's solid gold armor. They might fawn over her and court her prized interviews, but they're all too happy to throw shade now that her vulnerability has been exposed. Me. I'm the vulnerability.

One anonymous source confirms Tessa Shepherd personally contacted the Crier to request her daughter be awarded the highly sought after position. While the younger Shepherd's academic record had been good, she wasn't a standout student and there had been speculation amongst the staff that the placement had been a mistake even before the Harbor Fund scandal. Tessa Shepherd did not return our calls or requests for an interview.

On some level, I've known she'd done that. She never told me that she'd gotten me the internship and I certainly hadn't asked, but I'd always suspected it. To see the truth staring at me in black and white on a backlit screen hurt a lot worse than unconfirmed suspicions. Back when I was sending applications out last spring, I'd been so hesitant about applying to major publishers. My GPA had been a respectable 3.5, but that wasn't in the scholarly league of most successful applicants. I hadn't wanted to stay in the city at all. I'd begged my mother to let me return to Connecticut, find a small local paper, and bide my time that way. I knew that having no internship at all wouldn't be an option, so I was hoping to shoot for the least painful experience possible.

Tessa had been furious that I'd even asked. "You don't leave New York City to find an internship in Connecticut. That's ridiculous. It's as if you're purposely aiming as low as possible, as if you want to actually destroy your career before it even starts."

She hadn't been entirely wrong. I've never wanted to be a journalist. I've never wanted to be a writer. I've never wanted to have anything to do with her publishing world at all. I couldn't say any of that though, so instead I dutifully collected letters of recommendation, writing samples, and filled out the applications. Apparently that had all been for show, Tessa had always had her cache of contact numbers at the ready to do her bidding. My cheeks burn as I understand now why I'd faced such hostility from the other interns. I had been handed what they had worked so hard for.

Unable to endure another rehash of the story, I close the browser and open my student email account. The first new message is from the Honor Board. My first hearing date is scheduled and I'm expected to present myself and any extenuating evidence I might have. I'm invited to bring a faculty member to serve as a mediator if I wished, but I couldn't bring an attorney. All hell will break loose when I forward this to Tessa. She fully anticipates I'll be leaving Barnard, but she wants it to happen under her carefully constructed terms. An attorney's presence is an important part of those terms. I have to assume now that more inappropriate demands will follow.

I scroll past a long list of welcome back campus-wide messages. Slaps across my face. Updated class requirements, invitations to join new clubs, promises of the college's commitment to a safe and vibrant campus. Messages not meant for me. I'm about to shut down the portal completely when I notice a message that looks out of place. The subject line simply says, *Dear Kennedy*. I don't recognize the sender's email address and considering some of the nasty comments that I've read online I am afraid of it. Is this someone who wants to hurl terrible words at me, someone who would get their jollies watching me fall even further?

I think about deleting it, unread. Mother always says critics only have power if you bother to listen to them. I don't have to listen. Mother also always says I'm the biggest disappointment of her life and she's made it clear that not listening to her has never been an option. If I have to listen to my biggest critic, what's the point in shutting down the lesser voices? I open the message.

Dear Kennedy,

I was able to find your address through the journalism department student email directory. I hope I'm not being too forward by contacting you, although I suspect I am. I'm certainly violating a legal trust, if not also a moral one. It's absolutely your right to share this with Tessa, although I hope that perhaps you'll consider the value in that.

My name is Rachel Patrick, and I first met your mother in 1998 when I was a student at Connecticut College. It's a long story, but the end result was she chose me to be your surrogate mother. I'd never come to you like this if I thought that news would be shocking- but I've seen the surrogacy mentioned several times by Tessa in interviews over the years so I assume you're well aware of that part of your background.

I've read about your recent hardships, and feel compelled to reach out and let you know I am thinking about you. I know you don't know me from Adam, but at one time we were quite familiar with one another. I have found there have been times in my life where I've felt so very alone even while being surrounded by other people. I don't know if this is the case for you right now, but putting myself in your shoes it seems it may be. As hard as it may be to imagine right now, this too shall eventually pass and someday you will look back and it won't hurt like it does right now.

I'm not trying to invade your privacy and I have no expectations from you, it's fine to never reply to this at all. I just wanted you to know that somewhere in this world, there is a woman who is thinking of you and wanting the best for you.

Sincerely,
Rachel Patrick

I stare at the screen for a few minutes. The fact that I have a surrogate mother is not a surprise. That woman has always been abstract though, as if she'd only existed for nine months for the express purpose of serving Tessa's needs and then disappeared into thin air after my birth. I've wondered about the woman occasionally over the years. Back in high school I'd read an article that suggested that babies carry a small amount of DNA from their surrogates, as it crosses the placenta during development and it becomes forevermore a part of their genetic makeup. More recently I'd seen a news report that suggested women actually kept some small bit of DNA from the babies they carried, for the rest of their lives as well. Chimera. That's the term for an individual who carries genetic material from multiple sources. That another definition of a chimera was a monster from Greek mythology doesn't escape my notice.

Any curiosity I've felt about the woman who carried me is weaker than my fear of Tessa's rage so I've resisted the urge to ask any probing questions. The identity and story of the woman who carried me seems pretty minor in the scope of my life. On the other hand, the wrath I'd face by violating one of Tessa's unspoken codes seems pretty major. I've stifled any questions and let my curiosity go.

Rachel. Her name is Rachel. Another thought occurs to me- how do I know the woman is even telling the truth? As she'd said, Tessa hasn't hidden this story; anyone could have picked it up over the years. She could be an imposter taking advantage of the fact that my name is in the news now. I'm not sure what her gain would be, but it isn't uncommon for scammers to go after my mother and her money. Tessa's legion of lawyers usually protected her, the obvious thing to do here is to forward this to them so that they can handle it. What if she's telling the truth though and what if she really just wants to offer comfort?

I google her name and the resulting hits are overwhelming. Her email hadn't specified her city, or even state. I add "Connecticut College alumni" to my search bar and that finally does the trick. A LinkedIn account pops up for one Rachel Patrick, Connecticut College class of 2001, librarian in Metzgartown, Pennsylvania. Any hopes of seeing what she looks like are quickly dashed. She's broken from headshot convention, and has a picture of a bookshelf as her profile picture. It's disappointing.

Maybe her face would have revealed something. I'm not sure what exactly I'd learn from it, but maybe there'd be some hint of truthfulness or some suggestion of duplicity.

I have a lot of questions and they aren't just about this outreach now. Becoming a surrogate is a pretty major commitment. Her body, her time, her mental health- it must have all been impacted during those nine months. There's the obvious motivation, I'm sure Tessa dangled a huge financial carrot. I've watched people subject themselves to my mother's abuse and demands over payouts that were likely to have been far less than she'd offered her surrogate. Had Rachel Patrick actually known my mother? Is it possible they had been friends? I thought of the small circle of women my mother described as friends, no, she wouldn't have related at all to a librarian. Did this Rachel Patrick have other children? I'm an only child. When I was younger, I always wished for a younger sibling when I blew out my birthday candles. If Rachel Patrick does have children, would they be almost-siblings?

I weigh the pros and cons of replying back. I'm curious, but I've also spent my entire life armoring myself so that no one would get too close. I guard my privacy every bit as carefully as Tessa guards her reputation. While my mother thrives on public attention, I take every precaution possible to avoid it. I reread the letter though and fixate on her final line. "*I just want you to know that somewhere in this world, there is a woman who is thinking of you and wanting the best for you.*"

I feel it, the faintest hint of something, a single strand of something that might be hope, kissing my skin. For a moment this woman's simple, kind words are a physical talisman that has floated through the ether to touch me. I am alone, I am always alone, but now suddenly I'm not. At least for a moment. There's an oblique otherness out there and through the power of her thoughts- I am momentarily seen and felt.

I pick up my guitar and begin to strum softly.

Takes three long years, to sell her beat.
Ran hooded down Greenwich Street.
Oh little one, she cannot see
The sun from the shadows of Greenwich Street.

The sound of my phone interrupts the moment and the fragile tendril of peace I'd felt floats away again. I reluctantly set my guitar to the side and grab the offending object. Tessa. My urge is to ignore it, to let it go to voicemail just this once. If I do that though, there will be a knock at my door eventually. Sighing, I answer it on the third ring.

"Kennedy, I've been thinking about it and maybe the best choice after all is to withdraw before they have a chance to actually hear this thing. I know we all want to take it through their little fake honor court and make them put it on paper that you didn't wrong the school in any way, but Phil thinks we might be able to reason with the school and agree to early withdrawal and promise we won't sue in exchange for complete expunction and a nicely worded letter absolving us of any guilt."

Us. I want to scream that there was no "us" in this fight and that I certainly can't be absolved of guilt when I've clearly done the thing. I say nothing and instead stare at my guitar, imagining my fingers running chords, until I don't hear a word she says anymore.

"Kennedy! Are you even listening? You're going into shut down mode again, aren't you?"

"Yes, mother, I hear you. I'm sorry. I'm just... well, I don't have much to say, I guess."

Usually, when we reach this part of the discussion, she angrily walks away. I know that she can't stand it when I "shut down," but ironically she doesn't want me to actually respond either. I am to be an acrobat. I am somehow expected to both feign interest and avoid participating in said conversation at the same time. This time, though, she just won't let go. Her words become more acrid and her pitch becomes sharper as she reverts to one of her favorite insults. It's one I've heard many times during my youth.

"Ungrateful spoiled brat. You've been given everything any girl could ever want, and you appreciate none of it. Vapid, ungrateful, spoiled brat."

She's losing control- the tough, unstoppable Tessa Shepherd has been reduced to pure emotion and I know that once this happens, it'll take days of silence to move beyond it. Most people would be horrified by this shrieking, cruel version of the woman America adores. I, on the other hand, spend most of my waking hours trembling at the thought of dealing with my mother's cold, biting commentary. It's a relief when she actually loses control like this. Satisfying even. Face to face, it can be terrifying. Over the phone though, it's a means to an end. I want nothing more than the days of silence that I know will follow this outburst. When the phone clicks in my ear, I sigh in relief and put it on the end table.

"I just wanted you to know that somewhere in this world, there is a woman who is thinking of you and wanting the best for you."

I glance around the lushly decorated main room. Gilded wooden frames adorn painted reproductions of plaster arabesques that cover the walls. Small glass topped sculpture tables of varying heights accent various areas in the room. A brightly colored cascading Moroccan pendant lamp hangs appealingly in one corner. It's a luxuriant room designed for intimate parties and affairs that would never take place.

The warm gold and orange tones, the plush fabrics, the carefully selected bohemian art- the intended effect is one of welcome. The problem is, none of it can disguise the cold foundation, the forever winter of my empty life. I drop my phone onto the cocktail table, stand up and walk toward the bedroom. I glance at the ornately carved queen sized bed and, for a moment, contemplate lying down and losing myself in a nap. But then I make a decision. I turn and look toward the closet, toward the place that houses my chic pink suitcases and as if I am sleepwalking, I walk toward it and begin to pack.

Chapter 5

Rachel

If there is a heaven, it's an eternal Saturday morning in September. The kind that starts with the glazy hint of frost kissing the tips of grass blades, but soon transforms to the sweet, fresh scent of green under the mid-morning sun. The kind that ushers summer's mosquitos and humidity away even as it promises that the gravel encrusted snowy roads of winter need not be considered yet. Here in the mere mortal realm though, we only get four or five of those a year. In the before, back in my happy years, they'd been the ideal quiet recompense for the week's hard work.

We'd had a system. Delta was in charge of the coffee station because she didn't burn that. Cooking had been God's way of humbling her, she used to quip. Bilbo would weave between our legs as we worked side by side and then we'd pile the eggs and toast that I'd cooked onto Delta's antique Wedgwood plates. My Mama had taught me that if you have pretty things, you should use them, not hide them away in a cupboard. Saturday mornings in September were made for Wedgwood plates, dippy eggs and warm, brown triangles of buttered toast. Then, as we sat across from each other on the back deck, we'd enjoy the kind of quiet, comfortable conversation that only two people who have been together for decades can appreciate.

Now I brew my own coffee. There are no fried eggs or toast these days. Cooking for one earns no gratitude and it's difficult to work through an entire loaf of bread before it goes stale. Instead, I prepared a bowl of cold cereal or hot oatmeal, depending on the weather.

I stepped out onto the back patio with my book tucked under one arm as I clung to my bowl and mug. It was an unseasonably warm September, with temperatures in the mid-70s, but I knew that it was a fool's summer. Fall was smiling petulantly around the corner. For now, the backyard was still a brilliant green. Even the giant oak that had long served as our traditional seasonal gauge gave no hint of the brilliant oranges to come. A large swath of freshly bloomed black-eyed Susans framed the sides of the patio, watching me with the practiced disinterest of professional courtesans. Nothing planted out here was willing to concede to autumn just yet.

There were some early hints of change though. The nestlings had moved on, the birds were a little quieter in general these days. The squirrels were starting to grow more active in their foraging. The animals always knew first. Soon a kaleidoscope of color would blanket the entire region as the first crisp breezes crept in. This time of year, just before autumn's appearance and just after summer's longest days, this had been our favorite.

It had been almost six months, but I could still picture Delta sitting in the empty chair beside me with her tiny hands wrapped around her mug as her green eyes scanned the great oak's branches.

"Now why in the hell do you think the Sheehan's cut down that tree in their backyard?" She asks irritably.

"I told you. They want to put one of those above ground pools in sometime next spring, they figured it'd be easiest to get it cut down before winter so they can get an early start in the spring."

She looks at me, her eyes blazing and replied, "A tree isn't an inanimate object Rachel. It may not walk around, but it moves. It grows. Those young branches there, they're going to move right along to a new spot five years from now. You don't just cut down a tree that's survived everything nature can throw at her to put in a pool you might get three month's use out of a year. It's a damned travesty, that's what it is."

Delta maintained that incandescent fire almost to the bitter end. Even when her formerly solid, muscular body had been whittled down to a mere 88 pounds and her glorious mass of curls were just a memory- even then she'd still occasionally whisper about some injustice that she felt I needed to fight on her behalf. I knew that she needed to see that fire in me;

46

she needed to know that her voice still made a difference in some way. I was her legacy. I'd nod and agree and try my hardest to look like I cared about anything other than the fact that the woman I loved most in the world was dying slowly before my eyes.

At the very end, after we'd made the decision to have hospice in our own home, either her medical aid Randy or I would bundle Delta up in her mother's patchwork quilt and carry her onto the deck. She'd lay perched in the lounger, impossibly small, and would stare at the oak as spring's first earnest attempts became clear. She wasn't really talking at all by then, but she could still see and feel and love. Randy would wait quietly in the background and I'd sit beside Delta and pretend it was a warm early September Saturday. I'd hold her hand and would quietly point out the new buds, the emerging squirrels, the birds busily nesting. I'd assure her that soon we would see everything fully bloomed and it would be our season again.

Just like every other time I sat out on that patio these days, I closed my eyes and strained to feel her. I had this fantasy that if I listened hard enough, I'd eventually hear her whisper my name. If I inhaled deeply enough, I'd catch the slightest whiff of her Hawaiian plumeria perfume. I wished and prayed for a sign, a message, a hint, every single time I sat out there. Every single time I was left wanting.

"People waste way too much time pining away for the dead. There are plenty of living people who need our attention." Delta says because I've apparently read one too many obituaries in her opinion.

"Come on, be real. I'm surrounded by dead poets and dead novelists writing about their dead lovers and dead mothers, all day, every day, at work. Dead people have things to say too." I insist.

Delta gives a little chuckle and tips her mug toward me, giving me the solid point. It isn't often that I score the win, so I smile back and accept it graciously.

Now the one voice from the great beyond that I most desperately wanted to hear remained silent. Annoyed at myself for persisting in the wasted exercise, I glanced at the book that I'd impulsively grabbed the previous night. I'd read it during my college years as part of a philosophy class, but as was often the case with required reading, I hadn't given it my full attention. Straining, I tried to recall what had been notable about the author- Viktor Frankl. He'd been a holocaust survivor, but he'd also been uniquely qualified to dole out wisdom on meaning and purpose. There was a background in both medicine and philosophy, as I recalled.

As I read through the Foreword I felt quite ambivalent about the entire exercise. There had been a number of grief books throughout the prior six months that I'd skimmed through. They hadn't helped. They'd just left me feeling impotent. There was a spark missing in my own spirit and in its place a troubling numbness had taken refuge. Time wasn't fixing it either, instead I felt the numbness grow with each mundane morning routine. Some part of me had been anesthetized and a spate of grief books hadn't reversed that.

Frankl believed meaning could be found in one of three ways. One could find it through meaningful work, and through the act of ordinary love, romantic or otherwise, and by displaying extraordinary courage during times of trial.

That was the heart of the matter, wasn't it? My work paid the bills and was pleasant enough, but it hardly inspired any grand purpose. I wasn't saving lives or changing the world. As for courage, I wasn't a particularly cowardly woman, but I'm also no hero. That left love. I had no children, I barely had a relationship with my parents, and I'd only loved one woman in my life. Meaning had ceased to exist when Delta ceased to exist. I was an island.

I swallowed the last bit of coffee and walked back inside. Like most of my weekend days of late, there wasn't much to be done but I kept a meticulous schedule for the few obligations I had. Some light housekeeping work, my morning walk with Susan, and my latest project. I'd adopted the practice of personalizing and sending two to three résumés out every Saturday. The job hunt wasn't desperate; there was nothing wrong with Metzgartown or Metzgartown Library. This was an exercise in curbing the restlessness that plagued me. I needed something to make it feel as if the simple act of waking up had a purpose again.

Résumés had been carefully crafted and sent to targeted cities along the east coast. Most of my adult life had been spent in Pennsylvania, but parts of me were scattered along the Atlantic seaboard. The idealized scenes of my earlier childhood had never left me, if I returned to one of the cities I had previously called home, it would be a continuum. I'd pick up a path that I'd already started. There wasn't a real preference for any one location - each one offered a good balance of familiarity and adventure. Each one would also come with unique challenges.

The problem was that despite my carefully crafted résumé and diligent follow-up attempts, thus far nothing was panning out. The lack of responses wasn't a complete shock. By the time I was in college, certainly by my graduate school years, the writing was on the wall for the print world. Many of my wiser and more attentive peers had dabbled their toes in Library Sciences but quickly abandoned it for more employable career fields. I'd stubbornly hung in there, clinging to both my love of books and my love of order. I was born to work in a library. Lately, I'd been trying to think outside of that box. The reality was I could only do so much with an MS in Library Science. If that failed to land me a position, then perhaps my much broader undergrad degree in English would open other doors. If I persisted, an opportunity would knock eventually. This was the promise I made myself.

Today's résumés would go out to a small private school in southeastern Virginia and to the Navy base in Key West. The Virginia job was pretty standard and I had an already existing cover letter that I'd edit creatively. With a final proofread done, I hit "send." The Key West job was a little different; it was located on a secure Navy base. I opened the base webpage to explore it further.

Clear blue skies, palm trees, and a jet flying overhead dotted the landscape of the opening image. It was both familiar and different. I grasped at the fragments of memories that the photo elicited. I'd lived there for my first eight years of life. Brilliant sunsets. Roosters crowing. Running barefoot across the courtyard in our Sigsbee housing community with friends. Melting popsicles in our sticky hands. Forever summer.

Life at home was still sweet. When my father was out to sea on his Coast Guard cutter, my mother allowed me to eat in the living room in front of the television. She'd throw together easy hodge-podge meals that my father wouldn't have approved of. With bellies full and the soft golden glow of the sofa-side lamp changing my mother's face from pretty to beautiful, we'd curl up side by side to enjoy our books. Picture books graduated to first readers and by first grade I was already reading Nancy Drew. My obsession with books was born on a worn, plaid couch just a mile from America's southernmost point.

Those were the years when my parents' marriage was strong and happy, and my parents were the two people that I admired most in the world. When my father was in port, they'd hire a teenage babysitter and I'd watch as they walked hand in hand toward the gate that led into town. My dad worked hard then, but he hadn't had the same level of responsibility that anchored him later in his career. Appearances hadn't meant quite as much. They could still relax with drinks and go dancing with friends until the sun came up. Years later, I would wonder why they had retired to Charleston rather than Key West, because they never seemed quite as happy again as they'd been there.

I had still idolized my father then. When he was in port, he'd been a hands-on, involved parent. Even now, after all of the hurt and anger and resentment, I could smile at those memories. It's a bittersweet smile though. It was difficult to accept that the jovial, fun father of those tender years turned into the same man who'd forced distance between us later. I preferred to think of them as two separate entities. I preferred to pretend my original father, the one who loved and accepted me as I was, was still out there somewhere in the perma-sun of Key West.

A knock at the door interrupted my thoughts. Surprised, I glanced at the clock. I wasn't mistaken; it was only 10 am, Susan was early for our walk. I shook my head in annoyance because she knew how I felt about punctuality. I stifled a groan though because the walks were good for me and they were also good for Susan who was still on a long post-cardiac event recovery path.

"Come on in, I'm upstairs!" I yelled down.

As I began to descend the stairs, I heard the door open. I was about to hit the stairwell's turn when I heard the sound of a throat clearing.

"Um, Ms. Patrick?" The young voice clearly didn't belong to Susan.

Surprised, I stared down as I rounded the corner. Townsfolk had descended on our home right after Delta passed, dutiful bees to the hive to deliver casserole dishes wrapped up in honeyed words. But that time was over, the drop-ins had faded gradually until they'd stopped entirely. I was the only one still mourning these days. I couldn't imagine who would be visiting me now.

A young woman, girl really, stood awkwardly in the doorway. She wore an olive green backpack on one shoulder and clutched a piece of folded paper in one hand. She'd already dropped a black guitar case and a ridiculously bright, pink suitcase at her feet. For a moment she was a complete stranger but then I allowed myself to look at her, really look at her. Everything fell into place at once. Dizziness washed over me, as if I'd been dangling inverted for too long. I grasped the stair rail in an attempt to keep my balance and stared down at her as the foreign familiarity of her face revealed itself. I'd seen this face, or an altered, older version of it, on book covers and billboards and television commercials. Kennedy.

"Hi, I'm Kenna. Kenna Shepherd. You emailed me yesterday... at least I hope it was you..." The girl's voice was weak and tired.

I appraised her. She was no imposter. The resemblance was unmistakable even if she was wearing an expression I couldn't imagine ever crossing Tessa's face. The girl wore tight blue jeans, a baggy sweater, and black leather booties. The ensemble looked casual and thrown together but I suspected every piece cost a fortune. She was attempting a smile, but it only amplified the distress on her pale face. Breathe Rachel, I told myself, and I nodded an affirmation. She'd come to the correct place alright.

"Kennedy, or did you say Kenna?" I replied.

"Kennedy is my legal name, but I go by Kenna. It's a long story I'll explain some time, but the short version is that Kennedy always felt so... big." The girl explained.

I still felt a little shaky, but that made me chuckle. I could imagine just how much Tessa must love that. On still shaky legs, I walked down the last of the steps and motioned for her to follow me into the living room.

"Go ahead and sit down. I expect we have things to discuss but first I think this calls for me to hit my hidden stash of Scottish tea. I'll be back in a minute." I said, impressed with my own ability to keep my voice level and calm.

In the safe refuge of the kitchen, I gripped the edge of our Formica countertop and practiced a series of deep breaths. Kennedy was here, in our home. I was torn between the desire to dart out of the back door and run toward the safety of the old oak and running back into the living room to scoop the child up into my arms. Woman, I reminded myself. She'd grown into a beautiful young woman, but it was clear that she was in distress. Why exactly was she there though? *In my living room.* Was she in more trouble than I had thought?

Another thought occurred to me. Oh, dear God, did Tessa know that she was here? I'd have to find that little nugget of information out as soon as possible, but the possibility spurred me back into action. Problems didn't resolve themselves. I placed a kettle on the stovetop and dug through the pantry for a box of shortbread. Delta's prized teacups barely shook on their delicate saucers as I carried them over to the stove. I was back in control.

My kitchen timer chimed, warning me it was 10:15 am. Normally, I'd head upstairs to change for my weekly walk with Susan at this point. Instead, I called her and said there wouldn't be a walk today. As the water reached a rolling boil, I poured it over finely dried leaves from a half a world away and inhaled the earthy aroma that rose with the steam. We'd visited Scotland six years ago and discovered the brand. Delta wasn't much of a tea drinker, but I'd loved it and periodically ordered a replacement tin online.

"Why does this tea taste better on your lips than from a cup, Rachel?"

The memory grounded me. It reminded me of who I was and how strong I could be. When I walked back into the living room, I found Kenna perched on the edge of the pink wingback chair. She was ready to run, I thought. Small and terrified, she didn't look like she was about to turn twenty-one, she could have been thirteen years old. My natural inclination was to go to her, hug her, reassure her, but I resisted it and handed her the cup instead.

"Okay Kenna, can you tell me how you came to be here?" I asked, my voice quite steady. I'm quite adept at controlling my emotions, a skill born from years of working with children who could make a grown woman cry if she were too thin-skinned. A skill honed by six months of disguising grief in public. This felt like the ultimate test of that skill.

"Well, I googled you and found your LinkedIn account. Once I found out what town you worked in, it was easy enough to find your address."

I'd only created the account because the job search articles I'd meticulously read and studied had suggested it was critical in this day and age. Thus far it hadn't helped me find a job, but apparently it had blasted my location to the entire world wide web. That was a little disconcerting.

"And you drove over from the city this morning?"

Kenna shook her head and lifted her chin proudly. "I took the Martz bus from the city to Scranton, and then took a taxi here. I didn't think it was a good idea to bring my car. She can trace me that way."

I hoped she didn't notice just how tightly my fists clenched. "She? Tessa?"

Kenny flushed, "Yeah. I mean, if I took the car she'd have people looking for it. Plus, it's just one more thing that's really hers..."

"So she doesn't know you're here? Does she know you've left at all?"

"No. I didn't volunteer the information. I know this probably seems crazy, but I just needed to get away. I couldn't take one more day at Barnard and I can't take one more call from my mother."

It didn't seem crazy at all to me. I remembered quite clearly just how manic Tessa could be on the phone, the incessant demands, the undisguised insults. She was able to suck all of the oxygen out of the room even when she wasn't physically present. Crazy wasn't wanting to escape that, crazy was purposely subjecting yourself to it for nine long months.

"What about school though, surely this isn't the best time to take off?" I asked in as delicate a tone as I could muster.

"I'm done with the school," Kenna paused, then corrected flatly, "They're done with me."

I wanted to ask about the incident at the Crier. Perhaps it was being reported inaccurately. I wasn't sure if Kenna was a victim or if she'd actually created the mess she was in. I did know that she'd been hounded by social media, the real media, her school, and worst of all- Tessa. I could see how fragile she was and I knew it wasn't the time to push for more details.

"Kenna, I'm glad you came here. I've always wanted to meet you. You are more than welcome in my home! I have to ask though, why here? Don't you have a friend or boyfriend you could have gone to?"

Kenna's eyes shot downward as she confessed, "No, I don't really have any friends and there's no boyfriend. I thought about just heading out someplace new, alone, but the truth is when I read your letter, I realized I wanted to meet you."

I smiled at that and said, "I'm glad you're here. We have a lot of catching up to do, almost 21 years' worth."

My smile swiftly dropped though as another thought hit me, "Kenna, Tessa isn't going to just let you walk away without answers. She's going to want to know you're safe. I don't think she's going to take this very well though."

My mind raced as the full implications of testing Tessa's rage hit me. I'd signed a very explicit contract all those years ago. When Tessa learned that I had reached out to Kenny via email, she'd hold me accountable. I didn't have a huge savings account, but I did have this house and Tessa could easily go after it. I didn't want to face a lawsuit, but even more ominous, was the thought of facing the woman herself. I knew how toxic she was. The last time, I'd allowed her to bully and intimidate me. I'm not that timid 21-year-old college student anymore and I'd have a lot to say back this time. Everything could explode.

"I'm not calling her." Kenna said resolutely. It was the strongest her voice had sounded yet, and she was looking me in the eyes. Her steadfast gaze held a challenge.

I studied her for a moment. The girl had been beaten down by something in her life, but there was a spark of fire in there. Escaping Tessa, avoiding the media, that wasn't the act of a girl who was surrendering her fate- it was just the opposite. She was taking control of her own life, maybe for the first time ever.

"Kenna, don't you think she'll be able to trace you here?" I asked softly.

"I don't know, maybe. But I didn't make it easy. I withdrew cash and used that to buy my ticket and cab fare. I've kept my phone powered off. I didn't tell anyone. I just need time. I'll call her eventually, but right now I just can't."

I glanced back to the suitcase and guitar. I certainly had the space for her. I could set her up in the guestroom, she could... what exactly would Kenna do all day while I was at work? Read? Watch tv? Maybe that was exactly the kind of healing she needed, but something told me that Kenna already had plenty of solitude.

For the first time in a long time, I felt an alluring spark of curiosity. I had my own selfish reasons to keep her here. I wanted to get to know the young woman I'd given birth to. I wanted to hear about her life. I wanted to be part of the solution to her troubles. I had spent the past six months trying to find something other than work to wake up for each day, and maybe Kenna was an answer to that prayer too.

At that thought, I stood and asked for Kenna to follow me to the kitchen, then motioned toward the backdoor. I'd always thought best out on that deck, under the watchful eye of the old oak. We sank into the plush chairs around the glass topped table and I ignored the urge to rise again immediately to get a paper towel to wipe a streak. Stay here, stay now, I told myself. I gazed at the oak tree again. What would Delta have said at this turn of events? What would she have counseled?

"You're a caretaker, I love that in you but it also drives me nutty as hell. We don't need a cat, although I'm still not convinced that dirty, scruffy little ball actually is a cat. I'm not gonna waste my breath telling you to take it to the shelter though, I know better than to get between you and one of God's critters in need."

Delta would have thought this was absolutely crazy. She would have made that opinion crystal clear and then she would have completely accepted and supported my inevitable decision to help Kenna, in any way possible. She would have done it because she had a big heart. She'd have felt sorry for the girl, but almost just as importantly- she would have done it because she'd have known how much I needed this to happen.

Just a few hours ago, I had begged the dead to speak and then Kenna had knocked on my door. It's a solemn thing to have a wish granted from the dead. Such wishes don't come without strings. I'd be expected to use the gift wisely. Here in this backyard, this sacred space, we could get to know one another, but we'd be doing so on borrowed time. By bringing Kenna here, I'd be all but inviting Tessa to invade my sanctuary. I needed to protect both Kenna and this space. How could I connect with this young woman, keep her engaged, and protect both of us from Tessa at the same time?

The idea came swiftly. Kenna had taken a big leap, packing up and hitting the road to come here. She'd set the ball rolling- and maybe all I need to do is to keep it rolling.

"Kenna... how do you feel about road trips?"

The younger woman looked up quizzically and admitted, "I don't know, I've never had one."

"Wow, really? You're a junior in college and you've never experienced a road trip?"

Kenna shook her head and looked embarrassed. "I mean, that's not exactly Tessa's style, and like I said, I don't really have any friends. I've seen movies and read books about them, but I've never thought about one of my own."

I knew it was probably a foolish plan. There was so much that could go wrong. There was no guarantee we'd even get along once the pleasantries were over. I knew nothing about Kenna, other than the fact that she'd been raised by a woman I despise. While all signs indicated that Kenna herself had a rough relationship with her mother, I could learn that they were more alike than different. She'd clearly been raised in an affluent, privileged setting- the type of adventure I could afford might prove to be too challenging for her. Even if none of that was an issue, our personalities simply might not gel.

I flashed back to the warmth of her tiny body on my belly, her little fists clenched and raised in fury, the slightest wispy hints of blonde hair on her head before they fitted the cap over it. I remembered the surge of pride that was quickly followed by the crushing wave of sorrow as it sank in that I'd soon be handing her over to someone else. Someone I didn't even like. I remembered the way I'd wanted to clutch her against my chest, I wanted to refuse to say goodbye. I remembered how hard I'd sobbed in Delta's arms when she was finally taken from me. I'd have given anything back then for a few more hours, a few more days.

I was caught off guard by the tears that threatened to fall, I hadn't cried since Delta's death. I hadn't even cried at the funeral itself. I'd somehow folded in on myself, an empty polyester dress in a shade of grief, and blunted the pain. Tears were wasted, that's what I told myself almost every day. Yet now they threatened to spill out of me. I fought them off again and stared at the young woman who sat across from me biting her lip nervously and mind was made up.

"Okay, let's do it. Let's hit the road. I haven't taken vacation time in forever, I can afford a few weeks off. I need to visit a few cities anyway, to scope out where I want to go next. It'll be the perfect opportunity for us to get to know each other and get away from Tessa for a while."

"You're moving?" Kenna asked.

"I'll explain later. We'll have plenty of time to share everything. We'll hit the road; I want to visit Virginia Beach, Charleston, and Key West. We won't be staying at the Ritz though." I added in a warning tone.

Kenna slowly nodded, and I wondered if she regretted showing up yet. Then the younger woman smiled softly and said, "Wow, a real road trip. I think I'm up for that!"

"Okay, it may take a few days to arrange. In the meantime, we are going to get you one of those gas station cell phones and you are calling your mother. No, don't argue. I'm not going to be chased down for kidnapping. Call your mother, tell her you are fine, tell her you need some headspace and if she wants to hear from you again then she needs to back off."

Kenna frowned, but finally nodded in agreement. Then she asked, "Wait, what about the media? What if someone recognizes me?"

"That's a legitimate worry, but you and Tessa have done a great job at keeping your picture out of the media for a lot of years."

Kenna visibly winced and admitted, "I hate being seen, but honestly I think my mother's kept me low-key because she's always been ashamed of me. She's told me more than once that I don't sparkle."

She didn't sparkle. That was absolutely textbook Tessa, and my heart hurt for Kenna. What other horrible things had she heard over the years? What other terrible things had she been convinced of about herself?

"Kenna, I don't really like profanity, but once in a blue moon it is appropriate and I indulge. In the case of your mother, I'm making one of those exceptions. Tessa's an asshole."

Kenna's eyes widened and then she grinned. "She really is."

I smiled back and suggested that Kenna make herself at home. It was time to shift myself into logistics mode. I knew that I needed to work on finding coverage for work and a pet sitter for Bilbo. Kenna thanked me and headed inside to bring her belongings to the guest room. I leaned my elbows on the table, and rested my chin on my hands as I thought about the coming days. This wasn't just about rescuing Kenna. I could admit that. Thinking of the journey ahead gave me a feeling I hadn't experienced in a long time. Excitement. Closing my eyes, I listened again as a soft breeze whispered through the oak's branches and I smiled.

Chapter 6

Kenna

I prop myself up on my forearms as my mother stands over me staring intently. She doesn't say anything; her mouth is set, a firm, determined line. I've seen that look before. It's her work-face. Not the one she wears like lipstick for the public, it's the one she wears in her board rooms. I should feel relieved it's not the familiar cold, angry mask but in work mode she's relentless. I frantically look beyond my tangled bed sheets for escape. Mother leans down and, with her face still staring intently as if I were a thing and not a person, begins to lower her right hand to my face. With one manicured index finger, she begins to trace the contours of my face. Too late, I realize that every spot she touches disappears. She's erasing me entirely.

A tiny engine in my left ear and insistent pawing to my arm shifts the room and she is gone. Bilbo. Looking quite pleased with himself at his success in rousing me from my deep sleep, he proceeds to jump on my chest, demanding more attention. He's oblivious to the sleep-world I've just left behind and I'm grateful for that. The dream was disturbing as my dreams of Mother often are, but grounded by the little cat, I feel warm and safe again.

I sit up in bed and study my surroundings. The small, simple room is wallpapered with a fading floral print. The dresser and headboard are painted an ivory color and feature gold factory cut-out trimmings. A ceramic pitcher and bowl decorated with bright pink cabbage roses sit on the top of the bureau and a trio of pastel Parisian street scene watercolor prints hangs on the largest wall. I struggle for a minute to capture the right word for the setting and it finally comes to me. Cozy. It's the sort of coziness that HoHo attempts to simulate, but fails to actually replicate. The contrived comfort of a hundred designers on high-tech computers is soulless. This is the real thing. If this room were music, it would be ambient.

The bedside alarm clock reveals it's barely 6 am. This is ridiculously early for me and I throw the cat a wayward glance. I'm grateful he rescued me from the dream, but I am definitely not a morning person. I wonder if Rachel is awake yet. If the cat has these hours, I'm guessing she just might be.

Rachel. I hadn't known what to expect from her. I knew that Tessa had chosen her back when she was a young college girl in New London, CT and I'd made some assumptions based on that fact. Tessa's social circle isn't just moneyed, they're also sophisticated. Her friends are celebrities, politicians, tech giants, or they're women she'd known from as far back as her own Calvin Brook Academy days. Women who, like her, had been born into "old money," although none had descended from a family more affluent than the Shepherd dynasty. Her friends would never have actually bought any of the mass-market decor items that had made her famous.

My mother's male friends tend to be the "new rich" variety, self-made men who'd combined luck and opportunity with hard work to produce enviable lives. They're mostly loud and entertaining, often flamboyantly so. They hang around enjoying Tessa's largesse for however long she allows but they have a shelf life. The women, on the other hand, come from pedigreed backgrounds. They were born into their money. I am not sure if she deliberately avoids the self-made women of the world or if such women see through her charade and avoid her.

When I was younger she would occasionally connect with one of her male friends romantically, but it had always been a subtle, temporary thing and not something they'd share for the cameras and press. I couldn't remember a single time in my childhood that I'd gotten potential daddy vibes from any of them. Tessa is perfectly happy being the queen of her world and I think that means she'll never share her throne.

Rachel is clearly the exact opposite of the sort of person Tessa likes. Rachel is down to earth, neat, tidy, self-supporting, and attractive but certainly not attractive enough to garner much attention. She's quiet-spoken, dresses modestly, and seems content in her cute little home with her cute little cat. She's the sort of person that might buy an occasional Tessa product at the store, but she wouldn't have enough patience to watch the show. I've only spent a day with Rachel, but I am certain that she isn't a woman who cares what anyone else thinks about her home, her person, or her life.

The small slit between curtains reveals dawn's light and although it's much earlier than normal, I push myself out of bed. I'm filled with nervous energy. There is relief at escaping the city, excitement about the journey ahead, and terror at the prospect of speaking to Tessa. Rachel had made her expectation clear, and I know I'm going to have to make that call. I also know that I don't have the fortitude to stand up to my mother. She'll order me home and objecting to my mother's demands has never been an option. I want this time away so badly, more than I've ever wanted anything, but can I be strong enough to tell her that?

I'm not surprised to find Rachel in the kitchen- the fact that she's an early bird makes perfect sense. It fits right into the narrative I'm already building of her in my head. I know instinctively that she's efficient in every area of her life. She's the exact opposite of me. Clearly whatever tiny bit of DNA that might have crossed my placental wall hadn't contained that handy trait.

She smiles up at me. "Good morning. Hope you slept well."

"I did, thank you. And thanks for letting Bilbo sleep with me. I've never had a cat. It's nice waking up to a living, purring, stuffed animal." I reply.

She chuckles at that. "Oh, he'll wake you up alright! I was about to make breakfast, nothing fancy, eggs and toast. Does that work for you?"

I nod and walk to the back door's window to peer into the backyard. It's not a yard that's been sculpted by the hands of a professional landscaper, but somehow it's all the better for it. Wild flowers adorn the sides of the patio, a half dozen young trees are sprinkled around the yard, and there in the center of it all- a huge tree stands dominant and regal.

Beneath the tree is a crooked, simple black metallic bird bath that a robin is spinning his wings in madly at the moment.

I turn to look at Rachel, "It's incredible out there. So peaceful. You must love it."

She smiles, but it's a smile of habit and it doesn't reach her eyes. "It is peaceful. Truth be told, I haven't loved it like I should for a while now though. Sometimes the things that give you the most joy become reminders of all that's lost."

There is melancholy in the pitch of her words and I instantly regret whatever offense I've committed. I don't want to be the source of pain for this kind woman. As if reading my mind though, she hastily adds, "It's fine. It IS a lovely backyard. I'm fairly recently widowed and that yard often reminds me of what I've lost. It's a shame really, I ought to allow myself to appreciate it more again."

The words are said calmly, even briskly. She doesn't betray emotion when she says the word widowed and I'm not sure how fresh a wound is. I've been so wrapped up in my own crisis, it hadn't occurred to me that she might be dealing with her own. Until now, I'd just accepted Rachel's solitary existence. My own mother had never married, I've never had a real date. In my world, being a single woman is the default. I'm curious though. What kind of man had Rachel been drawn to? I immediately pictured someone strong, but simple, a man who worked hard and came home every night.

"I'm so sorry. I had no idea. Do you mind me asking, how long ago did he pass? We don't have to talk about this at all if you don't want to."

She smiles again, but there's a tightness to the smile. I'm an expert at hiding emotion, balling it up tightly and shoving it behind a casual smile. She's doing exactly that, now. "She, and I don't mind. It's been six months. Delta had breast cancer; we went through several rounds of recovery and then relapse over the years. We knew what was coming toward the end, so it wasn't sudden or unexpected. I suppose it was a blessing in some ways because we had time to say everything that mattered and a curse in other ways because it was so drawn out and agonizing to watch."

The fact she'd been married at all had been a surprise. The fact that her spouse was a woman though, isn't all that shocking. I've grown up surrounded by publishing and entertainment industry icons, same sex couples were almost as common as the more traditional variety. I had already assumed that despite her choice to retreat to a small town and the tiny whisper of a southern accent that tinged some of her words she probably wasn't a traditionalist. There isn't anything very traditional about being a surrogate for a complete stranger after all. I am very curious about the type of woman that Rachel would have been drawn to though.

"How long were you married?"

"Almost 5 years. It wasn't legal here until 2014, but we'd been together for 19 before that."

24 years. The significance of the numbers hits me. "So you were together when you met Tessa...?"

She nods, "Yep. Delta was there for me through my entire pregnancy. She felt your kicks and met you the day you were born. Tessa hadn't even wanted to allow me that much, but somehow the OB convinced her it was important I have a little time with you before the hand off. She'd left the birthing suite for a private room they'd set aside just for her to make some calls, and Delta snuck right on past the assistant she'd left guarding the door. I suspect they just assumed she was another hospital staff member, had she been a man it might have been harder."

She'd been propped up in the bed and had handed me to Delta, who had apparently been enamored by my tiny features. Delta had proclaimed me perfect and had joked I had Rachel's eyes. As she recounts this, I can't help but sneak a peek at her face. Her eyes are a soft, almond shape and are a very dark brown. My own cat's eyes are ice blue, mirrors of those found on my genetic mother. There is no resemblance to Rachel, despite my fervent wish there were. I'd once seen a unique German "word of the day" on social media that has stuck with me. *Fernweh.* Feeling homesick for a place you'd never visited. I understand it now.

On the day of my birth, after the cleanup, Tessa returned and found Delta in the room with me. She'd been livid. Delta and the assistant took the brunt of her fury, as apparently accosting a woman fresh in recovery from childbirth had been even beyond Tessa's pale- but the confrontation played out before Rachel's eyes and hurt her anyway. Delta agreed to having her purse searched to prove there hadn't been a camera or recording device.

"It was quite a thing to see Delta and Tessa face to face. Delta had never backed away from a fight in her life and well, you know Tessa. Fire and ice. I was tired, sore, and bleeding and I was already dreading how it would feel when they took you away and when they started with the caustic comments back and forth I broke. I just started crying, Delta broke away and came to me, proving that I meant more to her than winning the argument."

In the end, Tessa got the prize. Me. She wouldn't have known then that I'd turn out to be a booby prize. Rachel had kissed my forehead and then handed me to the woman who'd engineered me and they'd never see each other again. Rachel got the remainder of the promised money, spent the rest of her leave of absence from college recovering physically and mentally, and then returned to pick up the life she'd paused. She and Delta used the funds to cover the costs of her education. A few years later, Delta left the Coast Guard and the pair moved here to PA where they purchased the modest cottage with the remaining cash. Rachel became the town librarian and Delta took a position at the wastewater treatment plant. Here, they enjoyed a quiet, comfortable, all too short life together.

"You never wanted a child of your own?" I ask hesitantly.

"We did, for a while at least. After Delta left the Coast Guard we looked into fertility options. The irony is, it turns out I don't have working eggs. I can carry a child, but I can't produce my own. Delta couldn't do it; she loved me and would have done almost anything for me, but she did not want to be pregnant for many reasons, and I respected her choice. We toyed with egg extraction, I could carry her baby, but it seemed like a lot to put both of our bodies through with limited chance of success. We talked about adoption too, but something always held us back. At first it was practical. At that time, it was much more difficult for a same sex couple to even be approved for adoption. But then it was busy work schedules and our love of frequent travel. Then, by the time we started to get serious about our search, Delta had her first cancer diagnosis. Eventually, we just accepted we were not meant to be parents."

She's saying it in a calm, measured voice. She could be relaying a complete stranger's story, rather than her own. I know that she's hiding behind her stoicism and clearly has for a long time. Had being Delta's caretaker taught her that skill? I'm driven to tears by a mere cross look. Baring my most intimate heartbreaks would have reduced me to hiding in my closet again. Was I born this way, or has Tessa engineered this too?

I hate my softness, my weakness. If I'd been a stronger person I wouldn't be sitting here now. I'd have never allowed the forces around me at the Crier to make me feel so small. I wouldn't have felt so inadequate and incapable of actually doing my job. I wouldn't have sought a quick escape from what should have been an easy assignment. I wouldn't have done such a stupid, selfish thing. I would have believed in myself and something as simple as making a phone call wouldn't have utterly overwhelmed me.

As a fresh wave of shame washes over me, I feel myself tighten again. The treacherous sinews of my physical body tightening, clenching, in concert with the knotted fibers of my thoughts. For just a while I'd escaped and felt relatively normal. I'd allowed myself to forget that I'd ruined my life in a spectacularly public fashion and that there was no coming back from this.

"Hey now, no need to look so sad. We had a very rewarding life together. A child would have been wonderful, but I cannot be so ungrateful as to complain about what we had. In the end, everyone leaves this earth. No living thing escapes that fate. We're all on a schedule, a calendar, we just don't know which day is meant to be our last."

Rachel's mistaken my shift of mood as a result of her story, rather than my own selfish concerns. I feel guilty about that now too. I really don't deserve the kindness that this woman is showing me. Selfishly, I want to wallow in it though.

"She sounds like an amazing person. I'm glad you found each other." I reply, sincerely.

"She really was. When we first met it was quite forbidden, and not just because she was a woman. She was a service member and this was in the days of 'don't ask, don't tell' and to further complicate things, she worked for my father. I was a senior in high school then, barely younger than her, but it crossed yet another invisible line that was forbidden. When my father found out he was furious. He threatened to destroy her career. He just couldn't wrap his mind around the idea that his own little girl had initiated that first kiss, so he made Delta the bad guy."

Her voice has grown distant and she looks away abruptly as if she's shaking away the memory. Glancing at the clock she says, "We'll have plenty of time for me to finish this story, but it's already 8 am. Let's get ready and head into town. We need to get you that phone."

The phone. For a little while, I'd forgotten about that little part of the deal I'd made. Dread weighs my feet down, but I force my legs to lift them and make my way to the guest room. Once there, I focus on an exercise I rely on when I'm facing demons. I struggle to invent lyrics to calm me. Every line I think of is unoriginal. Someone else has already birthed them. I give up and accept that this is going to probably kill me. After dressing, I walk slowly down the stairs and see Rachel watching me with a wry grin.

"I know this is hard Kenna, but you look like you're 8 years old and about to face the school principal. Really, you don't have to have a long conversation. You just need to say what you need to say and then hang up. This is for the best, I might not like Tessa but even she doesn't deserve to worry the very worst has happened to her child. And frankly, I don't want to be looking over my shoulder the entire time we're driving down I-95."

I nod and swallow hard but don't speak, and then follow her to the beat up black Saturn in the driveway. The drive into town is filled with town tidbits and gossip. Rachel knows everyone, which is probably par for the course for a small town librarian. Every time we pass another vehicle, Rachel waves and then casually name drops. Oh, that's John the postmaster; that's Anita, she's published two books; hey there's Maggie- she just had twins.

Curious, I ask, "It seems like a friendly town. Did they welcome you and Delta with open arms or was it hard at first?"

She laughs. "I don't think they knew what to make of us for a while. Most figured out we were a couple pretty quickly, but I think a few of the older folks didn't quite get it until years later when we actually married. People here are friendly though and we chose to get involved in the community from the start. Truthfully, I need this change but I'll miss a lot about Metzgartown when I move on."

I don't say it, I'm thinking that what she describes sounds too good to walk away from. I would give anything to feel safe and welcome in a community like this. I've always yearned to belong somewhere but there really isn't a spot for me. I've never fit in my mother's publishing and marketing world, or with her beautiful celebrities, or with her old money friends. I don't fit in at Barnard amongst the intellectuals and activists. I could hide in a small town like this for a while, but I wouldn't truly fit here either. I'm too odd, too private, and I know despite my ambivalence toward the trappings- too privileged.

We hit the town perimeter and soon pulled into a nearly empty pharmacy parking lot. My heart is thumping loudly in my chest, I don't want to go in there. I don't want to face strangers, but more importantly, I don't want to get a device to call my mother. I look at Rachel and think about pleading for reprieve one more time, but as if reading my mind, she just shakes her head.

"I have to run across the street to talk to a girl who works in the cafe, she's my usual pet sitter, I'm hoping she's available on short notice. Just come over when you get the phone." She pauses and then adds, "Do you need money?"

That question makes me want to laugh. No one in my life has ever asked me that, but given my circumstances it's a fair question.

"No, I'm okay for now. I pulled $1200 from the bank before leaving New York. It's not much, but it should get me through a few days."

She bursts out laughing. "Oh, Kenna, we are going to have a budget talk really soon. Okay, I'll see you at the cafe."

Inside the drug store I walk to the register, behind it are colorful racks of cigarettes and next to them are a few neat rows of pay-as-you-go phones. Feeling as conspicuous as I might have felt had I been buying condoms, not that I've ever had occasion to do that- I eye the models. A clerk comes over and I steel myself for this exchange.

"Can I help you?" She asks, sounding completely bored as she asks. I study her wide, freckled face and realize there's no recognition in her eyes. Relieved to be so anonymous in this small town drug store, I'm about to pick a phone at random when another thought occurs to me.

"Actually, not quite yet, I'll be back in a bit."

I beeline for the hair care aisle and study the boxes of hair color. My own pale blond tresses have never been colored, in part because Tessa would have had a fit but truthfully it has always been the one feature that I am regularly complimented on. I don't want to look like me right now and I certainly don't want to look like *her* either. The huge selection of boxes is overwhelming. How am I supposed to know if creams are better, if semi-permanent is preferable to permanent, if brand A is a better quality than brand B? I've got a general idea of what I want, something quiet and demure, something brown, but choosing an exact shade and brand feels impossible. Frustrated with myself, I finally stop at a random grouping of boxes and choose one that shows a picture that resembles Rachel's dark brown hair.

Next, I wander until I find the stationary supply and gift wrap section and eye the items hanging along the wall. I grab a pair of scissors from the hook. I know what I'm contemplating is crazy. My regular stylist would self-combust if he knew what I was planning. So yeah, maybe this was crazy, but I happen to be feeling a little crazy. What does something as silly and vain as hair style matter in a world where my character is far more flawed than my appearance could ever be?

Ten minutes later, I've completed the task, including the scary part. I try not to think about what's in the bag I hold, but it may as well be a loaded gun. I eye the bag warily, as if it will go off at any moment. This phone will open a portal to a world I've been trying desperately to escape. Clutching it, I slowly walk across the wide parking lot and the nearly dead main street into the cafe. Rachel's sitting on a red vinyl covered bar style seat at the counter, listening attentively to an animated young waitress. She looks over as the bells over the door announce my arrival and waves casually, but I pause and watch her for a moment.

The waitress throws her head back in a hearty laugh, even as her hands whip through the air in pantomime. Rachel is smiling warmly at her and nodding encouragingly, clearly in no rush to end her story. It's striking how genuine a listener she is. That's a gift. Most people ask questions but don't really want to hear your answers. Most people feign their interest in you because it's expected of them. That's been my experience anyway.

As if reading my mind, she turns and waves me over. "Kenna! This is Sherry. She's going to take care of Bilbo while we're gone. Sherry, this is my niece I was telling you about..." She looks at me pointedly.

"Nice to meet you." I reply then turn back to Rachel and hold up the plastic bag so she'll know I've completed my mission.

I sit down beside her, mostly to listen, as she and the waitress continue their chat. When they wrap up their conversation, we finally make our way back to the car.

Belting myself in, I turn and ask, "Niece?"

"A lot easier to explain than... well this." She says motioning back and forth between us.

She has a point. I'm not exactly sure how to refer to our relationship. We're strangers, even if it feels like I've known her for a long time already. Clearly we're not mother and daughter, and those very words come loaded with all kinds of dark baggage so I wouldn't have wanted them associated with her anyway. Niece. It works.

She interrupts my thoughts, "Alrighty, so do you want to get it over with now in the car, or wait until we're home?"

The novel normalcy of our time in the cafe with a friendly stranger had made me brave. I want to be part of that world where people sit and laugh with ease and every word isn't loaded. I want it badly enough I think I might be able to face my biggest demon. Sitting in Rachel's modest little car, windows down, radio playing 80s tunes from a low volume, makes me feel free. It won't last though. This is a breath mark, a grace rest. My opus to mother hasn't been marked with a final double bar. I push the thought away and focus only on the now. This is the moment I feel strong so this is the moment I'll take the leap.

I pull the phone out, inhale deeply, and with a shaking hand dial the familiar number. On the third ring a young voice answers and I realize that Mother must have foisted her phone onto her assistant when she didn't recognize the number.

"Hi um, is Tessa there? This is Kenna, I mean Kennedy."

I've barely finished my name when I hear my mother's voice. I had imagined that perhaps she'd sound frantic, panicked even, by my absence but instead she's confident and cold. She's exactly who she always was.

"Where are you?"

"I'm okay, I'm in a safe place."

"Dammit Kennedy, where are you?"

"Mother, I don't..."

"Kennedy!" She interrupts and the ice encrusted facade breaks as her anger reveals itself. "We've been working way too hard to somehow fix this mess you have created, and you decide now is the right moment to run off and hide? Tell me where you are and I'll send a car immediately."

I close my eyes and for just a moment, I want to tell her. It's an insane urge, the exact opposite of self-preservation. I've been conditioned my entire life to confess all sins of thought, word and deed to her though. I can only find salvation if Tessa deigns to offer it. She's always had that power over me and I'm not sure I can resist it. I look helplessly at Rachel and her eyes are both sympathetic and worried.

"I'm in a safe place." I repeat dully. Then taking a deep breath, I say in as strong a voice as I can muster, "Mother, I'm not going back to Barnard for the hearing. I'm sorry. They can expel me. I'm not fighting this. There's nothing to fight here, not only is it true that I did what they're accusing me of, but it's also true I don't want to be there."

I glance back at Rachel, she hasn't asked yet about the Crier. If she's surprised by my words, she doesn't show it. Her face holds no judgment at all, only empathy. She nods slightly, encouraging me to continue.

Feeling stronger, I cut off Tessa's protests and say, "I won't be reachable for a while. I need time and space. I'll be in touch eventually."

I hear bitter laughter from her end and she says so very coldly, "Oh, Kennedy sweetheart, you won't last a week. Did you forget who controls the purse strings here? I'm not sure I'll answer the next time you call. I've honestly never been so disappointed in another human being in my life."

The phone connection is severed, but instead of the usual shame it brought, I feel a surge of anger. This was supposed to be my turn to hang up on her! She's ruined that too.

"It sounds like that went well!" Rachel offers cheerfully and I turn to glare at her. At the mischievous look on her face I can't help it, I burst into laughter.

"Let's get home and start prepping. I'm going to try to keep the schedule loose because I know that's the only way to really enjoy a road trip but I can't handle leaving everything to chance. I'm going to create a loose schedule, book our first motel, and plot out routes. We can also start packing, well I can- I suppose you're still living out of your suitcase. The plan is we'll leave in two days."

Two days. Tessa has two days to find me. I hope it's not enough time.

Chapter 7

Rachel

"Work hard, play hard. All work and no play makes Johnny a dull bitch, or something like that."

We'd always subscribed to the value of working hard, but Delta loved to push the outer limits of her favorite mantra more than I did. Throughout our relationship, she'd often work a full-time job and take on extra odd jobs on her off hours. I wasn't exactly a slouch, since graduating from college I'd always been employed. I didn't typically earn supplemental wages though- my contribution tended to be one of servitude. I cooked, cleaned, ran errands on my off hours. That model worked well for us and together we earned enough to both pay our bills and enjoy the play side of that mantra. For almost 24 years, we filled passport pages and photo albums with the fruits of our labor. Our journeys had always been a partnership, I could no more imagine traveling without Delta than I could without a suitcase. When Delta died, I'd had the painful realization that I hadn't just lost the love of my life- I'd also lost most of the things that previously brought me joy, including travel.

Now, I'm going to rediscover that joy. I glanced into my open suitcase and inspected the tidy rows of neatly rolled, wrinkle-proof, clothes. I'd spent years perfecting that efficient system. There were more tops than bottoms, everything in muted neutral shades. I'd added a sundress in case a special occasion popped up. A pair of sandals, a soft cardigan, and a very modest toiletry bag were expertly squeezed into the remaining space and the end result was a carry-on sized suitcase that would meet my needs for two full weeks.

I grabbed the bag and walked toward the stairs just in time to see the bathroom door swing open. Again, I forced myself not to stare. It was going to take some getting used to that. When I'd come home from work the evening before, Kenna had surprised me with her new look. She'd somehow managed to use a combination of mirrors, ponytail elastics, and Youtube videos on the old desktop to pull off the feat.

"I still can't get over it. You look beautiful." I hadn't been lying.

Kenna smiled at that and I studied her. She was objectively beautiful. The deep espresso brown she'd dyed her hair had a startling effect on her eyes. They were brighter, more vivid, nearly hypnotic. She'd cut a good foot of length off as well, perfecting a short blunt bob that ended at her chin. Her face looked more angular within its new frame, giving her a sophisticated edge. There was a paradoxical effect though. At first glance, she resembled Tessa less without their shared blonde tresses but if a person were to study her more closely, her features seemed to mirror the woman who had raised her more than ever before. The effect was disconcerting and I certainly wasn't going to tell her about it.

"But do you really think that I look different?"

I understood what she was asking and there wasn't a way to answer her honestly without ruining everything. "No one is going to connect you with your mother now. If they look for her, they might see her. But they won't think to look for her."

Sitting at the dinette, we opted for a quick toast and coffee breakfast. We'd fallen into an easy conversation about Bilbo and his peculiar habits. Talking to Kenna was an easy thing; we shared a cadence that allowed us to walk in matched steps throughout a conversation. I'd feared our dialogue might prove to be an awkward, forced thing- but instead, Kenna seemed genuinely curious about me and my life. She hadn't shared much about her own yet but that would come. When I told the story of how Bilbo originally found us, Kenna revealed that she'd never had a pet. Tessa had a few small purse dogs over the years but they'd never been particularly friendly and it was always made clear they belonged to Tessa not her.

She shrugged and admitted, "Anything that wasn't in my room belonged to Tessa. She always had the last say too on what got to go in my room so maybe even that stuff never really belonged to me."

She glanced through the wide doorway into the living room and eyed the pile of gear we'd readied. Her eyes lingered on the guitar and she added, "Except that. That's mine. No matter what she says."

"I'm glad you have that."

Another thought occurred to me then. I glanced back toward the luggage and a prick of anxiety teased the back of my neck. We'd been sitting here longer than I'd anticipated. Lifting my wrist, I narrowed my eyes when I saw the time. 7:09.

The quick breakfast hadn't been as quick as I'd hoped it would be. I'd planned for us to be on the road at 7:00 and we hadn't even loaded the car yet. Realistically, the earliest we'd be able to leave the driveway would be 7:30 at this point. That was an optimistic timeline. I wasn't sure where in my planning I'd gone wrong- I rarely get it wrong when it came to timing.

Kenna noticed my consternation as I studied my watch and asked, "Is everything okay?"

I smiled reassuringly and explained, "Yes, it's just that I thought I had this better planned. We're running a little later than I'd have expected."

"Are you worried we'll be late for something?"

"No, no it's fine. I just like to get out ahead of the traffic so that... well, it's difficult to explain. I just like to have a plan and stick to it."

She suddenly looked a little nervous, as if she were chastised by my words. She'd internalized them, allowing herself to believe that I blamed her for the few pointless minutes we'd supposedly lost. I'd noticed over the past few days that Kenna embraced taking blame for anything that didn't go perfectly. That was Tessa's doing, I was sure of it. It was a habit she needed to break though, and that was going to be hard if I was constantly making her nervous about schedules. Did it really matter anyway if we didn't stick to a preplanned schedule perfectly? I didn't want to be a contributor to her constant guilt and self-consciousness, I already owned enough blame for the upbringing Tessa's given her. I needed to get a handle on my own issues before they contributed to hers.

"Kenna, really. This is not a big deal. I have some control issues of my own and I'm struggling to let them go. This has nothing to do with you at all. Let's rinse these dishes and just get on the road and enjoy our adventure. My goals on this trip are to figure out where I want to live next, and to learn how to embrace spontaneity again."

We loaded the car up and I carefully adjusted my seat before looking at the young woman beside me. I'd long ago mastered the art of hiding my thoughts, but Kenna's face was an open book. She was feeling the same emotions as me. There was nervousness, but there was no belying the excitement as well. The open road promised new views and neither of us knew what those would be, but sometimes, the promise of *different* was even better than the promise of *good*. This was a pathway to new beginnings and the one sure thing we had in common was the need for new beginnings.

As we made our way down Cottage Road, I confidently took on each familiar curve. Passing Maggie's home, I waved to the exhausted looking woman who carried both babies in her arms. As we rounded the bend through a small birch forest, I slow instinctively to glide down a slight hill, knowing it was a popular crossing spot for deer. Speeding up, we exited the foliage. The Murphy's old mare stood at the fence line, seemingly uninterested in the passing Saturn, but I waved anyway.

Leaving Cottage Road, a lump began to develop in my throat. We'd only be gone for two weeks, but this trip will likely change the way everything here looked. I knew it. When I returned it would be just long enough to pack. I'd find my new home on this trip, I was sure of it, and a person can't truly have two homes. Metzgartown would soon be a memory, like so many other homes from my past. While I was desperate for something, anything, to change- one part of this metamorphosis weighed heavily on me. I'm not sure how Delta would have felt about this.

Delta had loved Metzgartown from that very first day we'd rolled through in her old beat up Ford Ranger. As we'd exited the lush green hills for the small main strip we passed through the loop twice. On our second pass, we slowed to study the storefronts and the faces of the people we were passing along the sidewalk. Looking at the storefronts beyond the faces, Delta pointed out the similarities to her hometown in Mississippi.

"It feels like back home," she says as she leans her head out of the open window and inhales deeply. "Except you can actually breathe." She adds.

I understand the reference, Delta has never hidden her distaste of the ever present blanket of humidity that suffocated everything beneath the blazing Mississippi sun.

We park and take our third trip down Main Street, this time on foot. We're taking our time, eyeing each storefront that we pass, judging silently. No words are needed, our body language and facial expressions are always in tune. With each raised eyebrow, slight shoulder tilt, slowed pace, there is deliberation and a verdict. When we reach the dark enclave of Paddy's Irish Pub, Delta eyes the walls that are adorned with firefighter hats and old black and white photos, and turns to me.

"This will work."

And it did work. Townspeople had been a little reluctant to welcome us, not because of our relationship status, but because we were newcomers and newcomers are always viewed suspiciously here. The towns children were the first to come around, latching onto my story time hours with wide eyes and excited giggles. Their mothers soon followed suit. Delta drew attention from their fathers, albeit she hadn't set out to do that. She'd never been one to preen when people paid attention. The men in town were respectful in their furtive glances, but they clearly appreciated having a physically fit, curly haired, sassy young woman nearby. That appreciation deepened when they discovered that she could match any of them when it came to swapping fish stories around the heavily shalaqued bar top at Paddys. She wasn't a flirt. She was equally friendly with the wives, and that made her safe to talk to.

When the townsfolk finally understood that we were there for the long haul, the invitations to dinners and parties began to arrive. By the end of our first year in Metzgartown, we had started to joke about the fact we'd someday die there. Neither of us could have known that day would arrive for Delta just seventeen years later. Death is inevitable, but like most people- we preferred to imagine that such a day was so far away, an abstract thing to be ignored and forgotten.

As Kenna and I passed the library that had brought me to the town to begin with, I acknowledged a small swell of pride. I've done so much with it, growing it from a book repository, to a central hub of the community. It's a place where people gathered for clubs and events, where support groups held private evening meetings, a place where people sometimes fell in love and in at least two cases- it had served as a wedding venue. I'd made my mark here, and when I left I wouldn't be quickly forgotten.

And then there it was. The turn off to the state highway that would lead us to Interstate 81. This was the spot where everything would change. Keeping my eyes on the road, I said aloud, "Here we go!"

"When was the last time you left Metzgartown," Kenna asked.

"Well, I go into Scranton once every few weeks to run errands and visit the veteran's cemetery, but I haven't left for an overnight since last year. Delta and I took a short trip to Lake George that spring. She wasn't truly well enough to travel but she'd refused to admit it, to be honest it was pretty miserable. Our last and great big road trip was a summer vacation on Ocracoke Island a few years back."

Delta had been good then. She'd been issued another all clear just a few months prior and we'd naively believed that the bad times were behind us. We'd made the drive to Swan Quarter, NC and then taken the ferry to the island. Unencumbered by the anxiety that had dominated so much of the prior year, it had been an almost perfect getaway. For a whole glorious week, we'd soaked up sun, gorged ourselves with fresh seafood, and spent our evenings with drinks and live music. A memory surfaced though, and I gave a small grimace.

"Everything was almost perfect. Almost. We had a stupid fight while there one night, I'd wanted to make reservations at a certain restaurant, but she'd insisted we didn't need them and wouldn't commit to a time. Sure enough, when we showed up there wasn't a table. I was so angry because it was our last night on the island and there's this famous scallops dish there that I'd been salivating over ever since seeing a picture of it in a travel magazine. Now we'd never get to try it, all because we didn't have a reservation. In the end she promised we'd be back and I could try it again. That never happened, but what do I care now? I don't even remember the name of the place..."

It's like that. You cared about the small things, the socks in the middle of the floor nuances, at the expense of the big things. What did it matter if I hadn't been able to try the recommended scallops dish in Ocracoke in the long run? It'd meant nothing really.

"I don't really do that, to be honest, I don't really argue about the small stuff or the big stuff." Kenna replied, and I realized I must have said the thought aloud.

"Not ever? What about with your mother?"

Kenna laughed, but there was a brittle edge to it. "Especially not with my mother. It's not worth it. No one's allowed to be angry or irritated by her. I've seen others try, former assistants, boyfriends, nannies... at the first hint that she's done something to hurt someone else she strikes. Anyone who orbits Tessa understands quickly we're not just protecting her image from the public, we're also protecting it from herself. We're all expected to play along- and nowhere in that image is a woman who irritates others."

She might be young and utterly beaten down in spirit by Tessa, but Kenna was astute. And why shouldn't she be? The girl was well educated and, in just a few weeks, she'd be 21 years old. Her fragility and soft voice made her seem younger, but it'd be a mistake to view her as a child. I needed to undertake a course correction, as Delta was fond of saying. I'd been infantilizing Kenna without consciously meaning to. I needed to view her as the grown woman she was. It was time to broach the one subject I'd been purposely avoiding.

"Kenna... I need to ask, what happened with The Crier?"

Kenna turned and stared out of her window and, for a moment, I wondered if she was just going to refuse to answer. Finally though, she replied, "I shouldn't have been there at all."

She hadn't wanted to stay in the city over summer break. She hadn't wanted to intern with a major publisher at all. Tessa had other ideas and had pushed her into the position. From her first day on the job she'd found it difficult to fit in. The office pace was frantic. Everyone seemed to be hopped up on caffeine and relentless ambition. Her fellow interns shunned her from the start. She described the article that she'd come across, the one that revealed her mother's influence on the hiring decision and added, "Knowing that now, I can't really blame them. I didn't deserve to be there."

She shared how every morning she'd force herself to leave her apartment. She'd try to ignore the knots in her stomach and plow ahead, but it didn't really matter how sincere her desire to improve was. Whether the task was as simple as collecting a large coffee order for the office from the nearby Starbucks or as complicated as fact-checking a human interest piece, Kenna seemed to get it all wrong every time. The criticism felt constant, she was incapable of doing anything correctly the first time. The staff was a little kinder than her fellow interns had been, but they didn't quite disguise their impatience and annoyance with her at times.

After a few weeks, it became clear that the other interns had formed a solid group. She'd overheard references to their nights out together, sometimes punctuated by moaning and one-upmanship over who had the worst hangover. It wasn't that she'd wanted to hang out with them socially. They'd so thoroughly rejected her at work it was hard to imagine ever being able to relax with them away from the office. Still, it stung that no one ever bothered to even ask. It felt even worse when she'd learned some of the younger staff members were starting to join the group on their off time. She was truly an island.

Making matters worse, Tessa would check in frequently and demand updates about what she'd accomplished. Kenna would attempt to keep her answers short to avoid sharing just how bad it was and over time the impression she gave was of a completely different reality. Everything was good. Everyone was nice. She was fitting in just fine. They liked her. Yes, she was learning a lot. Yes, she was putting her best foot forward. Yes, she'd probably get a job offer. As time went by, the stories became more fanciful and she felt trapped in a web of her own lies.

She knew that she wouldn't get a job offer, she fully anticipated a miserable review at the conclusion of the internship, and she hoped that Tessa wouldn't find a way to read it. Surely there were HR and privacy rules that would at least spare her that? The end result though was unavoidable- Tessa would be furious that she didn't get an offer.

"It felt like I was faking being an intern, pretending to be a would-be journalist. It's a lot of work to fake who you are all day, every day, and I was just so tired. The others... they started to get their byline assignments, it's the thing every intern dreams of. Part of the big draw at The Crier is the fact they promise everyone one article. You know going in it's going to be something small that very few people are actually going to bother to read, but it's just the cherry on top. It'll go on every résumé you send out when graduation approaches. I knew they wouldn't be happy about giving me one, and for a while it seemed like maybe they just wouldn't. And then, the harbor story came up and I was the only one left, so I got stuck with it."

Kenna grew silent again and I gently prodded, "And it was just too much?"

With a sigh, Kenna replied softly, "It was just too much."

She described the feeling as paralysis. She'd wanted to do the assignment, she'd wanted to follow all the steps exactly as she'd been taught- but just wanting it hadn't been enough. Instead, she'd stared at a blank word processing document on her screen and the phone on her desk for days. With each passing hour, she'd grown more overwhelmed about the now dwindling amount of time she truly had to research and write the story.

"Tessa knew about the story and she started pressing me, she wanted to see my completed copy before I submitted it. So I was getting nudges at the office by my supervisor, and my phone and computer are both sending me these reminder alerts about the deadline, and now my mother is pushing too. I knew whatever I wrote wouldn't have been good enough for her anyway, but there's no way I could have just not written anything at all."

Through her rising panic, she finally mustered enough fortitude to read through Buzz article about the project again, and attempted to wade through some of the cited city documents although they proved to be pretty difficult to sift through. She was able to scrape together a barely acceptable article that would pass a plagiarism check. The problem was, she hadn't actually reported anything new- she'd just rewritten what the Buzz had already reported. The interns had been well schooled on the expectation that they would do actual leg work and find new angles and sources for whatever story they'd been assigned. Now, with mere hours left until the firm deadline she had nothing to add and made the fateful choice.

"I was drowning and I needed a lifeline. I considered just fessing up and saying I couldn't complete the assignment, but remember, I have Tessa on top of me too. She's furious by this point because she knows she won't have time to proof whatever I'm writing before the submission deadline so I'm now lying to her and telling her I think it's a good piece and she will like it. And that's when it comes to me, just make up a source who gives a few new but not very important details about the project. I know this is one of the worst things a journalist can do, but maybe this is such a small story no one will care. It's not like I'm going to make up new information, I'm confident the other reporters had already done their own fact-checking on the earlier stories so I am just adding a tiny new spin on what they wrote with a fake source. It wasn't a big deal, but it was also a huge deal."

It turned out it was exactly as small of a story as she'd judged, The Crier fact-checkers had barely bothered to even read her piece and hadn't bothered to actually check back with the phony email address she'd created and supplied. This was a huge mistake on their part, but it didn't absolve the person who'd made the overt decision to falsify a story. When the story printed, Kenna was filled with relief, assumed that was the end of it, and hoped to finish her internship in complete obscurity. Tessa had criticized the final product, but she'd been satisfied enough that it was actually completed that she had been fairly mild in her critique.

Then, just as she let her guard down, the Buzz retracted their original story. The chain effect was instant. "My supervisor called me and said I needed to come into the meeting room, and I somehow knew. When I walked in, there were several people already seated. My supervisor was there, but so was his supervisor. There was a third person as well, a woman from HR, and when they introduced her I knew what was happening."

She'd fought a rising panic attack as she sat at the boardroom table, facing her accusers. With her chest clenched, and her stomach rolling, she'd just sat there and dully nodded and gave simple yes and no answers. She hadn't bothered trying to deny doing what she was accused of, or to make excuses. In the end she signed the forms she was handed acknowledging her guilt and agreeing to sever her ties with the Crier immediately. She stared at the highlighted portion of the contract she was handed that made it clear her lack of journalistic integrity would be reported to her school. She was escorted to her desk area and handed a box to fill with the few belongings she'd kept there and walked right out of the building.

"The shame was unbearable. I can't stand to think about how it felt walking past everyone with that box. No one said goodbye. No one said anything; they just stared as I walked past them. I refused to look at anyone, but I could see one of the other interns out of the corner of my eye and he had this smirk on his face. I wanted to just run at that point but I somehow kept it together until I got into the garage, and that's when I let myself lose it."

I could hear the pain and regret in Kenna's voice as she relayed the full scale of her humiliation and, had I not been driving, I would have hugged her. She'd made a huge mistake, mistake might not even be the correct word to use in this context because she'd chosen to break the rules on purpose. But there hadn't been malice in that decision. Being let go was a reasonable consequence, the rest of the fall out seemed extreme and unfair. Had she been anyone but Tessa Shepard's kid it never would have happened. She'd have taken her licks and moved on to do the hard work of rebuilding her reputation. Had she lamented something like, "my life is ruined!" it would have been hyperbolic. But she was Tessa's daughter, and her life had been ruined in some ways.

"Kenna... you know this is going to pass, right? There are a lot of lessons here, and once you learn them you can truly move past it."

I kept my eyes focused on the road, but my peripheral vision allowed me to see the girl turn and gaze once again out of her side window.

"I guess." She finally replied. "But I'm not just trying to move past the stupid thing I did, I have to figure out who I really am. I don't know where to go next."

I struggled for some nugget of advice, something wise and perhaps motherly to impart, when the van in front of us suddenly slammed on their breaks. Cursing softly under my breath, I managed to control the car and avoid hitting the minivan, but a sea of red lights around the bend warned we'd be there for a while.

We were three hours into what should have been a seven hour trip and from the looks of things it would prove to be much longer. Kenna and her need to grow and discover might be the center of this topic, but I clearly needed to address my own issues as well. I knew that it needed to start with letting go of the onward march of the digital clock. If we were delayed, well, so what? It was okay. We wouldn't get there too late, because there wasn't really a "too late". Unless someone died, a small voice said in my head. I blocked the voice out. No, we were okay, we could wait.

In the stagnancy of the traffic lockdown, I could safely face Kenna.

"I think maybe none of us are born to be just one person, one thing. We all have the potential to choose many different paths and there will always be forks. No one walks a straight path, Kenna. This is your fork."

Kenna nodded, as if she agreed. Between her tight frown and the way her eyes still faced downward though, as if direct eye contact would break her, I know she hadn't really bought it. Part of me wanted to push the subject more, to force her to consider all of the dreams she might secretly indulge in. I wanted her to acknowledge that those dreams were still possible. A bigger part of me knew it wasn't the time for that yet.

I reached up and spun the radio dial until I found an easy listening station. John Mayer crooned and I smiled at Kenna before joining him in my own not-quite-awful voice. Kenna was silent for a few minutes, but as the last chorus began, she hesitantly joined in. As soon as it ended, Fleetwood Mac's Landslide began and I found myself smiling in earnest. This had been one of Delta's favorites. As I softly hummed along, a soft angelic voice piped in alongside me. In surprise, I looked at Kenna.

Her voice was softer and higher pitched than Stevie Nicks, but she sang in perfect harmony.

When the song ended I gave a low whistle and watched as Kenna's cheeks flushed. "Wow! Beautiful! I didn't realize you were a singer."

As soon as the words left my mouth I chuckled, remembering the guitar that she'd thrown in the backseat. Of course she sang.

"I'm not really, I'm not a singer I mean, I enjoy song writing though..." Kenna confessed.

"Really? That's interesting! Have you always been into music?"

"I got a guitar for my ninth birthday, and I became a little obsessed with it. I'm okay on it, nothing great to be honest. I've taken several music composition and music theory classes though, it's been steadying but nothing super special."

I shot her a look. "I don't think I believe that. If you've been playing this many years and have the ability to sing like *that* then I think you're downplaying it."

Kenna shook her head. "No, I'm really not. I mean, like I said, I'm okay. I'm really not good though. Back in high school, I actually played in a talent show and didn't even make the second round. It's okay though, that's not why I write and play. I do it for myself. It's just always been a way to get the things out that I couldn't actually say aloud."

Traffic had begun to move again and I inched the car along until the line of vehicles accelerated to nearly normal speed. My mind was still occupied with the latest revelation of Kenna's talent though.

"Was Tessa encouraging with your music?"

Kenna didn't answer for a moment as she carefully considered the question. "It's kind of hard to say. I mean, she's the one who got me the guitar and lessons. She never really complained about my singing or playing and you know my mother, not complaining or criticizing is kind of the highest form of compliment. But I wouldn't say she actually encouraged it. She didn't bother to ask if I'd continue with music in college. She'd never have suggested I play in a public setting. I guess the kindest way to put it is she tolerated my music. Tessa doesn't tolerate much, so I always appreciated that."

Not for the first time in recent days, I fought the urge to share the full truth about what I really thought of Tessa. Tessa had taken the beautiful baby that I had grown for her and had crushed her tiny spirit before she ever really had a chance. If Kenna didn't "sparkle", as Tessa complained, it was only because Tessa had snuffed that right out way back at the very beginning. Fury filled me as I thought about that. Worse than the fury though, was the guilt. Eventually, I'd have to be brave enough to broach that topic. Eventually, I would need to apologize.

Chapter 8

Kenna

It's reflexive, I try to turn my own core into solid iron to survive what's coming. My stomach muscles tighten and we dive beneath the deep gray of the Chesapeake Bay. There are tunnels in New York, but nothing like this. The tunnel's walls loomed imposingly around the two lanes of traffic that slowly churn through the passageway of what Rachel called the Hampton Roads Bridge Tunnel. Willing my eyes to actually move was a feat, but when I glance to the side I regret it immediately. The shoulder is impossibly narrow. At any moment, we'll nick the wall and start a chain reaction that'll trap dozens of vehicles here. I sit white-knuckled, but when I glance at Rachel, none of the fear I'm overwhelmed by is parroted on her face. In fact, she looks almost jubilant.

"Never thought I'd feel this happy about hitting rush hour traffic in the ole HRBT!" She says cheerfully.

"I can't imagine driving this thing regularly. And you were just a teenager when you lived here, right?"

Rachel smiles and nods. "Yep. This tunnel signified independence and freedom though. When we'd hit this tunnel, it was to head off for day trips to Busch Gardens up in Williamsburg, or weekend sneak-aways to Richmond. The tunnel meant we'd escaped my father's watchful eyes, but more than that it meant we were moving on to something exciting. I get the same excited buzz in here that I get when I'm driving past a lit up airport runway at night. The whole potential for adventure, don't you feel it?"

Up ahead, a nearly blinding semicircle of light grew larger. Escape. I reply, "Well I guess I do a bit. I'm sure I'll feel it even more when we're completely out of this death trap though."

Rachel laughs at that, nods toward the windshield as we exit the tunnel, and says, "As you wish!"

When we'd entered the tunnel, I'd only had a quick glimpse of the body of water we'd be traveling through. Now, we're on a bridge that stretches ahead for miles. Seagulls rest along a guardrail that separates us from the Bay below. A dozen small boats span the bridge as fishermen take advantage of the shade that it offers and the schools of fish that are drawn to it. In the distance, huge mammoth gray Navy ships are silhouetted against the landscape. Emerging from that tunnel, we've entered a new world.

"Well, some things sure haven't changed," Rachel mutters as we approach a long line of nearly stalled traffic.

I sing along with Tracy Chapman as I continue to eye the scenery around us. We've been stuck in traffic long enough that even the Bay has become tiresome. Inching forward, one car length at a time, we finally complete the length of the bridge. Back on firm ground, exit signs begin to make their appearance and we're moving at a fast clip. The renewed speed doesn't spur new conversation. We're both firmly locked away in our own heads. The radio makes our silence okay.

When we pass a set of signs, Rachel straightens in her seat. I've spent a lifetime studying my mother, reading her moods. The ability to know what's coming before it hits you is crucial when you have a mother who is a master pitcher of insults and vases. I'm using that skill now as I watch the tension creeping into the rigor of Rachel's posture. Her jaw clenches as she glances at the car's mirrors. The radio is no longer able to soothe the silence.

"Hey, are you okay?" I ask.

She nods but still doesn't speak and then we're crossing three lanes of traffic to barely make an exit. The signs we'd recently passed indicated the thruway to Virginia Beach was still a few miles away but our exit said, "Little Creek".

"Pit stop?" I prod. I'm not a prodder. Where am I finding this strength?

As the car slows at an intersection she clears her throat and answers.

"Little Creek... it's technically part of the city of Norfolk, it's where the Coast Guard station was. Still is, I imagine."

I remember her casual comment yesterday about meeting Delta for the first time at her father's Coast Guard base. Now I understand her tense posture and voice. This is more than just another old haunt; this is where it had all begun. Sacred ground. We wind the Saturn through deeply potholed and litter-strewn city streets until we find ourselves in a line of cars that's slowly progressing through a military gate.

"Get your driver's license out." Rachel instructs and I do so even though I'm confused.

"I didn't think just anyone could drive onto these kinds of installations? Don't we need special permission of some kind?"

"I guess we'll see," Rachel says tightly.

Whatever hopes she might have had that the gate guard would just waive us on are quickly dashed as he explains we need either a military ID card or to be sponsored by someone already on the base. Biting her lip, Rachel explains that we want to visit the Coast Guard part of the base and asks if it was possible to arrange a tour. The guard directs us to a small, white building next to the gate and suggests we inquire there. We follow his instructions and park in the small lot that's adjacent to the building. Once inside, a polite young man listens as Rachel explains our request and leaves to make a phone call.

"I don't know Rachel, it seems like they're pretty strict here." I caution.

"I know," she admits. "But I felt pulled here. I'm not one for spontaneous pit stops. If something told me to stop, then I have to believe we are meant to be here."

I don't have the chance to reply, because the young uniformed man returns quickly. He explains that someone from the Coast Guard station will soon be there to escort us in.

Rachel smiles and thanks him and we make our way to a small row of hard plastic chairs that line up the waiting area.

As we wait, I watch the steady line of truck drivers make their way to the desk to receive passes to complete their deliveries onto the base. The service members who are dealing with them are more interesting to watch. I've never had any direct exposure to the military so my sum knowledge of service members is a Hollywood version. The friendly, young, uniformed people bear little resemblance to those characters in movies and television. On the screen, the service members are usually men- hardened, bearded, commando types who are always in motion. Chasing someone, killing someone, running from someone.

I realize again that as encompassing as my education has been, I'm embarrassingly unfamiliar with the lives that most Americans lead. I'm painfully aware of just how little I can relate with real people in the real world. Two years of college has helped a bit, but a single gender, highly selective college campus in the middle of New York City doesn't necessarily offer a much more realistic worldview than my Hollywood created screens. I'm not comfortable in my mother's gilded world, but I am equally uncomfortable in a world full of normal, real people.

I turn to Rachel, wondering if I can explain my observation but the tight look on her face makes it clear she isn't interested in idle chatter. She's nervous. I don't know why it surprises me that she's as susceptible to nerves as anyone else, but it does. She glances at the silver watch on her wrist at regular intervals. In fact, as I watch- there seems to be a cadence to it. Soon the pattern reveals itself. Blink, blink, blink, blink, glance to the wall behind the counter where a wall clock hangs, blink, blink, blink, blink, glance to her wrist. It's as if she's comparing the two, determined to find a flaw. Repeat.

I'm now ridiculously watching the clock too and the pattern continues for several minutes. The front door swings opens and a young woman in a dark blue uniform nods at us. "Hi, I'm Seaman Hatcher, I understand you're looking for a tour?"

Rachel clears her throat and explains, "Yes, we're actually just passing through and I thought I'd show my-" she glances at me, "daughter... The station. My father and wife were both stationed here back in the 90s."

I feel my eyes widen at her choice of words, but Seaman Hatcher doesn't visibly react to it. Daughter. I understand why she said it. It'd be too hard to explain my presence otherwise. Identifying me as her niece had seemed to work well enough back in Metzgartown. I don't need to read too much into the word, the apologetic look she throws me tells that story. Still, a barrage of emotion came with that word. In a way, it wasn't a lie. She *had* given birth to me after all. But legally, emotionally, for all practical purposes, she isn't my mother. She's a near-stranger.

The young woman smiles even wider at her words. "Oh wow, cool. I've heard a lot of stories about what it was like here back then. There's an auxiliarist who comes in here every once in a while. He retired about ten years ago and sometimes talks about the olden days."

Rachel, a woman who is clearly only in her early forties, snorts at that comment. "Yes, back in the olden days, it looked a little different around here."

Soon, we're following Seaman Hatcher's government truck to the Coast Guard portion of the base. A large, rather picturesque white building looms ahead. It would have fit perfectly up in New England which makes it seem a little out of place here in southern Virginia. After parking, we walk toward it in silence. Rachel is lost within herself and I know without being told that she's retracing the footprints of ghosts.

"The main building was built in the 90s, was it here when you lived here," the young seaman asks.

Rachel nods, "95, they opened it in 95 not long before we left for Connecticut. Most of the time we lived here in Virginia my father, and then my wife, were in the old building."

Seaman Hatcher asks curiously, "Didn't you guys have trouble getting collocated with your dad? Nowadays, they wouldn't allow a spouse to be stationed with a father-in-law."

Rachel chuckles. "Back then, it wouldn't have flown either. But neither would a marriage between two women. No, we first met when Delta was stationed here."

Hatcher smiles and wiggles her eyebrows, "Ooh, forbidden love. I'm just guessing your Dad wasn't thrilled about that. Where's your wife now?"

Rachel's smile falters and she says simply, "She's passed away."

After a slightly awkward apology, Hatcher leads us into the building. I watch Rachel's eyes widen as she looks around.

"It really hasn't changed much at all," she murmurs.

As Seaman Hatcher points out various offices and rooms, we follow along silently. When we pass a door labeled, *Officer In Charge*, Rachel stops. "That was my father's office."

Hatcher apologizes and explains that it wouldn't be appropriate to go into it and Rachel waves her off. She isn't here to see her father's old office. We follow the labyrinth hallway to a large open space that's populated with a few cozy looking sitting spots, and Hatcher explains it's known as the Day Room. Rachel begins to walk along the perimeter, studying the many plaques and framed photographs that hang on the walls. When she abruptly stops at one photo, I hear a long, slow exhale between pursed lips. I walk over to view it myself.

"Kringle Crew!" Seaman Hatcher helpfully interrupts. "They were the small boat crew that successfully saved the lives of 11 college kids from the Vessel Kringle during a bad nor'easter. It got a lot of attention because the dude who owned the Kringle also owns the waterpark here in Norfolk. Two of the people saved were his own kids; the rest had been their friends. He's super generous with us to this day. Every year he throws us a special party on Coast Guard Day, and sends free tickets to the park all the time."

I study the photograph. A large mustached man stands between a younger man and a petite woman- all in uniform. The woman stands with her chin tilted up, a slight smile on her lips. Cocky. Wild curls have rebelliously escaped from what's clearly supposed to be a tight bun. I recognize Delta from the photos at Rachel's house, although she's much younger in this one. Younger than I am now, I realize with a start. I'm uncomfortable as I compare our trajectories. There's no real direction to my life, I am symbolically adrift. This woman, girl really, younger than myself, saved the lives of those who were quite literally adrift.

As Rachel stands transfixed, Seaman Hatcher says excitedly, "Oh! That's her, right?"

"Yes. She'd have liked this. She was proud of her Coast Guard years long after she got out, she would have gotten a kick out of knowing she'd left a mark here in Virginia," Rachel says softly.

Something's cut her invisible bindings and the tension that had been stiffening her spine is relaxed. We continue a tour through the main building and then head down to the docks to see the moored small boats. Apparently, they're all quite different from the boats that had been there in the 90s and Rachel expresses much less sentimentality as we admire their silver and orange trim. Stopping at the docks edge, she gazes out across the water and I can only guess at her thoughts. Whatever they are, they're not sad. She's closed her eyes and is breathing in the sea air deeply, a hint of a smile curving her lips. Here, the memories are clearly good.

She turns and smiles at Seaman Hatcher and asks amicably, "What about you? Are you going to make a career out of this?"

The young seaman grins and says, "Ma'am, I'm going to be Commandant one day!"

Rachel laughs aloud at that and says, "Delta would have approved."

Soon afterward, we walk back up to the parking lot and pause to say our goodbyes. Rachel digs into her purse and pulls out an old dry cleaning receipt and writes her phone number and email address on the back. She hands it to the young woman and instructs her to get in touch if she ever needs anything. Seaman Hatcher thanks her. A quick hug follows and we're now following her back toward the gate.

Back on the road, I comment, "You're really good at that, aren't you?"

"What's that," she asks

"That people thing. You know how to make other people feel comfortable. Back there, you had our tour guide ready to hop in the car and join us on the trip. If you'd asked, she would have said yes. Somehow you have a way of being a non-stranger, right away."

Rachel laughs at that. "Well her boss might have had something to say about that, but thank you. That's really sweet to say."

Relaxed now and smiling, she reaches and finds an 80s music station. I assure Rachel that I know the oldies, my generation loves the 80s. She snorts and mutters something about breaking out her old phonograph machine and turns up the volume. Def Leppard makes way for Journey. Duran Duran. Cyndi Lauper. Dire Straits. Phil Collins. Whitney Houston. A-ha. When Nena starts singing about 99 red balloons floating by, we finally exit the highway and make our way toward the center of

Virginia Beach. Within minutes, we're on a busy street dwarfed by tall beachside hotels, surf shops, bars and restaurants. We slow to a crawl to gawk at the strip.

"Wow! This has certainly changed in the last 24 years. When I was here last there were a few larger hotels, and a whole lot of small mom and pop type places."

It's mid-September, past the high tourist season, but the sidewalks are still busy with families, groups of teenagers, hand-holding couples. At a red light a panhandler boldly walks up to the car extending a cardboard sign that reads, "Need money to feed dog," although there's no dog in sight. I instinctively glance at the door lock to ensure it's engaged, just as my mother had taught me. Rachel on the other hand, lowers her window, and hands him a $5 bill. He offers her a blessing and runs back to the curb.

"That was nice of you. I don't think he really has a dog though," I comment.

She glances at me and says, "Kenna, we all have a dog, and eventually we all need a little help in feeding him."

I smile at her. There's a kindness in Rachel that's uncommon in my world. The stark contrast between the woman who'd given birth to me and the woman who raised me has never been so obvious. Had Tessa sensed that kindness? Had that made Rachel seem easier to manipulate, or was there some latent part of Tessa that actually admired the trait? And why had Rachel agreed to be tied to a woman like Tessa? I suspect that while money had been her primary motive in the surrogacy, she may have also been moved by the idea of helping another woman bring a child into the world. I'd been the dog that needed to be fed back then.

We're finally at our hotel, The Coral Breeze. The hotel has taken artistic license with its name, as my quick googling back at Rachel's house had confirmed there isn't actually a coral reef anywhere near Virginia Beach. The location is beachside though and that's our number one requirement. After a quick check-in at the sparsely decorated lobby counter, we board a suspicious looking elevator and hit the number 7 button. A loud grinding noise sounds and only after it subsides does the small box begin its ascent. I remind myself that this is okay. This is supposed to be humbling. Still, I breathe a sigh of relief when the doors open and reveal a long dark corridor.

After making our way to our room, I steel myself to whatever might be behind the locked door. Inside though, it's not as bad as I'd feared. The small room is a few decades outdated and the tap water has a peculiar musty smell but there are two beds with seemingly clean bedding and a wide balcony that overlooks a bustling boardwalk strip and the Atlantic ocean beyond it.

Standing on the balcony, I inhale the sea air deeply. As a child, I'd enjoyed beach vacations in far more stunningly beautiful places. Greece, France, Antigua, Curacao... those were the playground beaches of my youth. When we visited such beaches, we'd stay at opulent resorts. I'd taken them for granted, didn't everyone vacation that way? This hotel wouldn't have passed muster even for a quick airport layover. This experience is special though, this is my first beach escape without Mother's approved care team tethering me down. Here, no one has expectations; no one is watching and judging. For the very first time, I understand why poets and writers sometimes describe the ocean as a vibrant symbol of freedom. Beyond the ocean's horizon, there is an entire world waiting to be seen. A world I could allow myself to be lost in. The possibilities are suddenly endless.

"Let's hit the boardwalk. I'm feeling like it's time for an iced cold beer and a plateful of fried calamari." Rachel interrupts my thoughts from behind me.

"Sounds good!"

On the boardwalk, we weave ourselves around the myriad of dog walkers, joggers, and lollygagging children. Various genres of music waft from open doorways. When we find a restaurant with beachside outdoor seating, we sit down and I eye the bar menu. Rachel reminds me, "Not yet, your birthday is next week, wait and make it special."

Ah yes, my birthday. The twenty-first birthday is significant because of the tangential legal drinking age. I've been enjoying an occasional glass of wine or cocktail for many years though. We've spent enough time abroad where it just isn't a thing that's questioned. Here in the states, if I travel with Tessa or one of her assistants, it's also quite normal for me to order whatever I want without the server raising their eyebrows. I am Tessa Shepherd's daughter, a member of the untouchable class, after all. Remembering my recent downfall, I correct myself grimly. Not so untouchable after all.

I glance up at Rachel who is studying me and I suspect she knows what, or rather who, is in my thoughts. She doesn't prod though, she just allows me to move past the moment. As our waiter drops off a pair of water glasses and takes our order, Rachel raises her water in a mock toast.

"To new beginnings and old ghosts."

"Cheers," I reply as we clink glasses.

"Did you and Delta spend a lot of time down here," I ask.

She turns and looks at the ocean and then smiles back at me. "Yes, we really did. She was a creature of the sea. Delta didn't really sunbathe, she just ran straight for the waves. Sometimes she'd have a surfboard in her hands, other times she'd hit the water and just swim back and forth. We'd spend hours at the beach and then we'd change in the public restrooms before heading out for dinner. There also used to be a really fun 18+ club down here on the oceanfront, maybe it's still here? Anyway, no one ever actually checked my ID so they'd wave me in with her and we'd sit in the back to watch people dance and make fools of themselves. I always felt so alive down here."

It's pretty difficult to picture the modest, proper woman in front of me sneaking into loud nightclubs. 18 year old Rachel must have been very different than 42 year old Rachel. It's a hopeful thought. If Rachel could change, it was possible I could too.

I want to ask more about Rachel's own childhood but before I have a chance to do so, a loud, booming voice with an exaggerated Texan drawl punctuates the air.

"Kennedy? Kennedy Shepherd! What in the hell are you doing slumming here in Virginia Beach?"

The deck spins. I grip the table as I struggle to catch my breath. The stylish voice of Bruno Mars from the deck's speakers fades and is replaced by a loud siren in my head. Every hope I'd dared to allow is tossed into a giant funnel and redirects into a black pit. Sforzando. I've been an idiot. I can't just disappear. I would always be recognizable to many as

Tessa Shepherd's daughter. We haven't made it 24 hours on the road before discovery. Squeezing my eyes shut for a moment, I take a deep breath and then finally look up at the sunburnt face that hosts a familiar smug grin and glassy eyes.

"Hi, Zach," is the only reply I can muster.

Chapter 9

Rachel

Kenna's eyes were huge, pale blue saucers as the color drained from her cheeks. You have got to be shitting me, I thought, resisting the urge to say the words out loud. Something had changed since we'd left Pennsylvania and it feels dangerously fleeting. Kenna had begun to relax. She'd been opening up. Like an early spring tulip, the girl's petals had softened at the edges, the potential of full bloom was imminent. And now, just when I'd started to feel hopeful, this boisterous intruder threatened everything.

"I almost didn't recognize you with that hair, what in the hell did you do, Kennedy?" he drawled slowly, flashing a toothy smile.

His eyes narrowed though as he studied her, he considered her newly shorn dark tresses, then his gaze dropped to the parts of her body that were not as visible to him from her seated position. His grin grew even wider and he shook his head. It's not apparent to me if the look conveys approval or disapproval at her changes. His face was ruddy, his eyes glazed, it was obvious that the man had been imbibing in something chemical. Perhaps he'd had just too many drinks or perhaps he'd been smoking something stronger. Whatever the cause, there was an air of belligerence about him that troubled me.

Kenna visibly shrank before my eyes. As her body curled inward and sank deeper into her chair, I sensed her struggle to disappear entirely. The young woman who'd begun to share parts of her life and had offered moments of sincere laughter was gone again. She'd been replaced by a pale copy with downcast eyes.

She stammered softly, "Yeah, um, I guess I got it cut..."

I cringed at the note of weakness in her voice and then I immediately felt guilty for it. It wasn't her fault she was this way, I reminded myself. I interrupted by thrusting out my hand and saying, "Hi, I'm Rachel."

The intruder glanced and didn't bother to hide his disinterest but a lifetime of training must have kicked in as he reluctantly shook my hand before replying, "Zach, Zach Calvin."

At my barely perceptible nod and lack of reaction he added pointedly, "The Fort Worth Calvins."

I have no clue who the Fort Worth Calvins might be. Was this a reference to his family? The name of a sports team? A religious sect? Rather than admit my ignorance or feign interest and risk extending the introduction to a full conversation I just nodded again. He turned his attention back to Kenna.

"Jesus, Kennedy, there's some crazy shit in the news about you. What the hell happened?"

Kenna bit her lip and said, "It's a long story."

What I really wanted to do at this point is jump in and speak for her. I wanted to dress him down and send him on his way. I've dealt with unruly boys before, I knew exactly how to put them in their place. I fought the urge though. This wasn't my battle to be fought. I couldn't allow myself to become just one more person in her life who didn't allow her to think and feel and speak for herself.

He didn't take her subtle hint and pressed onward. "I bet, your mama must be going crazy over all of this. Tessa always was a little high strung!"

At that even Kenna managed a tiny smile, but she continued to hedge. "It's complicated."

"What are you going to do? Are you going back to school?" He looked confused for a moment then said, "Wait, shouldn't you be there now?"

Kenna nodded, but instead of clamming up again or allowing him to push her into revealing more than she wanted she pivoted back, and I felt a spark of pride. "Aren't you supposed to be back at school too? Somewhere in Texas?"

"Gig 'em! Yeah, baby!" He whooped.

Kenna and I glanced at each other and then back at Zach. I had no clue what he was saying, but he wasn't perceptive enough to pick up my confusion.

"Heading back next week, Calvin Corp takes precedence over cadet corp. A&M knows it too. They'll hold the line for me." He said, jutting his chin out proudly.

His phone sounded a text alert and he glanced at it, furrowing his thick brows in annoyance before shaking his head. "The old man. He can calm his tits."

Then, without warning, he lifted the device he'd just been texting on and turned it toward us and I heard the sickening sound of a faux camera shutter. Kenna quickly objected, "Wait, no, what are you..."

"Relax, Kennedy, I won't show anyone. Besides, you don't look that bad with dark hair." His eyes squinted again, as they had when he'd first appraised her and he added, "Actually, maybe you look even better with it. I always like blondes, but maybe this is working for you."

With her panic evident, Kenna reached out and grabbed my hand across the table. An uncommon fury began to rise and I struggled to keep my tone civil.

"Kenna doesn't want any pictures taken. In fact, she'd rather you didn't mention this meeting to anyone."

With his toothy grin back in place, Zach replied, "Sure, mums the word. Even if you still haven't told me how you ended up in this shithole."

Kenna didn't answer, she just stared at him with wide eyes as she squeezed my hand even harder. As both Zach and I awaited her response, she remained still, frozen. That's when I realized that the problem wasn't that she didn't want to answer- it's that she physically couldn't.

"We're visiting an old friend." I said tightly, not bothering to hide the note of animosity in my tone anymore.

"Sucks to be them." He said, as he glanced down the boardwalk and shook his head at the scene. "The old man is bidding on a new Navy Housing project, I'm supposed to be shadowing him but if you ask me it's a waste of time. Can't get out of here soon enough, nothing but screaming kids, a bunch of fat people who have no business in bathing suits, and gang bangers here."

I was still too troubled by the way he'd responded to my comment about the photo to focus on his rude comments so I pressed onward.

"Okay, can you please delete that picture now then?"

I stared challengingly at him and he met my gaze directly, before half of his mouth broke into a sneer.

"Lady, not sure who you are, but me and Kennedy are old friends. She knows I'm good for my word."

I glanced back at Kenna, who sat silently watching the exchange. She obviously didn't know any such thing. She looked down and mustered enough strength to say, "I'd appreciate it Zach, if you could please delete it."

He rolled his eyes and opened his phone screen, and dramatically touched it as if he were complying with the request, when a text alert sounded again. His brow furrowed as he read the incoming text and he shook his head.

"Christ. It's Daddy and I'm being summoned again. I better go or I'll be listening to his lecture all the way back to Fort Worth. See you later Kennedy. Hopefully someplace better like back in St. Barts."

"But, Zach, did you-"

"Yeah, it's all good. Later!"

Kena stared silently at Zach's retreating back and I reached across to squeeze her hand again. "I'm sorry Kenna. I never would have imagined you'd run into someone you knew here."

When she looked up, she had tears in her eyes. "It's not your fault. And I'm just lying to myself if I think I can escape who and what I am anyway. I don't believe he deleted that picture, he's going to have it in circulation in minutes."

"How do you know him," I asked, not bothering to deny the likely truth of her words.

"His father and Tessa are friends, maybe more at one time, I don't know. But they popped up on several of our beach holidays ironically enough. His father's huge in real estate development and somehow we ended up running in the same circles. Or at least our parents did anyway. Then we ended up going to high school together at Calvin Brook. You should have heard him- trying to convince everyone the school had been named after his family. It wasn't by the way, it was named after John Calvin, but he actually tried to convince our classmates it was true. The whole Calvin clan are a bunch of loud mouthed, obnoxious, arrogant jerks. They're the type of people who exaggerate their Texas drawls and pretend to be all down homey and real, but they'd never have the time of day for anyone who was actually homey and real."

I'd picked up exactly that vibe from the young man. Over-privileged, obnoxious, and immature for his age. He'd been exactly the kind of guy that Delta would have deliberately taunted. Back in our younger years, Delta had certainly garnered more than her fair share of male attention- and she could pick out the slime balls easily. She'd enjoyed toying with them as they confidently leaned in and offered drinks and saccharine compliments. I'd never suffered that kind of attention, I've always been the sort to blend more seamlessly into the background. Mousy, that was the word I used to describe myself despite Delta's protests. It was true though. I'm the sort of woman who can quietly blend into a wall. At times in the past, this had bothered me just a bit, but the flip side was I haven't had to suffer many fools.

"He sounds like a peach. Okay, let's say the worst case scenario is he still has the picture and he does go public with it. We'll probably be long gone before it gets enough attention to matter."

Kenna shook her head emphatically. "It'll happen faster than you can imagine. Are you on instagram? TikTok? Snapchat? Zach's not exactly an influencer, but we have plenty of mutual contacts from school who are. As soon as one of them shares the picture he took, it'll go viral."

It was true that I wasn't overly familiar with social media, but I had trouble imagining that people would really care as much as she feared.

"Even if that's true, I have a hard time imagining it'll be a topic of conversation for long. We will be moving on soon enough, I just don't think this will be the emergency you fear." I said.

She shook her head. "Even if this miraculously doesn't go viral before we leave Virginia Beach, the damage will be done. Everyone will know what I look like now. They'll recognize me in Charleston and Key West. It keeps the story alive that much longer, and Rachel there's something else you're not considering... he got you in the picture too."

Her words hung for a moment before I understood her point. Tessa. If she saw the picture, she'd surely recognize me, even all these years later. When she did, she would be furious and that's when the consequences would happen.

"I'm not worried about that," I lied. "I'm not hiding anything. Let them see me."

That secret bank of Delta's voice inside my heart sounded again.

"For a girl that doesn't care, you sure look like your heart is breaking in half Rachel. I hated keeping this whole thing secret, like what we have is something we should be ashamed of. That's just ridiculous. There's not a damned thing wrong with us. I wanted to shout it to the whole world, including to your stubborn Daddy. I wanted that, but I never wanted this. I never wanted it to happen when you weren't ready. To hell with him though. To hell with the whole world. We are not the ones who are fucked up."

I shook away the memory, I was stronger now. I could face this head on. Yet for all my newfound bravado, I had a sudden urge to get far away from the restaurant. I paid the check and we walked a little further down the boardwalk before the sound of waves crashing along the shore lured us toward the tideline. We peeled off our shoes and gingerly stepped onto the cool sand. With each step we took, each deep inhalation of hearty, salt air, we moved further away from the dark cloud that Zach had forced upon us.

The unseasonably warm temperatures that had blanketed the east coast didn't fool the ocean. We dipped our feet into the shallow, translucent edge of the tide and it's cold enough to make Kenna shriek and she was laughing again.

After a moment she turned and said, "He's wrong. This place isn't a dump. I think I really like it here. No, it's not Palm Beach, but there's something real about this place. An energy. It doesn't feel like it just exists for the tourists either, in spite of all of those-" she gestured at the hotels behind her, "You can tell most of the businesses cater to locals too.

I can see you here too Rachel. You're waiting to hear about a job here aren't you?"

Somehow I'd managed to forget about the job hunt. I'd conveniently put it aside because it was easier to focus on Kenna and her problems. I nodded and sighed. "I am, and I do love it here obviously, but I'm still not sure. It feels in some ways like this would be taking a step backwards. A lot has clearly changed here, but it's no secret that my memories are the real draw to this spot. I'm not sure if I'd actually love living here as much without Delta. I lived in a lot of places as a girl after all, and I wonder if she was what made this one really stand out."

"Was it hard? Moving when you were younger? Not growing up in one home, one spot?" Kenna asked.

I motioned for her to follow me as I traced the serpentine fringe of the wet shoreline. Had it been difficult? Certainly there were challenges. There had been difficult goodbyes to friends, teachers I loved, and favorite parks and beaches I was sad to leave. You don't know anything other than the reality you are born into though. Perhaps our version of normal looked quite different than many other families, but it was absolutely normal to us. Wasn't this the way it is for all children? Before moving to Pennsylvania, every stop was temporary. Given our transient nature, our family learned to seek out every sight, every adventure as quickly and thoroughly as possible. When Delta and I settled down in PA, it was different. We'd landed there with the intention of staying there for the long haul. For a long time, it'd been exactly that. I thought I'd found my forever home.

"We thought that was it, and we thought that somehow life would be easier when we were firmly rooted somewhere. In a lot of ways, it was wonderful, but the truth is that sometimes I really missed my old vagabond lifestyle. There's something to be said for discovering new favorite places, being able to reinvent yourself every few years. I didn't anticipate I'd miss those things as much as I did. We tried to make up for it, we traveled a lot! But as wonderful as travel is, you don't have the opportunity to really dig into a place the way you can when you're going to be there for years. Permanence is such a strange thing for me, it offers sanctuary but I find myself wondering what I'm missing out on."

The truth is that not every move had been filled with the glow of promise. The inglorious end to my childhood had tainted that last official military move with a cynical, sepia brush. Our unceremonious exodus from Virginia Beach to New London had felt more like a shameful escape under cover of darkness, than an exciting adventure. It was the only move that I'd ever experienced that had been an act of running away from a place, and not toward one. No, I correct myself, not a place- we'd been running away from a person. Although I'd made some fragile semblance of peace with my father over the years since, everything had changed after he found out about my relationship with Delta. The memory chilled me far more than the icy water that stings my feet.

It'd been a frosty November evening, and we'd sought refuge in a small Italian restaurant in Norfolk's Ghent neighborhood. Although the world wasn't as accepting of same-sex couples back in the 90s, there had always safer spaces in which to hide- and Norfolk offered more of those spaces than many cities. The Ghent section of the city was particularly safe and welcoming for same-sex couples. In Ghent, no one blinked an eye when Delta and I walked hand in hand down the street. We occasionally visited the cafes and restaurants there, and then as cold weather moved in and the beach became less attractive, we found ourselves retreating there more often.

We had finished dinner that fateful evening and exited into the damp, crisp air, huddling together. At a curb, we waited for traffic to abate and Delta leaned in for a kiss. I didn't register the blue Chevy slowing and stopping right next to us at first. Then Delta physically pushed me away. Shocked, I glared at her and then realized she was actually staring in horror toward the road behind me. I spun around to see my father in his beat down old Tahoe. He'd lowered the passenger seat window and was staring at us. He didn't yell, at least not at that moment, but he said in a firm voice, "Get in Rachel."

I didn't attempt to argue with him, I just shot Delta a terrified glance and entered the car. The ride home was torturous for its silence. My father and I sat side by side, silent as if we were complete strangers. I didn't dare a glance at him. I hunched against my door and blinked back the tears that threatened to spill. Part of me wanted to try, to apologize and explain, to promise I was still his little girl. I wanted to tell him about Delta. About her fearlessness. I wanted to explain about the way Delta found humor in everything. I needed him to understand how kind Delta was to me, how she encouraged me and understood me. The words wouldn't come though, I was too scared to start that conversation. It wasn't until we walked into our house that he'd turned around and confronted me. I'd never seen him so angry.

"What in the hell was that?" He'd demanded, ignoring my mother's attempts to ask what happened.

"I'm sorry Dad... we just..." As I stammered beneath his hard gaze, he shook his head with disgust and held up a hand to stop me.

"You are never to see her again. Do you understand? If I ever find out you're cavorting with her again, not only will you not get one cent of college money, but I will make sure her career is ruined."

I'd made a half-hearted attempt to reason with him, but the tone of his voice and stillness of his posture had made it clear there was no point. Back then, at the age of seventeen, I hadn't found my voice yet. Instead I headed to my room, holding my head down meekly.

We hadn't actually stopped seeing each other. Had any teenager ever really stopped seeing a love interest at the demands of their parents? We went underground, inventing excuses to get away. We met in quiet, dark places. I knew from the way that my father refused to look at me, that he'd figured that out too. Our home felt increasingly stifling as my father clung to his disappointment and anger. My mother certainly didn't approve of my relationship with Delta, but she was angry with my father too. She wanted us to pretend everything was fine, but neither my father nor I were any good at faking fine. So, my parents argued more often, and I stayed away as much as possible.

In the end, when Delta's request for early transfer netted her orders to New London, I submitted a last minute application to Connecticut College. My high school grades were good, I was a strong essay writer, and in return the college offered me a partial scholarship. Delta and I were reasonably sure that between the two of us working, we could cover the rest of my tuition costs and our modest living expenses. As it turned out, we overestimated our ability to do that- but at the time it felt like it'd be easy to do.

When I broke the news to my parents, neither seemed surprised. My mother just looked tired and overwrought while my father sat stone-faced and had nothing to say at all. He didn't follow through with his threats to affect Delta's career, but he also didn't arrange any departing awards or farewell fanfare for her. He chose not to speak to either of us at all. It would take many years of cohabitation, a few health scares, and a changing world before my father began to speak to me again. It took still more before he would mention Delta at all. I've visited Charleston a few times over the years at my mother's behest, but Delta never accompanied me. She went to her grave without having made amends with my father.

"Rachel, did you hear me?" Kenna asked.

"Whoops! Sorry, I guess I was a little stuck in my head there for a while."

"No problem, I understand. I know you have a lot on your mind. I was just asking if you thought maybe we should turn back now, I think we've gone a few miles down this beach and it's going to be getting dark soon."

"Good idea, I could use a shower anyway."

Even though we were supposed to be walking back to the hotel, we couldn't resist a detour for an ice cream stand. Sitting on a bench, with our cones in hand, we watched the dusky sky roll in. Although we didn't mention him, it was clear that we were both still a little spooked by Zach. I couldn't help but periodically glance around to make sure he wasn't about to reappear and every time I did my eyes would meet Kenna's and it was obvious she was doing the same thing. I glanced back toward the ocean, and the fear mellowed and I relaxed again. Nearly finished with our cones, I motioned toward the hotel behind us and we walked back to the room. It'd been a really long day- between the driving and the memories.

After showering, I was more than ready to crawl into bed and sink into sleep. As I relaxed beneath the sheets and felt my eyes begin to close, the annoying trill of the bedside telephone ring jarred me. Kenna sat upright in her own bed and gave me a questioning look.

"It's got to be the front desk, no one else knows we're here." I said before answering.

The cold, clipped voice on the other end wasn't the unfamiliar voice of a hotel clerk though.

"Hello, Rachel!"

I looked wildly at Kenna, whose face made it clear she understood immediately and wasn't surprised at all. I closed my eyes and replied, "Hello, Tessa."

Chapter 10

Kenna

I know as soon as the phone rings.

In biology class, we'd studied a unit about the role of evolution in the natural, instinctual fears that human beings suffer. One powerful fear we read about was a fear of snakes. Humans are programmed to fear them because historically snakes held grave risk to primates. In our modern world, we're taught to differentiate between good snake and bad snake. If our home is even further progressed we are taught that there are no bad snakes, just bad ways to handle them. We learn to handle them carefully or to simply avoid them entirely. The fear though, that part isn't taught. Studies showed that even infants reacted to the sight of a snake with measurable fear. We're just born knowing there is potential danger.

Had I sensed the danger, even as an infant?

There are baby pictures of me. In those staged photos, I'd typically be posed alone, with a HoHo Nursery prop or two, looking for all the world like a content and loved baby. There are even a few publicity shots of my mother holding me. I suppose to the general public the pictures are sweet evidence of a lovely mother-daughter bond. Tessa and her adorable miracle baby. When I study them closely though, I see something else. I see the fear in my eyes. I suppose I'd just been too frozen in terror to even cry at the moment the shutter was snapping. I see it though. I'd recognized the snake.

When the phone rings, that ancient instinctual alarm sounds in my head. Before I have a chance to warn Rachel though, she's picked up the handset. I reach over and will my trembling fingers to turn on the lamp. The viper has always been watching, waiting, with glassy cold blue eyes. Nothing's escaped her notice. I know that Zach's photo is somehow the cause of this. She's had but a peek at her prey and has swooped in for the kill.

"Hello, Tessa," Rachel says, in a tone that a complete stranger might have mistaken as strong and unflappable. By now I am no stranger. I hear it, the hint of vulnerability. Tessa would have heard it too.

She holds the phone close enough to her ear that I can't hear Tessa's voice and Rachel won't look at me as she listens. It's hard to gauge which version of Tessa has attacked. Is it perhaps Public Tessa, smooth as butter with an expertly crafted smile and faux-friendly voice? This is a woman who can reach out and pat the hand of a crying mother on a television screen. Afterward, hundreds of thousands of fans will offer her accolades, any sympathy for the bereaved woman are an afterthought. The fans of this Tessa would defend her in our current situation if they knew about it, they'd be angry and upset on her behalf. Public Tessa won't crack though. She'll hold her head high and smile dotingly at the daughter who has so wronged her. But no, Rachel wouldn't get that mild version. I'm sure of it.

It's more likely that she's talking to my clipped, controlled, ice queen mother. Ice Queen Tessa leaves no doubt as to who the boss actually is. She shuts down disagreements with a penetrating stare and she's seemingly impervious to emotional appeals. Of the many flavors of Tessa, this is the most frequently present version in my life. This is who she reverts to when the cameras stop filming. This is the face I normally associate with the word "mother." That she's able to so cleverly disguise this face when on camera has always been a marvel to me.

This isn't the worst version though. The worst version is saved for her most intimate contacts. Her personal assistants, the men who stick around long enough, and me. This version surfaces when the iron grip she holds on her emotions is somehow breached. This version is pure fury. Angry Tessa doesn't issue cold, biting words. Instead her face contorts and the veil of beauty that she hides behind floats away. Now the shouting, the shrill screaming, ensues and the words are painful, even terrifying. Angry Tessa is capable of anything and she makes sure that her target knows it. She'll threaten job loss, legal action, and general life-ruination, and the thing is- she isn't lying. She's perfectly capable of destroying any of those things. Angry Tessa is also capable of striking physically. A glass might be hurled on a wall just behind her target's head. Sharp nailed claws might dig into a little girl's arms as she's forced into a deliberately frigid shower. I know that Rachel won't win in a battle against Angry Tessa.

Rachel is occasionally speaking in short one or two word sentences, yes, no, I see, punctuated by long periods of silence. She wouldn't have been able to maintain that cadence if she were being confronted by Angry Tessa. The Ice Queen it is.

Rachel breaks in and takes control. Her voice wavers a bit, but there's no mistaking the grit in it. "Look Tessa, I'm well aware of what I signed, but it's been 21 years and Kenna is a legal adult now. She initiated the contact, not me. I don't think even your lawyers can do anything with this."

More silence follows, Rachel's face turns redder and she's looking at me- rolling her eyes.

"No. No, we will not. If Kenna wants to speak to you then she can contact you, I'm not keeping her prisoner, but she's not a child to be summoned home."

Eventually, she puts the receiver against her chest and asks me quietly, "She'd like to speak to you. Do you have anything to say to her?"

I shake my head forcefully. I know that if I get on that phone, Tessa will beat down every bit of resolve I've somehow mustered. My sincere attempt to move on with my life will collapse instantly. There will come a day when I can no longer avoid her, I'm not a fool, but we aren't there yet. I can't move forward with her noise in my head.

"She doesn't want to talk yet, and I have nothing else to say. I know this seems like an impossible thing for you- but be patient. Kenna will contact you when she's ready." Rachel says sternly, just before placing the phone back on the receiver.

She gets out of bed and begins to pace back and forth across the narrow swatch of carpet at the foot of our beds, "That woman! She's insufferable."

She quickly glances at me and adds apologetically, "I'm sorry, this is your mother I'm talking about, I should be a little more careful with my words."

"No, you're not wrong. She is insufferable. How did she find us?" I ask, although I already know the answer.

"Your pal, Zach. Apparently, he kept and shared our picture on social media and it quickly made the rounds. One of her assistants saw the picture and told her. That woman's been having them call every hotel on the strip to look for us."

I roll over and bury my face in the misshapen, suspicious smelling pillow. I had known this would happen. Everyone puts everything on social media even when they promise they won't. My mother has spies everywhere. This outcome is completely inevitable.

Almost as bad as being confronted by my mother, are the others. I cringe to imagine what our mutual contacts are saying at this very moment. The comments section of his picture must be lit up. Poor little Kennedy Shepard, social outcast, fired, expelled, humiliated, sitting at a Virginia Beach boardwalk restaurant with a box dye hair job. Had anyone asked me a few days earlier if I had any pride left to be trampled on, I would have said emphatically that the answer was no. It turns out that would have been a lie.

I know that Rachel is stressed out over my mother's threats and angry on my behalf. I'm not sure that she understands just how deep my wounds are though. My mother has bemoaned my idiocy, my ugliness, my hidden character flaws my entire life. She's reinforced her harsh comments with a bevy of staff who rarely brought themselves to even look me in the eyes. I'm sure that my classmates have seen it in me as well. And now, they can enjoy publicly ridiculing me on social media. She didn't make those flaws up though. Any illusion I might have had of secretly being a decent, worthy human being have been utterly exposed as fraud by my appalling choices this summer.

There have been times over the years, moments when I've felt so utterly alone, so unlovable, that I've fantasized about doing something drastic. If I disappeared from the world, no one would notice- except my mother. She wouldn't be devastated either, just angry that I'd caused yet another scandal. I don't actually want to die though. As nonsensical as it is I've retained some ridiculous spark that wills me to keep living, keep suffering, keep waiting. I'm not sure exactly what I'm even waiting for, but I haven't been able to give up that tenuous grasp of hope that somehow my life will change someday.

Sometimes I wonder if my mother even understands how damaged I really am. I wonder if she understands her role in that- the way she's chipped away at me with a verbal hammer my entire life, leaving a battered and scarred form. Does she imagine that this is the normal state of girlhood? That we all wander around, shamed and broken? She had to have learned that skill somewhere. It was carefully nurtured and honed long before my birth. My mother didn't just wake up one day and suddenly decide to wield that hammer.

Although she's a force of nature, Tessa hadn't actually sprung from the wild, already a fully grown adult woman. She never spoke of such personal matters but I could fill in some of the gaps. Her mother had passed away in childbirth and her father was certainly too busy running an empire to be emotionally available to her. It would have been a stretch to even call him a single father because that term brought a completely different image to mind. I'd gleaned that Grandfather had been all, but missing from my own mother's life until she'd reached the age of majority. A cold and cynical man, I've never felt any attachment to or from him. I've also never witnessed any affection displayed between him and my mother. I know that even with her unparalleled success as an entertainment and media mogul, he's never fully approved of her career choice. Television, after all, is a tool of the commoners. He's tolerated her though and that seems to be a lot more than what she offered me. I wasn't even offered the tiny kindness of tolerance. Something is so wrong with me that I don't even rate tolerance.

"Kenna..." Rachel interrupts my thoughts.

Feeling a bit like a petulant child I force myself to roll over and face her. Her forehead wrinkles as she stares silently at me. I know that she wants to hear that I'm okay, but I can't find the voice to console her. Feeling my eyes fill with tears I give a small shake of my head and reach over to turn off the light. I drift off to dream about my mother again. This time she doesn't just erase me. She swallows me whole.

Chapter 11

Tessa

Employees came and went. Assistants, marketing advisors, interior designers, textile artisans, graphic artists, editors, writers, photographers, drivers, chefs, gardeners, housekeepers- they were all replaceable. Phillip Cross, Esq. stayed. He was the one constant in her life. He'd been bequeathed to her by her father when she'd reached the legal age of majority and had proven himself to be loyal, punctual, attentive to details, and above all else- he knew how to keep a secret.

"Well, what did you discover? Do we have legal recourse?" She asked impatiently.

Phillip picked up a pair of wire frame reading glasses from his desk and twirled them by the frame absentmindedly. He was dressed as dapper as always, she noted, in a muted charcoal suit with a forest green silk tie. He looked tired though, and that alarmed her. She knew he was in his early 80s, he wouldn't be around forever. She needed him to help her one more time though before retirement.

"I've been over the contract with a fine-toothed comb and I don't think you have a case. Assuming she's telling the truth about Kennedy contacting her first, well, it puts the ball in Kennedy's court. As a legal adult, she's got the right to reach out to whomever she wants. Kennedy didn't sign a contract, after all."

She cursed silently. It would have been unreasonable to force her own daughter to sign a contract about this, but she wished fervently she'd thought to do just that when the girl turned 18.

"So I'm supposed to just sit idly by and allow this woman to kidnap my child? God knows what she's filling her head with. And what if she somehow convinces Kennedy to turn on me? They could do something crazy, like write a tell-all together."

Just a few hours earlier she'd had a certain young Hollywood starlet on the show to discuss her bestselling memoir. The young woman was Hollywood royalty; her father was a famous director, her mother an actress who'd won three academy awards. The starlet had used her family connections to quickly climb the industry ladder and had landed several lead roles in A-list movies. Then, when she finally had the world's attention- she'd dropped a memoir that revealed titillating stories about her parents' serial infidelities and mutual abuse. Tessa had been forced to don a mask of sage counsel and faux concern. She'd spent the entire interview pushing her unease aside but now she indulged in it.

"Do you hear me Philip? A TELL ALL. That is what these kids do now! They don't bite the hand that feeds with their teeth anymore, they do it with a computer keyboard. I won't have it. She needs to come home now."

Phillip sighed and rubbed his face. "Tessa, you're not going to like this answer but yes, you should just sit this one out. There is no scenario here where you try to strongarm either of them and come out a winner."

"Can we at least offer a bluff? There's no way some... librarian," she spat the word out as if it were profanity, "is going to fully understand her own legal rights. Could we issue a letter threatening legal action, have it delivered to her by courier. She'll probably assume it's akin to a subpoena."

"We could issue a stop and desist notice, yes. The problem is it's utterly unenforceable and if she calls your bluff and you persist in trying to scare her off, the legal table can turn. You could be the one accused of harassment. Don't forget, she also has Kennedy in her ear. Kennedy is no fool, Tessa. She's smart, educated, and she's seen your legal actions enough times she might just be the one who calls your bluff."

"Dammit!" Tessa yelled, slapping the palms of her hands against the top of his massive desk. Phillip didn't flinch. He'd spent most of his adult life navigating Tessa's complex legal needs and more complex emotional issues.

"Tessa. This is my advice as your legal counsel, yes, but also as a longtime friend who has known you for most of your life. Let this go. Give Kennedy the space she obviously needs right now to sort out her own life."

She stood and walked over to the great window that overlooked the street that lay some 43 floors below. She knew that technically, he was correct. What was that old saying? If you love something, set it free. It wasn't in her nature to let someone else win a fight though, and by walking away she was allowing both Rachel and Kennedy to win. She turned back around and studied Phillip again. He really was looking ancient. Perhaps it was time to find his replacement. Someone equally trustworthy, but younger. Someone who still had a modicum of fight left in his blood.

Chapter 12

Rachel

When I'd awakened, there was a weight laying squarely on my chest. For a brief moment, my lungs were unable to expand. I'd gasped for air and then rode a wave of relief as the reality of wakefulness sank in. I pressed a cool wet washcloth to my eyes because there was nothing about the face in the mirror this morning that suggested refreshment. I've always been cursed with recurring puffiness under my eyes. If I carefully ensured at least eight hours of sleep, didn't overindulge on alcohol, and hydrated frequently, it was a manageable problem. I wasn't a vain woman but it bothered me enough that I did try to manage it. Last night's tossing and turning hadn't been kind to me and I'd spend the day looking and feeling slightly under the weather. As she'd reliably been depended upon to do, Tessa had injured me again.

Hearing Tessa's voice directed at me after so many years had been surreal. I'd heard her voice occasionally. Although I'd tried to avoid it, sometimes a commercial might flit across the television. Someone flipping channels might pause for a moment on her program before I urged them to keep looking. Once, at the Johnson's Labor Day party I'd been forced to watch her entire segment during a charity telethon. Those encounters had rankled, but they'd been one way conversations. She hadn't even known I was watching. This time... she'd said my name.

"You'll regret opening your door to her. Believe me Rachel, I can hurt you in ways that you can't even imagine."

She hadn't even said it in a particularly menacing tone, she wasn't implying physical harm. Yet that voice had the same effect as a sample of bitter melon once had on me. It made me physically shudder. Still, a stranger might have heard it differently; perhaps, they'd even have noted wry humor in her tone. They didn't know her as I did. I knew better. I knew that she could keep me busy and financially strangled for years with litigation. I knew that she could go after my savings account, my house, my job, my reputation in the community.

It wasn't the fear of those consequences that was the worst of it though. That wasn't why I'd spent my evening tormented by dark, shadowy dreams. So much more powerful than the fear, was the guilt. For over twenty years I'd tried to convince myself that Tessa's animosity and cruelty had been singularly focused on me. I'd even allowed myself to question the legitimacy of my own memories. Perhaps I'd overreacted. Perhaps I remembered wrong. Perhaps she hadn't actually been quite so bad.

As it turns out, she was even worse than I remembered. I'd left a helpless infant with her, and walked away. Kenna wasn't whole- you didn't need a medical degree to see that. She lacked any hint of self-confidence; she was terrified of her own shadow. She was a hothouse flower that had been restrained by a too-small pot and denied the nutrients that would have allowed her to grow and thrive. I was afraid to ask her just how bad it had actually been. Perhaps there was nothing I could have legally done to stop the handover, but my choice to participate at all in the process at all had aided and abetted Tessa. Without me, there would be no Kenna. I'm not sure if that was an indictment or not. At what point was it morally reprehensible to bring a life into a chaotic, toxic world?

I've been curious about the infant I'd given birth to, she's crossed my mind many times over the years. I've wondered, hoped, and prayed that she was happy and healthy- even as part of me didn't believe she would be in Tessa's care. On the few occasions that I'd seen a reference to her in the media, the details had been scant. I could allow myself to indulge in the fantasy of Kenna's happy childhood. I would wonder if motherhood had perhaps softened Tessa, I'd hope it had. It was clear now though that those brittle, harsh edges hadn't been worn down with maternal hugs. It's been nearly 21 years and I don't know if that damage can be repaired. With Tessa hot on our heels, I've been reduced to triage. I could not undo almost 21 years of harm.

I glanced once more in the mirror, took a deep breath, pasted a smile that belied the bags under my eyes onto my lips and opened the bathroom door.

"Good morning!" I called cheerily to the bundled body on the bed. Kenna moaned and then shot her hands up to rub her eyes.

Clearing her throat she replied huskily, "Morning. What time is it?"

"Almost 7," I replied even though I knew it was precisely 6:57 am. I'd trained myself to round up or down and answer vaguely whenever anyone asked me that question. I knew that my proclivity to clock chase would be viewed oddly by most people.

Nodding, she sat up slowly. I busied myself by making my bed but I could feel her watching me. The questions hung in the air between us, unspoken, unrelenting. Neither of us wanted to start the day with a discussion about Tessa, but she was there nonetheless.

Kenna was up and in the bathroom, leaving me with mundane busy tasks around the room. When she emerged, she was dressed and had brushed her newly shorn and darkened hair. While her younger, more elastic facial skin didn't quite mirror the bags I suffered, she still looked tired. As if reading my mind, she grabbed a pair of tortoise shell sunglasses off the bureau to disguise the fatigue. I was determined to push past the night, to salvage what we could of both this day and this trip.

"We can go down and grab some breakfast, then I was thinking this would be a nice day to show you a site away from the beach. The infamous Mount Trashmore!"

At her quizzical look I laughed. "You'll see." Then studying her closer, I couldn't help asking hesitantly, "How are you this morning? I know you were upset last night."

She sighed and shrugged. "I'm okay."

I shot her a piercing look and she clarified, "I'm okay at this very moment."

It wasn't a complete lie I suppose. She wasn't breaking down in hysterics. She seemed to be functional enough. This alone was progress from the previous night. Perhaps okay is the best we could hope for. Perhaps it actually was enough.

"Alright, we don't need to talk about last night right now. There's enough time for that later. Let's just get out of this room and see where the day takes us."

By mutual agreement, the day first took us to a nice breakfast at a boardwalk cafe. This was one of the mysteries of traveling. I've always had a light breakfast appetite, except when adventuring with Delta. On those beloved trips, I'd awaken famished and we'd indulge in ridiculously rich meals, consuming more calories at once than we normally did in an entire day. She'd always outdone me though.

"I want some traitor eggs, mmm, and one of those giant cinnamon rolls I saw in the glass case too. How about you?"

I glance over at Delta's trim frame. Where does she put it all? Her appetite for food is as ravenous as her appetite for life in general. She's grinning at me, waiting for me to ask for the punch line.

"Traitor eggs?"

"You know, Benedict Arnold!"

My stomach growled as I studied the plastic menu and settled on a full scale Farmers Breakfast. Kenna ordered a much more modest yogurt parfait. As we sat across a knotty pine table, I inhaled the salt air and willed myself not to study every face in the periphery. I didn't want to make Kenna more nervous than she already surely was, but after the previous day's experience I half expected to see paparazzi popping out of every hidden corner. The few times that my resolve wavered and I scanned the crowds, I found only disinterest.

"So tell me about this mountain we're going to see today." Kenna suddenly asks.

I chuckled and replied, "Well, calling it a mountain might be a bit of a reach. Mount Trashmore was actually an old landfill area, later beautified and turned into a popular park here. In the summers it's a popular spot to walk and picnic, in the winter it's a favorite sled hill for the local kids. It's a special place for me because Delta and I went to a fourth of July fireworks show there for our first real date."

She leaned in smiling, clearly eager to hear more details. "How did you guys meet anyway? I mean, I know she worked for your father so it must have been through the Coast Guard, but what was the first introduction?"

I stared at my plate and poked the remaining egg yolk with my fork for a moment before replying. Swirling my yolk art about the plate absentmindedly, I considered her question. I'd never shared the full story with anyone else. Delta and I had never agreed to keep our origins secret, but over time it became clear that the story was something precious and private. I couldn't ask her permission now. She wouldn't be hurt or angry by anything I shared. The truth was that I wanted to allow Kenna in though and bonding with her over a story that was uniquely ours might bring us closer. Perhaps in turn, she'd open up to me. Then I had an idea.

"I tell you what. I'll share our story, but let's make a deal first. I reveal something, you reveal something."

She was alarmed, I could see it in her face and I cursed myself silently as I realized that she probably thought that I meant to push for details about life with Tessa. "Not what you think, I'll tell you about how it began, and you share one of your songs with me. Deal?"

Her eyes widened at the request, but she didn't immediately discount it. After staring at her bowl for a few moments, she lifted her head and said, "I think I can do that, one song."

I nodded and smiled and then waived our waiter over for the bill.

"Okay, mountaineering we go!" I said with a grin, hoping it conveyed just how silly that term was in the context of what we'd actually be doing.

A short while later, we were driving through the oceanfront area, navigating the maze of storefronts and businesses. The hotels, ice cream stands and putt-putt golf shops quickly disappeared from view and were replaced by single story brick ranch houses and vinyl sided cottages. Those were the neighborhoods I'd presumably be house hunting in, if I were offered the middle school job. It was a nice area, but I struggled to imagine myself there. Could this become my new world? Could I fit in there as a 42 year old widow? There were so many homes, so many people- I'd show up knowing no one and then what? As a child I'd started over several times, had I completely lost those skills? It was different, I reminded myself. My parents had always been there. I'd never been truly alone. We drove past the suburban landscape and I saw the park sign ahead, we pulled off the congested road and into the parking lot.

As I steered into an open spot, Kenna looked around, clearly confused. "I don't get it, where... oh, wait!"

"Mount Trashmore! Ta-da!" I announced with a mock flourish as I motioned toward the vista we now faced.

Kenna rewarded me with a laugh. A genuine, joyful laugh that wasn't forced and faked. Mount Trashmore, which should have been more aptly named Mound Trashmore, was surrounded by parking lots, green spaces and scattered playgrounds. To the right of us lay a mirror-surfaced pond that was surrounded by walking paths. Earnest joggers ran up the long stairway to the top of the grassy mound, dog walkers made their way around the pond, and children flew kites at the modest summit of the former landfill.

We parked and made our way toward the stairs, ascending in short order. At the top, the view revealed it was a little more elevated than it had appeared from the parking lot.

"Well, it's not a mountain," she commented, "But it is pretty."

She wasn't wrong. I smiled and told her, "The best part about Mount Trashmore, is the fact it even exists. Once upon a time, this was something ugly. The waste of thousands of humans over dozens of years, marring the scenery, stinking up the air. Somehow, those same humans were able to take a place of ugliness and transform it with new purpose and life into something enjoyable and lovely."

The grass was freshly cut, Delta used to describe this fragrance as *"a green you can taste"*. Our cottage yard was heavily treed and our summer season was short, the sun doesn't bake the turf in the same way. This smell, it brought me back to other homes, other years. We made our way toward the center of the structure and it was the most natural thing in the world to just drop down for a sit. For a while we were silent and Kenna was as lost in her own thoughts as I was in mine. I allowed my body to fall backward and I lay staring at the robin's egg blue sky above. I spied a navy jet, tiny and miles to the east, but even from this distance I could hear the roar of its engines. The sound of children's laughter was much closer, and stronger, and for just a moment I allowed myself to relax beneath the familiar Virginia sky.

As Kenna reclined in the grass beside me, I asked "Are you doing okay?"

"Yeah, I think I am." She hesitated and then asked, "Rachel, why are you doing this?"

I smiled at her and then turned to study the sky again. "I'm not entirely sure. Your eyes are so sad Kenna, there's a pain in you that no girl your age should be feeling. There's some primal part of me that wants to reach in, find it and heal it. This isn't all altruistic though, I'm also trying to heal my own sadness. I haven't felt whole since she left"

"Tell me how you met her."

I closed my eyes, conjuring up the image. Wild curls. Glittering green eyes. Huge smile framed by caramel round cheeks, dotted with a tint smattering of freckles.

"When I was a younger child I loved going to my father's work. We'd get to ride along sometimes on the boats, and it felt special being part of this small Coast Guard family. As I got older, it became kind of a drag. Teens can be snotty, and I was no exception, so back in high school I'd started to beg my way out of events. When school ended that year though, I was so excited that I'd finally be a senior. I was willing to be a little more gracious toward my parents again. I spent the summer deigning to gift them with my presence a little more often than I had before. I think maybe subconsciously I knew I'd be leaving soon for college and part of me wanted to enjoy that last grasp on childhood. My father invited us over to the station for an Independence Day morale BBQ on the lawn and feeling extra generous, I actually agreed to go. The party was on the third, Dad knew most people would have their own plans for the fourth. July 3rd, my favorite date."

That world didn't exist anymore, Delta didn't exist anymore. The father I'd so admired back then had ceased to exist too. When you were living in the moment though, it wasn't possible to truly understand how finite it all was. Don't we all secretly hope that we are the exception to the rules of time? We might even be immortal. Then, one day, something happens, you see your aging reflection in the mirror, really see it, and you know you've been fooling yourself. You can't go back and relive it again and remembering can be a beautiful thing, but it can also break your heart.

I took a deep breath, and allowed myself to feel the pain as I described the gathering we'd found ourselves at. There were about 40 people there, between the crew members and their guests and most of them knew my father. As the Officer In Charge, he was in high demand for introductions to the newer guests. I dutifully followed behind him, next to my mother who had a pasted on smile and friendly hello for each person we met. When I was certain that we'd shaken every possible hand in sight, I wandered off alone to find a soda. Popping the can top, I surveyed the scene.

My mother had also successfully broken away from my father's side and she now stood with a few other wives, laughing easily at their conversation. Sometimes, senior enlisted member's wives could project an image of standoffishness. My mom called that "putting on airs" and she had no time for it. She was the type of woman who literally rolled up her shirt sleeves and got to work feeding the troops. She didn't have a desire to wear her husband's rank. The only people she had ever wanted to impress were God and her husband, and I frankly wasn't sure which of those entities she wanted to impress more. She sometimes drove me a little nuts, but at the same time I loved this down to earth side of her.

And then there was my father. No one would have accused him of being too accessible and friendly. As he spoke with some of his subordinates, his posture revealed the distance he kept in his work world. When I'd been younger it had been different. While he had always tended to be fairly quiet, he'd been willing to open the house and lawn for a party. In those days, other men and women his age would laugh with him, clap him on the back as they told stories, and to my young eyes the whole group would turn red and shiny as they drank their adults-only beverages. He hadn't seemed to have a care in the world in those days. Time, experience, and responsibility had changed him.

That time and experience meant that he was the oldest and most senior member of this crew. As a result, no one else on the crew had a kid that was close to me in age. Watching the young children and tweens group up together, I sighed. The fact that I'd accompanied them to the event made my parents happy, but I was bored silly and I began to regret my decision.

A voice behind me said, "You look as excited as me to be here."

Turning, I saw a teenage girl smiling at me. She was a few inches shorter than my five foot six inch frame and had an athletic build. A small constellation of freckles danced across her face, and her green eyes sparkled- but it was her hair that was the showstopper. Dark, wild curls danced defiantly around her head and shoulders. I smiled at her and attempted to focus on her face, but I couldn't help glancing back repeatedly at the wild mass of curls that seemed to be its own entity. It would have been utterly bizarre to reach out and touch one, but that's the exact urge I had.

"Ha, yeah, you know how it is. I'm Rachel, and I'm peopled out already."

The girl smiled and her face transformed, as small crinkles framed her eyes and large dimples appeared in each cheek. Butterflies danced in my stomach when I saw that smile, how had I even noticed her hair before? I could only focus on her face, and it was the most beautiful thing I'd ever seen.

"Delta, yes like Delta Force or Delta Dawn," the girl replied in a strong southern accent, rolling her eyes and making it clear she'd heard dumb jokes about her name before.

I glanced around, I knew most of the families there pretty well and I knew that Delta didn't belong to any of them. Someone new, someone close to my own father's age, must have transferred in.

"I'm Bob's, well, Chief Potts' daughter. Who's your dad?" I asked, looking around curiously. I couldn't pick out any new people who might be old enough to be Delta's parents.

That smile appeared again, and Delta answered, "My Dad is Jeremiah Patrick, but everyone calls him Jay."

She waited a moment as I scanned the crowd again for an older crewman and then added, "And right now he's probably sitting third chair in at the VFW, in Pass Christian, Mississippi, yelling at the bartender that she's pouring weak again."

I shook my head, and replied, "I don't get it..."

Delta laughed and explained, "He's an Army vet. When his only child decided to join the military though, he steered her away from the Army and somehow she ended up in a Coast Guard recruiting office in Gulfport. After boot camp, they sent me here, to Virginia."

It hadn't occurred to me that I might be speaking with one of my father's young seamen. Delta was young, I was sure of that, but it was more than her age that had made it difficult to make that connection. There was a wildness about her, emphasized by those haphazard curls that now danced in the slight breeze. Normally, the young seamen I met were restrained in my presence, flocking together tightly, as if protecting themselves from the watchful eyes of the older members and their families. Even now I could see them gathered under a pavilion, avoiding the crowd. Delta didn't seem interested at all in insulating herself within that group.

"Oh, wow, I'm so sorry! I just assumed you were around my age." I replied, feeling embarrassed.

"I probably am. I just turned 18, in March," Delta replied with a wink.

I'd certainly met young seamen before at my father's stations, but there'd always been such respectful and necessary distance, they'd seemed more mature and advanced than their years. It wasn't that Delta struck me as immature, but she felt approachable and familiar; she felt like an actual peer.

"I'm 17, as of last month," I admitted. Then I added, "I still have one more year of high school, so jealous you're already out living your real life!"

Delta laughed at that, "Well, I guess I am, but my real life is pretty full of mowing grass and washing dishes and painting boats. Everyone tells me this gets better after a while. Maybe once I go to school for my specialization, but right now, this doesn't feel a whole lot different than doing chores back in Pass Christian. It pays better than my Daddy ever did!"

"Will you be in Virginia for long?"

"Probably a year or so, then I'll go off to school to become a boatswain's mate- like your father! Someday I'll be the big Daddy on station," she quipped with another wink.

Delta's voice was a low and gritty drawl. Later, much later, when I had a chance to visit the place she'd come from, I'd come to associate that voice with the fertile silt that lined the Mississippi, the very delta that had inspired her name. Back then though, I'd simply found myself entranced by the otherness of it. Between the voice, the wild curls, the freckles and sparkling green eyes- I felt like I'd been struck by lightning. My entire body registered this shock. My extremities buzzed, my lip twitched, and I was unable to control any of it.

I glanced back at the group of seamen who were taking turns glancing at the older men and women, and then surreptitiously passing a small glass bottle around. Although their civilian clothes were evidence that they were not on duty, they were also likely underage and just plain discouraged from drinking at a family event. These young adults had been highly trained to be organized and aware though and they functioned regularly out at sea as a unit- not as individuals. At that moment they were using every bit of that training to rotate as a group so each member had a chance to stand with their back to the older crowd. Then one by one they'd take a long chug from the hidden bottle. It was amusing to watch, but I worried Delta might want to go join them. If that happened, I wouldn't be able to follow. I had to keep Delta talking.

"Did you always want to join the Coast Guard?"

At that Delta threw her head back and gave a throaty laugh. I felt my pulse quicken again.

"No ma'am. First, I was going to be a fisherman like my father. He wanted me to have none of that though. Then I thought of being a worker out on the rigs, apprenticing somewhere to get a trade and then heading out there with big oil for big money, but Daddy wanted me to have none of that either. Then I wanted to join the army like he'd done at my age and, well, you can guess how my father felt about that. One day, I sat him down and said 'look Daddy, I'm done doing what you want. I saw this commercial, and I'm going to a Coast Guard recruiter in Gulfport'. I really said it more to get a rise out of him because I was done listening to him say no but to my surprise he said, 'alright then.' So I guess I joined to spite my Daddy. Jokes on me though, because he seemed pretty damned pleased when he came to watch my boot camp graduation."

I laughed at that. I knew a thing or two about old fashioned and at times overbearing fathers. My own father had never even hinted I should consider the Coast Guard as the end of my high school years drew closer. He'd commented more than once that his boys, as he called the men who worked for him, were quality people but that they could be a rough talking crowd when they were underway. My entire life, my father had tried to protect me from the rougher edges. He wouldn't have wanted me around that kind of talk, the harsh demands, the long, hard days. Instead he had pushed college for years- his daughter could be a nurse, a teacher, even a lawyer. Anything she wanted. Anything she wanted, as long as it felt like a safe and traditional career path.

As if reading my mind, Delta asked, "What about you? What are you going to do with your life?"

"I'm honestly not sure. I guess college, and then maybe teaching or something like that. I'm kind of a book nerd, so I'm thinking maybe teaching English..."

I felt smaller suddenly, I knew I sounded unsure and less than passionate. The girl before me had gravitated toward exciting, active professions, and here I was sounding like a timid mouse.

Delta nodded approvingly though and replied, "That's cool! I'm no good with kids, but I do like books."

Soon we were comparing reading lists, exclaiming happily when we found commonalities. When I shyly admitted that I still sometimes broke out my childhood Judy Blume books for comfort, Delta nodded seriously and replied, "Girl, that Margaret, she's a trip. My mama passed when I was 10, Miss Judy filled the gap there for a while."

I murmured an apology for her loss and asked, "What was she like? Your mother I mean."

Delta smiled that crooked smile again and replied, "Mama was a show stopper. That's what my Daddy always said. She was creole, her people were French and Spanish and African. Daddy met her when he was bringing a haul of shrimp over from Bay St Louis. He'd stopped at the restaurant her auntie owned and she'd been his server. Show stopper. Not only was she gorgeous, but she could cook! Soon he was sniffing around the Pass on the regular and promising he'd buy her one of the big houses down on the strand."

She laughed at that story and added, "She ended up settling for a 40 year old cabin on the edge of town. Lived there happily too, until breast cancer took her."

Her childhood was at odds with mine because she'd been forced to grow up fast when she lost her mother. She'd taken over as the woman of the house; she cooked the meals and cleaned their small cabin. Her father gave her the space and freedom of an older teenager. She tended her mother's vegetable garden and when she began selling excess produce alongside baskets of shrimp at a roadside stand, people in town started treating her as a young adult rather than a child too.

As the natural conversation flowed with ease, we walked together to pick up plates of food and then headed to another quiet spot along the outskirts of the main group. I caught my parents glancing at us a few times, but they didn't seem troubled by my choice of companion. I knew that if Delta had been one of the male seamen it would have been very different, but for once I was grateful for the gender biases that had always subtly influenced our home.

My stomach full, I let myself flop back into a full recline on the grass. Delta mimicked the move and we stared at the clouds passing overhead. The momentary silence was comfortable, even as I was acutely aware of Delta's lithe body beside my own. I turned my head and glanced at the girl beside me. She had closed her eyes and had a small smile on her face. What was she thinking about?

As if I had said the words aloud, Delta said, "Rachel, do you have a boyfriend?"

"No," I replied softly. The truth was I'd never had one of those. I'd been asked out a few times, I'd even accompanied Bradly Tapper to his senior prom a few months earlier, but when he'd leaned in for a kiss I'd practically run away and he'd never expressed an interest again.

"Girlfriend?"

I was unable to stop the widening of my eyes and slight drop of my jaw at that question. No one had ever asked me such a thing before. No one had ever hinted that might be an option. I knew that plenty of women did have girlfriends, but no one had ever supposed I might be the sort who would do that. No one had ever known that secret part of me.

I knew I'd been quiet too long, but answered, "No. I'm single."

I was afraid to look at Delta, but forced myself to turn my head. She was smiling again.

"Me too. So what do you think about spending tomorrow with me? We could meet at the boardwalk, hang out, and then head over to the fireworks show at Mount Trashmore together."

Balling my hands inward so hard that my nails dug into the soft palms, I fought to sound cool and casual in my reply. "That'd be fun."

Delta nodded her understanding and we arranged a meet up time and place. Then groaning with the effort, she then sat upright and glanced back over to the other seamen who seemed to be paying a little too much attention to us now. It was clear they'd been talking about us, although whether the comments were flattering or judgmental, we did not know. Delta looked at me and shook her head and said, "I hate to do this, but I better get over there before those boys get themselves in trouble. I'll see you tomorrow!"

After she left, I sat alone for a while and considered the conversation. Had I just agreed to a date, or was it simply a meet up between two new friends? I wasn't entirely sure and I was afraid of getting my hopes up. I snuck glances at Delta and the young men watched her laughing as she playfully punched one in the arm. I saw the moment she took her own turn with another hidden bottle someone had produced, tipping it back quickly and coolly. I still wasn't sure. Could Delta be like me?

My mother interrupted my thoughts, "Hey hon, we're ready to head out," and we began our goodbye rounds, then made our way back to the car.

"I noticed you spent a lot of time with Patrick," my father commented, once we were all belted in.

If he disapproved, it wasn't immediately obvious in his tone. His use of Delta's last name reinforced her relative position in his life, but he didn't sound annoyed or suspicious.

"Yeah, she seemed nice," I offered.

"She's a good kid, haven't had any problems with her," he replied, and then just that easily, he dropped the subject and turned up the radio.

Sighing with relief, I shut my eyes and once again replayed my conversation with Delta. It might be a date, it might really be a date, I thought.

Sleep did not come easily, but when I awoke the next morning I felt energized and excited. I put on a pair of denim shorts and a white shirt that I knew would emphasize my narrow torso and then brushed my shoulder length brown hair under a hair dryer until it shined. Adding a kiss of lip gloss, I appraised myself in the mirror. Almond shaped brown eyes, a small button nose, and a perfectly normal mouth stared back at me and I frowned. The problem wasn't that I felt ugly, but I also knew I wasn't truly pretty. I had an average face, easily forgettable, no one ever stared at this face in adoration. Delta- well, she had an extraordinary face. With her freckles and dimples, some might call her cute but I suspected she was going to be one of those women who people call beautiful one day. Could she really be interested in me?

At the boardwalk I walked to the bench we'd agreed to meet by and scanned the crowd nervously for Delta. The summer crowd was in full swing, and I had trouble finding her small figure in the melee. Then, through the sea of faces, I spotted a wildly waving hand.

Smiling broadly, dimples on display, she pushed past a family and almost broke into a run for the last fifteen feet of distance between us. I felt my insecurities and doubts slip away as she reached out to hug me enthusiastically.

"Her girl, you look great!" Delta said, and for a moment I actually believed it.

"You too." I replied, definitely meaning it. Delta wore a short denim skirt that highlighted her muscular, tanned legs, and a pink crop top that revealed her tight, surfers abdomen. Her hair was pulled back, held at the nape of her neck with a thick clip but stray curls bounced around her face. I worried I'd looked too long, and had trouble meeting Delta's gaze. I still wasn't quite sure what this meeting actually meant. Above all I wanted to ask, "Is this a date?" but I didn't have the courage to ask that question out loud.

"Let's go grab a bite to eat because I'm starving." Delta suggested, and as I nodded I felt the back of a small cool hand touch the back of mine. It just rested there, waiting. I looked Delta in the eye, and saw that she was staring intently. Biting my lip, I made a decision and did the most natural thing in the world. I turned my hand and clasped it around hers, and then we began to walk slowly down the boardwalk.

Chapter 13

Kenna

Rachel isn't just reciting an old story- she's living it all over again. Her life is a symphony and she's in the translucent fringe of the opening movement. With her retelling, I can picture myself beside the two girls she describes. A silent witness, a ghost of Christmas yet to come. The shadows of those girls exist again, as real as our flesh and bone filled bodies exist now. The barely perceptible halo of sadness Rachel always wears momentarily lifts as Delta is alive again.

I'm afraid to break the spell because it's drawn me in, but I say, "And you made it work. You were both so young but it somehow worked. The kids that I went to high school with broke up with their old boyfriends and girlfriends years ago."

It's all abstract, of course. I'm an observer of relationships- never a participant. Boys have asked me out on dates or tried to convince me to fool around at the rare parties I attended back at Calvin Brook. My instinctive reaction has always been to shrink back from them. Even the times that some part of me had wanted to say yes, my words and my body would say no. There've been a few quiet crushes along the way but I've never had the confidence to pursue them. It's not just my fear of rejection though. My early attempts at actual friendships with other kids taught me the cold, hard lesson that when someone wants to spend time with me, they're usually just hoping to get closer to Tessa.

"We got lucky; it's as simple as that. We fell fast and hard and despite it feeling like everything was against us, we managed to make it work. That doesn't mean it was easy though, a couple doesn't survive that many years without learning some tough lessons along the way. Keeping it secret for so long took a toll, and then my father's reaction when he found out- well, I thought that might really end it. There were others who didn't approve, but none of them seemed to matter as much as my father. Yet somehow it didn't drive us apart. With each challenge, we only grew closer. We also were fortunate enough to have supportive friends and then there was Delta's Dad. He loved his little girl more than anything and only wanted her happy. He liked that I made her happy. That helped a lot too."

"Are you still in touch with him," I ask.

"Yes, although not as much as I should be, to be honest. I think when we talk, it reminds us both of how much we have lost... we just find it easier to keep contact minimal."

Despite her devastation over losing Delta, part of me is envious of her memories. She's alone now but for most of her life she'd been with someone who loved her. She'd been seen and heard. She'd been adored. It's a life I see in the movies and hear on the radio, not a life I imagine I'll ever be able to have.

"Being here, does it bring you closer to her?" I wonder.

She thinks about it for a moment and then replies, "It brings me closer to the Delta I first met, but not the one I spent most of my life with. It's been a lot of years since we were the two girls who climbed this hill to watch the fireworks. The thing is, people grow and change. The woman I spent my life with, the woman I married, and the woman I said goodbye to, wasn't the same girl I knew here. We spent most of our lives together in Pennsylvania, and Delta permeated every inch of our home even after she was gone. I don't necessarily feel her here any more than I did there."

What's she looking for then, if it's not Delta? I believe her when she says this trip is about both of us, she's not on the journey just for me. I don't think this is just a middle-aged exercise in chasing her youth. She isn't the type of woman who resents her age and besides- she's only in her early forties. She's mentioned her parents several times during her story, maybe she's seeking the younger version of them. Idealized parents who supported and encouraged her. When she speaks of those happier times, it's hard to connect them to the parents she describes after Delta came into her life. If it's hard for me to relate the images, it must be nearly impossible for her.

This is a language that I don't have a handy translation app for. I don't have the urge to visit any old haunts, there isn't any particular time in my life that I yearn for or look back on fondly. There were quieter moments, times when I hadn't needed to tiptoe around in fear of gaining my mother's attention. There were days, weeks sometimes, when she would be gone from the house. Those were times of peace. But peace doesn't equal happiness. Peace is simply the ability to sleep without worrying about being woken up by a screaming tirade. I'm not exactly sure what happiness feels like.

"I know you're not close but you forgave them eventually? Your parents, I mean." I say.

She folds her hands together, still looking at the sky, and says, "I suppose I did, at least to a degree. It took a lot of years, I started with Christmas cards, and then one day my mother called to wish me Happy Birthday and that opened the door just a bit more. Then about five years ago my father had a heart scare and with Delta's urging, I flew to Charleston to see them. When we saw each other, it wasn't as if everything was suddenly okay. But, I knew I still loved them and they still loved me, so we pushed past the awkwardness of being face to face after so many years and survived the visit. I went back again a few years later for a quick visit, and it was even smoother- but there was still too much forced politeness. Distance."

"And soon you'll see them again." I comment, referring to our next planned stop in Charleston. We haven't discussed it much at all, we've been so hyper focused on getting to Virginia Beach.

She nods and sighs and then sits up. "So we've sure talked a lot about me today. It's starting to get late and I think you owe me a song."

I'd managed to forget this part of the deal. A wave of fresh nausea washes over me although I'm not sure just why I feel so nervous. At this point, Rachel knows my every vulnerability. She knows how my mother feels about me, she knows about my inability to shed my dependency on her despite the fact that I loathe it, she knows how flawed I am, that I'm a liar and a cheat. She knows that I have no clue what might come next. Yet, knowing all of that, she's still here. She isn't going to run away horrified if my song actually sucks.

My thoughts are interrupted by the sound of laughter and a big red bouncy ball that lands squarely in my lap. Startled, I sit upright and glance over to see a boy smiling widely as he toddles over toward us. Rachel reaches over and grabs the ball and says, "What's this? A giant red apple?"

The boy laughs, "Ball!"

Rachel looks suspiciously at the ball and says, "I believe this is actually a tiny red airplane. What do you think, Kenna?"

I shake my head, unsure of her game.

"Ball!" The boy repeats, laughing with delight.

"Perhaps it's a big red ladybug!"

"It's a ball!" He says, his cheeks round with hilarity.

"Oooooh, wait! It *is* a ball." She repeats, with a smile.

She tosses it back to him

His father stands nearby and smiles and waves, as the boy runs back to him with the ball. I look at Rachel, she's still watching the child, smiling. She would have been a good mother, I think. The image that evokes makes me sad and I try to push it away quickly.

"Alright, Kenna, let's go!" She says, and we decide to skip the stairs, opting instead to run down the hill itself, the sun and wind in our faces as we make our way back to the car.

When we arrive back at the hotel, we head back to the room where I wearily eye the guitar in the corner. I'd been thinking a lot about what I might actually play. My self-preservation instinct is to play a cover of something well known but I know that she wants to hear my original material. The problem is, my original material tends to be personal and raw. I've never been permitted to speak my fears and pains out loud, so instead I've learned to channel them into my notebook and eventually onto my guitar strings. Opening myself up that way to another human being hasn't been an option. Still, Rachel sits on her bed waiting. Her intent gaze makes it clear there will be no backing out of the deal.

I take a deep breath and pick up the guitar with my shaking hands. Gingerly, I carry her to the foot of my bed and study the soft, maple curves. Curves like a plump woman, that's what my old music teacher, Raul, used to say. When I was younger I pretended it was a she, and that she was a powerful, protective woman. She was maternal, although I never dared call her mother. Instead I privately called her Auntie, that was safer than mother. Sitting with Auntie and Rachel, I feel nervous... but also safe. I run my fingers along her well-tuned strings and search my invisible playlist. Finally, I find the track I want. Homeless.

My first shaky strums feel awkward and unfamiliar and I stop and glance at Rachel.

"It's okay," she says softly, then nods for me to try again.

Big inhale, exhale, inhale, exhale... I begin to play again.

Big town girl, small town dreams
Sits alone on 51st street
Taxi cab slows down on cue
She looks away
She's a creature of the moon.
Not going back, not tonight
Gonna claim this curb
Hang in tight
Maybe she will stay here for good
Nothin' back in the neighborhood
Maybe she will embrace the street
Curbside living, won't miss a beat

She won't be homeless
She'll just be free
She won't be homeless
Don't pity me
I won't be homeless
With the moon over my head
I won't be homeless
I'll just be free

When I finish the last note I keep my eyes downcast and await Rachel's critique. She's silent though and the only thing I can read into the silence is disappointment. I bite my tongue and study the floor again. I hear her make a tiny noise. I look up to see her kind, brown eyes glisten with unshed tears.

"Kenna... that was incredibly moving."

I feel the cursed heat reach my cheeks and turn away to hide the blush, murmuring, "thank you."

She's not faking her emotion. The song has obviously touched her. I'm not sure just how much of that reaction is organic. A perfect stranger, someone completely unfamiliar with my story, probably wouldn't have reacted so strongly. Still, this is more than my own mother has ever displayed the few times she's heard me perform. Maybe it hadn't been completely awful.

"Have you ever thought about pursuing a career in music," she asks.

The idea startles me. I haven't thought about anything like that. I can barely speak to strangers; I certainly can't perform in front of them. The irony is that I'm in a far better position to pursue professional music than most musicians. If I had real talent and a real interest, I could have access to a myriad of connections and open doors. I'd been born to a blazing, shooting star after all. It's never even been a fantasy though. Standing on a stage and performing for thousands of screaming fans, the mere thought of it fills me with a gut wrenching anxiety. No, it's not an option.

"No," I answer truthfully, "I don't think I'd want that. Even if I could somehow guarantee I'd avoid stage fright, I wouldn't want those kinds of crowds. Maybe there's something I could do with music that wasn't quite so in the spotlight but I'm not really sure what."

She looks contemplative and says, "Well, the one thing you have right now is time. Time to figure that out. It doesn't have to be something on a huge stage though. You could give music lessons, teach children to sing and play. You could write songs in the background, for other artists to perform. You could even perform at a smaller level, in cafes and on street corners. I know Tessa's set the bar pretty high on what success looks like, but her brand of success is only one version. There are millions of successful people who are perfectly happy without being at the very top of their field or in the center of the stage."

I try to imagine a world where I'm earning enough money to actually support myself. The only image of normal that I can conjure is Rachel's little cottage. My own future won't be in that cottage though and I don't have the skills or tools to duplicate what she has. What she says makes sense, most Americans, most people, don't live on palatial estates in Greenwich. Most people don't employ a private driver. Most people don't own not one, but two, Piaget watches- watches they never wear because the latest iPhone is easier to read anyway. Most people find a way to feed and shelter themselves without their mother's bottomless credit cards and the promise of their grandfather's fortune. They live normal lives. But how much money does a person even need to make a normal life happen? I'm embarrassed to ask the question out loud!

I've spent my entire life being handed whatever shiny object I wanted or needed. I rarely even notice cost. I have some vague, abstract idea about what Tessa's primary house is worth because of news articles and HoHo decorating specials, but I can't put that into context with the real world. The car I drive, the clothes I wear, the makeup that fills my dressing table, the handbags I carry, the electronic devices that are so casually tossed in those bags- the cost of any of it is theoretical. It could cost anything, it wouldn't have mattered. The boots I wear now, had they been a hundred dollars? A thousand? Ten thousand? I don't remember. Are they the equivalent cost of a normal pair of boots? A small car? A cottage?

I don't think I've ever been particularly greedy. I've never been demanding. I hadn't asked to be born into a world of limitless purchase power. It's been my reality though. I wasn't alone, this had also been the reality of most of my peers at Calvin Brook. That was our normal. But now, I've run to a new normal and I don't understand how it works yet.

"I do need to figure out something." I admit. "I can't go back to her, but I can't stay here in this world if I don't have a way to support myself."

Rachel nods. "I can help out during the transition but you're definitely going to have to find a path. I know this may be hard to understand now, but you will appreciate it so much more when you're earning your own way."

"That's not very hard to believe at all, the hard to believe part is that I'll be able to do it. Rachel this is a stupid question but I have to ask. How much do you need?"

She looks confused, "How much of what do you need?"

"Money. How much money do you need to just live a normal life?"

"Ah, well that depends on a lot of factors. There are a lot of different models of what so-called normal life looks like. It's going to vary depending where you live, how big your house is, if you have children or pets. It's not just cost of living that differs in various places, job markets themselves pay very differently. Your first goal should be to save enough to cover basic housing needs."

We spend the next hour discussing what cost of living really means. I discover that I'm even more out of touch than I'd feared I was and I feel wave after wave of apprehension hit me, almost in time with the beating surf just outside of our motel room balcony. Still, even with my fears confirmed I somehow feel better. Rachel has a way of organizing the process that makes it feel attainable and she does it in a way that doesn't make me feel stupid. My complete lack of understanding when it comes to personal economics isn't entirely my fault. She's fully convinced me of that. People aren't just born intuitively knowing those things. Their parents are supposed to train them, teach them, and prepare them for independence. Tessa had done none of that. The good news is it isn't like gymnastics, Rachel explains. I don't need to have formed that foundation from early childhood to master it now. I can pick up those skills at any age and now is as good a time to start that effort as any. Even as a stanza of doubt continued to sound softly in the background, I am hearing the first whispers of hope.

"Thank you," I finally say.

"You're more than welcome," she replies casually and I hold up a hand to stop her from brushing this lesson off as no big deal.

"No, really. Thank you. I am still completely clueless about what I'm going to do but you have this great way of breaking things down that makes them feel not so overwhelming. Also, I need to apologize. I feel like a needy emotional vampire. This is not all about me. I know today was really big for you too. I didn't mean to drag you from your memories of Delta."

"You didn't. I still experienced all of those memories. You just gave me something else to think about in addition to them. Believe me, Delta was not a wallower. This is exactly what she'd want me to be doing. I'm glad we're starting to talk about ways for you to move forward! That said, I think I am going to go for a little walk. Are you okay alone here for a while?"

"Yes, go!"

From the balcony I watch her walk away, her head turned eastward, as she watched the ocean that runs parallel to the boardwalk. The further she walks, the smaller her figure grows, but even from the distance, I can see she continues to watch the horizon for some hint of her beloved.

Chapter 14

Rachel

With the sun dropping to the west, the long line of towering beachside hotels cast a silhouette of monolithic shadows upon the golden sands of Virginia Beach. I paused to remove my sandals, and stepped onto the shaded and chilled sand to approach the awaiting sea. It was a bit choppy and the breaching tide was tipped with gray foam peaks. The water wasn't my center of focus though. I was studying the spaces left behind. Whenever the tide retreated I'd search for bits of shell and glass to collect. This part of the beach didn't typically produce many significant, intact shells- just the broken fragments of formerly lived lives. For a moment, I indulged in the image of stepping clumsily through a vast field of crushed bones. It was tempting to linger in the melancholy thought, imagining the fragments as a metaphor for Delta's too-short life.

Before the moment could dig in, wrapping morose tentacles around the part of me that was feeling a hint of peace, a strong gust of wind whipped the sand into my face. I reflexively spit out the few fine grains that found their way into my mouth and chuckled. The chuckles were soon a true laugh, any passersby would have thought me crazy. Delta would throw a playful, fistful of sand at my face if I'd ever called her life half-lived. Absolutely nothing about her colorful, passionate years on this planet had been half-lived. The years might have been abbreviated, but she'd greedily seized every moment of them until they were finally torn from her grasp. The tide's ebb may have won in the very end, but Delta had fought it valiantly.

What would Delta have thought about Kenna? The truth was that she'd been kind and generous, but her generosity wasn't limitless. She found it difficult to understand people who were prone to self-pity and who lacked critical self-reliance skills. From the time her mother had passed on, Delta had been forced to grow up and take responsibility for her own happiness. It simply hadn't been in her DNA to feel sorry for herself, even when she was literally dying from cancer. Part of me suspects that she would have been at least a little impatient with Kenna's neediness. I'd been the buffer to that harder side of her. I wanted to comfort the world, she wanted to teach it to save itself.

I do wish Kenna had a little of Delta's fight in her. On an intellectual level, it was absolutely understandable that a lifetime of emotional and verbal abuse, coupled with the challenges of being the daughter of a very public figure would stunt and inhibit her growth. It was understandable that her spirit felt weak and incapable. But Kenna had been born with the exact same potential for personal growth and survival as any other human being. She needed to find the will to fight, even if it was only half as hard as Delta had fought. I felt uncharitable for the thought; it was hypocritical considering my own juxtaposition in Kenna's life. My own contribution, or lack thereof, to the woman she's become was as much a factor as her timidity and inaction. I too was culpable.

It was complex. I felt sorry for the girl, empathetic for the way she'd suffered. I'd have felt that way about anyone in this situation though. This was something more. There was a sense of responsibility at play here; a promise whispered in the distant past that I hadn't consciously made. I had no legal obligation to Kenna and no one would have faulted me if I'd turned my back on a grown woman, a stranger really, with whom I shared no blood ties. The feeling of responsibility persisted anyway. It weighed heavily. I'd helped to bring a life into the world, I couldn't simply walk away now.

There was the awful crux of it. I wasn't just helping Kenna because she was a random human being in need of assistance. The desire to help her, to save her, came attached to thousands of pounds of unwanted baggage. There was a term for the feeling that fostered my need to save her. It was a word that terrified me. A word that had started as a whisper when I first heard her name on the radio, but with passing day grew louder and bolder. A word I didn't want to own, because I knew it would hurt too much. Maternal.

I wasn't Kenna's mother, I again reminded myself. We didn't share a common ancestry, I hadn't raised her, we were just two strangers who'd once spent nine months together. A sweet memory of her soft kicks deep within my womb suddenly surfaced, and I forced the image away. We don't owe each other anything. I had no right, no claim, to an emotional connection. She was another face in a long line of people I just wanted to help. That's what I tell myself. It made me think of another time I'd mentioned talking to a stranger in need at the library, looking to Delta for permission I didn't really need to help him.

Delta laughs, that full throaty laugh, the one that sounds like tobacco even though she's never smoked a day in her life. "You never met a stranger, Rachel. Remember that time you brought the wrong guy home for dinner in New London? You ran into him at Costco and thought he was my coworker Bob, and for some reason he didn't bother to tell you how backass wrong you were. He latched onto you like you were the best friend he'd ever had. I sat there staring at the fool, wondering if he was addled in the head or if he was just hungry. I kept shooting you the look and you kept ignoring me. Every time I'd try to catch your eye you'd throw more food on his plate and pretend you had known it wasn't my Bob all along. And damned if Fake Bob didn't end up coming back every few months for another meal."

She was right. I wasn't particularly outgoing by nature. I was introverted, reclusive even. But that part of me wasn't really about avoiding people. I enjoyed the company of other people, but in moderate quantities. I'd always found it fairly easy to relate to the strangers I met along the way as long as the interactions were in small, intimate groups. Kenna was certainly more familiar and relevant than Fake Bob had been. Stranger wasn't the right word to use for her. There didn't seem to be an actual word for what she is though.

When I'd first started toying with the idea of a road trip, Kenna hadn't been part of the picture. I'd spent those six months after Delta's death in a suspended state or numbness. It wasn't that her death was a surprise, we'd known it was inevitable by the time the end came. Knowing that and accepting are two different things though. I'd spent those last days watching her, wanting to steal every moment possible. I should have slept when she slept but I couldn't. I was afraid to close my eyes. I was afraid that the moment I let my guard down, she'd leave me. It turned out I'd been right to worry about it, she waited until I left the confines of our cottage. There had been a freak late season storm the night before and I'd gone outside to shovel the walkway. She slipped away quietly in the brief twenty minutes I'd dropped my guard.

After she was gone, I shut down physically for a while. My body tasted sleep, real sleep, again and it demanded more. During the first few weeks of mourning, my need for sleep was insatiable. I'd sleep nine, ten hours a night and still wake up feeling as if it wasn't enough. Eventually, that did subside and I went back to work, back into the community. I started walking with Susan. I attended a few social functions. I found new projects to keep me busy. I'd never really recovered my balance; I swung wildly from a state of perma-exhaustion to a wild restlessness up until the moment Kenna arrived on my doorstep.

The desire to escape the silence of my cottage and the lonely monotony of life without Delta was what had first inspired me to consider moving. Perhaps starting over in a new place, with new people, would spark that part of me that had been asleep since she left. I wanted the thrill of meeting new strangers, relating to other human beings, finding my place within a community again. I wanted a reason to wake up in the morning, something more than the body's stubborn insistence that it be fed and moved because one's body doesn't care very much about one's lack of motivation. A road trip seemed to be a possible solution when I tried but failed to nail down the place that would be my fresh, new start. So, it had been on my mind all along. Kenna, well, she had given me the final push to put it into action.

Now my attention was divided. I was no longer just seeking to heal my own broken life, my new focus was to fix Kenna's as well. She needed a fresh start, she needed it even more than I did. I wanted to gift it to her; I wanted to inspire her to believe in a brighter and stronger future. I wanted to guide her toward a life of meaning. All of my wanting wouldn't make it happen though. She had to want it badly enough herself and I wasn't sure if she had it in her. Perhaps the core of strength a person needed to thrive in this world was made of chalk. Perhaps it could be washed away, broken apart, crumbled under a cruel maternal hand. Or perhaps it was granite. Perhaps it needed only to be carefully mined and polished. I had to think there was a chance or we wouldn't be on this trip.

A trio of sandpipers interrupted my thoughts and I was ejected from the darker parts that I normally pretend don't exist. I couldn't help it, I watched with amusement as they ran back and forth along the waterline. As each wave rolled in, they scattered, only to return at the exact moment the water receded. In unison, they ran for the newly wet sand and pecked madly for unseen crustaceans. Only a brief moment later, they scattered again as a new wave hit. Distracted, I almost didn't hear the man calling at first.

"Hey, hey lady." A voice called rustily from several feet away.

I looked up toward the boardwalk to see a man of indeterminate age sitting on a bench, waving at me. He was wearing a pair of grimy gray cargo shorts that had surely been blue at one time, a torn black t-shirt, and a sun-faded ball cap that advertised the local minor league baseball team. I wasn't sure what the draw was, but I walked toward him.

"Can you spare a few dollars so I can feed my dog?" He asked.

He looked vaguely familiar and I struggled to place him. Then I realized that it was the same man I'd handed cash to on Atlantic Avenue a day earlier. This time though, he had a leash attached to his hand and on the other end of it sat a fat, scruffy, tan creature that might actually have been a dog. As I eyed the pitiful creature who was now waving her tail enthusiastically, I broke into a laugh, wishing Kenna were here to see this.

"Sorry, I don't have any cash on me this time. I do have this granola bar." I held up the unwrapped snack I'd casually tossed into my jacket pocket at the last minute. "Would you like it?"

He nodded approvingly and I ran up to him to hand it over. I stopped to pet the now happily panting animal. He might have gone awhile between meals, but she sure didn't look very hungry. She looked as if she'd been enjoying plenty of feasts. I smiled as she pawed excitedly at my legs, and asked, "What's her name?"

"Stella. Like 'Stella!'" He said, yelling the name dramatically in a reasonable impression of Marlon Brando. His missing front tooth and the smokers hack that quickly followed might have ruined the effect but the dog's tail wagged even harder.

I reached down to pet the scruffy animal and commented, "Stella is sure a happy girl!"

The man said, "Ayup. She likes pretty ladies."

"Well, aren't you a charmer? I'm guessing Stella is so happy because she's got someone in her life who loves her." I replied with a smile.

He grinned his wide toothy grin again and admitted, "Summa God's creatures are easier to love than others. Between the two a us, she's the easy one."

"Oh I don't know, it looks to be pretty mutual."

I didn't know what combination of life choices and bad luck might have led this man down the path to where he is, but clearly his life hadn't been easy. Yet here he sat, persisting. He wasn't alone in the world either. Even if Stella were the only loving presence in his life, he had an anchor. A reason for being. Everyone needed an anchor.

Glancing back toward the main strip, I felt a sudden desire to be with Kenna again. It might be very temporary, but for now, for this journey at least, Kenna and I could be anchors for one another. I turned to the man and smiled again.

"I hope you and Stella have a good day."

"You too, lady. God bless you." The man replied sincerely.

The exchange left a warm feeling in my gut and the more difficult thoughts I'd pondered earlier dissipated. I willed them away, at least for the moment. I was reminded that sometimes what the heart needs most is not to escape from the now- but rather to escape to it. In that afterglow I headed back up to the room, eager to see Kenna again. My good intentions were short-lived though, because the minute I opened the door I saw Kenna standing there with the suitcases packed and an anxious look on her face.

"What's going on?" I asked cautiously.

"We're getting the hell out of here, that's what!" Kenna replied, in a higher pitched, more animated tone than I'd ever heard before. My stomach dropped, something awful must have happened. I could only think of one thing that might be awful enough to elicit this degree of passion from her.

"What happened? Is it Tessa?"

"No, it's not Tessa." Kenna said, sounding nearly hysterical now. "It's... THIS!" she said, lifting her shirt slightly. There on her torso are a few scattered, tiny red marks, that had been highlighted by obvious scratching.

"I don't understand, what am I looking at?"

"Bites! Bed bug bites!" Kenna shrieked.

"Oh, shit."

Chapter 15

Kenna

Crushed under the weight of failure. I'm racked with guilt about the way we've left town. Rachel isn't here to just take a stroll down memory lane. It isn't all about sentiment. This is supposed to be a fact finding mission. She's seeking her new home. She would box up her earthly belongings, sell her beloved cottage, and relocate to start anew. There are the obvious job concerns and housing market. There's also the question of how welcome she'll feel in the community itself. It needs to be a place that a single woman can feel safe, a place where she'll find open arms and acceptance as a member of the LGBTQ community. I've prematurely punctuated the stop. I've ruined it.

My reaction to the insects might have been extreme, but it's still true that I couldn't have stood one more night in that hotel. I pictured tiny bugs crawling all over me as I slept, making a new home inside my suitcase, biting, digging, moving. Could they be in my ears? I wasn't a super squeamish person normally but this has completely freaked me out. This never happened at the Waldorf Astoria. I immediately regret that thought.

I glance to my right again, Rachel's been sitting silently in the passenger seat for almost an hour now. It's hard to tell if she's angry or just disappointed. Tessa had always made it abundantly clear, at least to me. Rachel is more restrained in general and I'm not sure how to read her current silence. I bite my lip, I haven't seen her angry before. Is it all bubbling up in her, will she explode soon in a mass of harsh words and threats?

As if reading my mind Rachel sighs. "I told you Kenna, it's okay. Bed bugs are a good reason to check out of a room, and Virginia Beach feels finished. I wish you'd unclench your hands, you look like you may break that steering wheel in half."

She doesn't sound angry, maybe a bit frustrated, but I'm not sure if that's because we've left early or if it's really about my childish reaction to the bugs. She might also be reacting to the way I've been pushing her to admit I'd let her down. There's an order of operations to these things though. You did the thing wrong, Tessa punished you with silence and you waited for the other shoe to drop. The tense buzzing in your head, a swarm of a thousand bees, expands and moves until it fills your entire physical body. Taut, you wait for the inevitable explosion- sometimes you even nudge a bit to stop the prolonged torture. When she finally did explode, you felt both regret and relief.

After the explosion, you could carefully tiptoe into the apology stage- and that's expected to last a while. Tradition dictated that apologies would last at least as long as the prior stages. And then when you get the brief nod that you've groveled enough, you're allowed to pretend the thing hadn't happened and you can move on.

How long the stages last depends on the crime committed. If you spill a glass of soda on a white gown that she's forced you to wear to an award event that you'd never wanted to attend to begin with, the cycle can be relatively quick. Within just a few days you might be all the way to the pretending it never happened stage. If it's something big though, like say- being expelled from Barnard for academic dishonesty- well that could conceivably take a good year to work through.

"Kenna!" Rachel yells, and I realize I've been so lost in my own head, we've drifted off the road and onto the shoulder.

"Shit, sorry." I say. "I was lost in thought, I didn't even hear the alarm."

"What alarm?" She asks.

"The lane alarm, the one that sounds when you leave your lane." Before I even finish speaking it dawns on me that such an alarm might not be standard issue on all cars and my cheeks flush.

Rachel sighs and then replies, "I'm the lane alarm in this car, Kenna. Stay in your lane."

Feeling even more sheepish, I hyper focus on the road. I'm not Kennedy Shepherd anymore, I remind myself. I am Free Kenna, Kenna Of No Obligations. Kenna who can speak. "Look, I know you're upset about this whole thing, we really could have just changed hotels..."

"Kenna!" It's the closest she's come to raising her voice at me, "I told you, it's fine. We're moving onto Charleston, because it's time to move on. I got what I needed in Virginia Beach. Please stop apologizing and explaining. I don't know how to make this clear, it is not an inconvenience to me to change my plans. Road trips are all about spontaneity, and frankly that's a skill I'm working on for myself too."

"All right." I reply, although I'm sure that my tone makes it clear I'm still not completely convinced. "Are you going to call your parents and let them know we'll be there earlier than planned though?"

Silence. The unease kicks in again; this feels all too familiar.

"They don't know." She says.

"Oh? It won't be a problem when we show up early?"

She sighs and admits, "They don't know we're coming to Charleston at all. I thought about calling before we left Metzgartown but I didn't want to get their hopes up. To be honest, I hadn't completely committed to this stop in my own head."

This isn't the Rachel I've come to know. Forthright Rachel. Confidant Rachel. Unwavering Rachel. The slight waver in her voice betrays her.

"Is this because of Delta? You mentioned before you'd been back to visit, so I assumed you'd worked past all of that."

"We've certainly tried. I have been to visit several times in recent years, but the visits were always short and there was always a protective distance between us. They actually offered to come to the funeral. It felt so... unreasonable. They couldn't make amends with her while she was alive, but they wanted to pay respects to her after her death? I love my parents and I'll always be sad for our lost years, but there's a part of me that is still pretty angry. Still, my father's health continues to decline and I've come to appreciate how short life can be. I want something more. I just wasn't certain when I planned this all that I'd actually make that exit to take the next step."

Everything she says makes perfect sense, but I'm still distracted by her vulnerability. I've been lost in the repeating chorus of my own family drama and had completely missed how complicated this next stop was for her. Then another thought occurs to me. I'm pretty sure I know the answer before I even ask.

"Rachel, do they know about me?"

"No, they don't. My pregnancy was during the no-contact days. We didn't have any reconciliation at all until after the move to Pennsylvania. I'd signed that nondisclosure agreement, but the truth was I used it as a crutch. I didn't want to tell them because I wasn't sure how they'd react. I was already their weird, disappointing, lesbian daughter. I didn't want to add yet another layer of weirdness to the story. Carrying a baby for Tessa Shepherd would have been just way beyond anything they could have wrapped their minds around."

I point out the obvious issue. If we show up together in Charleston, they'll want to know who I am. They'll speculate, maybe even recognize me if the media has circulated Zach's picture enough. Even if they don't have a clue, they'll want to know why Rachel has a random stranger tagging along. The niece story won't work with them. Rachel confesses that she's been thinking about this problem herself and has run through a number of scenarios.

"I've decided to just tell them the truth. It's easier than a lie. They may not approve, but at this point in life, I'm not craving their approval."

I can appreciate the simplicity of the plan even if I can't quite shake off the anxious feeling that nags at me. If Rachel's parents don't approve of me, it might color the way that she views me. Seeing me through their eyes could change everything. I might become a person she doesn't really care for. It's exactly the kind of thinking I'm trying to overcome though. The constant refrain of self-loathing is exhausting. I repeat the line I've been practicing in my head for several days. Rachel chose to carry me and give birth to me, I'm not a burden that had been foisted on her without her consent. Still, a competing voice whispers, "You don't sparkle."

We spent another hour following a state highway out of the cities that comprise Hampton Roads until finally we are in a sea of picturesque farmland. Periodically small clusters of houses appear, a bored deity having tossed random little brick ranchers onto endless fields in the middle of nowhere. Then fluffy white debris begins to appear along the roadside. Odd wads of tissue paper or handfuls of insulation of some kind, I assume at first. As the strange white piles grow though and begin to cover nearly empty, dry fields, I finally ask, "What is that?"

"Cotton bolls, it's harvest time. When the picking machines come in and do their thing, they can't get it all. Some of the cotton escapes and dots the landscape."

For all my worldly travels, this is brand new scenery. Rachel turns the knob of her radio and finds the perfect soundtrack of background music. A staticky radio station belts out ancient sounding country music. The music periodically disappears entirely- washing us in silence, but then we round a curve and some woman is again singing about standing by her man. The tunes are perfect for the backdrop but I miss the consistency and choice offered by my satellite radio. Still feeling a little chagrined by my earlier comment about the lane alarm, I resist the urge to say the thought aloud.

Signs indicated we're nearing the interstate. As we hit the small town of Emporia that signals our entry onto Interstate 95, Rachel suggests we stop for a quick fuel and restroom break. Spotting an Exxon ahead, I pull up to a gas pump.

Once the car is gassed up, I head into the service station to find the restroom and Rachel. It turns out to be a single occupancy toilet, so I wander the aisles as I wait for her exit.

"Hey there." A voice says.

I look up and see a man standing too close. He's slightly older than me; his red goatee is flecked with what I assume is tobacco and I can smell the beer on his breath. His low-slung baseball cap must be a temporary prop- his face is deeply tanned and his nose shows evidence of peeling. It's not a particularly unattractive face, but his eyes are unsettling. Bloodshot blue eyes stare at me and his mouth twists into something that might have been his attempt at a grin. It looks more like a grimace.

"Hey," I reply, nervous from the interaction. I don't like talking to people I know, I especially don't like talking to strangers.

"You live around here?" He asks and he leans slightly forward. Instinctively, I shrink back.

"No, just traveling through."

He grins again and lowers his eyes to my chest where they seemed to purposely linger. The small store is brightly lit, a cashier stands bored behind the counter and a half dozen patrons are walking around the aisles but I feel trapped and alone. Prey. I'm locked up, in a not-unfamiliar way, I don't know what to say or do.

"Cat got your tongue girl?" He presses.

I manage the tiniest of head shakes, but the words still won't come.

"Kenna, everything alright?" Rachel asks from behind me and relief floods my body.

"Um yeah, I'm going to the bathroom though if you want to wait here..." I stop short of saying, "Because I'm scared this creep will be here when I come back out."

She nods and stares at the man, who now looks annoyed.

"Your mama says run along, little girl." He says with a sneer, but he glances at Rachel's firm stare and walks away without another word. She shakes her head at me but doesn't say anything else. Afterwards, we leave the smells of fried chicken, ammonia and gasoline behind and I'm already driving toward the interstate's entrance ramp before she breaks the silence.

"Kenna, that guy. He was bothering you."

"Yeah," I admit.

"And you just stood there and let him?" She asks gently, but the words still sting.

"It's not like there was anywhere I could have gone. You were in the bathroom and I didn't want him to follow me to the car."

"You can always tell someone who is bothering you to leave you alone. If it doesn't feel safe to walk away, you can always yell for help even. I'm honestly having trouble imagining how you handled living in New York. What did you do there when these situations arose?"

I think about it. It's true, there were all sorts of strange people in the city and some could be aggressive. Homeless people who screamed at demons I couldn't see, street hustlers who tried to convince me to check out whatever they were selling out of their trunk, construction workers who whistled and yelled words they must have imagined were compliments. It's never quiet in the city. I've avoided most of the noise though by hiding either on campus or in my apartment. If someone on the street makes me uncomfortable then there's always a shop I can duck into, a cab I can hail, other pedestrians that I can hide behind. I try to keep my time on the streets as minimal as possible though. I'm not exactly familiar with the city I inhabit- and that's by design.

"I guess I'm a little sheltered, even in the city I tend to stay in my bubble- and usually if someone tries to talk to me I walk away quickly. Somehow that feels a lot easier though when there's a crowd to walk into, to be lost in, than standing just face to face with someone like that."

It sounds lame, even to my own ears. I don't know how to explain this to her though. I wasn't just protected as a child, I was completely isolated. I'd lived in an ivory tower, no one could get to me. Every single person I'd ever come into contact with up until college had been carefully selected and curated. It had never been left to chance that I might be exposed to someone Tessa would deem undesirable or unsafe. My mother was a lot of terrible things, but she wasn't casual when it came to safety.

Within our house, there had always been a strict lineation between the household staff that had the privilege of addressing Miss Kennedy and those more temporary, anonymous faces on the periphery, the gardeners, the caterers, the groomsmen. A polite hello was all that was allowed from those on the outside and they were carefully monitored for any deviation from that expected norm. When we left the safe confines of the house, there was always someone there to hold my hand and guide me away from strangers. We stayed at exclusive properties, if it was particularly trafficked then we'd take extra precautions like reserving an entire floor of resort rooms. Kennedy Shepherd was never left to mingle.

When I'd finally gone off to Calvin Brook, I'd been overwhelmed by the sheer number of people that were suddenly part of my inner bubble. Calvin Brook was very small, with just over 200 residential students in grades 7-12 in attendance, but that was far more than I'd ever been exposed to before. Still, we were well-insulated. Almost every student there would have been a juicy target for the media, and more ominously, almost every student there would have netted a tidy ransom. Gradually, my bubble grew, but it was still within safe and guarded confines. My exposure to anyone like the man at the gas station was non-existent.

When college application time came, we found ourselves suddenly thrust into a much larger world. There was a seeming disconnect in our parents minds between the sheltered lives of our youth, and the fact we were now expected to embrace the greatest institutions in the world-many in larger cities. Most of my classmates were eager to make the leap, they'd spent years planning their debut into the "real world". Everyone seemed to have a plan or a dream except me.

I'd been terrified by the whole application process. Not just because of the looming reality of leaving my bubble, but also because I had no clue what I wanted to actually study. Every time another career quiz was set before me, I'd panicked. I'd obsess over every question, choose an answer, reread and then change my answer. Who was I? I had no clue. I certainly had no clue who I wanted to be next.

Tessa was quickly fed up with my ambivalence and did what she always tended to do- she took control. My positive reports from English classes, combined with her own publishing background, convinced her that I would make a good journalist. When she said journalism though, she wasn't really talking about me becoming the next Christina Amanpour. She was picturing me on a television screen on a show like Entertainment Tonight. Part of me suspected that what she was really doing was cultivating her own evening news promotion expert. I have no doubt that she'd carefully considered what I might do for HoHo and Shepard Productions in general.

My reluctance to actually join some semblance of the bigger, more real world, outside of the confines of Calvin Brook wasn't strong enough to empower me in a fight against Tessa so I did what I always do. I obediently filled out the application forms, wrote the essays that her staff writers would edit, and submitted the packages to the schools she'd selected. My sole act of defiance had been sending that one extra package to Barnard. When the acceptances came in, I made my one independent decision in life, I selected Barnard. That I didn't actually want to be in the city; that was my way of compromising in a deal Tessa didn't know we'd even made. She was predictably furious though, and further compromise had been required- this time in the form of a journalism major.

Life in the city was every bit as terrifying as I'd feared it would be. I learned quickly to keep to myself as much as possible on campus and to retreat immediately to my off campus apartment when I wasn't in class. On weekends I'd usually drive home to CT, where thankfully Tessa was an infrequent visitor. She split her time between New York, Chicago, and LA, giving me plenty of time alone. While I'd come out of my shell a bit at Calvin Brook despite its remoteness, the city had an opposite effect. I'd crawled right back into that shell and had no desire to leave it again. Until The Crier incident.

I glance at Rachel, her eyes are closed. I'm not sure if she's actually asleep or just resting them but I'm thankful that the subject of my complete inability to handle a stranger is seemingly finished. We've lost another radio signal and I spin the dial to a pop station, as we speed through the North Carolina stretch of I95. The roadside signs are getting interesting. Interspersed between signs touting cheap gas, fireworks and hotels are huge colorful billboards that advertise a marvel called, "South of the Border." I can't tell at first if it's a resort or a restaurant, but some of the signs begin to advertise gift shops and meeting someone named Pedro. I'm starting to get the idea that it must be a large tourist attraction. When one billboard includes a three dimensional hot dog and the words, "You Never Sausage a Thing," I laugh and decide we have to stop.

Just as I've relaxed, another sign appears. "TESSA LIVE!" and there she is. My mother's much larger than life face, lit up and airbrushed, beaming with her fake, friendly, beautiful smile. She's staring directly at me as we speed by. Apparently her tour is stopping some 130 miles away in Charlotte according to the billboard. We quickly pass it at 70 MPH, but it lingers through the rest of the state, an unwelcome heartburn after a quick bite of something harsh.

We near the border and the billboards increase in frenzy. At the picture of Pedro's friendly face, I shake off my mother's image. I've decided to fully embrace the spirit of road tripping and obviously that means we need to see this wonder. I know it's probably out of Rachel's price range to actually stay there and we need to get on to Charleston anyway, but I have enough cash left that I can at least treat us to lunch. I plan to wake her after we park.

My surprise is foiled though as Rachel stirs beside me. She asks sleepily, "Where are we now?"

I smile and explain, "Almost to South Carolina but I have a surprise! There's apparently a big resort just across the border, appropriately named "South of the Border." I thought we could stop and I'd treat for a nice lunch. I don't know about you, but I could go for some ceviche!"

Just then a tower topped by a large sombrero comes into view and from the passenger seat I hear Rachel begin to laugh. As I ease onto the exit, her laugh grows louder.

"What's so fu..." My question dies on my lips as the full glory of "South of the Border" reveals itself.

Chapter 16

Rachel

I hadn't laughed so hard in a very long time. My stomach muscles hurt and tears ran down my cheeks as I fought to reign in the contractions that wracked my body. Every time I looked at Kenna and then at the figurine cutouts that sat in front of the car's bumper, the laughter would start anew though. Kenna studied the life sized photo props with her mouth open and eyes wide. She looked around again at the kaleidoscope of color that surrounded us and then slowly shook her head. When I failed to rein my laughter in quickly enough she turned and glared at me.

"Alright, I get it."

"I'm sorry, I just... a Mexican resort! On I95! In South Carolina!" I began to laugh again.

"How was I supposed to know? This isn't exactly my stomping ground." Her voice shifted then from annoyance to wonder, "I'm so confused though, what exactly IS this place?"

"It's more like, what isn't it? Restaurants, gift shops, arcade, kiddie rides, and I suppose more. We'll explore a little but not until after lunch, I'm starving."

We entered a dimly lit, but cheerfully decorated restaurant. The tile floor, cactus murals, and strategically placed giant sombreros were a good effort at whisking us thousands of miles away- but the menu made it clear this was an All American experience.

"Would you like the tacos, the cheeseburger or the BLT?" I asked Kenna.

She giggled. "I guess ceviche is out. Tacos it is!"

She paused then and looked around again. "Uh, Rachel, don't you think this is all kind of..."

"Kitschy?" I asked.

"I was thinking something more along the lines of racist. I mean, it's pretty much all a giant caricature of Mexico, right?"

I considered it, it wasn't an invalid point. "I think it started out that way, but I don't think anyone- even the staff here, is under the illusion this is representative of Mexico anymore. There's some appropriation going on here, but it seems to be done in good fun. I don't think there's any harm intended."

I could see she was unconvinced and she glanced at the menu again. "You know what? I'll just have the BBQ sandwich."

Interesting. Until now, Kenna had been preoccupied with her own troubles. She'd shown curiosity about my story, and an appropriate level of sympathy about my recent loss- but she'd seemed pretty detached from the larger world around us. It'd been difficult fleshing out just who she was, what she believed in, how she felt about world affairs with the ghost of Tessa smothering her. I wasn't sure how I felt about what she'd said here, I'd have to think about it some more, but I was happy to see her assert an opinion. It was expressed in a pretty mild manner, it was a start though.

"Good choice. You should have the full South of the Border experience though while we're here, buy a giant pencil at the gift shop, grab an ice cream cone across the street, pose with the big gorilla for a picture!"

Kenna asked curiously, "You seem pretty familiar with this place. Is this some mainstream American thing that everyone except me knows about, or have you been here before?'

I smiled, "Been here, done it. I'd been here several times as a child, back when it was in its true heyday." I said, gesturing toward the nearly empty dining room. She nodded in understanding.

"Later, Delta and I made several road trips down to Florida and we always made a pit stop here. I know you're not quite sure about being here, but I'm glad you stopped, because no road trip down the east coast would be complete without popping in."

Kenna nodded thoughtfully and looked around the brightly decorated room. The amber lamp overhead cast a golden glow across her face, creating the illusion of a soft spotlight. She looked so young under the golden hue, she could pass as a child. I felt an almost visceral urge to reach a hand out to brush her soft cheek but I reined it back in and instead asked, "Tell me about your own vacations. You didn't do road trips, but surely you traveled a lot?"

Kenna nodded. "Oh yeah, we traveled pretty frequently, especially when I was younger. Most of the time, we'd stay barricaded in some private estate or exclusive resort though- we didn't really go out and experience the local culture. Oh wait, there was this one trip to Portugal where I'd been given a special role to play and we went out then."

HoHo had offered a book series about twelve years earlier, called "HoHo Heritage". Each volume was the approximate size of a traditional Time Life book and focused on a different culture. Readers could purchase them individually or subscribe to the entire series at a discounted rate. They'd proven to be very popular. The books featured home decor, furnishings, and nuanced little life-space touches that would instantly transport a homeowner to the theme country. While the homes and rooms featured were actually based in the United States and Canada, Tessa had decided to include actual photos of the original habitats and furnishings that had inspired the pieces. For reasons that Kenna didn't know, Tessa had decided to attend the Portuguese shoot in person and had brought her with.

They'd traveled with a small convoy of photographers, make-up artists, personal assistants, and nannies from Lisbon to the small medieval walled village of Obidos. There, the population had been deemed small enough and quaint enough, Tessa and Kenna could freely roam the streets with only minimal private security at their side.

Kenna described walking the cobblestoned streets under the bright midday sun, the smells of baking breads and pastries emanating from bakeries they passed, old men holding out tantalizing tiny chocolate cups full of ginja for them to try as younger men ran through the streets carrying casks of port and wine to waiting trucks. Tessa, who never stopped to smell the roses anywhere, actually did stop when a small child stepped shyly out of a doorway to hold up a bouquet of flowers. She'd smiled and graciously took the bouquet, closed her eyes, and drew it to her face. Inhaling the sweet scent, she then reached down and ran her hand softly over the eager child's head. *Thank you, sweet baby.* She'd said and Kenna felt something she'd never experienced before.

"Jealousy. She'd never spoken to me that sweetly, that tenderly. I remember just reaching for my nanny's hand, and she squeezed mine in return so I think she knew it too. Don't look so sad, I was over the feeling a minute later. The child went back inside and my mother spun around to the photographer and said, 'tell me you got that! I don't have time to do this again.' and I realized it had all been set up. I was only eight years old, but I got it all in an instant. The whole thing had been a set up. The child, the men in the background, the supposed freedom on the streets. None of it was real. It was a facsimile of real though- and that's the sad part. We could have just done it real, but Tessa leaves nothing to chance and had to control the entire scene."

I shook my head. The life Kenna described included a bounty of riches and yet had been bereft of even the smallest hint of kindness. By Kenna's accounts, and I didn't doubt them, their home had been cold and loveless. Until now, some part of me had believed that Tessa loved the girl, in her own damaged and stilted way. I was beginning to accept Kenna's truth though. Something was broken in Tessa, she'd never developed that critical maternal string that is required for a species to survive and thrive.

I hadn't liked Tessa from the first time we met. She'd struck me as cold and calculating from the start. She'd had a special way of making me feel really small and inconsequential despite the fact I was carrying her child. I'd grown to truly despise her during the pregnancy. Our conversations became increasingly hostile as her phone interrogations grew in frequency. Where was I? What had I eaten that day? How many hours of sleep did I get? All too often, I got the answer wrong. It was perfectly reasonable, for example, that I might have some pizza. I was pregnant and pregnant women sometimes crave things like pizza! But if she asked and I was truthful, she'd demand to know what kind of pizza.

"Did it have sausage or pepperoni on it? You know those can cause listeria and then there's the sodium content to worry about. Did you even bother to read the books I sent? Do I need to remind you that you're carrying my child?"

More often than not, I'd hang up and find myself pacing, simmering with anger, or drowning in tears. That Tessa was somehow able to obsess over the healthfulness of pepperoni on pizza, but didn't seem to care if she kept me in a constant emotionally fraught state, was an incongruity that Delta just couldn't get over.

"That woman is batshit crazy Rach. Can't you just stop talking to her?"

I explain for the hundredth time that I can't legally avoid her. Part of the contract I'd signed had explicitly required me to return any requests for contact within a 24 hour period.

"But what in the hell is she thinking? Pepperoni is bad for the baby, but driving you to tears isn't?" She presses impatiently.

"Delta, I have to take enough crap from her. I can't handle taking it from you too."

She'd backed off then, as much as Delta had been capable of backing off of anything- which wasn't completely. Through most of my pregnancy, she'd been reduced to muttering under her breath and shaking her head whenever Tessa's name came up. Tessa had a roadmap to "How to Build a Perfect Baby," and my emotional wellbeing hadn't made the checklist. Thankfully, it had made Delta's list.

None of that meant I didn't defy Tessa. I wasn't so deeply under her control that I'd lost my own sense of autonomy. My parents might have broken my heart, but they'd provided me with a healthy childhood. Unlike Kenna, Tessa did not have the advantage of crushing my spirit since birth. But perhaps my biggest strength came from the fact that I had Delta. You couldn't help but feel a little fearless when Delta was on your side in a fight. Still, I kept my rebellions subtle and secretive.

My boldest move had been when I'd felt Kenna's first fluttery movements. I'd instinctively hidden them from Tessa. I hadn't done it out of contempt. I'd just wanted to grasp and hold the experience close to my heart, a primordial sensation that belonged to me and me alone. When I entered my fifth month of pregnancy and the ultrasound technician highlighted the dancing infant in my womb, Tessa had asked irritably, "How can she not feel that?"

The tech met my gaze and paused too long as she sought an appropriate response. Tessa noticed and her eyes narrowed before she said, "I see."

She didn't explode until the tech packed up her gear and left the house. When we were alone though, I saw yet another face on the woman. Her features contorted as her entire body seemed to turn bright red with rage.

"How dare you keep that from me? Have you forgotten whose baby that is?" She shrieked.

I'd instinctively stepped back, needing to be further from her. My hands shot across my belly protectively. At that moment, I feared she might actually strike me.

"I... I know, I'm just, it's only been recently. And you can't feel it yet from the outside. Delta tried. I didn't think it was a big deal..." I lied. I'd known it would be a huge deal, but I hadn't wanted to share the moment. Not yet. I'd wanted some part of this baby that would be just mine.

She turned her back on me and walked to a window. She stood there for several minutes, silent, while I struggled to calm my breathing and heart rate. I was afraid of what she might say or do next, but by the time she turned around again the wild look on her face had been replaced by a calm, if cold, look of composure.

We avoided any further major outbursts throughout the rest of the pregnancy, but the interrogations and vaguely threatening comments never ceased entirely. When I gave birth to Kenna, I'd been filled with both crushing heartbreak and monumental relief. I would never have to deal with Tessa again, or at least that's what I had assumed back then. I pushed aside my vague concerns about her fitness for motherhood and allowed myself to imagine that the baby that I handed over was being raised in a safe and loving home. I'd assumed that a sweet infant would be just the tonic needed to coax a softer, kinder Tessa out within the confines of her own home. I'd simply never dreamed that she'd raised our daughter without a hint of the normal compassion and pride a mother is supposed to feel.

"Oh," I said softly, as the word hit me. Our daughter. That was a problem. That fragile thread of connection gave Tessa's every painful word and action new meaning. It meant that I was and am on some small scale, culpable. I'd given her the baby after all.

"Kenna I..." I began, but then stopped. What did I say here? Did I apologize for giving birth to her? What kind of message would that send to a girl who already felt she was unworthy of love? It was too cruel. I shook my head.

"Kenna, I am so impressed with what a kind and thoughtful young woman you are. You didn't have the best role model, yet you've grown to become a wonderful human being."

Kenna looked down at her plate and shook her head, "Don't forget what started all of this. I'm a coward and a liar."

It was an instinctual reaction. I pounded a fist on the table so hard our glasses of iced tea slid around on their condensation powered bases across the faded, laminate table top. Kenna jumped at the sudden move, but I wasn't letting it go that easy this time. I leaned across the table, targeting her unnaturally wide blue eyes with a face I knew was red and tense.

"Stop that. You need to learn to take a compliment, and you've got to learn to forgive yourself for making mistakes. Every time you do that, you're letting her win. When someone compliments you, say thank you. Internalize the compliment a little even as that little voice tells you that you're not worthy."

The younger woman blushed and bit her lower lip, "I'll try. It's really hard, but I will try."

And she would, because that's the kind of young woman she was. She learned, she tried to do better. She grew. And there was a spark of hope then. Maybe it wasn't too late. I offered her a smile of approval and I wondered if she could read my thoughts. Turning, I waved the waiter over with the check. Kenna reached out and snatched it from my hand, reminding me it was supposed to be her treat.

"Thank you Kenna! All right, let's go hit that gift shop before we get back on the road. Giant pencils, trust me- you need one."

Chapter 17

Kenna

This isn't my first visit to Charleston. I'd been maybe 6 or 7 years old when we'd come down for a charity event that had really been an excuse for my mother to schmooze it up for a long weekend with a tall, dark haired man. I can't remember his name or whether Tessa's ulterior motives had worked, he'd been a short blip on our radar- but I do remember his house. It was a huge, stately Georgian style home in the historic district. Two of the four stories featured white rail lined porches that ran the entire length of the home, and fragrant flowering plants spilled from giant boxes beneath each window. It was situated just one street in from the waterfront which had been impressive, but the primary feature of the home for me had been a resident ghost. Tessa had laughed away his story of the supernatural houseguest, but I'd believed him.

Our host gave us a full tour of the house, including the revelation of a secret room behind a bookcase. The dark paneled, windowless space was anchored by a huge, colorful oriental rug. Polished brown leather couches sat facing the wide stationary wall where a huge red and gold painting hung. My mother had been drawn to it, sucking in her breath before murmuring, "Exquisite."

"It's a Klimt," our host explained. "It may seem strange to hide it away here but sometimes you want a private, creative space to retreat to. Obviously this isn't my normal home office, but some of my best work actually happens here." He said as he nodded toward the small desk in the corner.

He'd turned to me then and confessed, "The ghost can't come through the walls you know. Most people don't know this, but ghosts need open doors too. I hide here when I don't want her around."

I'd stared back, wide-eyed and unable to actually speak, clutching my Nanny's hand. He smiled and winked. There had been no malice in that smile, even in my childish mind, he looked more sad than scared.

Now older and wiser, I wonder who his ghost was. What had he actually been hiding from in the secret room?

I don't like associating anything on this road trip journey with Tessa and our previous life. I want to see Charleston through fresh, unbiased eyes- so I force the memory away. It isn't very difficult at the moment, given our surroundings. Nothing about them resembles that majestic home on Tradd Street. Our hotel isn't in the historic district, Rachel explained that even the least expensive options there are twice as much as on the outskirts, so we stop before reaching town at a seedy looking roadside motel in North Charleston.

The mention of finances makes me feel uncomfortable, I've used up about a third of my cash reserve and I don't like that Rachel's taking on the financial burden. I know that the $800 that I still pocket won't pay for everything, but I can cover something. Besides, it feels especially ridiculous to worry so much about finances considering the balance in my checking account and the stack of credit cards in my wallet. I haven't wanted to touch any of it because I knew that Tessa would track my every step that way- but now she knows who I'm with and surely she'd also have Rachel tracked through her own digital banking footprint. There doesn't seem to be a reason to stubbornly avoid my accounts now.

"Rachel, I've been thinking. Maybe it's time for me to start using my own credit cards." I suggest.

She smiles at me but shakes her head. "No Kenna, I was going to take this trip with or without you, so this isn't a burden."

The trip seems awfully last minute for someone who already had it on the books. I mention that and she sighs at my unwillingness to just give her the lie gracefully.

"I was planning it. I just hadn't committed to it. I needed a push to follow my plan, and that's what you gave me. I don't mind paying as long as you don't mind slumming it. You know the second you use one of your accounts, your mother will know exactly where we're staying. And besides, didn't you tell me she was actually named on all of your accounts as a co-owner?"

"I don't think it matters anymore if she knows where I am. We kind of made it clear I'll be back when I'm ready to be back. And yeah she is, but it's moot because even if she wasn't I'm sure she has some nosy contact who could tap into my accounts and share any recent charges."

Rachel shakes her head, "No, that's not what I meant. What I mean is how do you know the cards still work? She'd threatened to cut you off and it seems to me that implies she will remove your access to everything."

As soon as she says the words, a dawning horror creeps over me. It was one thing to allow Rachel to cover costs all the while knowing I could easily do the same if needed. It's quite another thing to imagine not having access to those funds at all. Would my mother really go that far? I know the answer immediately. Tessa. Of course she would.

"Oh god, you're probably right. I need to find out for sure. What am I going to do if she has? This trip isn't going to last forever!"

I know Rachel's taken just two weeks of vacation time at work, one way or another this trip is ending in just 10 days. Am I really supposed to have my entire life figured out in ten days? This is a hill too big to climb, too soon. The only realistic options are to earn enough money to support myself or to crawl back to Tessa and beg for forgiveness. I obviously have no skills or ability to support myself, so that really leaves just one option.

A cramp shoots through my belly at the thought. I picture Mother's face. Icy eyes filled with fury. Smug near-smile on her thin lips. She'd make me beg and grovel and there still wasn't any guarantee she'd relent and let me have the shattered pieces of my life back. If I were anyone but her daughter, she absolutely wouldn't. It won't be love that motivates her either, if she does grant me absolution. My only real hope is that she'll do so to protect her own image.

"Kenna, breathe," Rachel instructs. "You certainly can go back and ask for whatever you need. That's not your only option though."

I rub my eyes and try to understand what she's saying. It's my only option. But then realization dawns. Is she saying she can support me? I can't let her do that. I've already let her do far too much for a woman who owes me absolutely nothing.

"I can't let you do that." I say, as I try to retract the sting in my eyes.

"I wasn't suggesting that I could financially support you in the long term, although you're welcome to stay for a while as you get on your feet. What I'm saying is this is a big world, and you are a smart, talented woman. You can make your own way in life. Tessa doesn't have to map your life out or even financially support it. Maybe it's time to start thinking about who you are and what you really want, without Tessa being part of that equation."

I stare at her, confused. I know exactly who I am. I'm Tessa's daughter. That's it. The grand sum total of all I have ever been and all that I will ever be. I don't need to figure out what I really want because that's irrelevant. I'm the sheet music, not the bard. Sheet music doesn't compose itself.

The thing is, it's not just me. If my time at Calvin Brook taught me anything, it's that there are plenty of other people in the world who exist only as an extension of their parents' ambitions. Most of my classmates came from similarly privileged and dysfunctional homes. The default was the same no matter how our parents made or maintained their fortunes. Most of us were expected to get in line and follow the family trade. Protect the family assets. Grow the family portfolio. Our school's official mission statement described us as "the progeny of America's finest families." People immediately think that progeny means children, offspring. It's the primary definition after all. No one seems to bother reading all the way down the dictionary page to the last definition. A body of followers, disciples, successors.

If our parents were in politics, then we mastered public speaking and learned to dress conservatively so we could serve eagerly as campaign trail props. If our parents were in business, we went to Harvard, bought our first companies at a young age, and in turn invested the profits into the family industry. If our parents were in the entertainment industry, we focused on our appearance with plastic surgeons and private trainers and then we plastered our pictures all over social media to a legion of fans. We existed as extensions of our parent's lives. We didn't create our own reality. No one ever told us how to do that.

"Those are things I don't exactly know." I admit out loud.

"And that's okay." Rachel says. "You don't have to know it all right now, but these are things you need to start thinking about sooner rather than later. The first step is realizing you're allowed to do it. You are allowed to find yourself."

I nod as if I understand even though I'm completely lost and go into the bathroom to clean up. My immediate financial problem doesn't leave my mind though. I can't see an obvious end to this journey except the one that ended at Tessa's door. For Rachel's sake though, I need to avoid admitting that out loud again. This trip isn't just about me and at the very least I can shift the focus to Rachel and her needs. Surely I could fake enthusiasm and hopefulness for the next ten days. I will accept my fate afterwards.

After returning to the room, I feign a smile and ask in as casual a voice as possible, "So tell me about your time in Charleston. How long were you here?"

"Four years, from age 11 to 15. We were here right before Virginia, and right after a few years in Boston. My father was at the small boat station down in the historic district. Back then, we actually lived in Navy housing in Goose Creek because the Coast Guard was so small, we didn't have our own."

"Boston isn't on your short list though?"

"No, it was only a few years and my father ended up being gone for most of it, so I just don't have any strong feelings or memories about it. Plus, as odd as it sounds, I like the idea of traveling in one direction on this search. It just appeals to me to travel in a straight line."

I nod. "And obviously, you must remember Charleston fondly if you're considering coming back?"

She smiles, "I do, although to be honest it's all kind of blurry. My early childhood memories are dominated by Key West because we lived there the longest, seven years. And Virginia stands out the brightest because that's where I met Delta. Still, what I do recall of Charleston is lovely, my family was still intact and reasonably happy here, our weekends were full of exploring the area. There's no bad baggage associated with this city."

"When do you think you'll reach out to your parents?"

She's silent for a moment. As she gazes out the window, I study her profile. Her normal air of confidence has disappeared. It makes her look younger. Sometimes I forget just how young she actually is. Maybe it's the loss of her wife, maybe it's forced her to adopt a serious and seemingly unflappable countenance. Or maybe she'd always been older and wiser than her actual years. I've heard the term 'old soul' before. Maybe that old soul is what drew a free-spirited and passionate Delta to her when their story began.

"I'm thinking it's really late and we've been going all day, I'm ready to crash already. Let's order a pizza to eat in the room, then get some sleep. We can get up tomorrow morning, head downtown and enjoy some sights and a nice lunch and I'll reach out to them afterward."

I nod in agreement. I'm clearly a fan of delaying confrontation and I selfishly prefer to enjoy at least one nice day in town with Rachel without the baggage of family drama. I have no idea what to expect once she does contact them, but I assume they'll be happy to see her. When she tells them about me though, well, I was sure I wouldn't exactly be welcomed with open arms.

For all of my issues, I've never felt particularly self-conscious by the nature of my conception and birth. I knew other kids at Calvin Brook who had been surrogate babies, it was a perfectly reasonable fertility option in this day and age. I'd also spent time online researching the process out of curiosity. Apparently, I'm a little different because my mother hadn't chosen to go with surrogacy due to infertility or other medical issues. The way Rachel describes being selected is really different than the way it's done normally. Or maybe there has just been an evolution of the process?

These days, parents are called *intendeds* and the selection process is done through private agencies that carefully screen surrogates. Modern surrogates know exactly what they're signing up for, no surprise reveals like Rachel experienced. It seems that in most cases, the agencies seek women who have already experienced pregnancy and are raising children of their own. A naive, young college girl like Rachel wouldn't be an ideal candidate. Perhaps privileged people like my mother are still able to procure their own surrogates though. Perhaps even now, Tessa would be able to ignore convention and soft rules to bind an unexpecting young woman to her.

Still, it's never been something I've been overly sensitive about. Now though, I'm suddenly feeling a bit self-conscious about my conception. Rachel's parents are normal people- and she'd presumably be telling them the gritty details including the why of it all. What if they look at me as some sort of circus freak?

It's about her, not about me, I remind myself again. This is Rachel's family, her home search, her moment of reckoning. For the past week, although it's felt so much longer than that- she's been supportive and caring. She's put my needs first. I realize that my appearance has to have dredged up some complicated feelings and memories, but she's never displayed even a hint of it. She's been far kinder to me than my own mother has ever been and there must have been a cost to her for that kindness. This is my chance to reciprocate. Whatever her parents think of me is their business and hers. I'm determined to just be by her side, supporting and encouraging her. I will mimic the caring model that Rachel's given me all week.

"You're so quiet Kenna, what's on your mind?" Rachel asks.

"I was just thinking about time. It's strange how a unit of time can feel very different, depending on how it's spent. An hour of road trip time stretches on much longer than real life time. I feel like it was ages ago that I was in New York- but it's actually only been six days. It's so strange. So much has changed."

"You're right. And a road trip is different from any other kind of travel. There's something about an interstate highway that nearly wipes out the memories of before. Each ticking mile marker brings you further away from the person you were at the start. That said, by the time we finish this trip you're going to be sick of me." She says, smiling.

"Ha, I don't think so. I already kind of feel like I've known you my whole life!" I reply without thinking.

"Well, Kenna, that's because you have."

Chapter 18

Rachel

"Most sailors fear fire the most. Fire onboard is devastating, there's a good chance it'll be a total loss but the way I see it is you can take lots of steps to avoid ever having a fire and if you catch one early enough, you can control the outcome. Most passengers on the other hand fear sinking the most, which never made sense to me. It's a waste of fear. Boats generally don't just sink for no reason. I blame the Titanic for that nonsense.

Me? You just know I gotta be different. The monster under my bed is pitchpoling. See, when you're in heavy seas you always face the bow forward. Steer into the waves. Seems to break the laws of nature but most times it works. You're gonna live to see another day. If your vessel gets turned sideways though, you get stuck in the trough and in heavy seas you can capsize. I don't even worry about that so much. I can control that- I just steer the boat into the oncoming waves. Problem solved. Until it's not.

Once in a while you might get stuck in a storm that's so bad, the waves build and become boogie monsters, real boogie monsters. Even the ablest coxswain and sturdiest boat can't take on that kind of monster. You steer into it and it's just too much. The boat flips, end over end. Pitchpole. I picture it sometimes when I lay in bed. Nearly black sky, inky waves that you can only just barely make out with your naked eye. Then you can't see any sky at all because the thing, the wave, is on you. That's the thing I fear most. I fear it because I can't control it."

The soothing massage of hot water jettisoning from the shower nozzle overhead made it easy to ignore the rust stains that run the length of the shower wall. It had been a restless night. Delta had showed up in my dreams, but she hadn't come as some Jacob Marleyesque guide, leading me to greater truth. Instead it had been the Connecticut years Delta who visited. Her substance proved to be more recollection than apparition. This Delta still had the glow of a golden tan, healthy muscular legs, and her eyes were still bright and unstained. This Delta had still smelled of diesel fuel and salt water, not the bleach and urine scent that hovered at the end. I didn't usually dream of those days, it wasn't a luxury that my brain normally allowed. This trip has triggered that invisible wire.

I wasn't sure how to interpret it. Clearly my subconscious was digging up old memories for a reason. I couldn't help but wonder, would Delta have approved of this visit? She'd been the one who'd encouraged me to take that first phone call from my mother after so many years of silence. But at the time, Delta had believed that there would come a day when they'd also accept her. A day when she'd be invited into their lives. That opportunity was forever lost now, there would be no reconciliation for her.

I slipped into the casual sundress that I knew my mom would approve of and with that realization came annoyance. I told myself I wasn't consciously trying to impress her, but the truth was I did care what she thought. My mom had never been openly critical of anything I'd worn or said, but she had a way of smiling politely that conveyed her disappointment all the same. I didn't want to see that smile today. I just wanted to be wholly and completely accepted by her.

As I began to dry my short, dark hair, I tried to remember a time when my mother had ever been anything but kind to me. The fact that she really hadn't, didn't make today any easier though. Her love and pride in me had been absolute during my childhood, so how had she so easily swayed to my father's side after our estrangement? I supposed I understood it just a little after spending so many years with a devoted partner myself, but it still hurt. Mom could have been a source of healing and reconciliation rather than his apologetic supporter. My father had started this cold war and I knew he was the one I should be angry with. The truth though, was that my hurt had instead focused for many years on my mother and her unwavering support for him. What was it about mothers and daughters that made it so damned complicated?

Satisfied with the results of my hair dryer, I exited the bathroom only to find an empty bedroom. A note was laying on the tv bureau and for a moment my heart rate quickened. Had Kenna left me?

Going to grab coffee and donuts. Be back soon!

The small act of service made me smile. Just a few short days ago, Kenna wouldn't have taken it upon herself to do this. She'd have been afraid to borrow the car without asking and afraid to venture out into a strange public space alone. She still had a long way to go, but the foundation was there. She was physically healthy, well-educated, attractive, and sweet-natured. I absolutely believed that she could go on to have a productive and successful life despite her upbringing. Now I need only convince her of this. She needed to see herself as more than an accessory or appendage to Tessa's ego- and I believed there were signs she was starting to do just that.

The sound of the door opening interrupted my thoughts, and Kenna walked in balancing two coffee cups and a small box in her hands.

"Okay this part of Charleston may be sketchy, but check out these donuts I found. The guy at the front desk told me they're the best around and if they taste as good as that bakery smelled he wasn't lying!"

"That's very sweet Kenna! I usually do savory for breakfast, but I'm going to make an exception this time."

Unlike our room in Virginia Beach there was no balcony overlooking the ocean here. Instead, the small room was dark and claustrophobic; its solitary window overlooked a mostly empty parking lot. Eyeing the yellowed walls and brown polyester bedspreads wearily I suggested, "Let's eat this outside, I saw a picnic table in that small patch of grass on the other side of the parking lot."

The donuts proved to be every bit as good as the desk clerk had promised. As Kenna bit into her bacon and caramel concoction, she closed her eyes with pleasure.

"My mother, you know she hates donuts." She offered casually. The comment was so relaxed, so normal, I was momentarily taken aback. Normally the mere hint of Tessa in a conversation was enough to scare her right back into her shell.

"She's missing out," I replied, trying to match her casual tone.

"Mmhmm. It's not just because of the sugar and carbs, there is that too though which is a shame. I mean, maybe if she ate a cookie she'd be a nicer person. But for some reason, she associates donuts in particular with the working class. You know, cops and construction workers, PTA moms, that kind of thing. It's funny though because if you open a HoHo kitchen edition, you'd see beautiful layouts featuring plates full of colorful donuts. I think they even sell an actual donut fryer. She's so far removed from reality, it's ridiculous."

I smiled at her candor and replied, "Well, one thing that can be said for my mom, is the fact she's never met a baked good she didn't like. She's terrific in the kitchen, she likes to try to replicate the goodies we'd find elsewhere." I glanced at Kenna, "Ha, it just hit me, she's probably looked at that HoHo donut fryer and considered buying it- her sense of frugality would have won out though."

She chuckled and then began to lick caramel frosting from her fingertips. We weren't in a beautiful setting; it was just a sunburnt patch of grass alongside a poorly maintained parking lot. I could spy two dumpsters against the hotel wall some twenty feet away. For the moment though, we were two ladies enjoying tea at the park. It was a comfortable, enjoyable thought.

"All right, let's head up, wash our hands, and then hit the town!"

High on sugar and caffeine, we made our way toward the heart of Charleston. The Charleston of my mottled memories was situated around grand historic homes and buildings. Brick and cobblestone streets crisscrossed through public and private gardens that bustled with people. I remembered the smell of carriage horse dung mixing with the fragrant natural perfume of the gardenia and jasmine that grew everywhere. The Charleston of memory was a curious mix of historic homily and the modern crunch of too many people and vehicles converging on the same spots. When we arrived downtown, it was clear that nothing had changed.

We navigated through crowded streets, following signs toward a public parking lot. After parking we walked toward Market Street where there was a long, mostly contiguous, brick market spanning the length of four city blocks. The well-known tourist attraction, first built in the 1790s, was popular for its age and historic significance. Antiquity wasn't the only draw; it still functioned as an actual marketplace. We wound our way through the crowd, occasionally stopping to inspect some of the artwork, foodstuffs, and souvenirs that overflow from vendor stalls. I was particularly drawn to the basket weavers- Gullah artisans intricately woven the native sweet grass into decorative and usable baskets. They worked their craft alongside tables that were piled high with the finished wares.

"I really want one." I admitted to Kenna as we watched an older woman use skills that had been passed down to her from generations of ancestors to create a small, lidded basket.

"You should buy one then!" Kenna replied.

"They're so expensive. It's absolutely a fair price for the artistry put into them, but it'd be a pretty frivolous purchase." I explained.

"Rachel, if I am expected to learn how to budget and restrain spending, then I think you should be expected to learn how to splurge on yourself once in a while on- what was the phrase you used? Oh yeah, frivolous purchases."

The artisan, who until that moment had been working silently, interjected. "This is not so frivolous, you know, this is six hundred years of history that you can touch. It is a living history."

I reddened a little at the older woman's words, as I realized that we'd been speaking louder than I had realized. I hastened to reassure the woman that I'd meant no offense. The older woman just shook her head.

"No matter. You see it now. This one here, you watch me make it, but it's not just a thing of here and now. My mother taught me this, her mother taught her. And so it goes all the way back, all the way across the ocean to Africa, across the years, to another people, another time. The basket is in my hands now but it does not just belong to me. It belongs to the grandmothers, yes? And maybe, if you buy it, it belongs to you too."

I felt my thrifty resolve weaken and reached for my purse. When Kenna chuckled softly, I threw her a sour look. Turning back to the woman I smiled and admitted, "You're a good saleswoman, I'll take that one over there."

The woman smiled broadly and exchanged the desired basket for the offered cash. As she handed it over she nodded toward Kenna and said to me, "Someday you pass this to your daughter, then it belongs to her. Some things are meant to belong to more than one woman."

Feeling a bit like the wind had been knocked out of me, I stammered a thank you and led Kenna toward the open doorway onto the street. The artisan's parting words wrapped themselves around me, both desired and unwanted at the same time. She'd taken a scour brush and worked at some small part of my skin- exposing the pink, vulnerable layer that hadn't yet been toughened by the sun. Yet when I glanced at Kenna, it was clear that the younger woman had missed the significance of the comment and the strong reaction it had evoked in me.

My thoughts were interrupted by Kenna's hand on my arm, she was suddenly pulling me along the sidewalk to a set of wide cement steps. There was a sense of urgency to her move, and I was confused at first, but then I saw him. A teenage boy sat on the center of those steps, playing his guitar for a small crowd. Kenna stood transfixed, humming along to the chorus of the Paul McCartney song he was performing as she watched. When he was finished, she mimicked the people around us and drew a dollar bill from her pocket to throw into his guitar case.

"He was great! I've seen some pretty incredible buskers in New York, but they're not usually that young." She said enthusiastically as we began to walk away.

"He was pretty good," I admitted, "But you're even better."

Kenna shook away the compliment. "Nah, there was something so charismatic about that kid. The crowd loved him!"

"Kenna, I'm serious. The crowd would love you too."

An idea began to form, although I wasn't sure just how to put it to words without scaring Kenna off.

"I totally get why large crowds intimidate you. I'd feel the same way. But what about something like this? There might have been ten people there. That's not bad. Maybe taking that kind of risk, putting yourself out there, would make the smaller steps seem easier."

Screwing her face into a dramatic look of horror, Kenna said, "You can't be serious. You want me to play on the street?"

"I'm just saying that these are strangers, small crowds, and you saw he had quite a few dollars in that guitar case. It might not be a bad way to gain both confidence and a little income."

"Hm, I just don't think so. Stop looking at me like that, I'm not saying no, I'm just saying I don't think so. Anyway, why do we always end up talking about me? Isn't today about you? When are you calling your parents?" Kenna countered.

I was impressed. She's quickly learning how to push back. It was a skill that every girl needed. "Young grasshopper learns fast. Actually, I've decided not to call," I raised a hand to stop her protest. "We're just going to drive over. I don't feel like explaining this twice to them."

She looked at me pointedly and raised both eyebrows. The gesture made me laugh, I had a feeling she was trying to imitate my trademark single brow lift, but the result was a rather spooked looking face.

"Seriously, we are. Right now, in fact. Let's just get this over with."

She sighed and then said, "Okay. But one question first." At my curious look, she continued, "Why did you call me a grasshopper?"

Feeling old again, I groaned and spent the remainder of our walk explaining the origins of the quote and the genius behind the old television classic, Kung Fu. As we reached my trusty old Saturn, Kenna smiled and said, "Rachel... sometimes, you're very strange. I like that."

"Oh, Kenna. Get in the car."

My parents lived about twenty minutes from the downtown area in an area called West Ashley. Although the town was suburban and well-populated, a veneer of the earlier days still persisted. Huge grand oaks, magnolias, cypress, and crepe myrtle trees lined the roadway that led to their house. The road was heavily shadowed as a result and it had a slightly haunted feel. Signs marked turnoffs that led to historic gardens and plantations. It was as if we'd been transported to another world.

Then the trees thinned and a golf course community revealed itself. Motioning toward the tidy cluster of houses ahead I said, "That's them."

"You sound more resigned than nervous." Kenna remarked.

"I am. There's nothing for me to prove here. I don't want to hurt them, but I just want to have my say. I don't have any expectations, I'm not sure what the response will be... but we'll know soon." I explained as I pointed ahead to a house that proudly displayed a Coast Guard flag.

Their home was a modest sized one story house that was surrounded by a well-manicured lawn. I knew my father wouldn't be using a lawn service, this was the product of his own hard work and a good deal of chemicals. My Dad had never bought into the science of toxicity. He'd been working with harsh cleaning agents, paints, fertilizers, and weed killers his entire life. They'd probably all contributed to his health woes, but my father was notoriously stubborn and I know he'll cling to his spray bottles until the bitter end.

Although it was September, it was still hot enough in the low country that the hydrangea was still in bloom; they were oblivious to the calendar that northerners followed. This was one of the things that had first drawn my mom to the south despite having been raised in the greyer, cooler surroundings of the Oregon coast. No matter where we lived, we'd always had huge, expansive, beautifully bright flower gardens. The further south we'd lived, the brighter they'd been and the longer they'd thrived. Charleston gifted her with gardens for most of the year.

After parking, we sat in the car, silent for a moment as Kenna allowed me to gather my thoughts. When the cheerfully painted yellow door swung open I was unsurprised. My mom had always been a devoted window watcher. A slightly smaller, significantly greyer version of me cautiously stepped out onto the front porch to inspect our car more closely and I inhaled sharply. It'd been almost three years since we'd last seen each other and my mother seemed to have aged significantly in that short period of time.

I looked at Kenna, faked a smile, and said, "Let's go."

I knew the instant she recognized me. The curious furrow between her brows relaxed and, for a brief moment, she shined with a huge smile. She tempered it into a smile that was more self-conscious. She was afraid to look too eager, too excited. This wasn't just a normal adult child's homecoming. It hadn't been that simple for a long time and we both knew it. She walked cautiously toward me and then as she extended her arms shyly, I allowed myself to fall into them.

"Mama."

My mother pulled back and for a moment I allowed myself to sink into her warm, almond shaped eyes. "You've come home." And then almost as if it were an afterthought she added softly, "He's out back."

I watched as her eyes darted to the left, catching the exact moment she noticed Kenna. When she looked at me again, I could see the questions in her eyes but she wouldn't just blurt them out. My mom was nothing if not a polite and gracious hostess.

"I'll explain inside." I promised anyway.

We followed her into my parent's comfortably decorated, tidy home. In the living room, I made a beeline for the pristine, floral couch and Kenna followed. Mom sat opposite us, on the matching love seat, and shook her head in wonder.

"I can't believe you're really here. This is just the loveliest surprise Rachel. I've missed you so much. So has your father, in fact I think I should go get him."

Although I felt pretty ambivalent about facing him, I nodded my approval. I only wanted to do this once and I was ready to get it over with. After she left, Kenna turned to me and asked, "You okay?"

She actually cared, I realized with a start. Despite her own troubles, at this moment she was squarely focused on mine. I smiled and nodded. It was surreal to be sitting in my parent's living room with Kenna, but I realized that the truth was I actually was okay. I felt strong and capable, and Kenna's warm presence at my side gave me strength. At the sound of footsteps, I looked toward the doorway that separated us from the kitchen and the backdoor beyond it. My father stood there now, his hair was barely thinning, but the rest of him was showing his age. He walked toward me, his limp more pronounced, he was favoring his left leg more than he had the last time I'd seen him.

I stood and nodded at him because I couldn't think of actual words to say. When he was just a few feet away he said fondly, "Well, look at you!"

"Hello, Daddy." I greeted him and reached up to hug him.

I stepped back and saw my parents were both looking at Kenna and then glancing at each other, they were clearly wondering who she was. "Mom, Dad, this is Kenna. She's... well, she's sort of a friend."

My father looked again at the young girl beside me, a girl who would have been far too young for me to be dating, and I watched as his face changed from confusion to concern. I realized what he was thinking and quickly added, "I know this is going to be a shock, but I was her surrogate mother."

A moment of silence followed, and then finally my mother said sweetly, "Maybe we should sit down, would anyone like a glass of iced tea?"

Chapter 19

Kenna

For the first time since leaving The Crier, I've slept undisturbed for an entire night. I have been a captive every night since my Great Shame to disturbing dreams. When dark visions of my mother and the world she'd created weren't tormenting me, I lingered on the edge of a shallow and unsatisfying sleep. Fragmented slumber. Something's changed. I work through the invisible calculus and I realize what I've forgotten, at least for the moment. Tessa. I've been so hyper focused on Rachel and her parents, I haven't had time to think about Tessa.

Bob and Lacey hadn't been what I'd expected. I hadn't known a whole lot about them before we arrived at their sweet little Charleston home, but I did know that they'd hurt Rachel and rejected Delta. I was defensive on Rachel's behalf. We'd quickly bonded and it's impossible to imagine anyone rejecting her. More surprising though is the realization that I also feel protective of Delta. As the stories have grown, I feel as if she's someone I know, someone important in my life. Instinctively, I want to defend her. Knowing their past history, I'd expected a very different version of Rachel's parents. In my mind, Bob and Lacey would be as cold and remote as my own mother. Tessa serves as the model for all parental failure.

Reality is quite different. Lacey is every bit as warm as Rachel, her soft voice and familiar brown eyes are as comforting as Bilbo's purrs had been. She's a hugger by nature and there were several occasions that she'd doled one out to me the previous evening. When she gazes at Rachel, I see a mixture of love and sadness. There's no recrimination or judgment in the longing stares. Just a mother who misses her daughter.

Bob's a little harder to read. He had spent much of the evening sitting in a well-worn armchair, nodding politely as Rachel, Lacey and I talked. When Lacey suggested barbecuing dinner, he'd quickly stood and escaped to the kitchen to prep the meat for the grill. It wasn't that he was unkind in any notable way, but it was clear he wasn't entirely comfortable with our presence in the house. I wasn't sure if his awkwardness was about his complicated history with Rachel or if it was really about my surprise existence.

I was a curiosity. That's something that normally would have made me extremely uncomfortable- perhaps to the point of having an actual panic attack. I've always hated being the center of attention and I'd found myself in the spotlight several times the prior evening. It felt different though. For the first time that I can ever recall, that curiosity has nothing to do with Tessa. In fact, Rachel had left the identity of my mother out of it entirely. She'd simply described my mother as a woman she'd met in college who was seeking a surrogate. Rachel's parents clearly didn't recognize me from any media chatter and I'm appreciating the chance to be something other than Tessa's daughter.

Lacey asked relatively harmless questions about my own childhood and college life that I artfully skirted with vague. I used to ice skate, no other sports though. No, I've never been to Oregon but I'd sure like to visit. What are winters like there, Rachel? I definitely prefer my English classes, but I'm not too shabby at the sciences. My grandparents? Just a grandfather really but we didn't see each other very often. When Rachel casually mentioned the fact that I played guitar, Bob became a little more animated. He'd owned a Gibson when he was younger. That led to a discussion about music in general, guitar players in detail. It was a relatively short conversation- but it mattered because I'd finally fallen on his radar as something other than a strange apparition that had sprung from his daughter's womb.

Throughout dinner, Rachel updated her parents on her own current situation. I noticed that she was spotty with the details. Charleston itself was supposed to be one of her potential relocation spots. Instead, she described this journey as a trip down the coast to investigate possibilities. The impression she gave was that our stop in Charleston had been a quick side trip to visit them. I began to wonder if maybe she'd actually made up her mind already about the city. Maybe I'm the one who is mistaken, maybe Charleston is already out of the running.

There was one subject that never came up and its absence was glaring. As we sat across from one another at the dinner table and discussed everything from the weather to Rachel's vegetable garden, we each skillfully avoided any mention of Delta. There had been a few times when I thought she might be mentioned, conversations where it would have been natural to include her name, but when those tiny awkward moments appeared the conversation would suddenly change. It was as if there were an unspoken agreement between Rachel and her parents to avoid Delta at all costs and I found the efforts dizzying.

Since I'd first arrived in Pennsylvania, Delta had been ever-present. I couldn't see the woman, but most days she sat firmly beside Rachel and I. Calmly watching, our silent witness rode every mile in that old Saturn with Rachel and I. I knew that Rachel wanted, needed even, a frank discussion about the ways her parent's rejection of Delta had contributed to the pain of her loss. She needed to give voice to the hurt in order to move past it. It surprised me that she chose not to broach the subject.

Now as we prepare to sightsee a bit before our planned return to Bob and Lacey's home, I look at Rachel curiously and decide to brave the subject.

"So I couldn't help but notice that Delta never came up last night."

She'd been running a brush through her hair and her hand pauses mid-sweep for a second. I've caught her off guard. Good, it's about time we reversed roles for a change.

"It didn't seem like the right moment, but I'm not planning to avoid the topic forever. I know this conversation needs to happen, but I didn't want to shut them down the minute we rolled into town."

Rachel has this perfect way of raising one eyebrow whenever she feels that I'm being less than fully honest or forthright- it's a skill I've been trying to mimic. I turn to her and focus on my right eyebrow and attempt to raise it. My earliest attempts had resulted in a clown-like pop of both eyebrows. This time I try to focus on the brow that I want to keep lowered, rather than the one I want to raise. As my eyes squint with the effort, Rachel stares at me in confusion.

"Is everything alright? What's happening with your eyes?"

I burst out laughing. The sound of my own laughter still catches me off guard. It always sounds so clumsy, whatever place in my body that creates laughter has no muscle memory. I've laughed more in recent days than I had in all of the years leading up to this though, it's starting to feel almost natural.

"Nothing wrong, just being silly. I'm also a little antsy to see what happens next." I admit.

"Next?"

"Yeah, part of me wants to see you take your parents to task for Delta. She deserves it, right?"

Rachel looks at me thoughtfully. "I've been framing my disappointment and anger toward my parents as a result of something they'd done to me. But something about the way you just said that made it click. It's really Delta they wronged."

"Does that make you feel more forgiving toward them, shifting the hurt from yourself to Delta?"

"No. Actually, it makes me angrier. You're right. I need to stop delaying, this is just going to hang over us until I say my piece."

She walks to the window and stares down at the parking lot for a minute and then spins around. "I'm calling my mother and letting her know that we'll be over earlier than we planned last night."

When we arrive back at her parent's house, there's less trepidation walking through the front door than there had been the previous night. I feel as if it's a homecoming of sorts. I've imprinted on this house, I'm no longer an alien to it. Lacey cheerily opens the front door and waves us in. Bob is at the hardware store, she explains, as she gestures for us to follow her into the kitchen where she's canning the excess of a big pot of tomato sauce she'd made for tonight's dinner earlier in the day.

Rachel comments politely on the delicious smelling sauce, and gives her mother a brief cursory hug, but I can see the tightness in her posture. She's like a rubber band that's been stretched taut and I know that at any moment she might either snap or fly.

"Mom, I'm glad we have a little time before Dad'll be back. I had a few things I wanted to talk to you about."

Lacey keeps her eyes trained on the canning task before her and nods silently. I'd have thought that she was completely oblivious to any underlying tension but for the fact her hands grip the jars hard enough that her fingertips have grown white and I'm a little worried she'll shatter the glass itself.

"We have to talk about her mom." Rachel prods. When there's no reply she pushes forward. "You guys really missed out. She was an incredible human being. Everyone who knew her loved her."

Lacey carries a handful of utensils to the sink and begins to vigorously rub them with her bare hands as she rinses them under the faucet stream. Still, she remains silent.

"Mama! Stop. Look at me."

Slowly, Lacey drops the utensils into the deep farm style sink and turns to face Rachel. It's then that I notice the tears in her eyes.

"Mama, you hurt Delta and that hurt me." Rachel repeats, now that she's sure that she has her attention.

For a moment I wonder if Lacey has been permanently struck mute but then she answers in a soft cracking voice, "I know. I regret it so much, I hate that I lost so many years with both of you. I'd do anything to go back in time and do it all differently."

"I just don't understand why. I get it, you don't approve of our lifestyle- whatever that's supposed to mean, but you eventually spoke to me again. Why not her?"

"I think we should go sit down, I'll try to explain whatever I can." Lacey replies, so we follow her into the living room. "When your father found out about your relationship... it was such a shock to both of us. We just had no clue you even liked girls. We'd always pictured you growing up, meeting a nice boy, marrying and having children," she glances at me and blushes, then turns back to Rachel.

"To be honest, I thought maybe it was just a phase and if we left you alone you'd outgrow it. Your father thought that maybe you'd been pressured into it by this older woman."

"Mom, she was 18 years old, I was 17. We were peers." Rachel replies, with a pained expression.

Lacey nods and closes her eyes. "I know that now, but I was struggling to find an answer. You know how I was raised, I couldn't just shut that off. I couldn't accept that God had just made you the way you are. So if it wasn't Delta's fault... then it was somehow mine."

Rachel tries to interrupt, but her mother waves her off and says that she realizes just how wrong she'd been. She'd realized it a long time ago even- but by then it was too late. She knew that Bob could not let go of his feeling of betrayal, even if that feeling was completely unjustified. He'd stubbornly clung to his belief that Delta had violated some magically binding honor oath to the military and her command, and you know how Bob Potts' world was a very black and white place. He may have felt uncomfortable with his daughter's sexuality, but with enough time and distance he could move past that. As ridiculous as it sounded to my ears, he apparently hadn't been able to move past Delta's disrespect of her uniform.

I'd sat silent through the entire exchange, it really wasn't my business. Yet neither woman had asked me to leave or even glanced at me in a way that suggested I wasn't wanted there. Knowing I was crossing a line that I should probably avoid, I'm unable to stay silent. "You guys knew about the cancer, right? You couldn't even find it in yourselves to forgive Delta and reach out then?"

Rachel looks surprised at my interruption, but her mother takes it in stride.

"We did. Rachel hadn't given us a lot of details though. Our conversations over the past twenty years have been all too infrequent and there seemed to be some unspoken agreement between us to just avoid the topic of Delta. Rachel made a few comments here and there about returning from treatment with her, but they'd always been presented in a very calm and reassuring way. We truly had no idea it had progressed to the point it did. Believe me, I regret not being there for either of them during that time, so much. It's not a real defense I know, but I swear, if I'd known it was terminal I would have been there. Then when we got the word that she'd passed away I was so ashamed- I couldn't find the words to express that shame though. Not until now anyway."

She turned back to Rachel and said, "I am deeply ashamed Rachel, and I sincerely apologize for not being there the way a mother should have been there, when you both needed me most. I am so sorry you couldn't depend on me to help out during Delta's hour of need. I would do anything to turn back the hands on the clock and do everything differently."

Rachel's eyes fill with tears and she instinctively glances at the watch on her wrist at her mother's mention of time, and I'm unsurprised when she stands and walks toward the couch. Her mother stands and hugs her and both women stand crying as they embrace. I feel awkward and am all too aware of the fact I'm an outsider to this reunion. I'm not quite sure what to do with myself though so I murmur a comment about going for a little walk and let myself out the front door.

The house stands on the periphery of a golf course and there's a paved walking path around the green. I begin to make my way around the curving path, my mind solidly focused on what I'd just witnessed. Reconciliation. It's hard to know as an observer whether there has been a true substantial and lasting change between Rachel and her mother. By outward appearances though, it looks hopeful. Rachel's mother had hurt her, perhaps unintentionally although she had to have known the pain that her lack of support had caused- but Rachel seems willing to forgive. Is it that simple?

I can't help but compare them to my own mother and myself. If Tessa were suddenly standing before me and she demonstrated the humility and regret that Lacey had shown Rachel- would that be enough to change our lives? Could the thickened scars that criss crossed my soul fade? Could my heart soften toward her? Could I forgive her then?

It's a moot question, I know Tessa doesn't have it in her to be humble or apologetic. She'll never admit to any of the wrongs she'd done, she'll never accept any of the blame for the damage she'd done to me before I ever had a chance to figure things out on my own. If she apologized for every terrible word, every hurtful name, every ostracism, every threat, every pinch, every slap, every lonely day, every alienated night, could I forgive her then? Could I move on with her in my life? I don't think so. That's the crux of it. She's done such a great job at raising me to dislike, even hate, myself- I don't have anything left to do with those feelings other than to mirror them back to her.

Lost in my thoughts, I hadn't realized I'd completed the short loop and am rapidly approaching the turn off that would again lead to Rachel's parent's house until I see the craggy figure standing at the end of their driveway, staring at me.

Cautiously, I wave as I begin to approach him.

"Hello Kenna." Bob says. He sounds slightly weary, as if he's still not quite sure what to make of me.

"Hello Mr, um... Bob." I say, remembering their insistence on first names the day before. It was easy with Lacey, who feels enough like Rachel to me to connect the blood dots, but with Bob there's a formality that emphasizes my otherness.

"I wasn't expecting to see you ladies until later this afternoon. Is Rachel inside?"

"Mmhmm, she's with Lacey having a private conversation. I thought I'd give them some space and enjoy a little walk. This is a beautiful neighborhood you have here."

The effort to sound casual and friendly is difficult. I force myself to look him in the eyes, and keep my body rigor limited to my lower extremities the way I'd so frequently practiced at the office. I know my fake smile is slightly twitchy and hope he doesn't notice. The intensity of his gaze makes me suspect he does though.

He glances toward the house and I know he is torn between wanting to escape my awkwardness and wanting to give his wife and daughter the alone time they clearly need. He sighs, and looks back at me.

"Did you walk the short loop, or the long one?"

"Short I think, it took all of fifteen minutes."

"Let's give it another go." He says, and begins to walk toward the path. I'm momentarily taken aback, I hadn't expected that. Reluctantly, I follow.

At first, we walk silently, not exactly side by side. He's always two steps ahead of me- close enough to see me in his peripheral vision, but far enough to leave no doubt he's in the lead.

"She doesn't usually talk to me, you know?" He says.

"Rachel?" I ask, feeling slightly foolish as soon as I do.

"Yeah, she calls once in a while, if I answer she asks for her mother. The few times she's visited, she doesn't seem to have anything to say to me. Yesterday was the most she's had to say in years."

I'm not sure how to respond. My loyalty lies with Rachel. She doesn't have much to say, that's because if she starts to say everything that's really on her mind to him, it might close that door forever. He slows his pace now and we walked as a pair, side by side. I glance over and try to read his face. It's difficult, he hides his emotions well. Craggy features, grey-green eyes, too many worry lines for a man his age. I wonder what's aged him so much. Was it his family strife or had a lifetime on the sea done that? Maybe both.

My continued silence doesn't seem to unnerve him. He asks, "What about you? I didn't get how long you've been in touch with her."

I count backward and realize with a start it's been just over a week. It doesn't seem possible, but ten days ago I had been someone else entirely.

"Ten days." I say, and he stops abruptly.

"Ten?" He asks, now looking searchingly at my face.

"Yeah, I'm not supposed to be here. This all just kind of happened so fast, out of the blue."

"The parents who raised you..."

"Parent. Mother. It's complicated." I say, simply.

He nods. He understands complicated things.

"My daughter, she's a good woman. She would have been a good mother."

"Yes..." I'm unsure how to respond. It seems to me that a compliment like that belongs to Rachel and is wasted on me.

"How's she really doing?" He asks and I think his voice sounds smaller. I can see the end of the path up ahead and I suddenly stop. He glances at me, his mouth tightens, but he pauses too.

"She's doing, hm, too well some days. She puts on a smile, and goes to work, and stops to chat with everyone she sees. She's working hard not to be a downer, pretending everything is normal and okay. She's incredibly lonely. She's still hurting so much and doesn't let anyone in. She just pretends to. She pretends to be okay."

To his credit, Bob doesn't ask what his own role is in Rachel's stunted grief. He looks down toward his feet and I sense shame in the gesture.

"We offered to come up, you know. Afterwards I mean." He says.

I know what he means, Rachel had mentioned it herself. They'd offered to come to the funeral. Yet still, even now- even with blunt evidence of Rachel's grief in his face, he can't bring himself to actually say Delta's name. His obvious efforts to avoid mentioning it are louder than if he'd shouted her name across the golf course.

"Yeah, she told me. It was a little late then Bob, wasn't it?"

I hadn't meant to be cruel, but as soon as the words are out I hear it. I hear the steel and ice in my voice. The familiarity of my tone, the chill I'd manufactured, I hear it all. My mother's voice. With the realization comes a strange sensation, a swift plunge into vertigo- the world around me shifts quickly and uncomfortably. With a sharp intake of breath, I turn and begin walking quickly toward the house. This time he walks a few steps behind me.

200

Chapter 20

Rachel

The door swung open a little too quickly and Kenna's face was just a little too red as she walked quickly past us and into the kitchen. My father was close at her heels, but she hadn't held the door for him. He didn't look angry though. Bob Potts, the unflappable old man of the sea, looked rattled. I shot him a questioning look.

"Rachel." My father said, by way of greeting. I'd always hated that salutation, it was impossible to decipher. Was it a welcome, or a warning?

"Dad." Two could play at that game.

Kenna was only gone for a moment and then walked back into the room with a glass of water in hand. She didn't raise her eyes to look at any of us directly but I could see she wasn't in any real distress. Maybe she'd just overheated a bit under the midday Carolina sun? Dad offered her the slightest of nods though. A silent acknowledgement that she both read and accepted. I'd pry get the full story out of her after we left. Then, my father dropped his eyes to the floor and began to limp toward the back door. An unexpected hint of frustration bubbled, it'd been building since we first arrived. Did he really think this was it? We were just going to pretend everything was normal now? He owed me more than polite greetings and goodbyes.

"Going to your workshop? I'll join you." I said in a firm voice that left no room for refusal. I'd learned that trick from him.

The corner of Kenna's mouth curled up, just a hint of a crooked smile to encourage me. I didn't dare look at my mother to see her reaction. I knew how much she hated confrontation of any kind- she was undoubtedly hoping that we could spend the entirety of this visit precariously balanced on niceties and polite conversation. If anyone was going to be confronted about unspoken past injuries, she'd prefer it to be her. She would happily do his emotional heavy lifting if it meant ensuring a peaceful home. This was something I'd waited too many years for though and I wasn't going to give in and let go this time, not even to placate my mother.

"Alright." He said simply, still not meeting my eyes as he led the way to the back door.

His workshop smelled of cedar and paint. It was a throwback to many garages and sheds of my youth and it was tempting to let myself indulge in a retreat to happier times with him. Hardboard hung along one wall above a workbench, displaying tools that had been neatly separated and hung. Beneath the work surface were shelves lined with small cans of paint, each label facing outward to display the brand. He'd written the color names and serial numbers in sharpie, in neat capital letters, above each brand name. Shelves and bins along the side walls store various sized cuts of wood and hardware. Everything here was as precise and orderly as the man who now stood at the workbench. Bob Potts' entire life had been built around everything being in its proper place. He functioned best under the rigid auspices of tidy organization. I was the one thing he'd created that hadn't conformed to that expectation.

I watched him pick through a bin of leftover bits of wood. He built beautiful bird feeders that he sold at the local flea market a few times a year in bulk. I could see a long line of miniature houses peeking out from the shelf that was positioned high above the work area. His current work in progress looked to be a miniature barn. As he dug through the excess trimmings, he pulled out several thin pieces that could easily be cut down and sculpted into tiny accouterments that would be affixed to the exterior. I'd watched him hone this craft throughout my childhood. His large, calloused hands would carefully work tiny, delicate pieces of wood. It'd always seemed to me to be an unexpected softness in an otherwise hard man. In those days the birdhouses had been created as gifts, although I realized now that the act itself had surely been his own form of therapy. He didn't talk about the rescue cases that hadn't ended well with me, but

I'd heard enough whispered conversations over the years to understand that they affected him. Working with his hands in a peaceful shop must have been his own form of meditation. These days though, it was for spending money.

Delta paces back and forth in a pair of white cotton underwear and a black Nirvana t-shirt. She's rhythmically running her hands through her hair in frustration, the result being an even wilder mass of curls than usual. She looks as if she's been caught up in a tropical cyclone.

"Chief Daddy has gone too far this time. He does not want to start this fight with me." She says angrily, her Mississippi accent more pronounced than usual.

I cover my face with my hands, this is my worst nightmare. Delta confronting Daddy could only lead to disaster.

"The man is a rock!" She fumes. "I'm nominating your mama for sainthood because I don't know how she manages to sleep beside a giant fucking rock every night."

She's furious about his refusal to sign her leave request. She had tried to explain how much her father needed an extra deck hand. It was the height of the season and both Hawley and Tibedeux had disappeared at the last minute for other jobs. She really only needed two weeks to help him out, but she hadn't had enough leave time on the books. She needed a leave advance, and Chief Potts doesn't believe in borrowing leave. He doesn't believe in it for the crewmembers he actually likes, he sure doesn't believe in it for her. I'm starting to worry about just how angry Delta is though and where this will lead.

"You need to be careful. When you get like this, you don't always control what you say. If he finds out we're still seeing each other it's going to be a lot worse than just denying leave." I caution.

Delta's mouth tightens and she glares for a moment, but she doesn't deny the accusation. She knows she has a big mouth when she's angry.

She walks over to the dresser and picks up the small red and white bird feeder. It'd been designed to look like the station and he'd done a passable job. He hadn't made it for her. I'd stolen it from a stack of other feeders that were stowed in his garage. They were intended to be Christmas gifts, my mother's idea. Gifts for family and close friends. He might eventually notice one was missing but I don't think so. He'll probably never touch them again. My mother handles the holiday stuff after all.

"There's gonna come a day when your Daddy and I have our words." She promises me as she slams the feeder back onto the dresser, breaking the tiny cupola from the carefully constructed roof.

I shook away the memory. I'd waited too long to speak, too many years. Not even Delta could stop me now. "Dad, are we going to keep doing this forever?"

Focused on the task at hand, he continued to look down at the piece he was marking with a hand whittled pencil. For a moment, I wondered if he'd heard me at all but then he replied.

"I guess not."

I stared at his back. He wasn't going to make this easy, I knew that he was still hoping I would change my mind and just walk away from this confrontation. I was emboldened by the discussion I'd had with my mother though and I was tired of holding my tongue. I took a deep breath and plunged ahead.

"She died, Dad. You never made it right with her and she's dead now."

He seemed to freeze then. His shoulders and arms had stopped moving, his back barely moved with each breath.

"I know." He said, and his voice was raspier than usual. "She... she was something special."

"Yeah, she was. Did you ever forgive her Dad? Because you should know... she forgave you. Toward the very end, she even begged me to forgive you. Said you were a stupid, proud, old man but we'd need each other."

He turned to face me. His face was reddened, although not in anger. He was working his jaw, and I realized he was fighting a quivering chin. He didn't speak for a minute as he fought to reign in the emotion that I could see was threatening to erupt. He nodded his head.

"It took me too long, but yup, I did. And I guess I am a stupid, proud, old man. I didn't know how to say it. If she'd called me and asked, I would have told her. I just didn't have it in me to take that step first."

My eyes teared up at the pointlessness of it all. The years, decades really, that had been lost. This was a reconciliation of some kind happening here, but I wasn't sure just how deep it went. There wasn't any way to actually make up for all that had been lost. Nothing that had happened could be undone. The heavy blanket of grief had weakened me though. From the moment my mother had offered, begged even, to come to the funeral I'd fought to keep my righteous anger. Balancing that anger with my grief was exhausting. Now I just craved peace and healing.

"I've missed you Dad, you and Mom both." I admitted.

"We've missed you too, Rachel." He paused and struggled to find the words that he knew I needed to hear. "It hasn't been easy missing you. And your mother, she's had to bear the price for my sins. It's not easy watching that either. There've been too many empty moments. Holidays, the times our friends shared their family stories and pictures, the quiet table, those were the price we've paid. Your Grandma Beanie would have said that it's been our penance."

He wasn't a man I'd ever seen as vulnerable. He hid emotions behind a calm but stern exterior. This was the closest he'd come to letting me in and it was working. The natural empath in me acknowledged and regretted the sadness in him. I wanted to ease his pain and tell him it was over. His penance was paid. I wanted to tell him that I forgave him and that we could move past it and enjoy a happier relationship. I couldn't quite give him that total absolution though. I pictured my beautiful wife. Some transgressions stung so deeply, so thoroughly, they rotted the flesh they touched and ruined mobility forever. He wouldn't ever be able to apologize to Delta, the wound might heal but there would always be a scar. Maybe there could be baby steps though, maybe we could recover some small piece of what family meant. I couldn't give him everything, but I could give him something.

"Dad, I want to try harder. We can't do that though if we pretend she never existed. Delta is a big part of me. She may be gone physically, but she's never going away in here." I said, pointing first at my head and then at my heart.

He nodded. "I understand. I'd like to try though."

And then I walked to him and hugged him and there in his arms I allowed myself to be that little girl again for just a moment- that little girl who adored her father. We both knew this wasn't a complete exoneration. It was something soft though, some hint at reprieve.

When we separated, he turned back to his work bench and without looking at me said, "By the way, I like the girl."

"Kenna?"

"Yeah. She's a good one. I can tell. Has spunk too."

"She is. Honestly, she's far better than she should be." I confessed. When he turned and looked at me questionably, I continued. "Her family life has been complicated. There's a lot of pain there."

He said, "Maybe it's not too late for them either."

Understanding his point, I smiled softly but then shook my head. "Unfortunately I really don't think so, it's different. There isn't any foundation at all for her to lean on. She's been completely beaten down her entire life."

I saw the look of alarm cross his face and I added, "Not physically, not that I know of anyway, although I suppose even that's possible. But emotionally, mentally, the girl has been severely neglected and abused. It turns out I pretty much handed her over to a sociopath."

"You wouldn't have known that then though, right?"

"Not exactly, but I had an inkling. By the time I figured it out, it was too late. I was already pregnant and locked in legally. I chose to ignore my concerns and lied to myself for a lot of years. I'd convinced myself she was out there somewhere- happy and healthy."

"She seems fairly happy and healthy to me." He observed.

I was taken aback for a moment as I realized she had been in good spirits since arriving in Charleston. It was as if the further away from Tessa she was geographically, the more she could breathe. It was delicate though, I knew. The new, freshly painted layer of contentment could be washed away by a light shower. It was going to take more than a few days of freedom from Tessa and the public eye to heal the parts of her that were so badly injured.

"I'm not sure how much of that is what she wants you to see. I think she's working hard right now to convince herself and the rest of the world that she is happier and healthier. Maybe in time it'll even be true. But my gut tells me that she's still in a lot of pain."

He nodded and said, "That gut, it's called parental instinct."

White noise sounded in my ears and I started to deny his words, but stopped myself.

"I have no rights to that. I'm not her mother." I said firmly.

He raised his right eyebrow, the exact mannerism I'd duplicated myself thousands of times. I knew that he thought I was wrong. He stopped short of disagreeing with me out loud though.

"Whatever you are to her, she's lucky to have you." He looked away again and added, "I don't think I'm going to get much work done out there today and I suppose your mother has been in there cooking up an early supper. Let's go see."

I smiled at him and for once I was relieved he was a man of few words. He reached one of his large, knobby knuckled hands out and placed it on my shoulder. Our eyes locked for a moment and he squeezed my shoulder gently. I nodded my understanding and then we walked toward the house together.

The smell of lasagna in the oven permeated the entire house. Kenna and my mother were chopping vegetables for a salad, the younger woman was laughing about something. It was such a domestic scene, it brought a smile to my lips.

"Hey, what's so funny?" I asked.

Kenna held up a piece of red pepper and said, "There was a baby pepper inside it!"

"Oh, yeah that's always fun to find."

"Really? This happens a lot?"

I explained that the more mature the pepper, the more likely the phenomenon was to occur. My mother interrupted and shared that the correct term was carpelloid.

"Ah yes, mom's the master gardener and produce expert." I said.

Kenna said, "I'm going with baby pepper! So cute!"

Mom turned to my father and said, "Bob, I'd love some cucumber for this salad. Would you mind taking Kenna out to the garden and showing her how to pick the ripe ones."

He nodded and motioned toward the door. As soon as they left the house my mom turned and said, "She's a really sweet girl, but that was kind of strange."

"Really? What happened?"

"Nothing bad, but she asked if she could help and when I got out the veggies and said she could prep a salad, she was clueless. Not just about what the inside of a pepper looked like- she didn't know to wash it all first, which knife to use, how to hold the vegetables as she chopped or sliced. Rachel, the child didn't even know how to peel a carrot!"

I wasn't sure whether to laugh or cry at the story. This was exactly the kind of scenario that I was worried about. Kenna was a smart young woman but she was completely unprepared to live independently without a disposable income. I was sure if I asked her how she managed to feed herself in New York, her explanation wouldn't have involved cooking at all. She'd have depended on deliveries and take out. There was no way to explain all of this to my mother though, not without getting into the dangerous territory that would out exactly who Kenna was. Kenna didn't want anyone, not even my parents, to know the details of her background and I would respect that.

"Yeah, she had a very different kind of upbringing. We're working on getting her up to speed on the basics though."

Mom shook her head as she dried her hands on a dishtowel, and unknowingly echoed my father's earlier comment. "Lord, that poor child. I'm glad she has you in her life now."

"I just hope I'm up for the task. It feels like there's so much ground to cover in such a short amount of time. There's no way I'll be able to teach her everything she really needs to know to live independently."

"Oh, I don't know, it seems to me a person doesn't have to know everything at once. None of us are born that way. We pick it all up gradually over a lifetime. I'm 65 years old, and I'm still learning new skills. Just keep dropping the lessons, she'll pick up enough to make it work."

I thought about her words, they rang true. When I'd left home at the age of 18, I'd had a basic foundation in life skills but there had also been a lot to learn along the way. Mom had taught me culinary skills, but I couldn't balance a checkbook. Dad had taught me how to check the oil in the car, but I had no experience dealing with a garage mechanic who wanted to overcharge for services. I did have Delta though and we'd learned together through trial and error. I wished Kenna had someone in her life that she could rely on that way, someone to learn and grow with. She had me now though, and I would do whatever I could to make this transition to independence easier for her. Maybe I couldn't cram in lessons for every life skill right now, but if we could work around Tessa then I could at least remain in her life and answer her questions. I could be her someone.

Chapter 21

Tessa

She lifted the rhinestone embedded reading glasses onto her face and read the investigator's notes for the third time. Rachel Patrick, née Potts hadn't done a whole lot with her life. Rather than taking the overly-generous gift she'd received for incubating Kennedy and investing it smartly, she appeared to have wasted it all. She was a small town librarian in the middle of Nowhere, Pennsylvania. She owned a small cottage, a 13-year-old car, and an embarrassingly small pension fund. She'd apparently married the girl she'd been living with in Connecticut, although the girl had died about six months ago. Tessa remembered her all too well- a short, wild-haired thing that'd had the audacity to sneak into the birthing room before Kennedy was removed despite the clear rules in place about guests.

The investigator had discovered a recently opened LinkedIn account that revealed that she was currently job shopping. That explained a lot, Tessa thought. She was obviously short on funds and anticipated the loss of her job for some reason. She'd contacted Kennedy- Tessa was sure of it although she couldn't prove it yet, as part of a scam. She was looking for a second payday from Tessa, but she would soon discover that Tessa never paid twice for the same merchandise.

She wasn't sure where the pair had run off to now, the last known location was Virginia Beach, Virginia but when the investigator had showed up at the hotel they'd used, he'd been informed they'd left in a hurry without completing their originally booked stay. The clerk hadn't known why they'd left early, but Tessa had an inkling. They'd been given a heads up that someone was on the way to the hotel. She wasn't sure who the spy was, it wouldn't have been Phillip or her long time top assistant,

Allison. It could have been one of the underlings though. She hadn't spoken about the investigation with anyone else, but there were several junior assistants who had regular access to both she and Allison's offices. They could have been snooping and stumbled upon the information. Perhaps she should fire them all and start fresh, just in case.

For now, Kennedy's location was a mystery, but that was fine. Although it wasn't in Tessa's nature to be patient, she couldn't imagine she'd be waiting for long. Eventually, one or both of the pair would be in contact to ask for money. Even if Kennedy wasn't complicit in Rachel's scheme, the small amount of money she'd withdrawn before running off wouldn't carry her much longer. She was a girl who'd been raised to enjoy the finer things in life; she wouldn't be able to stand slumming it forever with her low-rent partner in crime.

Still, it stung to imagine the things the librarian was filling her daughter's head with. Rachel had been a clever young woman, well-spoken for someone who hadn't benefited from the type of education Tessa valued. With age, she'd likely grown shrewder because that's what women did. They suffered the indignities of their softer flesh and weaker bodies with a devil may care public face and grew harder. They learned to use those bodies and soft voices to their advantage. They turned what was once vulnerability, into a weapon. Why would Rachel be any different? Yes, Kennedy was getting an earful.

Her daughter was the exception to the rule. She'd tried to toughen her up, to strengthen her spine, but the girl was hopelessly weak. Even as a small child she'd drooped and withered on the sidelines, a sad plucked dandelion. She'd excelled at nothing and seemed to fear everything. That she'd found the resolve to run away could have signaled an actual spark of something passionate in the girl but Tessa knew that this wasn't true defiance. This was simply the act of Kennedy once again giving into her fears and hiding. Rachel was taking advantage of her weakness but Tessa wasn't going to indulge the pair in their game.

Tessa lowered the glasses again, allowing them to dangle from the chain around her neck, and rubbed her eyes. She really didn't have time for this drama right now. They were getting ready to launch this year's HoHoHoliday line, and the project was always the biggest feat of the year.

Her own show would unveil the new products. The special HoHoHoliday edition magazine would be thicker than usual, and would undoubtedly outsell any other this year. It didn't end there though, she'd also be making the rounds on the morning programs to share the recipes that her lab kitchen had concocted in her signature product line mixing bowls and display stands. Somehow on top of it all, she'd complete four more stops on the Tessa Live! Tour as well.

It was exhausting and some days she wondered if it might be time to scale the empire down. Although Botox and skilled makeup artists helped her look years younger, the fact was she was about to turn 65 and she felt every single one of those years. She tightened her lips, no, slowing down wasn't really an option. Her father had continued to run his businesses until well into his 70s. This was the natural order of things, Allister Shepherd continued to serve several boards, he'd do it until he died, just as his father had before him. Tessa would do the same. This made her think of Kennedy again and the familiar fury filled her. Where had she gone wrong with the girl? Not for the first time, she wondered if the sperm bank had mixed up donor samples and given her the byproduct of a mindless, aimless hack.

She had to get her full focus back on HoHo, and in order to do that, she needed Kennedy to be found and returned and that librarian woman cut from their lives like a cancer. Shaking her head she picked up the phone and dialed the investigator's number.

"I need you to dig deeper. They're paying for gas and hotels with someone's card and if it isn't Kennedy's then it has to be this woman's. I don't care how much you have to pay and what rules you need to break, get a trace on her spending and find her that way."

She hung up without waiting for a response and rubbed her eyes again.

Chapter 22

Kenna

We've spent five nights in Charleston and we're both ready to move on. I hadn't wanted to be the one to bring it up because I didn't want to rush Rachel. I'm happy that she's clearly made progress with her parents, but I'm eager to see where the interstate takes us next. I'd thought about bringing it up casually, but couldn't find a way to just work it into conversation gracefully. Rachel had solved my dilemma by suggesting at dinner last night that it was time to hit the road again.

What I hadn't expected was the flood of emotion I felt when we said goodbye to Bob and Lacey. Rachel felt it more keenly than me. I'm not sure that she'd come to complete peace with her parents, but they had clearly reached an enviable place of compromise. There were long hugs and tears in eyes and promises to reconnect much sooner "next time." Maybe that was to be expected, they were her parents, after all. The real surprise was how deeply saying goodbye affected me. Bob put his hand on my chin and gently raised my face to look him in the eye. He said firmly, "You always have a port in the storm here."

I was touched, I know he's not a man who offers gentleness easily. I've softened one of his harsh edges and in turn he's made me feel welcome and wanted. When I turn to Lacey, the real tears begin to roll. She's smiling at me so tenderly and earnestly, I'm able to pretend for a moment that she's my real grandmother. A stab of regret strikes me, were we making a mistake by leaving? She draws me into her arms and says quietly in my ear, "We love you, Kenna."

I have no clue how to respond to that. No one has ever said those words to me before. I've never considered that I might actually be lovable.

I don't know what the correct response is. I'm unsure if it's expected for me to repeat the sentiment back to her, but that feels too awkward. I settle on, "Thank you so much for everything."

She puts her hands on my cheeks and looks directly into my eyes, "You come back sometime, dear."

I'm afraid to speak, afraid that in just a few weeks I regress in my mother's control and be someone unrecognizable to Lacey. I won't come back at all. I'm saved from the awkward moment by Rachel who swoops in and grabs my arm.

"I'm sure you guys will see her again." She says confidently and I'm strengthened by the conviction in her voice. It makes me feel hopeful. Finally, wiping tears, we make our way to the car. As we pull away from the little house, Bob stands by Lacey's side, one arm around her waist and they wave sadly.

On the ride back to the hotel, we don't speak about the painful goodbye. Words aren't needed, it's clear we're both feeling emotionally exhausted. Instead, we deflect and begin to talk about the long ride ahead.

"It's about 12 hours with no stops..." Rachel warns.

"If we split the drive, that's not too bad."

Rachel seems unconvinced and suggests that we keep our plans flexible. We won't reserve a room ahead of time for Key West, we'll give ourselves the freedom to arrive in one day or two. That way, if we see an interesting place to stop along the way we can stop and explore it. This way, we won't be beholden to driving it straight through.

"Look at you, Ms. Flexible! You're not as glued to the clock now." I comment.

Her cheeks flush and she replies, "I guess not. Was it so obvious before?"

I laugh, "It was kind of hard to miss. It seemed as if you thought you might keel over if you were a minute late on your schedule."

She admits, "It's been a thing. I've always been very punctual-growing up in a military family will do that to you. But honestly, it's gotten much worse in recent years. I think it was that great invisible clock that I always felt hovering over Delta. Suddenly every minute, every second, mattered more than ever. The truth is I've been feeling a little imprisoned lately by my watch. Having to be flexible on this trip, it's been good for me."

"That makes perfect sense. I'm glad you're relaxing a little with it. So maybe our start doesn't have to be too early tomorrow?"

She laughs and says, "Nope, not budging on that. I'll always be a morning person!"

I playfully groan, but agree that it would probably be for the best to start early.

When morning comes, we go about the now familiar routine of loading up the car and settling our account. I've decided to take the first driving leg, I've come to appreciate the surge of control that strikes when I get behind the wheel with Rachel at my side. My own mother has never ridden as a passenger in my car. My driving instruction hours had been handled by a professional, something I hadn't minded at all. I can only imagine how stressful it would have been if she'd been by my side, barking orders and criticizing my every move. I rarely found myself in a car with my mother in recent years, on the occasions I did it was always with a private driver at the wheel.

We hit the highway and I tune into an upbeat pop station. Lacey had handed off a few well-read paperbacks and Rachel is almost immediately nose deep into a romance book that features a shirtless man in pirate costume on the cover. It strikes me as ironic, given her orientation.

"You read male-female romances?" I ask incredulously.

"Sure! Why not?"

"I thought that if you weren't interested in men, you wouldn't be interested in those."

"It's men I'm not interested in, not books. I read about all sorts of things I can't personally relate to. Give me a good story, and I don't care. Don't give me that look- yes, it's a trashy romance novel, but the story itself is actually pretty good. The main protagonist is actually a really strong woman; she's disguised as a pirate to avenge her father's death. What she doesn't know yet is that she's going to fall in love with the seemingly villainous pirate leader. It'll turn out that he's quite redeemable. I'm sure at some point he'll save a boatful of kittens or something- but it's a fun story nonetheless."

I laugh and tell her to go back to her pirate. There has been an awful lot of talking in my life lately and I'm content to just hum along with the radio. I embrace the widening gulf between this car and New York and allow a surge of freedom to wash over me. With each mile marker that we pass, a weight that's been bearing on my shoulders for almost 21 years, grows lighter. Soon I'll be floating.

After almost six hours on the road the gas gauge needle is pointing more south than west. I tell Rachel and she studies a map on her phone. On her suggestion, I agree that stopping a few miles ahead in Cocoa to refuel and grab lunch sounds good. I'm ready for a little break. The sun overhead feels as if it's frying me through the windshield. Already, we've crossed that invisible line where the sun beating down on the car shifts from being barely perceptible to nearly roasting us.

After pulling over, Rachel volunteers for the chore of pumping gas- while I go inside the station to grab a couple of water bottles. Opening the drink cooler, I allow myself to linger for a moment- enjoying the chill that emanates from it. Just as I turn around, I hear a voice quietly say, "'Scuse me, Miss?"

Standing before me is a young man who looks to be in his late teens or early twenties. He wears a filthy baseball shirt that doesn't fit correctly, my guess is that it isn't his, especially considering the baggy jeans he wears on the bottom. He's well-tanned and smells of stale cigarette smoke and body odor. What strikes me the most are his eyes. They're a deeper, darker blue than my own and they looked so weary. The bags under and heavy lids above hint at an exhaustion that belongs to a much older man. Instinctively, I default to my normal terror at a stranger addressing me. It pulses through my core for a moment but this time as my eyes scan the scene around me and outside the window, I can see Rachel still standing beside the car at the pump. I take a deep breath, and reply, "Yes?"

He looks down at his well-worn gray sneakers and says, "Miss, do you have a few dollars to spare so I can get some water and something to eat? Been walking since Jacksonville."

I remember passing through Jacksonville several hours before. Taken aback I ask, "Walking? That must have taken you all day."

"Twelve days actually." He corrects. "Trying to get to Melbourne, I think maybe two more days and I'll make it."

Twelve days, this man has been walking for twelve days in this heat. I can't comprehend it. My curiosity grows and I can't stop myself from asking, "Why? What's in Melbourne?"

"My sister. It's been a rough few years, she told me I could come to her when I was ready though and she'd help me make things right. Her husband has a job for me and they have the space but didn't want me there around the kids until I was ready. Been clean now for almost six months, I think I'm ready now."

I hand him one of the cold bottles of water and he drinks eagerly from it. I can see the clerk eyeing us and I give a little motion to indicate I'd be up to pay for it shortly. He doesn't stop watching though from his perch near the door.

"Don't you think she'd have come for you if you called?" I ask.

"Probably. I didn't want that though. I wanted to go to her, to show her I could. I need to show her I really want this."

I don't know his story. I don't know the story of any of the anonymous faces I see and pass every single day of my life. Sometimes though, I get an idea. The broken child in me instinctively recognizes when I pass a kindred spirit. A silent choir of broken children walking the streets of New York... Florida... wherever. Usually, we never hear each other's voices. Today, I want to hear more. I point to the register and say, "I need to pay for this stuff, why don't you follow me and I'll hook you up for lunch."

He looks embarrassed, but nods and follows me. Maybe he's recognized me too. The man at the register scans my items while keeping a wary eye on the stranger next to me. Affecting an air of bravado that I don't actually feel, I turn to the stranger and ask, "What's your name anyway? I'm Kenna."

That earns a tiny hint of a smile. "Kenny," he replies.

"Actually, Kenna. And you?"

"Kenny."

Now I'm starting to feel slightly annoyed. Was he making fun of my name? I know it's unconventional, but I'm trying to help him out. He could be a little cooler about it. "No, it's Kenna, not Kenny. Is that a problem?"

"No, Miss, what I'm saying is my name is Kenny."

At that, we both start laughing. I'm lost in the moment and miss the sound of the door opening until I feel a hand on my elbow. Turning, I smile at Rachel.

"Everything okay?" She asks, as she eyes the man beside me.

"Mmhm," I reply. "This is Kenny... and he's been out for a long walk. We're taking him to lunch."

She looks taken aback and narrows her eyes on the scruffy body at my side. I know exactly what she sees, it's what I'd seen at first too.

"Kenna..."

"Yes?" I say, sticking my chin up defiantly.

She shakes her head and pokes my arm with a finger, "Er Kenna, I don't think..."

I interrupt and reply, "Kenny needs to feed his dog and we're going to help him."

Ignoring both his confused look and her annoyed one, I lead the way through the door toward the car. A Dairy Queen is on the opposite corner, and I motion toward it. "Kenny, we're not putting you in this car buddy, but meet us across the street at that Dairy Queen."

Inside the car Rachel asks, "Have you lost your mind? It's fine to help someone in need, but we could have just handed him a few dollars and been on our way."

"Look, I know this may seem crazy, but I like him. He's been through a lot and he's on this incredible journey. You're going to have to hear it straight from him. You'll get it. I promise."

I glance in the rearview mirror to see if the young man has followed us as instructed. He'd grabbed what looked to be a nearly empty backpack from the sidewalk in front of the gas station and was now jogging behind us toward the street crossing. His pace slowed as we paused at the parking lot exit, and he watched cautiously. I realize he probably wonders if I've been lying or have maybe reconsidered. I am sure it wouldn't have surprised him at all if I threw on the turn signal and beat it for the highway ramp.

When a break in traffic appears though, I drive across the four lane road into the Dairy Queen parking lot as promised. He runs in behind us. I pretend I don't notice the relief on his face as we exit the car. I can sense his reluctance at being seen as too poor. Too needy. Too tired. Too weak.

Soon, we're settled at a shaded picnic table outside with bags of food and large milkshakes. I'm not sure when he's last eaten but it's been awhile judging by how quickly he stuffs the food into his mouth. After devouring a burger and most of a chicken sandwich, he slows down enough to look around. Seeing our eyes on him, a slow blush creeps up his face and he grabs a napkin to wipe his mouth.

"Sorry, I guess I was really hungry." He admits.

"It's okay, but can you tell Rachel your story?" I ask.

He shares the basics as he had done with me in the gas station, but well sated and more relaxed now, he gives more details. He's 22 years old and originally from the Orlando area. He doesn't speak about his parents and I don't press for details. I understand how that goes. He does talk about his siblings though. He was the youngest of four children. The oldest child, his sister Marie, is the one who got out. A bright and determined girl, she'd made it through high school and two years of community college and then married a nice guy with an HVAC certification. They had two kids, moved to Melbourne where business is booming and they're enjoying the beach life these days.

At about the same time Marie had started seriously dating her husband, Kenny's closest brother in age was introducing both Kenny and the oldest brother to a newly discovered love. Oxycodone. The mountain had always been stacked against them, he explains, but if he was ever to pinpoint when the rockslide began, that would have been the moment. Things spun out of control for all three boys. His oldest brother Pete died of a fentanyl overdose first. Then Marie left town and with her went the only healthy relationship in his life. Billy, the brother who'd first brought opioids into their lives, couldn't live with the guilt of Pete's death.

Eighteen months earlier, he had died of a not so accidental overdose. That left Kenny alone in Orlando.

With nothing to keep him there, he'd migrated to Jacksonville with a friend who had a pipe dream about opening a skate shop. His friend came from a more financially comfortable family and had a small nest egg saved that he hadn't been able to touch until he turned 21. As soon as he reached the legal age, he cashed it in and they headed for Jax with big dreams. The reality though, was that they blew through it all within a matter of weeks. Long before they ever found a space or inventory, they'd snorted and swallowed every penny. The friend took off, presumably back to Orlando, and Kenny hasn't heard from him since.

Desolate and now homeless, Kenny reached out to the only person left in his life who he knew would give a damn- his sister Marie. She was horrified to hear about his living situation and had begged him to go into treatment. When he pointed out his lack of health insurance, she'd vowed to help as much as possible financially but he wouldn't allow himself to take money from her babies' mouths. Instead, he promised to kick it on his own if he could come to her. Having already watched two brothers die from the epidemic, Marie couldn't watch a third go down that same path. She insisted that he had to be clean before he came to her.

"I didn't get clean right away. I kept using for maybe six more months- every day, I'd tell myself, 'okay today you do whatever you want and tomorrow is a new start. Tomorrow you have a new life.' The problem was, tomorrow kept getting pushed back. Then, one day I got into it with someone and found myself waking up in a hospital bed with a broken collarbone and nose. The nurse came in to give me meds and I don't know how or why but I looked at her and said, 'No, thanks.'"

The weary doctor he'd been assigned had been sympathetic but skeptical. Using the argument that withdrawals could put him at imminent risk of severe physical injury or death, the doctor had been able to place him in a bed for three days. Afterward, he walked out of the hospital and into a shelter where he managed to stay clean for the next five months with the help of Narcotics Anonymous and his sister's promise. That was when he reached out to Marie again and she'd offered to come get him.

"I didn't want that though. I wanted to come to her. I wanted to prove to myself I could do it. I thought about panhandling enough to buy a bus ticket but then I got to thinking about this movie, the documentary kind, we'd had to watch back in high school about some place in Spain where people walk hundreds of miles on a pilgrimage. They come from all over the world for this walk, and at the end they fall on their knees and you'd see these grown men crying real tears. At the time I thought it looked kind of stupid to be honest, but now I couldn't get it out of my head. I wanted that feeling, like I'd just walked a pilgrimage. So I started walking."

By the time he finishes his story, Rachel and I are both staring, entranced. She looks at me and nods her appreciation. I'd made the right decision.

"We'll be going through Melbourne, it's right off 95 right?" She asks.

He nods and I rush in, "Oh yeah! We could drop you off!"

He looks at both of us, one at a time and then turns back toward the road. After a few moments of silence he says, "I appreciate the offer Miss Rachel and Miss Kenna..." causing me to laugh out loud at the polite address.

He grins then and I can see even with his urgent dental needs, he could be handsome.

"Really, I do appreciate it. But I think I'm just going to keep on walking. I think I need to see this all the way through."

I nod in understanding. I know something about needing to finish a journey.

Chapter 23

Rachel

Our original intention had been to drive the entire 750 miles from Charleston to Key West in one fell swoop. It had been an ambitious plan. It's not that I particularly enjoy being compressed into a small car for twelve hours straight, but I truly was that eager to get back to a place I love. Thankfully, the two-hour detour we'd taken at a picnic table with Kenny had derailed that plan. Now, after having spent a night at a roadside motel just outside of Miami, I realized that we would have missed the very best part of the trip if we'd completed the journey on the previous evening. The Seven-Mile Bridge from Marathon to the lower Keys offered an unparalleled scenic view- one that could only be appreciated in daylight.

The water that surrounded us was a surreal turquoise, a rich fantasy color dreamt up with a child's crayon and imagination. That it might actually be real defied the laws of nature. Kenna had seen beautiful beaches before. Yet even she was momentarily silenced by the brilliance that surrounded us. Like me, she stared wide eyed at the marine landscape that challenged the beauty of the sky that reached down to touch it. Shades of blue dominated from all directions, dancing, oscillating, competing, as far as the naked eye could see.

"I had no idea," the younger woman murmured. "No idea at all that we could see this, right here in the States."

"It's been a long time since I've been on this road. Delta and I did the drive maybe ten years ago, and I remembered the beauty of it but in my memory it was never this... startling!"

"Was that your first visit back since childhood?" Kenna asked.

"Yes. To be honest, going back hadn't been particularly nostalgic. We hadn't gone to the Navy base, we'd focused on a part of Key West that I hadn't spent much time at as a child. Duval Street. Key West was quite the different experience as a grown woman with a license to drink."

Kenna laughed out loud at that. "I doubt you did all that much drinking."

"No, really. It was a fantastic getaway, but I'm surprised we were able to go home with our livers intact. There's something in the island air that just kills your normal inhibitions and precautions."

"You know what I see over there?" There's a slight slur to her words.

I squint and study the action on the sidewalk across the street. I've had more to drink this evening than I've ever had at one time in my life and everything is just a bit blurry.

"I don't know? Do you mean that guy dancing by himself? Or the shoeless woman who is smoking a suspicious looking pipe?"

Delta leans in with a very serious expression, until her eyes are just inches from mine and with a dropped, secretive voice she replies, "No... I see another bar."

With a loud whoop she begins to cross the street and I groan, chasing after her.

"We've had a lot already, maybe we should seriously take a break...."

Delta turns and quips, "We'll take a break after I dance on a tabletop somewhere. Until then... we're gonna drink like Coasties!"

I smiled at the memory and another thought hit me. "This is going to be one heck of a place to turn 21, Kenna!"

"Oh man, I actually forgot about my birthday the past few days. Ha, well don't have any crazy expectations, I've been sipping champagne at boring parties since childhood. I'm pretty restrained."

"In all seriousness, so am I." I admitted with a shrug, "I'm a fan of not feeling like poo in the morning." Kenna chuckled at that and a comfortable silence filled the car as we continued to enjoy the scenery.

I snuck a quick glance at Kenna. She'd rested her head against the passenger window and although I couldn't tell if her eyes were open or closed behind her large, tortoiseshell sunglasses, she was calm and relaxed. It was a peacefulness she'd been slipping more deeply into as each day passed. With each mile I felt more hopeful that there was a life for Kenna beyond the gilded prison that Tessa had consigned her to. The tranquility of my thoughts was interrupted by a loud pop, followed by a stomach turning silence from the old Saturn.

I instinctively hit the brakes and tried to steer toward the road shoulder but quickly discovered that the steering mechanism didn't seem to work either. Kenna was now sitting upright with a death grip on the handle above her door.

"Shit!" I muttered, as the car glided toward the guardrail beyond the shoulder where it mercifully made contact with the softest of touches. For a moment, we sat and stared straight ahead in stunned silence.

"Uh..." Kenna said cautiously. I closed my eyes, still reeling from the experience. Had that really just happened?

I opened the door and she followed my example. Kenna bit her nails nervously as I surveyed the road. The shoulder was wide enough that we were fairly protected from any passing traffic. I walked to the front of the car and inspected the small dent and scratch that the impact with the guardrail had caused. It didn't look serious enough to invest any funds into correcting. I was much more worried about what had gone wrong under the closed hood. I walked back around and pulled the hood lever to open it. Kenna and I then peered in to look at the engine. It was at this point that I admitted, "I have no clue what I'm looking at here. I don't suppose you've been hiding some secret mechanical savant ability?"

Kenna shook her head and said, "No, this is what OnStar is for."

At my cocked eyebrow, Kenna continued, "AAA?"

Still no vocal response, and Kenna threw her hands in the air. "Really? Now what?"

She was looking beyond me and suddenly exclaimed, "Oh my god, look! We're saved!"

I saw the minivan she was pointing to on the horizon, heading in the direction of Key West. I yelled, "Yes!" and as it neared I began to wave enthusiastically. Then, just as quickly as it had approached us, it was driving away from us. A small face in the backseat window staring curiously and a tiny hand lifted in a return wave. Then it was too far away to see the tiny face anymore.

"Seriously? Did that really just happen?" Kenna asked.

I cursed silently and reached into my pocket for my phone. I had a pretty good idea of what was going to happen next. I opened and held it up- and discovered that just as I had feared there was no signal. I thought about our predicament and remembered Kenny and his carless journey. I'd had enough standing around and feeling helpless.

"We passed through Cudjoe Key maybe ten miles ago, there were a few businesses back there although I don't remember seeing a garage... I think we're about fifteen miles out from Key West. We're at a crossroads and need to figure out which way to start walking. I don't think we should just sit here in this car, it's going to be 500 degrees in there soon."

Kenna shook her head and looked both directions before she sighed and said, "The whole point is not to go backward right now. Let's just start walking toward Key West. Maybe someone will come along and help us."

Just as we started walking, I heard the sound of engines and turned to see a pair of motorcycles gaining on us. Like the van, they flew right by. They had to have seen us, yet they hadn't even slowed down. Next, it was a red sports car. Then a half dozen other vehicles that were equally uninterested in us. Did they all think we were out for a leisurely stroll?

We hadn't walked far before it became clear just how foolish our attempt was. The sun overhead was merciless, there wasn't a cloud in the sky to blunt its sear and I was absolutely not in the right shape to undergo a trek in those conditions.

"I can't believe this." I muttered. "The damned luck of this happening here and now. Unbelievable."

Kenna didn't reply right away but she said grumpily, "I'm just saying, OnStar would be handy right about now. They find you anywhere. Haven't you seen those commercials where the car is in a ditch on the side of some remote mountain and help is on the way?"

As beads of sweat rolled down my temples and the wheeled suitcase behind me refused to fully cooperate on the sun-warped roadside, I fought to restrain myself.

"And once again Kenna, were you planning to buy me a newer model car? How about paying the monthly service fee for that? And then-" I gestured wildly toward the wide expanse of open ocean that surrounded us, "Were you going to arrange for a helicopter to fly right in with a tow truck dangling from a wire?"

The restraint attempt hadn't worked so well. But I was hot and fed up. I'd meant to replace that damned car a hundred times before. It had almost 200,000 miles on it and had been beaten down over the years on our many road trips. Even before Delta's death, it had been in the plans. Somehow though, I'd always convinced myself there was life left in it and that it would be better to trade it in later. Frugal to a fault, Delta would say.

"Sorry, I know I sound like a brat. I'm just hot, and my feet are killing me." Kenna complained. I knew without looking that the girl was still wearing those ridiculous black booties. They were completely inappropriate for this tropical climate. When we finally, if we finally, got into town I was going to insist on Kenna buying a cheap pair of flip flops to replace them.

We'd made very little progress because neither suitcase was handling the road well. Kenna still wore her backpack and had the guitar slung behind one shoulder and that wasn't helping the speed of our journey either. Then, as my suitcase hit yet another lull in the road, it lurched and I yelled in frustration as a wheel popped off.

"Dammit! Now what am I going to do?"

Kenna lowered herself into a squat, dropped the gear from her back, and wiped sweat from her beet red face with her t-shirt. "We're going to die out here." She observed, pointing at an actual buzzard flying overhead.

At the sight of the buzzard, I couldn't help it. I burst out laughing. Kenna gave me a cross look at first, but then joined me. We were bent over laughing tears when the pick-up truck suddenly appeared on the horizon.

"Oh my god, make him stop!" I yelled. This time we were taking no chances. We both ran into the center of the road and waved our hands wildly.

An old blue Chevy truck rolled to a stop and we cheered. Kenna stopped first and turned to me, whispering, "What if he's a serial killer?"

I pointed to my broken suitcase and said, "Good. Then our misery will be over soon."

The sound of a car door interrupted us and we watched as a bearded young man walked toward us. It was difficult to gauge his age, he hadn't begun noticeably graying yet, but the laugh lines at the edge of his eyes suggested he probably wasn't just some college kid.

"I take it that was your car I passed a mile back?" He asked.

"Maybe," I said, "Although I could have sworn it was about 50 miles..."

He grinned at that, and I realized he was a handsome guy beneath all that facial hair. When I glanced at Kenna, it was obvious she'd noticed too. This was the first time I'd seen that particular look on her face and I liked it. At her age, she should be noticing when a good looking man, or woman if the wind had blown that way, crossed her path. This was one of the more normal reactions to a stranger that she's ever demonstrated.

"I'm Jack," he said, reaching a hand out that I shook. I introduced myself and then he turned to Kenna.

"Kenna." She said, and I knew the pleasant tinge on her cheeks as he took her hand wasn't just from the harsh sun.

"I'm heading into town if you need a lift. I can recommend a tow company to send for your car."

"Town? Key West?" I asked.

He laughed at that. "Yep, not much by way of towns between here and there, just ten miles of mostly nature preserve, some houses and a small naval air station."

Kenna and I looked at each other, and I glanced back at my broken suitcase. With a sigh, I said, "Alright, we appreciate it."

As soon as I opened the passenger door of the quad cab a blast of cold air hit me. Any hesitancy I might have felt melted away instantly. They'd have to peel me out of this truck.

"Thank god," Kenna muttered from the backseat.

As we began the ride, Jack asked where we were staying. I explained proudly that we'd been on a road trip and were playing it by ear. No rigid schedules for these women, no siree! This was all about learning to be spontaneous and adventurous. We figured we'd find lodging once we got into town.

"Any recommendations? We're not looking for fancy, just clean and as inexpensive as possible." I said, thinking again about the broken down car. That was certainly an expense I hadn't planned on and our budget was going to be tighter than ever.

Jack dashed my hopes when he said, "I hate to break it to you, but summer is over. Rooms are hard to find, and I don't think there's anything in the Conch Republic that's going to qualify as inexpensive."

I swallowed hard, the truth was that I hadn't really thought out this part of the trip as well as I should have. I'd been seduced by the whole whimsical, impetuous nature of this journey. It hadn't occurred to me that we might get to a destination and not have an affordable option. I glanced back at Kenna worriedly.

Before I could vocalize my concern, Kenna said in a heavy, quiet voice, "it's okay."

"How so," I asked.

"I'm going to just call her." She said.

We both knew who the her in question was; Jack looked confused though. I was just about to voice my absolute veto to that plan when he interrupted with his own idea.

"I might have a solution for you ladies," he said.

I felt uneasy as soon as he said that. It was bad enough that we were his captives until we reached the town, he seemed nice enough but if he suggested that we shack up at his place then I'd know for sure he had a screw loose. If he did that, I might just open the car door at 50 MPH and scream for Kenna to follow suit.

"It so happens I have an extra room. It's nothing special, but it has a queen bed and I'm sure I can find an air mattress."

"No, thanks," we said in unison.

He lifted a hand from the wheel and pretended to smack himself in the forehead. "I don't mean at my house, I probably should have opened with that. I own a bar on the strip and we've got a few rooms above it. I usually give them to music acts that come down, right now I have a free one. I don't think I'll be double booked again for a while, it's rare that both are occupied at once."

"Wow, that's quite a generous offer. What's your going rate?" I asked.

"I guess I don't really have one, I mean, it's usually just part of the package to draw performers down here. Make me an offer!"

"We can do that!" I said enthusiastically.

We'd hit the southernmost Key and the civilization that came along with it. A weathered and industrial looking area morphed into something much more appealing. As we rolled slowly through town and made the turn into the heart of the city, we stared out at the vibrant color and perpetual motion that was Duval Street. Crowds of vacationers, cruise passengers, and locals milled about the sidewalks. Jack lowered our windows and we could hear live music pouring onto the street from every open bar door we passed. It was as if a wild carnival had descended onto the end of the world.

"Oh my god, this is..." Kenna began.

"Amazing." I finished.

"Amazing. The music, the bright colors, the people. How have I never heard of this before?"

Jack laughed incredulously and asked, "You've never heard of Key West? Where are you from? Another planet?"

"Something like that," She admitted and added, "I mean sure, I've heard the name of the town before, something about Ernest Hemingway I think and I'm sure I've seen a reference to it and a hurricane before. But I grew up in a very different kind of place, and this was not on our usual vacation destination list. This is not at all what I expected."

Jack chuckled as he maneuvered the truck into a side alley between buildings and then said, "This is us!"

He jumped out and grabbed my broken suitcase, Kenna and I shifted the rest of the gear between us and we followed him toward the noise and wonder of the main street. He pointed to a doorway on the left and said proudly, "Jack and Jett's".

"Who's Jett?" Kenna asked.

"My Dad. When I left the tech world I had a little nest egg but property prices here are as crazy as you can probably imagine. My Dad had sold a large parcel of family land back in Idaho and invested soundly. We'd been coming here annually since I was a kid and he was willing to cash it all in to finance this dream for me. I send him a check every month and he comes down a few times a year to enjoy the fruits of his investment. He's pretty hands-off though, it's my monster."

As we entered the building, a blast of air conditioning offered cool relief from the heat that had threatened to overwhelm us earlier. A short, stocky woman behind the bar looked up and said, "Hey Jack." She eyeballed Kenna and I, then narrowed her eyes at the suitcase in his hand and asked, "Who do we have here?"

"Shannon, this is Rachel and Kenna. They're going to be staying with us for a little while in the B room."

Her forehead furrowed as she studied us, making it clear that this was not a regular occurrence.

"Nice to meet you!" I said as enthusiastically as possible. Kenna said something as well but no one could hear it because at exactly that moment the band on the small stage in the back began their next number. The crowd that occupied the dining tables and bar stools went wild with applause.

Jack motioned for us to follow him and he led us through a door that had been labeled, Employees Only. Behind it, there was a door marked as an office to the left and a hallway straight ahead that led to a kitchen, storage room, and the narrow stairway to the second story accommodations. Upstairs, there were only two doors to choose from. Jack explained that a visiting act is staying in Room A, but that they probably wouldn't be around much as they'd paired the gig with a fishing trip. Opening the door to Room B, we found a modest-sized bedroom with its own bathroom. A queen sized bed dominated the room but there was room for a twin size air mattress on the floor beneath the window. A few posters displaying local scenes were framed and hung around the room, but it was otherwise a plain utilitarian space. The air conditioning worked well, the bathroom looked clean, and the window overlooked the fun chaos of Duval Street.

I smiled, "This will work, thank you so much."

Jack grinned and said, "There's one big problem with these rooms I should warn you about, I hope you don't mind the floor shaking from the music all through the night. Right now it may not seem bad, but picture this when you're exhausted at 2 am."

Kenna laughed, "At this price, I think we can manage!" and I nodded my agreement.

"Okay, ladies, feel free to come and go at will. Here's the room key, it's safe up here but I'm a believer in locks." He glanced at his watch and said, "There's only about 30 minutes until sunset. I suggest you get down to Mallory Square because you won't want to miss that. You're not going to reach a tow truck tonight, so you can take care of the car tomorrow."

I nodded, remembering the sunset experience quite well. "Absolutely, Kenna, you are going to love this!"

Soon, we were walking toward the end of Duval where crowds had already gathered. As we emerged from behind the buildings that had initially blocked the view, Kenna gasped at the scene. There, a few thousand people were crammed into a waterfront area that was the size of a few city blocks. They stood in groups cheering on performers of every imaginable ilk. There were the standard street buskers playing their songs. But there were also fire dancers, trainers showcasing dog tricks, magicians, acrobats, unicyclists, skateboarders, plate jugglers- all performing to admiring, jovial crowds that eagerly threw dollar bills into awaiting hats and jars.

"Oh my god." Kenna said.

"Isn't it glorious?" I asked, with a sigh. Then I turned and pointed toward the water. "Don't forget to watch that show too."

The sun hung mere inches above the water's surface, illuminating it into a brilliant sphere of oranges and golds. A large sailboat crossed the orb and was momentarily silhouetted, a perfect black cut out of a sailing vessel suspended in time and space. As the cacophony of

234

competing musicians and the crowds of observers behind us reached crescendo, we stood transfixed. We watched as the sun seemingly melted into the sea. I instinctively reached over and took Kenna's hand, then held my breath at the moment of climax as the brilliance dissipated into a softer, more subdued palette of coral and pink. I looked at Kenna and saw the tears in her eyes. I understood they weren't sad tears, they celebrated all that was good and lovely in the world.

Chapter 24

Kenna

The smell of new vinyl wafts through the thin sheet and I shift awkwardly on the air mattress. I'd insisted Rachel take the bed so that she could get some much needed sleep, but I'd ended up spending the night paranoid that the sound of my constant tossing and turning on the air mattress was disturbing her. My restlessness isn't so much the result of being uncomfortable- although there is a bit of that. The bigger issue is my mind continuously replaying everything I'd experienced the night before. I'd never have admitted it to Rachel or Jack, because they would have thought it either ridiculous or pitiful, but it had been the best night of my life.

Daytime in Key West had been a tropical kaleidoscope of pastel painted buildings, bright Hawaiian shirts, red faced tourists carrying cheery fruit-filled drinks, and an impossibly bright sun overhead. Nighttime had brought with it an entirely other sort of brilliance. Neon lights, brightly lit storefronts, and the omnipresent glowing ends of lit cigarettes, cigars, and joints worked in tandem with sounds of music and laughter to illuminate the small town.

I'm not convinced that I'd have a hard time getting a drink in the party town, but I'd decided to honor tradition by waiting out the final two days of my twentieth year before asking to be served. Instead, we had spent the evening strolling the sidewalks, perusing art galleries, and indulging in frozen key lime pie on a stick before heading back to Jack's place. Inside, we'd found a packed room enjoying a Tom Petty sing-along starring an older man who expertly fingered his electric guitar. There hadn't been any open tables, but we'd found a small counter top in the corner that could hold our sodas and enough floor room to stand and sway with the crowd.

The entire scene was raucous and yet it was somehow the most appealing place I'd ever been. The noise and inebriation of the crowd didn't intimidate me- instead I'd found it easy to blend in and become part of them. We were one living, breathing, writhing organism; we were no longer distinct and apart.

My entire life, I'd felt different and alone. Something fundamental had shifted. I knew no one here except Rachel and yet I was one of the crowd. We were one orchestra and I was a proud section member. Like everyone else in that room, a true hodgepodge of age, race, and style, I had belonged.

"Hey, there!" a voice yelled over the noise. Turning, I'd smiled when I saw Jack.

"Hey! This is great!" I yelled back. Rachel tapped my shoulder, smiled, and motioned toward the bathroom. Jack moved in to fill the small gap she'd left and soon he was singing the lyrics along with the rest of us. When the song had ended and the singer announced he was taking a break and would be back shortly, I turned to Jack.

"Isn't he great?" Jack had asked and I'd nodded enthusiastically.

"Everything about this place is incredible! If it's like this on a random Tuesday night, I can't imagine it on a weekend."

He laughed and said, "Believe it or not, every day is a weekend here in season. You notice the flux of day a little more in summer when tourism is slightly down but generally- this is it. Every day is a party in Key West."

"How did you end up down here anyway? You mentioned you were in the tech industry?"

He'd smiled and confessed, "I like to pretend that never happened, let people think I'm just a lucky beach bum who was born and raised here. But nah, I'm originally from eastern Washington state, right on the Idaho border. My father is a huge sports fisherman and we'd fly down to the keys every year during my spring breaks. We both grew to love this place. I did the grown-up thing and went off to college, Cal Tech, and after graduation found a job with a certain company you might've heard of in Redmond, Washington. I only lasted three years though, I just burnt out fast. Came down here for a short trip with my old man to sort my head out, and never left. It's home now."

I tried doing the math and trying to gauge his age but just couldn't figure it out so I asked, "Do you mind me asking how old you are?"

"Just turned 29, how about you?"

I'd felt a little embarrassed when I replied, "I turn 21 on Thursday."

He looked taken aback for a moment, then glanced at my cup.

"Soda," I promised with an apologetic shrug.

"You're mature for your age." He observed and I laughed, because no one had ever accused me of being mature for my age before.

I studied him for a moment, his brown eyes were clear and focused, giving no hints that he himself had imbibed at all. In fact, physically, he was in incredible shape. He wore a t-shirt advertising the bar, and I could see the outline of a firm, well-shaped torso beneath it. His biceps were well developed and tanned. The calluses on his hands made me think it wasn't the result of a gym- but instead the reward of hard work. He wasn't getting lost in the party, he knew restraint. As my eyes drifted down to his jeans, I suddenly realized I was inventorying the man right before his eyes. My face flushed and I glanced away.

When I glanced back up he was grinning and I had the awful feeling he knew exactly what I'd been thinking. Rachel saved me by reappearing at that moment.

"Sorry that took so long, I ran into the bartender we met earlier, Shannon. She was telling me about a lunch spot we have to check out that's away from the tourist traffic."

"Well you ladies enjoy the rest of your night. I'm going to need to put some time in at the office." Jack said and we said our goodnights.

Now in the fresh light of a new day, I'm lighter than I've ever been before. Unburdened. Rachel wanted to go for a walk, but something else was on my mind. After telling her to enjoy her walk, I take a quick shower and dress for the day. Pausing at the bathroom mirror I consider my reflection frankly. With my new dark tresses, my eyes stand out. Digging into the small make-up bag I haven't touched since our journey began, I take a minute to run mascara through my lashes to further highlight them. Then with a quick roll of pink lipgloss, I smile at myself and head downstairs.

It's barely 9 am, but the bar is already open. The kitchen serves breakfast and a roomful of tourists are already laughing over bloody marys, mimosas, and the occasional beer. Shannon, the bartender I'd met the night before, has been replaced by a tall brunette whose arms are covered in colorful tattoos. I walk to the bar and smile at her.

"Hi, love," She says in an Australian accent. "What can I get you?"

"Coffee? Can I get that here?" I ask, motioning to the bar top. She nods and walks back into a corner where a coffee station had been set up.

"Are you enjoying your vacation?" She asks, although I have the impression she's just being polite rather than asking out of actual curiosity.

"Yes, but it's not really a vacation." I wave off the comment when she looks up. "Long story. I'm actually staying here, in room B."

"Ah! So you're the one! I'd heard Jack had brought home a few strays. Welcome to the club. You know the last one he brought home never left."

I wasn't quite sure how to respond to that, is she saying he moved someone in with him? Maybe a woman? As ridiculous as it is, I realized it hasn't occurred to me that he might be in a relationship with someone.

"I see. We won't be in the way long. We have less than a week before my... friend... has to be back at work."

She laughs at that, "I thought the same thing. I'd just be here a few nights and then move on back to University. After just a few nights though I knew I couldn't leave. It's Key West." She says, with a shrug.

"Oh wait, you were the stray? And you ended up working here?" I'm feeling a little cautious, is she his employee or something more?

"Yes, love. Called my poor mum and told her I wouldn't be going back to uni just yet. Maybe someday. I ended up staying here for a few months, Jack gave me a job and I saved up to eventually get into an apartment with a roommate. That was two years ago. My girlfriend LaLa and I just put a bid in on our very own conch house!"

240

And just like that, I'm floating again.

"That's great! Congratulations on the house. I'm really envious that you were able to make a permanent move here. This place, it's magical."

"It can be." She agrees before adding, "But it can be a nightmare for the wrong person. An endless party sounds fun in theory, but the body and mind can only take so much. Some people show up here hoping it's the answer to all of their problems and figure out too late that they actually brought the problems with them. They look for answers at the bottom of every glass and eventually either burn out and move on or... well, stick around long enough and you'll see them."

My smile wavered at her observation. I'm not at risk of abusing alcohol or falling into drugs, but the part about bringing your problems with you- I'm never going to be baggage-free. I suppose that's something I'll have to accept wherever we end up. Maybe though, I need to at least start with trying to move past it all by figuring out exactly where I stood with the world beyond Rachel and Key West.

"Hey I'm Kenna by the way. I didn't get your name." I say, sticking out my hand.

"Oh yeah right love, I'm Tina. I better get those glasses washed. This place'll be a madhouse by lunch time."

"Nice to meet you, Tina, I'll be seeing you around." I reply, and then a thought occurs to me. "Oh hey one more quick thing. Is there a library here with public computers?"

"Need to check your email? Why not just use the one in Jack's office."

"Oh, I don't want to invade his space!" I say quickly.

"He won't care. It's the bar's computer, everyone who works here taps in. And we call it Jack's office, but once again- everyone who works here taps in. Just go into the back and through the kitchen. The bloody thing is slow as hell. Our Jack is funny like that. He started out working with computers but hates them now so he keeps the dinosaur around. Just wait it out; it'll work eventually. Password is password. Jack's not too big on overthinking things."

I nod and thank her again, although I still feel unsure. It might have been a communal computer for the staff, but I'm not staff. Considering what we're offering per night, I'm barely a paying a guest. Still, I'm feeling strong and capable this morning. If ever I am going to peek out at the world I've been hiding from, this might be the ideal moment.

I swallow my last sip of coffee and walk into the back area, through the kitchen, to the closed door that is labeled Office. I look around nervously, I'm not sure if it's better to dash in before anyone notices me or if I should wait and assure them I'd been given an okay to be there by Tina. The two cooks and a younger boy who I assumed was a dishwasher barely glance at me though, they're practically running as they move around the kitchen, their hands loaded down with plates and food items.

I shrug and knock lightly on the door. There's no reply so I cautiously turn the handle and walk in. I realize that calling the space an office is a little generous. It seems to be a catch-all space. A huge rack filled with cases of liquor lines one wall. File cabinets and stacks of document boxes line the opposite. A banquet table and six chairs take up the bulk of the center of the room. And in the back corner is a metal desk, crowned with a desktop computer.

Still feeling like I'm someplace that I shouldn't be, I sit down and type in the password. When sirens and flashing red lights fail to appear, I continue on- logging into the web browser version of Instagram. My account hasn't been updated in a very long time. I've never shared anything personal, just the occasional motivational meme, usually centered around song lyrics. My last shared image had been over four months ago- before the dreaded Crier experiment had even begun.

I go into my "followers" list, and scroll down to find Zach's name. My hands are a little shaky as I clicked his name. He's posted dozens of images since our encounter, most of them being selfies. As I scroll through them I find it- there we were on the boardwalk. My mouth was half open, eyes widened in horror, and I seemed to be reaching one hand toward the camera. Rachel's eyes on the other hand, seemed to be caught mid-blink. Great, I think, not only did this photograph out us to Tessa- it also happened to be an awful photograph in general.

The picture has over 1300 comments. I'm not going to bother scrolling through them all, but I take a peek to get an idea of what people are saying.

@FabianFantastico Are you sure that's her? It doesn't look like her.

@Jessi72920 What's up with her hair?

@Hanna_The_Banana_24 I like her hair, not everyone has to be blonde to be beautiful @Jessi72920

@Dat_Big_Nut Dufuq she doing in VB NEway

@Alison_Randolph_1994 Obv she thinks it'll make the Crier scam go away. WE WONT FORGET WHAT YOU DID TO @It's_Tessa!

@Tacosforbreakfastlunchdinner Your caps lock is stuck @Alison_Randolph_1994

@Alison_Randolph_1994 FU TACOS!

@Big_Tex_Zach Her hair is actually lit AF

@Jessi72920 Whatever Zach. We all know you're just trying to get laid

@Big_Tex_Zach I don't have to try darlin...

@TJlally You're all fcking gross. What's it matter what she looks like? The point is she totally fcked @It's_Tessa! over.

@Hard_Rock_Lvr23 Who cares?

@Alison_Randolph_1994 WE CARE!!!! TESSA DESERVES BETTER!!!

@LittleBlueRidingHood OMG I think I saw her! She was at a club in LA last week!

@JHnvsbsm Does anyone know what brand bag that is on the table next to her?

@Dancing_To_the_Moon

@Alison_Randolph_1994 She was adopted, thats why she doesn't care what happens to her so called mother

@Alison_Randolph_1994 NO SHE WASNT. SHE WAS A TEST TUBE BABY!!! TESSA IS HER REAL MOTHER!!!! ITS IN HER BIOGRAPHY!!!!! I READ IT THREE TIMES AND YOU CLEARLY DIDNT AT ALL!

@Jessi72920 Hey @Big_Tex_Zach- who the hell is Alison?

@Big_Tex_Zach IDK

@tyrese_Withers Hi @Big_Tex_Zach, I'm a local correspondent for WRJS, I sent you a DM

@Jessi72920 Aw Zachie's about to go viral

@SarahKentIII Hey guys just catching up, THATS @KennaFromCT? OMG she looks so different. Has anyone heard from her?

@KimberLee21 Love the new hair @KennaFromCT

@JulesLikesGirlsToo Me too @KimberLee21

@Alison_Randolph_1994 ITS FUGLY

@Jessi72920 Your ALL CAPS are fugly @Alison_Randolph_1994

@TMZ_Scout We'd love to chat @Big_Tex_Zach DM

@Can't_fight_the_reeeeper Hey I made $240000 in just 2 days with Netcoin! Check out link in bio to find out how!

@AndryDory I'm just here for the fight

@Lil_Neicey I think it's the same color as Kendall Jenner's new look

@KimberLee21 @Lil_Neicey Really? I love it! I wonder where they got it done

@TTTurner222 Who dat?

@Shileys_Mom Is that really Kendall Jenner??

@JustInCase3 @Shileys_Mom RU really that daft? It says right in the caption it's Tessa's DD

@T6289000 Whats DD?

@r2d2_poopoo @T6289000 Big tits

@Hanna_The_Banana_24 IDK whats happening here. Who are these idiots?

@Nancy_Lowen_Channel3 Check your DMs @Big_Tex_Zach

@ReesePiece I couldn't heart this more! I've been thinking of going dark too

@Libra_Rising DM me for my Only Fans link

I'd seen enough. I had been prepared to read blistering commentary, insults, and judgment. I had not been prepared for the shallow, often nonsensical, comments placed by distant schoolmates and strangers alike. Maybe it's because I've had a whole week to get over the initial horror of the photo or it might be the fact that Zach's feed is full of idiots. Either way, I'm feeling pretty darned relieved. Why would I allow myself to care what people like that think about me? For that matter, why had I ever cared?

Emboldened by my newfound sense of freedom from judgment, I open my email account. After scrolling through a dozen obvious spam messages, I reach one from the Dean of Students, Barnard College. I take a deep breath and open it. Skimming until I reach the part I need to see, the words jump out at me.

Your failure to attend your scheduled Academic Honor Board hearing is considered to be an admission of guilt, and your expulsion from the college is effective immediately. While this outcome is considered permanent and irreversible, you may direct a response in writing to the Office Of The Dean Of Students within 60 days for further consideration.

I had expected it, even hoped for it, but the realization that my tenure at Barnard is truly done now feels a bit like a punch to the gut. I'm free, but the taint from this will hang over my head for the rest of my life. Or rather, it will hang over the head of Kennedy Shepherd, daughter of America's sweetheart, Tessa Shepherd. Is it actually a factor if I'm not that girl anymore?

I'm spared the chance to obsess over it any longer when the office door opens.

"Hey, Kenna! Tina told me she'd sent you back here. Were you able to get online?"

Blushing at being caught someplace I'm still not sure I'm entitled to be in, I reply, "Yes I did, thank you. I'm sorry if I overstepped by coming in here..."

He waves off my comment, "Of course, you didn't. Call this the hotel business center." And then follows that comment with a wink. I feel my pulse quicken and for a change it isn't out of fear or panic. This is something much more pleasant. I've certainly known plenty of attractive boys and men in my life, some of them had been quite smooth in their come-ons even, but I've never felt tempted to actually explore anything with them. Jack, something about him makes me want to cast aside the old doubts and fears. I'm not the old Kennedy here in Key West, in this room, with this man.

"Where's your friend?" He asks.

"Rachel? She's off for her morning walk. She's usually up before the sun and wastes no time, she's obnoxiously cheerful when she does it, too."

He laughs. "Do you ladies have any plans for the day?"

"Not a whole lot, I think we're going to go tour the Hemingway House and Rachel mentioned something about a museum with gold doubloons and stuff that were found on the ocean floor that we should check out."

"Mel Fisher, yep, those are standard tourist must-sees. If you want, I can suggest a few other more out of the way places you might want to visit while here. First though, I wanted to let you know I talked to my friend Titus. He runs a tow service, and said he can get your car down here for a reasonable price. Here's his number, give him a call whenever you can. You won't want to leave the car on the roadside for too long- county will send their own contracted tow truck out and that'll cost a whole lot more."

I take the small piece of paper he holds and thank him. He starts to walk away but then as he hits the doorway he turns around and looks back at me. "Do you like boats?"

"Boats? Sure, I guess." I do like boats. One of my favorite holidays ever had been when Tessa had chartered a sailboat and crew in Greece, and we'd visited the islands. I'd only been allowed to leave at one port, but I hadn't cared. It was the actual experience of sailing that I'd loved the most- wind whipping my hair back. We'd only done it once though, because Tessa had found the whole experience too confining.

"I was thinking, I have a little Bay Reef, maybe I could take you ladies out for a tour of the Keys from a whole different perspective."

"Oh, that sounds incredible! Let me talk to Rachel, but I have a feeling she'll be all for it. Thanks so much for the offer."

"Your birthday's tomorrow, right?"

I'm a little surprised that he's remembered that little detail. "Yep, sure is!"

"What do you say? Birthday boat trip?"

"That sounds fantastic, we'd love that!" I reply enthusiastically.

He grins and says, "My pleasure. Have a good day Kenna."

After he leaves the room, the glow that fills me doesn't diminish, it grows. Have a good day? I am absolutely doing just that.

Chapter 25

Rachel

"Coo coo ca choo, what's eating you?"

We're walking off our hangover, a somewhat unique experience for me. Delta isn't the sort of woman who drinks regularly, but she's certainly had more experience with this sort of thing than me. She assures me that the best cure is copious amounts of water paired with a copious amount of sweat. It's 90 degrees this morning and humidity has to be near 100%. Sweat is not a problem. I feel unusually irritable. It's probably also a result of my overindulgence last night, but something else is annoying me. I remain silent as we happen upon a small, public garden that's situated off one of the side streets we've wandered down. I'm drawn to it because of its scent- a powerful aroma of plumeria, Delta's signature scent, but when I see the stone bench, I forget the scent and make a beeline for a seat.

"Nothing." I tell her, after she prompts me again. My voice makes it clear it's not actually nothing.

"Aw, come on Rachel. You woke up foul today, and I think it's more than those hurricanes you drank last night. What's the problem?"

I plunk down on the bench and narrow my eyes at her, and tell her. "Last night, That blonde. The trashy one with her breasts hanging out. She sure seemed to like you."

Delta's beautiful face breaks into a huge grin and I try not to smile back. It's difficult when her eyes crinkle that way.

She chuckles and asks, "Seriously? That's what has your tail up in a dander. You think I want some sloppy drunk chick who thinks that line in Living on a Prayer says 'It doesn't matter if we're naked or not'? Rach, she's not in your league. You're a rockstar. A librarian rockstar. I don't even know her name."

    I can't help it then, I laugh. I don't get jealous very often, almost never in fact. It must have been the copious amount of drinks we'd imbibed the previous night. Delta sits beside me and puts her arm over my shoulder.

    "You know what I love about you Rachel?"

    "My cooking? My ability to give a mean foot massage? The way I organize our closet alphabetically?" I ask.

    "Well yeah, all that too. But what I really love most about you is that you never, ever, fuck up Jon Bon Jovi lyrics."

I'd been exploring the quieter side streets that intersected with Duval for about an hour when the scent hit me. I wasn't certain at first, there were so many floral fragrances in this tropical climate but I sniffed again and it was unmistakable. Plumeria. It'd been Delta's scent of choice; she'd been introduced to it during our dream trip to Hawaii. A premature delayed honeymoon, we'd called it. We'd been living together for almost eight years by then, two self-supporting, tax-paying women who had established a community of friends and coworkers. We were as committed to each other as any pair of long term lovers could have been. We were friends, partners, lovers, everything to one another except legally married spouses because the world would take a little longer to catch up to us.

    "We don't need a piece of paper. Why are we waiting? Let's book that honeymoon suite. Let's go to Maui like we've dreamed of and say our own vows on the beach. Come on Rachel, a priest isn't going to make it any more real."

    She wasn't a woman who wore perfume very often, but after our premature-delayed honeymoon it would always be a simple plumeria scent when she did indulge.

    Following the essence, I came upon a small green area, filled with trees and flowers. The sign that fronted it said "Coffey Park" and I closed my eyes. I knew this place. Hallowed ground. We'd had a moment here on our last trip, a silly jealous moment of mine that had resolved and led to a beautiful day. As I walked along a small path, I spotted the source of the scent. A large, flowering plumeria tree. A skinny, knobbed trunk was topped by expansive limbs that were covered in the delicate, waxy white flowers. I knelt to pick one up that had fallen on the ground and held it to my nose as I closed my eyes. I allowed myself to pretend that she was there with me, but pretending wasn't the same thing as actually believing.

Just like I'd experienced too many times in the past six months, I felt tears of frustration sting my eyes at the undeniable lack of supernatural presence. I wanted to believe that some part of her still existed in some form. I wanted to believe that if I was patient enough or reached deeply enough, she'd reach back out to me. Maybe it was selfish, but I didn't want to let her rest in peace. She could do that when it was my turn.

Sighing, I sat on the bench and watched a pair of yellow birds I didn't recognize squabble. The park was perfect. The flowers were perfect. The birds were perfect. The weather was perfect. The only thing that wasn't perfect in the garden was me. The trip had been going well, I'd absolutely enjoyed most of it despite dealing with Tessa, bedbugs, and a broken car. Reminiscing about my childhood and my early years with Delta had been nice. Therapeutic, even. Reconnecting with my parents, seeing their remorse and love, touched me deeply. And then there was Kenna. Getting to know her, watching her unfold and unfurl against the tight ball that Tessa had wrapped her up into gladdened my heart and sparked something that felt an awful lot like pride. Feeling as if I was actually making a difference in the girl's life was the best feeling of all.

Yet even with everything going so right, something was still missing. Delta had left an extinguished lantern in my soul, and despite searching so desperately, I couldn't find the spark to light it. It felt unfair. I wasn't just sitting in my house, wallowing in my grief. I was actively trying to live a real life in the here and now. I was doing my part to find a flame of purpose.

I thought back to the Frankl book I'd read last week. He believed that you couldn't pursue happiness. I struggled to remember the exact words, something to the effect that happiness could not be pursued, it could only ensue. You needed to find the reason and then happiness could occur naturally as a result.

Once upon a time, supporting and encouraging Delta had given me a reason to be happy. I'd clearly transferred that role to Kenna. Introducing her to new places and ideas, helping her believe in herself, encouraging her to move past the pain of her childhood- all of that had been giving me at least the temporary facade of purpose and dare I say, joy. It was unfair though to put the burden of my happiness on her. I had learned from the loss of Delta that it was too much to place that responsibility on any one person. Too much and also not enough.

It was easy to lose myself in my own thoughts as I sat in the beautiful garden. This was my church and I could seek peace and understanding there. I replayed the trip so far. There had been moments of hopefulness, even joy. Watching my parents unburden themselves of decades of self-inflicted guilt and angst. Handing a stranger on a beach a granola bar to brighten his day. Buying lunch and listening to a young stranger's story, offering him encouragement as he fought to walk away from his demons.

Hadn't there always been such opportunities in my life though? Moments not dependent on Delta or Kenna. Introducing the children of Metzgartown to Charlotte's Web, easing Maggie's burdon with the twins, encouraging Susan to walk daily so she could fully recover from her heart attack, keeping the lights on late on Thursday nights so people like Johnny and Susette could attend a meeting and continue their sobriety- all of those were reasons to be both hopeful and joyous. The fruits of happiness hung invisibly all around me. By nurturing the trees, I could permit myself to pluck the fruit when it ripened.

The unfamiliar buzz of my phone interrupted my thoughts. I hadn't received a single call on this trip, something that wasn't a surprise. My friends back home knew that when I traveled I generally didn't carry the device. As a librarian, I'd lamented enough over the years about the advent of the screen age that it wasn't a surprise to anyone that it could be difficult to reach me via cell phone, except in cases of emergency. My first thought was that somehow Tessa had tracked the number down and the fact that the screen said "Unidentified Caller" didn't exactly assuage my fear.

"Hello?" I asked suspiciously.

"Hello, may I please speak to Ms. Patrick?" A polite voice asked. Not Tessa.

"Yes." I replied, trying to sound cool and uninviting. If it was a sales call, I wouldn't make it easy for them.

"Good morning, this is Jenna Oliver from Sigsbee Charter School in Key West. We received your résumé for the librarian position and we'd like to invite you to a panel interview. I see you are located in Pennsylvania, we can arrange a Skype interview at your convenience."

I was stunned. That my first real job bite would be here, while I was actually in town, seemed like more than just a handheld sign. It was a blazing, neon billboard. Such a sign couldn't be ignored. I knew that I could handle a Skype style interview, but surely I'd be an even stronger candidate if we could meet face to face.

"Oh, wonderful. This is pretty ironic, but I'm actually in town this week on vacation. I could come in, in person if that works?"

"Really! That is quite a coincidence. How long are you in town? Could you make it..." She paused and I heard her typing on a keyboard, "Tuesday morning?"

My heart sank, "I'm actually only here through Saturday. I'll be arriving back in PA on Tuesday, but I'll be available via Skype on Wednesday, if that works?"

As I said the words, the image of my Saturn, sitting on the roadside dead, crossed my mind. I pushed it aside. If we couldn't get it repaired in time, I'd have to come up with a plan B but this wasn't the time to be thinking about that.

I heard her typing further and then she came back and said brightly, "Mr. Thomas says he can fit you in on Friday afternoon. Will that work?"

"Yes," I replied excitedly. "Can you please email me the details? I'm out and about right now and don't have a pen on me."

She agreed to follow up soon, and we said our goodbyes. As soon as I hung up, I fought the urge to jump up and cheer. I'd wanted a sign, had prayed for one, and - I felt Delta's suntanned hand at work.

I needed to get back to the room and arrange the tow and then I had another urgent task- finding an interview outfit on an island full of t-shirt shops. When I arrived back at the bar, I had trouble restraining my jubilation. I waved to a heavily tattooed girl behind the bar, perhaps just a bit too eagerly, and made my way up to the room where Kenna was dressed and waiting.

"You're not going to believe what I did!" She said as soon as I shut the door.

"You won't believe what happened to me," I replied. "But you go first!"

"I used Jack's computer, and checked Instagram and my email! I know, that doesn't sound like a big deal, but oh my god Rachel- I did it! And you know what? It wasn't awful. In fact, I felt a whole lot like I just didn't care what people thought. It has got to be this tropical weather. I've never in my life not cared what people thought."

She radiated pride, that one small step had seemingly unlocked another door. It had been less than two weeks, yet I was watching her bloom right before my eyes. Her transformation filled me with pride. I'd helped create that beautiful young woman and then with a fierceness I'd been fighting for weeks I think- she's mine too.

"Kenna, that's incredible. You faced one of your biggest fears! What's next? Performing in Rockefeller Center?" I asked with a teasing smile.

She didn't laugh back though, instead she looked down shyly and said, "I've been thinking about that. Not Rockefeller Center, but maybe it would be interesting to take my guitar down to the square tonight. It sounds crazy, but everyone's a tourist down there, right? No one is going to remember me tomorrow. It'll probably be a whole new crowd of tourists."

I stared at her with my mouth agape for a moment. The idea was so stunning and yet so perfect- I couldn't immediately muster a response. As her face fell under my silence, I regretted the pause.

"Oh my god, Kenna, that's absolutely perfect. What better way to shed your fears and doubts and embrace a brave, wild new life?"

She looked back up at me and asked softly, "Are you sure? You're not just saying that because you're my... well, friend?"

"Yes, I'm sure. I wouldn't set you up for failure. Your voice is beautiful, you are beautiful, people will love it- and you can make a quick escape in the crowd if it feels overwhelming. I think it's incredibly brave that you even thought of this!"

Her cheeks turned an attractive shade of pink, and she looked away.

"I'm not sure what's happening down here, but I'm feeling alive. I'm honestly not sure I ever want to leave." She admitted, looking back at me pointedly.

"Kenna... I'm really glad you're enjoying it but I feel like it'd be remiss of me not to point out we've only been in town for one night so far. I know it was an incredible night, and the town and weather seem so perfect at the moment, but there's always a stark difference between vacationing somewhere and living somewhere. I want you to keep reaching for ways to challenge yourself, and keep getting out there amongst the living, but I think you should be careful with how much power you give any one place in making you happy."

"I know, I get it. I've been to a lot of really beautiful, fabulous vacation spots and always understood intuitively that living there wouldn't have been the same. But I'm just saying, there's something really magical here."

I wasn't sure just how much I believed what she said, it was a conflict for me. I loved seeing her happy and glowing in this way, but I also knew that the crash could be swift and painful if this was all based on a fantasy life, in a fantasy place. At some point, she'd realize that the things that made life so difficult in CT and NY were part of her- and she needed to address them or they'd resurface even here in paradise. I decided to let it go for a moment though, sometimes a person just needed to believe in paradise.

"I told you I had news. Wait until you hear what just happened."

I filled her in on the invitation to interview and she jumped up and hugged me. Then she pulled back and looked at me critically, "But Rachel, you do have one issue..."

"Interview outfit." I replied.

"Interview outfit." She confirmed.

"Let's figure out what to do about the car first, and then I'll ask downstairs- surely there's someplace around here that sells more than t-shirts and flip flops."

Prompted by my comment, she held out a piece of paper with a recommended tow driver and I made the call to Titus, who confirmed he would bring the car to his garage on the outskirts of town.

With those plans in place, we headed downstairs to find out where exactly the locals shopped. Just three hours later, we were walking back into the private area of Jack and Jett's with shopping bags in hand. In the hallway, we ran into Jack.

"Hey, looks like you did some shopping." He said, gesturing toward our bags.

I laughed and said, "Just a little. Hey, thanks for recommending your friend! I got the call that my car's at his garage getting a looksee right now."

"That's great, if anyone can fix it- Titus can. The man's a genius." He turned to Kenna and I couldn't help but notice that his smile grew a little wider.

"Oh hey, I forgot to mention it, but you might want to buy some hats. My boat doesn't have much cover, and the sun can be brutal out there."

As she smiled back, I asked uneasily, "boat?"

Kenna explained, "Oh I forgot to tell you! Jack has a boat, and he's offered to give us a tour by water tomorrow."

"Um, I hate to be a party pooper but nope."

Now they were both looking at me in confusion.

"I don't do that, no boats for me. I'll be puking ten minutes after we leave the dock."

Kenna looked horrified. "Seriously? You get seasick? How is that even possible? Your dad, Delta, surely you went on boats with them?"

"When I was younger, yes, but after my..." I stopped suddenly, unsure of how to continue in front of Jack. "After my early twenties, something changed. If I just step onto a floating dock, I start to get dizzy."

It took her a moment, but I saw the look on her face change from confusion to understanding. It was the pregnancy. I'd known women who said they'd never in their life experienced heartburn until pregnancy and then afterward it plagued them the rest of their lives. Others talked about the permanent changes to their breasts and waistline. It was truly a mystery to my doctors, but my strange carry-over from pregnancy had been sea sickness. We'd relocated to Pennsylvania a few years after Kenna's birth so it didn't come up often but on the few occasions I'd had to ride a ferry during our travels I always loaded up with meds and spent a lot of time on deck trying to breathe through the waves of nausea that somehow still snuck in.

"Seasickness isn't really in the gut Rachel, it's in your head. I'm telling you, if you believe you will be sick, you're gonna be sick."

"Delta...."

"Seriously, just trust me. Let's rent a boat when we get there, I'll prove it to you."

"Delta..."

"Hey, who's the expert here anyway? Trust me!"

"Delta I swear to god if you try to get me on a boat one more time, I'm not going to travel with you anymore. I'll just go solo. This is not in my head!"

She'd eventually relented, but I don't think she ever stopped believing I somehow had control over it. In a lifetime of good memories, it was almost refreshing to have a few not-so-happy moments to ground me. Life wasn't always perfect. Delta was the perfect woman for me, but she wasn't actually perfect.

"Um, sorry Jack. I guess we'll skip it..."

I turned back toward her and cut her off. "No way! Don't let me stop you. You guys should go and have a good time. We can pick up one of those disposable cameras so you can get lots of pictures to show me."

Jack interrupted, "She's right, you should absolutely still come. Don't you have a phone though?"

Kenna replied, "Oh, I don't want to put you out for just me, and no, I don't. Well I do but, long story. It's not working."

"Kenna, if you know anything about boats, you would know that it never puts a boat owner out to have to get underway on a fabulous day. Like I said, bring a hat. I'll meet you at the bar at 10 am. Have a great day ladies!"

He was gone before she had a chance to argue, and I was unable to stop the laugh that emerged.

"I like him."

She shot me a sour look. "Well, he's not so bad, but do you know how awkward this is going to be? What am I supposed to even talk about with him?"

"Where's that girl who was going on about how free and alive she felt here? Go, have fun." I said with a smile before adding, "And wear a hat."

Chapter 26

Kenna

I'd picked the ear of Shannon, the afternoon bar manager, about the process to play in Mallory Square. Apparently, it's fairly simple. Show up at the square two and a half hours before sunset, find the city kiosk, fill out the form and pay a 5 dollar fee. Find a spot, start playing, hope you don't die of embarrassment. She'd been excited for me, when she learned about my plan. "You have this! I'm just bummed I'm working and will have to miss it."

It still surprises me when people are nice to me. That a near stranger tries to encourage me that way makes me feel seen. Again, I feel as if I've jettisoned to a different world than the coldly empty apartment I'd left behind in New York. I use Jack's computer to look up the sunset and see it's scheduled for about 7:30 that evening. Rachel and I have decided to leave the bar at 4:30 to head on down.

With each step we take down Duval I feel the gentle, reassuring pressure of Auntie against my back. I hyper-focus on the sound of Rachel's rhythmic breathing as we navigate the thick crowds. My nerves are certainly triggered but I've experienced enough paralyzing anxiety in my life to know that what I feel now isn't panic. This is perfectly reasonable, I remind myself. All performers, even the greats, confess to nerves before stepping on stage.

When we reach the kiosk, I feel like an imposter asking for the form but the woman behind the counter doesn't blink, she just hands one to me as if I am a legitimate performer. I pause at the very first line though that asks for my name. I don't know that the woman will recognize mine, but I also don't want to take that chance- and I don't want a paper trail for Tessa to follow. Hesitantly I write Kenna... and then after glancing at

Rachel, who doesn't seem to be paying attention, finish with the last name Patrick.

After handing over the money and form, the woman wishes me luck and we walk around the square to find an unoccupied spot that isn't in the direct center of the action.

"Nervous?" Rachel asks.

"Nah, I do this all the time." I reply.

She nods and smiles.

"Remember, they're tourists. They're all happy, most of them are drunk, and you'll never see them again. Are you going to play original songs?"

I had thought about that and decided that this wasn't the time or place to debut something that no one could sing along to. I remember the boy in Charleston, people loved him because he played music that they already knew.

"Nope, I tried to come up with a short playlist that would fit the atmosphere down here. I've got three songs prepared. It'll be quick, and then we can make a run for it before the sun even actually sets."

She laughs at that. "You have to start somewhere."

Still, I don't move the guitar from my back. I scan the crowd, searching for familiar faces. Then I look along the periphery for other acts. A juggler is already gathering a small crowd. Not far from him, a trio is setting up a small tower made of ladders and chairs. Next, I study the waterfront where a few party boats seem to be positioning themselves to watch the sunset. Noise, movement, color. Everywhere my eyes fall. Aunty and I are perfectly still, the world whirls around us. Presto! Presto! Julian, my former composition teacher, instructs sharply. My arms remain limp at my sides.

"Kenna..." Rachel says.

I look at her, "I know. It's not that I'm afraid to perform. I mean I absolutely am afraid to perform, but that's not the problem."

"So what is it?"

"I don't know how to start." I confess.

"Put the guitar in your hands and start strumming." She suggests.

"That's helpful." I reply dryly, but now I'm able to do just that. As I begin to play people continue to walk by unaffected. It's as if they don't notice the girl with the guitar. Then I begin to sing Jack Johnson's Upside Down and a family of four stops to nod along. My voice sounds weak, I know I'm singing too quietly. Soon a couple joins them, nervously, I close my eyes and sing louder. Keeping them shut, I allow myself to get lost in the melody.

Upside down
Who's to say what's impossible and can't be found
I don't want this feeling to go away

Nearing the end, I fight the urge to drag it out- as long as I keep singing I don't have to actually open my eyes and face my listeners... but I can't delay it forever. When I hit that last note, I remove my fingers from the strings. I can still hear the cacophony of the crowd around the square but for a second I'm suspended above it all. And then, the applause begins. It's much louder and closer than I'd anticipated and I open my eyes to see a crowd circling around me. I scan the smiling faces until I find Rachel, who is grinning widely and giving me a thumbs up.

Still shaky, but this time from elation, I move on to my next choice. Looking Glass's Brandy. At the end, the crowd cheers again and more crumbled dollar bills are tossed into my guitar case. I follow that with my final song, Ed Sheeran's *Perfect*. By the time I play the last note, my body is slick with perspiration and my guitar case is full of money.

"Thanks, everyone." I say shyly to the crowd, as they wander off toward the water's edge to await the spectacular show nature would provide shortly.

Rachel walks up to me shaking her head, with tears in her eyes. "Kenna, that was wonderful. I'm so proud of you- and not just because you sounded so beautiful. You *did* it, you faced your fears!"

I reach up to hug her and begin to sob into her shoulder. They aren't really happy tears or sad tears, they're just 21 years worth of pent up emotion spilling out all at once and I'm not sure I'll ever be able to stop. Something has been released.

Chapter 27

Rachel

I was starting to actually worry. Kenna had cried throughout the entire walk back to Jack and Jett's. Not consistently. She'd sob, then stop and sniffle, look around at the passing tourists who eyed her curiously, and collect herself. Then a minute later I'd look over and the tears would be flowing again.

"Are you sure you're okay?" I asked for what felt like the hundredth time.

She nodded, but didn't attempt to speak. Speaking apparently reignited the tearworks so I didn't push. I tried to respect and mirror her silence, but I realized that sometime in the last ten minutes or so I'd transitioned from feeling worried to feeling exasperated.

"Kenna, seriously you have to stop. I swear I wouldn't lie to you about this, you were incredible. There's nothing to cry over!"

She sniffled and nodded, then fought to contain any further tears. It didn't work. She managed to sob, "I'm not sad. I just can't stop crying. I feel amazingly good actually, but..." She broke off, choking back another sob as new tears began to flow.

Understanding dawned on me. "It's a release. It's like we just lanced a boil and now everything awful is leaking out."

She nodded rapidly, sniffling as she said, "Ye, yes. I'm a giant pimple."

I burst out laughing at that and she began laughing with me. I was so relieved to see that she'd stopped crying, I was afraid to say anything else. I was equally relieved to see Jack and Jett's neon sign beckoning ahead. Kenna might be laughing now, but that much crying had done its damage-her face was splotched with red, her nose was running and her eyes were swollen. It wasn't a state that she'd want to be spotted in by anyone who knew her, especially Jack.

"Go in, and straight up to the room. Take a shower, gather yourself for a bit. I'll stay down at the bar." I instructed and she nodded as we walked in the doorway. After watching her make a run for the Employees Only area, I walked up to sit in the only empty seat at the main bar.

Shannon walked over to take my order and I allowed myself to relax as I scanned the massive crowd that filled the dining and stage area. Other than the bartender, I knew no one. It was an odd feeling to sit and observe in such a transient place. The majority of the people there were tourists, they'd switch out with another anonymous group tomorrow, ad infinitum. The crowd was festive but their lack of permanence tempered my own happiness as I watched them. I couldn't mirror their enthusiasm because I was too hyper-aware of how nameless they were. Everything felt temporary and fleeting there. I shook that thought away as Shannon returned with a fruity red drink that she'd promised would knock my flip flops off. I wasn't sure if that was a good thing or not.

"So how's the trip going?" She asked loudly, trying to be heard over the crowd.

"Very well! We're loving the island."

"Yeah, it's pretty hard to be miserable here. How much longer do you think you'll be around? Jack said it seemed a little open ended?"

"I guess I should talk to him about that, we'll actually be leaving Saturday. I need to get back to work, and my cat!"

She nodded, "Pennsylvania, right?"

"Yep, small town near the Poconos. It's not Key West, but it's actually a really beautiful area. If we end up moving down here, I'm going to really miss the mountains, especially in the fall." I confessed. I immediately pictured my oak, in its flaming coat of October.

She motioned that she'd be right back and I could see that the other bartender clearly had his hands full. I glanced down the bar to inventory the other patrons. At one end, was a large group of young women, one of them wearing a comb on the crown of her head that was attached to a long piece of white tulle. Several of her friends wore sashes that advertised their bridesmaid status. Next, there was a middle aged couple in matching T-Shirts that were stamped with the name of a competing bar, further down the strip. They were turned, with their backs against the bar, watching the band from a safe distance. Next to them was a pair of older gentlemen who might have been friends, husbands, or even brothers with matching beards.

Between the beards and me sat a quiet, middle aged man in a Hawaiian shirt. He didn't glance at me or at anyone else. He seemed to stare straight ahead into the mirror behind the bar as he slowly sipped a pint glass of beer. In the animated crowd, he felt out of place. Aloof and detached. Then again, I reasoned, I probably looked out of place to everyone else as well.

"Sorry about that, we've had three bachelorette groups in here tonight already. They're always so demanding." Shannon said, with an eye roll, as she returned to her spot behind the bar in front of me.

"Did you say you might be moving here?"

I hadn't actually intended to share that, it had just slipped out, but I nodded and said, "Yes, maybe. I'm in the middle of scouting out relocation options. I actually have an interview on the base on Friday for a librarian position."

"Really!" She said with a smile, "That's great! Oh shit, be back soon, drunks at table 9 are going to be an issue in 3, 2, 1..."

She walked away briskly and a raspy male voice interrupted my thoughts. "Housing in Key West isn't easy to find, and what you do find is going to cost a fortune."

I turned in surprise toward my neighbor, but he was still staring straight ahead. Had I imagined that? I stared for a moment and then he spoke again. "Librarian salary, I doubt you'll find anything you can afford here."

I was annoyed. He'd been eavesdropping on my private conversation and now he was offering unsolicited financial advice? I wondered if he was actually a local, a realtor maybe. He had an accent, I'd bet money it was New Jersey, but that didn't mean he wasn't local. Lots of people move to Florida from New Jersey. I balked at the idea of a sales pitch by a stranger in a bar.

"I'm sure we'll make it work." I turned back toward my drink and hoped he'd get the hint. He didn't.

"It'd be a shame to find yourself homeless."

It was such an odd comment and he said it in a tone that whispered a threat. Something wasn't right here. My anger gave way to alarm and I looked around for Shannon. She was standing across the room with a bouncer and a waitress, arguing with a group of thirty-something year old women who had clearly reached their limits. Completely uncomfortable now, I stood to leave. I could settle my tab later.

As I started to walk away though, he said, "My employer can help get you into a house."

Maybe I had imagined the threatening tone. Maybe he really was just a realtor. Relieved, but still annoyed, I turned around, fully intending to tell him I wasn't interested. But then everything changed. He continued. "She can get you into a house you can afford. You will be able to afford a lot. Or, you may find you don't have a job at all and can't afford anything. Sometimes jobs don't work out. Sometimes houses don't work out. She can help with all of that."

I froze. He was looking directly at me now, and there was nothing friendly in his steely stare. He wasn't trying to sell me a house. He was there for something else, or rather, someone else.

"She sent you?" I asked, although I already knew the answer.

He didn't bother to pretend that he didn't know who I was talking about. He gave a short nod.

"How did she find us?" I asked, feeling angry with myself for the slight tremble in my voice.

"It doesn't matter. There are a lot of ways to find a person these days."

"And you are?" I asked, trying to sound like I still had any control over this conversation.

"Donald Freeman, I'm a PI."

"Mr. Freeman, you can tell Tessa that..." My words died away as Kenna came into view, walking toward us. He wasn't looking in her direction and hadn't spotted her yet. She didn't seem to see me yet either-her attention was riveted to the dining area where one of the drunk women Shannon was dealing with was now yelling something about her rights.

I looked back at Mr. Freeman and finished lamely, "I don't want to talk to her."

"Tell the girl to go home Ms. Patrick. Send her home now, and you'll be well rewarded. But if you insist on keeping her away from her mother, you'll pay a very heavy price."

Kenna was just feet away now, and Freeman stood as he spotted her. For a moment I thought he was going to confront her, but instead he nodded his head toward her and then looked back at me.

"I'll be in touch soon." He said, and then he was walking toward the door.

Kenna looked at me questioningly, but as I'm about to respond a new figure walked up to greet us. As soon as Kenna saw Jack, her eyes lit up and a huge smile crossed her face. Oh. So that's the way the wind blew, this was starting to feel like more than just a mild crush. I couldn't enjoy it; my stomach was twisted by the confrontation with the PI. I was going to have to tell Kenna about it, but it could wait until the morning. She was glowing, positively glowing, at the moment. I'd let her enjoy one last night of satisfaction before I ruined everything for her again. Everything would change when she learned that Tessa had tracked us down and sent a goon after us. Key West and all of the happiness she had discovered here was going to be soiled.

Chapter 28

Tessa

"I gave her the message but my gut tells me she isn't going to fold. I've watched them and they're very attached. I think she's ready to fight back."

Tessa twirled the wine glass in her hand, watching a half an inch of chardonnay roll about the pristine stemware. Until now, Donald had been performing satisfactorily. He'd called in some favors and easily tracked the women through Rachel's credit card purchases to Key West after all. He had warned her that it might take a while to find out where they were staying once he arrived but as it turned out luck had been on his side. He'd gone down to a popular tourist event at sunset and in a crowd of thousands somehow stumbled upon Kennedy playing guitar of all things.

That Kennedy was actually performing for strangers and was doing it well enough to garner applause had been a true surprise. She hadn't realized the girl actually had talent. Perhaps she'd inherited more than her mother's eyes after all. Tessa thought maybe she could work with that, if she could get a top notch vocal coach and production team there might be a future there in entertainment. One big hitch in that scenario was her father. He thought musicians were a seedy lot- and in Tessa's experience that was a pretty accurate description. Still, it was a different world than the one her father had raised her in. Successful musicians were very lucrative and held a lot of media power.

The other big hitch was Kennedy herself. She was spiraling out of control and she'd apparently rather play to dirty street crowds than her own mother. It was obviously that woman's fault, she'd brain washed her. It infuriated Tessa. She'd given Kennedy everything a child could possibly want or need. The librarian had one single role in Kennedy's life. The rest of it, every meal and dress and pony and nanny and college itself, was the direct result of Tessa's hard work and generosity. Even after she'd brought shame and embarrassment to the Shepherd brand, Kennedy had been coddled and protected as Tessa undertook the hard work of finding an alternative path for her. How could the girl side with the librarian against her own mother?

"Donald, you're not being paid to lie down and let them trounce all over you." She said icily, fighting to keep the shrillness from her voice.

"Tessa, be reasonable. There's only so much I can say and do here. The Patrick woman knows what's at stake, and she knows there's an offer on the table. I can speak to her again, but I'm not going to risk harassment charges and I'm not going to make threats that I can't actually follow up on. Your problem is I don't think the woman is monetarily motivated. This is an emotional attachment, not a financial grab."

"Then stop talking to the woman. Let her soak in her emotional attachment. Kennedy needs to understand that an emotional attachment won't pay for her nails, or those shoes she's always buying. It's not going to pay for trips to the South of France. An emotional attachment won't replace her BMW or her tony city apartment. It also won't help that woman she cares about get a job. You're targeting the wrong person."

He sighed and she knew that she'd struck a nerve but then another thought hit her.

"Actually, no one can make this point better than me. I need to speak to her myself, face to face."

"You're not wrong." He conceded. "But if you can't get the girl on the phone and if I can't convince her to come to you, then you're still at square one."

"I know. I can't believe I have to do this, but I'm going to have to go there."

"Here? To Key West? Tessa, I don't know. This isn't exactly your scene..." He cautioned.

"Don't tell me what I already know. I'm certainly not happy about it. I have an old family friend that keeps an estate down there; I'll ring her up and see if a stay can be arranged. I won't venture into town. I'll send a car for Kennedy and bring her to me. The timing is awful; I've got very little time with the Live! Tour, but I can clear my schedule for the next two days. Stay put, I'll probably need your help once I arrive."

Donald was quiet for a moment, and then replied, "It might not be a bad idea, although getting her to come to you will be a challenge. You know that it's her birthday tomorrow, right?"

Dammit. No, she didn't know any such thing. Her assistant kept her personal calendar, and she hadn't reminded her. It was probably intentional- everyone seemed to be tip toeing around Kennedy's name for weeks. Still, maybe this would actually work in her favor.

"Good. You'll keep that Rachel woman occupied, and I'll send a car for Kennedy for a birthday surprise. I'll give you more details soon."

"I'm not going anywhere. We'll make this work somehow." He confirmed, although Tessa heard the doubt in his voice.

She hung up and continued to study her wine. Nothing had gone as planned so far, would this be the turning point? It was appropriate that it was Kennedy's birthday- that was what had started everything after all. She'd chosen the wrong surrogate. There was no getting around that now. At the time, Rachel had impressed her as being smart and diligent. She'd been healthy, unattached to her parents, and able to keep the entire arrangement confidential. The perfect candidate. What Tessa hadn't considered was just how much women changed when they hit the middle years. Rachel was only a few years older now than Tessa had been when Kennedy was born. She'd apparently never had her own child- and now like Tessa had felt then, she apparently regretted not checking off that box.

Not for the first time, Tessa wondered if she'd erred in not carrying the child herself. She'd seen firsthand though how much pregnancy drained a body. Even her friends who had the healthiest of pregnancies had suffered from crippling exhaustion- and every bit of research said that pregnancy at the age of 40 was much harder on a body than pregnancy at age 20.

Her father had not understood. He'd thought the entire arrangement was unnatural. Marry a man of means and have a child the normal way, he'd instructed, but Tessa wouldn't consider it. There hadn't been a viable candidate, although to be fair she could have found one if she'd really wanted to. She'd never wanted marriage though. Marriage to her father had made her mother weak and diminutive. Her married friends lived lives of no consequence. No matter how wealthy their origins had been, they ended up dependent on a man who they'd be stuck with night after night after night.

No, she reminded herself, a surrogate had been the right choice. The surrogate she had chosen had been the wrong choice. This entire situation was her fault. Kennedy had some culpability but she was young and obviously simple-minded. She lacked charisma and had never been a girl that drew people to her. Truthfully, it was all a bit embarrassing. Tessa had felt the silent judgment of her peers when they met her pale daughter. A girl like that would be easily swayed by someone as smart and devious as Rachel. Kennedy was Rachel's victim, and by extension Tessa was too. Tessa was smarter and stronger though, she'd win in this fight.

She swallowed the last sip of wine and then hurled the empty glass across the room. As it shattered across the antique, reclaimed mahogany floor, she smiled.

"Helena!" She yelled. "I dropped a glass! Please, see to it."

Chapter 29

Kenna

Rachel assured me that a t-shirt and shorts were appropriate dress for a casual boat trip. That was all well and good, but my wardrobe is severely limited and I want the sort of bright and cheerful graphic t-shirt I've seen so many people wear as they traverse up and down Duval Street. Venturing out with my ever-dwindling bundle of cash, I was looking at store windows. My mother would cringe to see me wearing tourist t-shirts and flip flops, but I've learned something from her. Quality over quantity. I skip the stacked bins that advertise deals like "3 shirts for $10" and instead found myself walking into a Margaritaville store.

300 dollars later, I walk back into my room above Jack and Jett's with a few bags full of t-shirts and multiple pairs of Reef flip flops. As I pull each colorful item from the bag though, I feel the guilt sink in. The Mallory Square money is helpful, but I can't continue to do this. I'm spending more than I can afford to lose. It's a lot harder to reign in the desire to shop without considering costs than I'd expected. Most of the world manages to do this, I remind myself. Still- it's hard.

Shaking off the thought, I remind myself that it's my birthday. Not just any birthday, it's my twenty-first birthday. Even more exciting, I'll be going out on Jack's boat. It's not exactly a date. Ge'd invited Rachel too. I had been nervous when she'd turned him down, but part of me is also very excited about the prospect of spending time alone with Jack. He's hard working, good looking, and most importantly- kind. I've watched enough movies to know that my reaction to him is perfectly normal.

That's the part that's quite abnormal though! I've never actually indulged in a real crush before.

Usually, when a boy talks to me, I feel sick to my stomach. I assume that they are only feigning interest because I'm Tessa's daughter. They can't possibly be actually interested in me. Every single thing that's wrong with my appearance, my personality, even my voice runs through my head in a laundry list of flaws. That list has been carefully constructed and edited by my mother since my early childhood. I can list a thousand things that are wrong with me before I can name a single one that is right. I know intuitively that my own perspective is suspect though. People seem to actually like Kenna the brunette. Kenna, the down on her luck, anonymous 21 year old. How could Tessa's laundry list be accurate if people genuinely like me when they don't even know who I am?

As a case in point, Jack had no clue that I was Tessa's daughter. I'm sure if I say her name he'll know who she was- but I'm feeling pretty confident that he's never watched her show or read her magazines. He wouldn't have had time or interest in anything HoHo or even the Shepherd fortune that sat at its foundation. When he looks at me, he saw Kenna- a new girl from up north somewhere. Maybe I'm all wrong, maybe he smiles that way at all the girls- but I think that maybe he looks at me as if I'm special. I think that maybe with him, I actually become someone special.

We've planned to meet at the bar at 4:00. He'll take me out and give a waterside tour around the island. Then, as the crowds fight for space to watch the sunset at Mallory Square, we'll watch the spectacular show, completely unencumbered at sea. Until then, I decide to bide my time with a tour of the San Carlos Institute, a Cuban heritage museum that features the story of Jose Marti. Tina had suggested it as a hidden in plain sight treasure. Although it occupies a prime spot on Duval, many tourists walk by the old building, never knowing about the historic treasure that lies within.

In the quiet, air-conditioned space, I take my time meandering around the many displays documenting Marti's fight for Cuban freedom and the plight of Cuban exiles. Losing myself in the story vignettes I read along the walls, I don't notice the man at first. As I leave one room for another though, I hear the soft sound of footsteps. I turn, surprised because I had been the only patron when I'd first entered. I notice a solitary man in khaki shorts and a Hawaiian shirt.

He's not looking at me, he's studying a bronze bust on a stand, but as soon as I turn back to study a grouping of framed photographs, I have the uncomfortable feeling of being watched. Not wanting to be rude, I resist the urge to turn around. Surely I'm imagining it. Feeling cautious though, I make my way to a stairway to the second floor exhibits.

Once upstairs, I move around a corner and wait. Sure enough, the man soon walks up the stairs. This time I decide to stand my ground. He looks surprised to see me standing there, looking at him. I wait for a smile, or a friendly hello, that might indicate he's just another tourist but instead he says, "Hello, Miss Shepherd."

I feel the room begin to spin and grasp the wall for support. I don't reply- speaking was impossible at this point.

"It's okay, I'm a friend. My name's Donald Freeman, and I'm here because your mother misses you and wanted to send you a birthday message."

My mother misses me? That sentiment is absurd, so absurd that it gives me my voice back.

"All I want for my birthday is for her to leave me alone." I reply, trying to sound strong.

He nods as if he'd expected that response. "She has regrets. She's also very worried about your health and state of mind. It's been difficult for her, and she needs to speak to you. I've been studying your background, you're not a cruel young woman. Do you really want to hurt her? What harm can a conversation have?"

"I told her that I would call her when I was ready and I'm not ready yet. Tell her I'm fine." It's not a lie, I am more than fine. I am feeling better than I ever have in my life.

"You know it won't be that easy. She flew all this way to see you. Give her 30 minutes of your time."

I gasped. My mother is here, in Key West? Where is she? I look around in a panic, half convinced she'll pop out from around a corner.

"Not here." He says, reading my mind. "She's in a private home, waiting for you. Thirty minutes Kennedy, that's all she is asking for. If you still feel this way afterward, she'll respect that."

My mother would never respect anything I did, he's either lying or she's hired a complete idiot who doesn't understand the woman he's working for. The problem is, she's not going to just vanish. She's going to continue to show up and interrupt my life no matter where I go. If I refuse to go to her, will she go so far as to actually walk into Jack and Jett's to drag me out? Mother cares a lot about her public image and that would certainly not fit the carefully crafted Tessa her public loves, but if she's angry and frustrated enough she might actually do it. She might do it with a tight smile, and make up a story afterward to explain it away to her legion of fans.

"What time is it?" I ask angrily.

"1:30" He replies after glancing at his watch.

I picture Rachel, a woman who has risked so much to whisk me away from my mother. If I don't do this and my mother shows up in person, Rachel would face her ire. Then I think of Jack- so uncomplicated and good natured. When she learns that he's housing me, Mother could lash out at him as well. She could hurt him too. She could hurt his business, scare away his patrons, shut him down completely. If my mother is angry enough- she is capable of anything.

I close my eyes and shake my head. "Fine. Thirty minutes and that's it."

"The estate she's at is on a private island, six miles from here. Don't look alarmed, it's connected by bridge- it's an easy escape." He says with a wink. "I have a car parked a few blocks away. I'll phone her and let her know we're on the way. I'll meet you out front in a few minutes. I strongly suggest you do not notify Ms. Patrick of your plans. She won't approve and may make this more difficult."

As I exit the cool, dusky interior of the museum onto the crowded sidewalk, I consider running. I could go get Rachel, her car is still being worked on but maybe the garage has finished whatever they needed to do. Maybe we can hurriedly pack our bags, jump in and take off for some other unknown place. Maybe if I go to enough places, I'll eventually find the one that Tessa can't ruin.

I know that plan is futile. As long as she's looking for me, she'll always find me. I need to find a way to stop her from looking. It's the only way to end the cycle. The sanctity of Jack and Jett's might be just two blocks away, but it no longer offers safe haven. No one else, no place, could do this for me. I have to do it for myself.

Donald exits the building and gives me a short nod to indicate he's spoken to her. With my stomach churning, I follow him to his car- a much too dark and sedate looking sedan for the Florida Keys. He opens the passenger door for me, but I push past him and opened the door behind him and climbed into the back seat. He shrugs as if to say, whatever, but I've made my point. We aren't friends or allies. He's my mother's servant. A chauffeur.

I try to compose a speech in my head on the ride toward the estate, but the further we get from the center of town, the more nervous I feel. It occurs to me that I don't actually know this man at all- how do I know if he's really someone my mother has sent? He could be whisking me off to meet human traffickers for all I know. For that matter, he might be legitimate but my mother could lock me up in a room and refuse to allow me to return to Rachel and Jack. It's a massive stretch but this guy has a shady air about him- she might even instruct him to cuff me and deposit me into a waiting helicopter. I know that these are fantasy scenarios, hardly likely to happen, but with Tessa one never quite knows just how far she'll go.

We turn off the main road onto a much smaller road that's heavily marked with privacy signs and blocked by a manned gate. My mother isn't going to be easily accessible to the masses after all. After parking, I swallow hard and follow the man to a large, ornate home that's flanked by tall palm trees. Each large window is shaded by a Bahama style teal hurricane shutter that serves as both decorative accessory and functional necessity. A polished set of double wooden doors that bears intricately carved birds of paradise remains closed as we climb the front porch.

The man doesn't turn to look at me or say anything, for which I'm grateful. He presses the bell and a young woman in a sundress opens the door.

"Welcome back Mr. Freeman." She looks at me and says nervously, "Hello, Miss Shepherd."

"Tania, hello. Kennedy, this is Tania, she's the property manager. She lives in the guest house."

I murmur a hello and will the bile back down into my stomach. I know who waits beyond those doors. She gestures for us to follow her in and asks politely, "Would you like something to drink? Some iced tea or cucumber water, perhaps?"

"Water would be nice," I answer meekly, following her through a large entryway. I'm afraid to look around, afraid of seeing Tessa. I keep my eyes planted on the floor until Tania says, "You can have a seat here. Ms. Shepherd will be here shortly."

Shortly ends up being a tortuous two or three minutes, minutes that feel like a lifetime. I hear her before I see her- the quick paced click of her heels as she walks along a wood floor toward the receiving room we are waiting in. And then, like a storm, there she is.

"Kennedy!" She says with a pleasant smile. I stand nervously as she reached her arms out to demonstrate a hug that is more air than flesh. She turns to Mr. Freeman and says in a warm tone, "Thank you so much Donald. Please feel free to go relax, Tania tells me the pool is a perfect 80 degrees."

Public Tessa it is. We are to pretend to be a normal mother and daughter who are enjoying the happy coincidence of finding each other here on this island. At least that's the impression we'll give until Mr. Freeman is out of earshot. I don't like the man, but I suddenly want him to stay. He ignores the silent look of pleading I send him and excuses himself, leaving me alone with my mother.

"Kennedy..." She looks at my hair and shakes her head. "I don't know what exactly you've done to yourself, you look terrible, but we'll get Duncan to fix that up when we get to New York."

I clear my throat and force the words out.

"I'm not going to New York, Mother."

"Kennedy, let's stop playing at this. You've made your point. You don't have to go to Ontario. It's time to come home though. I'll find a position for you at HoHo, and Donald tells me you've become quite the musician. We can work with that. I have plenty of contacts as you well know."

She's eyeing me shrewdly, her fake smile still firmly in place and I understand that this is her attempt to placate me. This is Tessa's version of making amends.

"Mother, I'm not going back to New York." I repeat.

The smile begins to tighten and before my eyes her face begins to transform. The ice queen is here. "I'm not sure what you're imagining doing in your new fantasy life, but let me spell out what you won't be doing. You won't be spending a cent of my money. You won't be contacting any of my associates to pull a favor. You won't be with your little friend either- she's going to have a very difficult time supporting herself without a job. She won't be able to support you."

I felt heat sting my cheeks as my own ire grows. "Why do you want me in New York? What can you possibly want with me? You don't even like me, Mother! No, don't try to deny it. You've never liked me. So why are you hell bent on bringing me home?"

I've surprised her. Her eyes widen at my open rebellion- that's something she isn't accustomed to. It only makes me feel braver and bolder.

"You're going to leave me alone. I don't want your money. I don't want Grandfather's money. I don't want to work at HoHo. I don't want to use your contacts. I just want to be left alone. You're going to give me my freedom, and you're not going to retaliate against Rachel for any of this."

That was it. She snaps, her perfectly made up face turns red as her mouth curves into a snarl. "You little bitch, you do not speak to me that way! You need to remember who you're dealing with, I am still Tessa Shepherd!"

At that I burst out laughing. She stares at me in confusion and I manage to speak between laughs, "You're... Tessa... Shepherd."

I get myself under control and finish, "You don't even know how to do this part correctly. You're supposed to tell me not to speak to you this way because you're my mother."

She begins to pace wildly and turns her back to me for a moment, before turning around with the friendly mask back in place. "Kennedy, I want you home because it's what America expects. We're a team, you and I. We always have been. Come home with me and we can grow closer now that you're maturing. As for your friend, she'll be rewarded handsomely for her kindness to you. I'll see to it she wants for nothing and from what Donald tells me, she doesn't have much now. It will change her life. Come home, and it'll be better."

If I were anyone else, I'd buy it. She's that good. I would believe the soft curve of her jawline, the serene smile on her lips, the friendly tone of her voice. I'm not anyone else though, I've spent my entire life watching my mother, the changeling, put on this act. If I go back with her nothing will change. She'll beat me down verbally, emotionally, until she breaks me completely. Rachel will eventually pay a price too- my mother has a long memory. There's no happy new beginning here.

This is the moment I'd fold. This is the moment I'd realize how strong she is and how weak I am. This is the point where I reluctantly realize I'll never escape her and that putting off the inevitable is a waste of time. I go with her and face my miserable future. That is what the old Kenna would have done anyway. I'm not that old Kenna anymore.

I think of Rachel's quiet, dignified strength. I think about the boy that we'd met, Kenny, and how he'd walked 175 miles to escape his addiction demons. I think of Jack's leap of faith when he left his tech career and bought the bar. And then, I hear her voice as clear as day. A strong southern accent, reminiscent of old tobacco, bayou spice, and sultry summer days. I've never heard the voice before, but I know exactly who it belongs to.

"You're so much stronger than her Girl, you just don't know it yet. Tell her to pound sand and get the hell out of there."

I take a deep breath. "No, Mother, I'm not going back. What I'm going to do is insist that Mr. Freeman drive me back into town. If he refuses, then I'll call a friend to pick me up. You're going to get on a plane and go back to your life. After that, you're not going to bother me again." She opens her mouth to object but I hold up a hand. "No, I'm not done. You're going to leave Rachel alone too. If you attempt to hurt her or harass me anymore then what I'm going to do is make a few calls of my own. I'm going to TMZ and anyone else who will listen and I'm going to start sharing childhood memories. Maybe I'll write a tell-all, I'm sure there are a dozen publishers who would get into a bidding war over that. I'm going to make sure the entire world knows the whole sordid tale of exactly who and what you really are."

She opens her mouth to speak but then closes it again. After giving me a withering but silent stare, she turns and storms out of the room. I remain standing in the same spot, unsure if she is coming back or if she's actually walked away from my challenge. A minute later a very timid looking Tania walked in with two glasses of water on a tray.

"I'm sorry Miss Shepherd, I didn't mean to come at an awkward time."

"It's fine." I say, waving her off. I feel buoyed, as if I've just run my first marathon. I want to jump and dance and shout. I stood up to my mother, I had the last word.

"I'll see if Mr. Freeman is available, but if he isn't I can have my brother Raul drive you to town."

"Thank you Tania." I say with a smile.

Ten minutes later her brother is driving me back into town, back toward Rachel and Jack. I try for just a moment to feel sad. I've just cut the last tie with my mother. There is nothing left inside of me that feels anything for her. All I feel is the unmistakable exhilaration of freedom. This was my coda.

Chapter 30

Rachel

I firmly believed that you knew when you walked out of a job interview if it went well and if you were going to be a desired candidate. You couldn't really know if they'd choose you as the best qualified person for the position, but you always knew if they *wanted* to. The three people who'd comprised my panel interview were smiling and shaking my hand warmly at the end of the process and I knew. They thought I'd be a good fit.

When Kenna asked how it went I found myself smiling demurely and saying, "Oh, I'm not sure. I guess we'll see." Some part of me didn't want to admit out loud that I thought an offer might be forthcoming. I hadn't fully explored exactly why I was feeling that way, but my desire to be offered the position was waning already. The panelists had all been friendly and would no doubt prove to be good coworkers and supervisors. The job itself had sounded easy enough for my skill set and it paid decently. I was having second thoughts that I didn't want to overthink just yet.

She shrugged and said, "Something will work out, I'm totally sure of that!" and then studied the olive-pepper-bacon-shrimp garnished Bloody Mary that our waitress had just dropped off.

"You're abnormally chipper this morning," I observed, "And clearly not hangover."

I knew what had caused the chipper part. Her date with Jack. When she'd mysteriously disappeared yesterday afternoon, I thought for sure that she was hiding out in town and purposely sabotaging their planned meet up. But just before they were supposed to leave, she'd come running into Jack and Jett's, her flip flops snapping as she took strong, purposeful strides. I'd been sitting at a table, studying an AAA map, already planning our escape but here came Kenna with a huge smile.

When I'd asked where she'd been she shrugged and said, "Oh, here and there. We'll talk more about it later but I'm going on a boat ride!"

I'd caught a bit of a mysterious inflection to her voice. There was something she wasn't telling me, I wondered if perhaps things had advanced with Jack. She was certainly old enough to indulge in a romance. I reminded myself that while in many ways she'd been stunted at a very young age, she was in fact twenty-one years old. And as if on cue, Jack had walked into the room. She'd smiled shyly at him and left me, to greet him. The pair departed shortly afterward. I hadn't heard many details later in the night because almost as soon as they'd returned, the daytime bar manager and a few of her friends whisked Kenna off for birthday drinks.

"So it seems like you had a good birthday!"

"The best. Really, the best ever! The boat ride was magical, you wouldn't believe how incredible the sunset is from the sea. And then last night with the girls, oh my god, I've never laughed so much in my life."

I smiled, she sounded like such a normal young woman, a carefree young woman. Was this really the same Kenna?

"And Jack?" I probed.

She grinned. "Jack... he was amazing. It's just so easy with him. Kind of like with us, you know how it's like we've always known each other. It kind of feels that way with him. Except it's different because I kind of want to kiss him."

I raised my eyebrow at that and then laughed. "But you didn't?"

"No, but there was this moment, we were looking at each other and it was as if we couldn't break our eyes away and I thought he might be about to do it. Then a giant party boat swept by us with their horn blaring and the passengers were all screaming and waving so that moment passed."

"Well, well, well. My little Kenna is growing up." I teased, but then it felt awkward because she had been my little Kenna and she really was growing up. She didn't seem to notice the slip though.

"Rachel, there's something I need to tell you." Her tone grew serious and she looked down to pick a cuticle.

"Okay, I'm all ears."

"First promise me you won't freak out," she said.

Did I strike her as someone prone to freaking out? I didn't think anyone who had ever known me would ascribe that characteristic to me. What on earth was she about to share? "Alright..."

"I saw Tessa yesterday."

If she'd announced, "A spaceship descended upon our boat yesterday and threw Mardi Gras beads at us," I'd have been less shocked.

"What?" I yelled. She shot me a warning look.

"Please, give me a minute! She somehow tracked us down and came down to confront me. She's staying, or was anyway, at a house on a private island not far from here. Yesterday afternoon she sent some goon to bring me to her."

My heart leapt into my throat. I knew it had to be the PI I'd met at the bar, the PI I very purposely hadn't warned her about. I was flooded with guilt for keeping his presence a secret.

"Are you okay? Did they hurt you in any way?"

"I'm fine. Better than fine even. Really, don't give me that look. Rachel, you would have been so proud of me. I did it! I stood up to her and told her off. I really think she got the message and won't be breathing down my neck anymore. I'm not gonna lie, it felt really good to do it, too."

I stared at her; it was difficult to imagine anyone standing up to Tessa and impossible to picture that anyone being Kenna. Somehow, she'd managed to find her voice and her spine in just a few weeks' time. I was confused about what exactly had transpired though so I asked her to tell me everything.

After she'd shared the entire nail biting story, I replied "Kenna, that's fantastic. Truly. I'm so proud of you. I know that facing her was your biggest fear and now that you've done this I hope that you can believe you really are capable of doing anything. You're free to actually think about your own future now."

"Yes! My future here in Key West." She said with a smile.

"So this is it, huh?"

She nodded, "I know you Rachel, there's no way you didn't blow them away at that interview. Look at this place! How can we leave here?"

She said gesturing around the heavily foliaged patio we sat eating brunch on. In one corner a man played Jimmy Buffett tunes and behind him, through the huge hibiscus bushes, I could see throngs of people walking toward the nearby Hemingway house.

"It seemed to go okay." I admitted, "But there's no guarantee they'll give me an offer. I still need to head back to PA in the meantime. I still have a job to do there, friends to check in on, I've got to start transitioning the library to the annual Halloween theme. Then there's Bilbo, and my house. If I do get a job here I'll have to sell it... and I need to visit Delta because who knows how long it'll be before I get back again."

As I spoke, I felt the sting of tears. I pictured my little cottage, the grand oak in the backyard, my sweet little Main Street in Metzgartown, my dear friends, the children I mentored, Delta's grave at the veteran's cemetery in Scranton. It was a lot to say goodbye to. So many years of my life were invested into it all.

"Oh, I know it's not going to be an instant process. I will be there to help you pack up and move, but Rachel I had a crazy thought."

"What's that?"

"What if I stay here for now, until you're ready to pack up? I didn't mention this earlier, but Jack's hiring wait staff right now- and I know he'd give me a job if I asked. I mean, I don't have a clue how to actually be a waitress, but I can learn. And I can play at the Square a few nights a week to earn extra cash. He's in no rush to get me out of the room- he said it's very rare they need both rooms at once. I just feel so alive down here. I don't want to leave just yet." She admitted.

I studied her for a moment. Despite the amount of the sunscreen we'd been slathering on, her skin was sun-kissed with a golden hue. Her eyes were bright, her voice strong. She was truly glowing. The broken child who'd showed up at my door just a few weeks before was healing. I knew that she would still face demons, there would be setbacks and challenges, but like a plant that sprang back to life overnight after a good watering- there was a lot of hope here. Yes, Key West was good for her. She belonged here, for now at least. Who knew what the future would hold?

"Kenna, I know you're loving it down here. It's not easy to wait tables though. It's hard work that'll have you on your feet for hours, sometimes dealing with difficult people. Are you sure that's the kind of work you want to be doing?"

"It's the kind of work I need to be doing." She said simply, and I saw the truth in her words.

"You know that even if they liked me, they might not offer me the job."

"They will." She said stubbornly.

I looked around again at the tropical splendor around us, and the crowds of tourists that never ended. We were in paradise, people fantasized about moving there. A person who had that opportunity would be crazy to turn it down. And Kenna would be there, it was yet another reason to say goodbye to Metzgartown for good. It ought to have been a simple decision.

I took a deep breath and said the words out loud. "There's something you should know. I'm not certain I want to move here."

"But why," She asked, startled.

"Because every day that I'm away from Metzgartown, I miss it a little more. I know that probably sounds crazy. Who wouldn't want to live here, right? But now that it seems like moving isn't just a pipe dream- it might be actual reality, I'm getting cold feet. I love my home, I actually love my job, I love the townspeople. This is all wonderful, but it feels so transient and temporary. I grew up in a very transient and temporary lifestyle and I've grown to appreciate the stability of permanence."

"Oh, I see." She said, and I could see that while she was attempting to look nonchalant, my words had crushed her.

"I haven't made any firm decisions yet. Like I said, I don't even have an offer to consider."

She looked away and I saw her blinking rapidly, fighting the tears. "I mean, I can make Pennsylvania work, I'm sure."

"Kenna, you are absolutely welcome to come with me back to Pennsylvania but you're clearly not ready for that. Why change your new plans? This place, it's great for you. Stay, earn some blisters and a little cash. Enjoy whatever's happening with Jack. Keep finding yourself. If I stay in Pennsylvania, well you know where to find me. We won't lose touch, I promise."

A tear escaped and rolled down her cheek and she asked, "Really? Do you really think I can do this alone?"

"You won't be alone. You'll still have me in your corner. You've already made friends down here and you'll make more. You'll never be alone again."

She nodded and smiled sadly, then she said, "There's something I didn't tell you, you're going to think this is crazy."

"What's that?"

"When I was speaking with my mo- Tessa, Delta came to me. I know, it sounds crazy but I swear, I heard her voice. She was encouraging me."

She looked at her feet, and I could see she was embarrassed. Tears sprang to my eyes and I said, "It doesn't sound crazy. Not at all. She would be so proud of you too. I have to admit, I've been begging her to speak to me since she passed. Maybe this is her way of doing that."

I grabbed her hand and squeezed it and she smiled at me. It was a genuine smile, one that was full of hope and I could see it now. She would be okay. She would pull this off, without me.

My purse began to buzz and I pulled my phone out. It was the school on Sigsbee. I glanced nervously at Kenna, and she nodded. I took a deep breath and answered it.

"Hello?"

"Hi, is this Ms. Patrick?"

"It is."

"This is Jenna Oliver, from Sigsbee Charter School. I know this is a ridiculously fast turn around, but we had a meeting after your interview and everyone was on the same page. We would absolutely love to have you here on staff. I'll email over a formal offer shortly for you to consider. We hope you'll be joining us!"

I closed my eyes and stifled a laugh. I could hear Delta clearly. It was near the end, she couldn't travel anymore but we'd pulled out a pile of photo albums to relive some of our old adventures. She had cuddled up against me on the couch, her big quilt covering us both, as we thumbed through images from our last trip to Scotland.

"Someday we'll visit again." I promise.

"No, I won't anyway." She says bluntly.

I plead- "Don't say that. We will have more adventures."

"Just waking up is an adventure, Rachel. You don't have to leave home for that. As for me, I'm going on the grandest of them all soon."

"I don't want you to." I sob.

"Don't be jealous Rachel, it's about time I get to go on a solo trip."

Snot runs from my nose and tears from my eyes, but I'm able to fake a small laugh at that and rest my head on her shoulder.

Delta's body starts to shake as a fit of coughing overwhelms her, after it passes she adds, "I know where home is. I'll be there, God willing and the creek don't rise."

"Miss Oliver, I am so flattered. I'm really sorry to have wasted your time, but I'm afraid I'm going to have to decline this offer." I glanced at Kenna, who looked nervous but nodded approvingly anyway. "As it turns out, I have another opportunity I need to commit to. I'm going to be heading home."

Epilogue

Kenna

"Oh my god, Shannon just Faced me from the other side, there are so many people in there! Did the entire town show up?" I ask, using a flyer I'd found on the table as a makeshift fan.

"Come on, it's not that bad. I think there are about 60 people out there and you know every one of them. Your closest friends and biggest fans. Come here, your face is melting girl. I need to powder you up again."

I glare at Celise. She stands there in her tiny red dress and cowboy boots, her long auburn hair tossed back in a casual bun, and she somehow looks fresh and perfect..

"Do you even sweat? Are you actually human?" I ask, grumpily.

"Someone's a cranky cow." She observes dryly and I throw my hands up in protest. I'd always wished for a best friend and when Celise had breezed through the front door of Jack and Jett's just weeks after I'd started working there, we had hit it off immediately. Almost five years in Key West have taught me the real meaning of friendship. It means having someone there to support you in the worst of times, celebrate you in the best of times, and above all- having someone to tease you at all times.

"Sorry, I'm just a little overwhelmed! And listen to my voice? Oh my god, why didn't I cancel last night's show? Everyone was so loud, I felt like I was screaming more than singing. Now I sound ridiculous." I explain grumpily.

My phone buzzes again, another Facetime request from Shannon. I groan. She's checked on me three times in the last 30 minutes, it's as if she's afraid I might run out of the back door if given the chance.

She's still behind the bar and it's hard to hear her over the rowdy crowd. As usual, Jack's WiFi seems to be running at dinosaur pace so the resulting video feed is a staccato, loud, hot, mess.

"What? I can't understand you!" I try yelling back into the phone, much to Celise's dismay.

"Your MOTHER-" She breaks away again.

My mother? Was she saying my mother was here? The connection fails entirely then, Shannon's face frozen with mouth gaped open and eyes squinted shut on my screen. I feel my pulse quicken the way it always does when I hear those words without context. It had been almost two years since my mother's last attempted contact, the longest she's ever gone, and I'd hoped that meant she understood I had nothing left to say to her.

A rapt knock at the door sounds and I swing around to face it. Celise, who is one of a handful of people who know my true background story, sees the look on my face and says angrily, "Oh hey-ll no. Not today."

She marches to the door and swings it open, her facial expression and body language leave no doubt she is ready to go to battle over me. The tension disappears though when we see the woman in the doorway.

"Rachel! Oh my god, you came! I thought you couldn't get more time off until Easter though?"

She runs in and scoops me up into a big hug. "I just couldn't miss this! Theresa actually went to the town manager and said if they couldn't find a temporary replacement, they needed to shut down the library for a few days because she was personally going to duct tape me and take me hostage to Key West whether they wanted me to go or not."

Tears of joy fill my eyes as I look into her soft brown eyes. I hadn't realized just how disappointed I'd been about her not being here. It's true that we haven't given anyone much notice. If we had planned this better, we could have arranged everything to coincide with Rachel and Theresa's visit in January- but we are nothing if not spontaneous. My therapist says that my recent proclivity toward said spontaneity is push-back against the rigidity of my childhood. It makes sense and I just accept this new part of me. That's me, Kenna on a dime! The plan this time was to keep everything low-key and simple. We decided to get everything organized with very short notice to keep the bulk of townies from turning it into a big ruckus. I've been sad about Rachel missing it though, I can't believe that with just three days' notice she's been able to pull it off.

"It sounds like I owe Theresa a drink or three and a big hug! The kids?"

"Back home. Don't get a sad look, this is not a sad thing. Do you have any clue how exhausting 14 year old twins are? I needed a vacation from them anyway." Her wry smile betrays the affection she feels for them.

However stressful living with two surly teenagers must be, I've never seen Rachel happier. Being in love looks good on her and so does being an almost-step-mom.

"I look forward to catching up with Theresa. Where is she anyway?"

Rachel's eyes twinkle. "Oh she's out there in the bar. With Mom and Dad."

I shriek. "Bob and Lacey are here? I haven't seen them in a few years now, that's wonderful!"

Celise interrupts, "Kenna... It's time. He's waiting."

Rachel pats my hand. I take a deep breath and risk one last glance in the mirror. The short, white, cotton sundress I wear is much simpler than the fancy princess gowns I'd dreamed of in my childhood. My long, artificially dark hair is worn down and held in place behind my ear by a plumeria decorated barrette. A pair of chic white sandals replaces the 3 dollar flip flops I usually wear, they'd been my only splurge. Then the door opens and I hear a murmur of voices until Old Daff Louie yells, "SHUT UP!"

The music starts and Rachel takes my arm. Celise precedes us out the door and leads the way into the bar, where a few cheers and an occasional wolf whistle greet her. Then we're following in her footsteps, walking toward Jack. Jack, who looks like he's been struck by lightning as he watches me approach him. Jack, who asked me to marry him six times before I'd surprised us both with an affirmative answer. Jack, who feels like home when I reach his side.

Father Keane's eyes sparkle and his nose is a bit red. It looks like Shannon has been keeping his cup filled. Still, he smiles and remembers his lines.

"Who gives this woman to be wed?"

I glance back at Rachel and nod. She steps forward and says, "I do."

I smile and mouth "thank you" to the woman who gave birth to me and then later taught me how to love and how to be loved. My family.

□

Authors Note

Motion of Intervals ends within the welcoming walls of Jack & Jett's, a stereotypical Key West establishment. It's the type of place that tourists and locals alike descend upon to celebrate life, push their limits, find community and forget life's challenges for awhile. In a bar like this, the stories write themselves.

Stay tuned for more from Jack & Jett's and the characters who find themselves walking through those doors. Kenna's new friend Celise has her own tale to tell in *The Four Baptisms of Celise Newman*- and that'll be coming soon!

Thanks for sticking around, hope you're here to enjoy the next round. In the meantime, your feedback is important to me and will help other readers decide whether to read this book. I'd be honored if you visited the site you purchased this from and wrote a brief review.

Blessings!
Kristy

Made in the USA
Middletown, DE
09 August 2023

36041248R00177